The Bonded

The Allseer Trilogy Book 1

Kaitlyn Rouhier

The Bonded: The Allseer Trilogy Book I

Copyright © 2015 by Kaitlyn Rouhier

Printed in the United States of America

First Printing, 2015

Createspace Paperback Edition

ISBN-13: 978-1517029630

ISBN-10: 1517029635

To the extraordinary league of writing motivators,

This is for you.

Chapter 1

The ritual was held in the Temple of Union, inside the vast hollowed heart of a glowing wraith wood tree. The tree itself jutted upwards, jagged spires reaching high into the heavens. In the glow of the moon it shone faintly, its ghastly bark throwing out a whisper of icy blue light.

The inside of the tree was a great hollowed core, forming a large circular room with nothing but dirt for a floor. It had been stripped bare, save for a row of wraith wood chairs at the back of the room. Robed council members sat quietly, waiting for the ritual to begin. They wore cloaks the color of the midnight sky, their faces hidden in shadow but she could feel them watching. Candles were the only light in the room and they formed a circle in which she and another Bondless sat. The faint light flickered and shifted, colliding strangely with the blue glow of the tree.

It was the sixteenth year in their cycle and now it had come to this. Reaching up, the girl tucked her ashen hair behind her ear and stared at the boy across from her. He returned her gaze, his dark eyes wide with fright. He had a full face, a boyish chubbiness to his body that only a growth spurt could take away. His wavy brown hair had been smoothed back and he ran a hand through it nervously, no doubt afraid her gaze picked apart some untidiness he had failed to notice.

Their clothing was customary for the Ritual of Union. Dark blue robes encased them, a silver sash tied tight around the middle. They'd removed the dark leather boots they'd worn before entering and they sat barefoot on the floor, their feet tucked beneath them. The girl tugged impatiently at a loose thread and she couldn't help but wonder how many Bondless children had worn those very same robes before her.

It was on this day that they would cease to be Bondless. Over the course of their youth, the Council had watched them. They had picked apart their personalities, studied their interests and dissected every action they had taken. It was with this information that they chose one boy and one girl to bond together. After the process, the two would cease to be apart. Their thoughts, minds and hearts would meld. It is said that the Bonded can know each other's thoughts without speaking, can find each other even if a great distance separates them. To be Bonded was an honor with no equal. To be given that special connection with someone was the greatest gift a Bondless one could be given. Such a bond would grant them the strength to face the Darkness that lurked outside the walls of Sanctuary.

It was also something the girl found completely and utterly pointless. She'd known her entire life that it would come to this moment. Sometimes she had watched the boys she'd been raised around, wondering which one the Council would see fit to match her with. As she'd gotten older, the allure of being permanently bound to someone had lost its shiny luster.

Now it just frightened her. The thought of giving her mind to another wasn't even something she could fathom. They'd tried to allay her concerns, her mentors assuring her it wouldn't be as terrible as she thought, but she'd known deep down that they were lying to her. And now she sat, watching the boy she'd be Bonded to with a dissatisfied frown.

It could have been anyone else and she would have been slightly more interested in the ritual but instead they'd chosen to stick her with *him*. His will was about as pudgy and pliable as his face. He was the kid that always did the right thing growing up, the kid that was first to tell the mentors when another had done something wrong. He would do anything for the good of Sanctuary and it grated on her nerves that someone could be so compliant. How could anyone not have an opinion of their own? How could anyone follow with questioning? It didn't make sense.

The only thing she was really looking forward to was getting her name. Throughout her youth, she'd always been referred to as the Bondless, or simply called 'Child.' During the Ritual of Union, they would finally be given a permanent name. To have an identity of her own after all those years was something she had been anxiously awaiting.

A soft rustling caught her attention and she glanced up, surprised to find herself staring at the Union Master himself. The man had always been a bit of an enigma. He commanded the lands of Sanctuary, keeping its citizens safe from the Darkness that threatened them. Along with the Council, he made the rules and kept the peace. Until their time of union, most of the children rarely saw him.

He was an old man, much older than she remembered. His thinning hair had faded to a dull gray and he had a sharp, weathered face that looked like it had been carved from rock. He wore the same robes as them; dark blue with a silver sash. They hung loose on his lanky body and swirled around him as he approached. He regarded them with hawkish eyes, his lips drawn into a tight line. She exchanged a nervous glance with the boy next to her.

With a gesture of his hand, the Union Master commanded them to rise. They stood, kneeling on one knee and bowing their heads to show respect. The Union Master nodded his approval and cleared his throat before speaking.

"Welcome, Children. It is good to see you both today. As you may already know, I am the Union Master. No doubt you've seen me throughout the years, but now I may properly introduce myself. From this point on you may refer to me as Master Nyson."

"Yes, Master Nyson," they spoke in unison, just as the mentors had trained them to.

"Ah, such manners" he spoke, his gravelly voice taking on a tone of approval. "You come before me today, two Bondless ones ready to take the next step in the cycle. As you know, the Council has watched you closely over the years. They have seen your desires, watched your actions and choices and have been amazed as you've grown before their eyes. We are all honored to guide you through this process. Shall we begin?"

She nodded, feeling her stomach twist at the thought but she managed to keep her expression passive. She didn't want the boy next to her to think she was as frightened as he looked. Even now she could see him wringing his hands nervously.

From the shadows, two men emerged. They were identical. Tall and lean, they wore the same dark robes as the others in the room. Both seemed dreadfully pale and their chin length white hair made them look like ghosts in the light. They bowed respectfully to Master Nyson before taking a seat before them. Each held a leather bag and from these they produced several vials filled with a dark liquid, parchment, ink, quill and a strange instrument with a needle sharp point. This was all done in silence, the strange men hardly looking at each other. Their movements were precise and almost comical, so mirrored were they that they barely seemed to be separate people at all.

The girl watched this with fascination, her eyes wide as she observed the silent exchange. "This is what it is to be Bonded," Master Nyson said. "To know the thoughts and feelings of another so deeply, you could mirror their movement without looking at them."

We'll share each other's thoughts, the girl thought to herself. It irked her that someone could be privy to the things that she thought or felt. She looked at the round faced boy and silently cursed her luck. She didn't want to be Bonded, not to him or to anyone. It wasn't her choice, but what other choice did she have? Much like everything else throughout her childhood, this was something being decided for her.

Nyson regarded her with a level gaze. "Are you disappointed girl?"

The girl checked her face, skewing her expression to something more agreeable. "No, of course not, Master. My thoughts merely strayed."

He nodded, his eyes hovering over her for a moment longer. "Very well. Let us continue the ritual. I could bore you with small talk, but I think you already know the importance of this. This Bond that you are to be given is unlike anything you've yet to experience. To succeed, you must treat your bond with the utmost respect. Treat each other well and you'll flourish. Now, I think it is time you both received a name."

At the mention of receiving her name, she turned her full attention to the man in front of her. He set a piece of parchment between them, dipped his quill and waited for Nyson to continue.

The Union Master shifted himself towards her and she met his eyes. She mentally forced her hands to be still, trying to keep her nervousness from showing. "It took quite some time picking a name for you, Child. Through your youth you've shown that you are spirited and intelligent. Your kindness and bravery are commendable traits and it is these qualities we smiled upon when we thought of who to bond you with. Your strength of character compliments him greatly and will bring him happiness and stability."

The girl smiled to herself as she listened, nodding in agreement as he listed off her more redeeming qualities. It was only when his face grew somber that the smile faded off her lips and she watched him with steely eyes. "One cannot just be made of good qualities, however. Be mindful of the doubt that plagues you, girl. We've seen it much over the years and we do not wish to see it lead you astray. You are curious about your new life and rightfully so, but curiosity can lead to trouble. Be thankful for the life you've been given and never cast doubt upon it. In this, your bond mate will help you. His dedication will reveal to you the value of devoting yourself to this process."

"Yes, Master Nyson. Thank you," the girl muttered, bowing her head. She bit back her frustration, glaring at the ground with enough force to burn holes through the world. Her cheeks burned and she was grateful for the dim light masking her embarrassment.

"Are you ready to hear your name?"

"Yes, Master."

Anticipation hung like a thick cloud and the girl found it hard to breath. She clasped her hands tightly, feeling her heart flutter wildly in her chest.

"From this day forth, you will take the name Kirheen. It speaks of strength and elegance, a perfect match for an intelligent beauty such as yourself." The girl nodded her approval, making sure to smile at the Union Master. She watched with great interest as the silent man before her wrote her name on the slip of parchment. He turned it towards her so she could see.

She whispered the name, letting it slip off her tongue. It felt good to finally have an identity, something she could claim as her own. It was a fine name and she couldn't help but grin as she memorized the letters on the parchment.

"Congratulations," the boy next to her whispered, touching her gently on the arm. "It's a beautiful name."

She was about to thank him when Nyson called for his attention. He turned away from her quickly, dark eyes shifting nervously to look at the Union Master.

"Ah, you're a dedicated one, boy. We've seen that much over the years. You are steadfast and loyal, always putting others first. You've a firm love of life and see good in all things. However, you're also doubtful of yourself. You are nervous and uncertain, lacking the strength of will to realize you are worth far more than you give yourself credit for. In this, Kirheen will help guide you. Her strength of character will help fuel your inner fire, showing you how to be courageous and confident." Master Nyson smiled at the boy, giving him a reassuring nod. "You'll grow to be a fine man. But you can't hope to be a man without a name. Are you ready to hear it?"

The boy said nothing, just nodded his head meekly. His eyes had grown large and he held his breath, waiting anxiously to hear his name.

"From this day forth, you will take the name Garild. It speaks of dedication and kindness, but also of a strength and confidence you will develop in the coming years."

"Thank you, Master Nyson," the boy said, bowing his head. If he was pleased with his name, he didn't show it. Instead he watched as the man in front of him wrote out his name in ink. Leaning over, Kirheen gave him a friendly nudge on the arm.

"Nice name," she said with a smile. "I think it suits you."

"T-thank you," Garild said with a stutter. He turned away from her, red rushing to his cheeks.

"Kirheen. Garild. You have been given names but you are still without a symbol. I've personally chosen a symbol for you. As I'm sure you've learned by now, your symbol is meant to represent two things found in the world that are unified. It is meant to represent a powerful bond, one that you will quickly develop. Your symbol is unique and special. It represents you both, unlike your names. To tarnish the reputation of your symbol is to bring shame to your bond. Do you understand this?"

"Yes, Master Nyson," Garild said while Kirheen nodded her head.

"Good. I want you to always remember that. It is very important. For your symbol, I have picked for you the sun and stars. It is a strong, yet subtle symbol."

This part of the ritual was one that Kirheen had found herself both curious and terrified of. The process involved having their symbol put into their skin using a sharp needle, a procedure that was supposed to be quite painful. Despite knowing that, it wasn't the process itself that scared her. What scared her more was the permanence of it. The symbol didn't come off. It would be in her skin forever making her a walking, talking advertisement for their bond. It would be a constant reminder that her life and her mind were no longer her own.

The silent twins took to work, creating the symbol on another piece of parchment. They drew the sun, hiding within its face a crescent moon and stars.

"This last part of the ritual is not without discomfort. It is through this pain that your bond will grow stronger. You'll carry your symbol not only in your heart but on your flesh as well." The Union Master pulled back his left sleeve and flipping over his arm, he showed them his own symbol marked in dark ink on the wrinkled flesh of his wrist. It was of an elegant fish with blue and silver scales. It looked to be leaping out of a pool of water.

"It's beautiful," Kirheen remarked. She wished nothing more than to move closer and inspect the design. The only thing keeping her rooted in place, other than humiliating the whole Council, was knowing she'd have her own symbol to gawk over soon.

"When you're ready," Master Nyson finished, stepping back into the shadows. The white haired men carefully set aside the design they had crafted, then took a moment to arrange two bottles of dark liquid within easy reach. Garild watched nervously as the thick liquid sloshed around within the glass confinement.

Kirheen spoke, trying to make herself sound eager. It was nothing more than false confidence to mask her nerves. "I'm ready," she said. Her words must have had the intended effect for Garild looked at her in shock, dismayed by her readiness. She was supposed to be strong and brave and she intended to live up to the impression she'd given them.

"You're going to let them put that in your skin," Garild asked.

Kirheen rolled her eyes. "Of course I am, silly. You're going to have to as well. It's part of the ritual." Her lips spread into a smirk, a solitary eyebrow rising as she challenged his bravery. "Unless you're too scared!"

He retorted quickly, trying to hide the fear in his voice. "I'm not scared!"

"Prove it!"

The man in front of Kirheen held a sharp instrument. He dipped it into one of the vials and the tip came away dripping with the foul looking liquid. He motioned for Kirheen to sit closer. As she drew closer, the man met her eyes and gently reached forward to grab her left hand. The closeness alarmed her and she nearly drew her hand away. He smirked, raising one brow in the same challenging expression she'd given Garild. She realized he was taunting her and she narrowed her eyes, giving him a firm nod to continue. Her sleeve was pushed back and her hand flipped so her palm faced the sky. He wiped her arm with a clear liquid that tingled as it touched her skin and then he readied the needle. Quick as a snake the instrument descended, striking into the soft flesh of her wrist. She gave a small yelp and would have pulled her hand away if not for his fingers gripping her tightly. With an intake of breath, she steadied herself. White teeth flashed, the white haired man amused by her reaction. She pursed her lips and allowed him to continue his work, feeling the slip of the needle poke into her flesh.

Garild watched in silence, his mouth gaping open like a fish. He gave a visible shudder as blood welled to the surface where the instrument had pierced her skin, injecting it with that shadowy ink. As the man smeared away her blood, the ink spread with it. He looked faint.

Kirheen watched as the man seated in front of Garild reached forward and tugged on his sleeve. He looked irritated. Seeing no response from Garild, he reached forward and tried to grab hold of him. Garild pulled back sharply, a look of horror on his face.

"It really isn't that bad," she said reassuringly. Despite her comment, she winced as the needle dove back into her wrist. "At least we only have to do it once." She smiled at him sheepishly and he gave her a look that said how little he trusted her words. He gulped down his nervousness and let the man take his wrist.

Kirheen watched him tense as the man gripped him, watched his eyes grow to the size of the moon as the needle was dipped and raised above his wrist. Whatever brave thoughts he'd had of surviving the experience left him in a rush of escaped breath as the needle touched his skin.

His eyes rolled back and he slumped onto the ground. At first Kirheen was alarmed and then the man holding her wrist burst with laughter. He had passed out in front of the Council and in front of Nyson. Kirheen felt a wave of embarrassment knowing that this was the boy she'd been bound to and for better or worse, she was stuck with him.

Chapter 2

G arild awoke with a start, feeling disoriented as he looked around. The familiar wraith wood walls common to Sanctuary surrounded him, but the room itself he'd never seen. He vaguely remembered waking in the middle of the night, but he'd been too tired to investigate his surroundings. He tried to think back on what had happened at the Ritual and felt his heart drop into his stomach. "Oh, Allseer..." He'd passed out in front of the Council, in front of Kirheen and in front of the Union Master himself. He was a fool, sure to be laughed out of Sanctuary by the rest of the Bonded.

The room was small and simply furnished. Two beds, one occupied by himself, took up most of the room. A small desk sat against the wall to his right beneath a large window allowing a pleasant view of the surrounding forest. Vibrant purple flowers filled a vase on the desk clouding the room with a scent he would have found agreeable if not for the dull throbbing in his temples.

As he went to prop himself up, pain flashed across his wrist. At some point bandages had been wrapped loosely around his arm, probably to protect the symbol that had been poked into his skin.

He had no desire to look at it. Doing so was likely to make him pass out again.

Soft footsteps echoed outside the room and a moment later Kirheen pushed aside a blue curtain and entered. Her face was rigid but her eyes twinkled as she looked at him. He knew she was suppressing laughter and the realization made him angry. He didn't want to see anyone right now, especially the one person he'd been hoping to impress.

"Finally decided to wake up, did you," Kirheen questioned as she moved to the edge of the bed. "I hate to tell you, but those strange men got quite a laugh. Guess it's normally the girls that have that reaction."

Garild looked away from her, his face turning red with anger and embarrassment. He pulled his burning arm to his chest and nursed his wounded pride. "Good to know."

"Oh, Garild. I'm just messing with you. Don't be angry." Stepping closer she took a seat on the edge of the bed. "If you want to know the truth, it hurt pretty bad. Have you looked at it yet," she questioned. "It looks pretty cool."

Garild shrugged. "I really don't want to look at it."

"Stop it! Take a look!"

Kirheen had removed the bandage from her wrist and held it out towards him. A dark color against the pale flesh of her wrist caught his attention. She hadn't been lying, it was interesting. A sun held the delicate crescent of the moon, stars dotting the surface around it.

"It's nice," he said, looking away quickly. Seeing the puffy red skin around the mark made his own wrist throb. "Where are we anyway?"

"Once they finished up the symbol, we were brought here. It's... our new home. They've already gathered all of our things from the Temple of Growth. We won't need to go back."

The temple was where they had been raised. Two long narrow buildings had served as their home throughout their childhood. It was where they had learned of the world, where they had learned of the struggle the Bonded faced, of the duties that were expected of them, of the powers they possessed that would one day be used to battle the Darkness.

It was strange to think they'd never go back. All of the people they'd grown up with were going to be Bonded soon. The time for playing was done. Now was the time to become an adult, to face their responsibilities.

Kirheen sighed, seemingly lost in the same thought he was. Her eyes shifted and she turned her attention back to him. "Our instructor is supposed to be coming by today."

"Oh? Do you know who it is?"

Kirheen shook her head. "From what I've heard, it's supposed to be one of the Council members. Apparently most of them are also instructors."

"Not surprising. They are supposed to be the best of the best," he said. He hadn't met many of the people on the Council.

Just like the Union Master, they weren't often seen until one became Bonded.

"Yes. Nothing like having someone here each and every day to help us learn about each other. I think having us share a room is going to take care of that just fine," Kirheen grumbled. She rose from the bed and strode into the other room, leaving him to his thoughts.

Garild winced at her words. He always had a hard time deciphering whether she was being serious or just sarcastic. She had always been an outspoken girl. Often he'd heard her openly challenge or question anything she deemed odd or interesting. She had no problem letting her thoughts be heard and he found himself envious of how easily she expressed herself.

It had never been that easy for him. Bottling everything up seemed to be a much better alternative. It also made him well liked, something Kirheen didn't have the luxury of. Her attitude hadn't earned her many friends over the years.

Although envious of her strength, a lot of her comments had a tendency to swing in his direction and she knew exactly how to hurt his feelings. It had never been a secret that she wasn't happy about being Bonded. He'd heard her rant more than once about the delicate nature of her thoughts and feelings and that an intrusion into her mind wasn't something she could tolerate. She'd vowed to keep her mind strong. If someone truly wanted in, they'd have to have the strength to break through those barriers. She'd been quick to assure him such a thing would never be possible.

Despite her brashness, he couldn't have asked for anyone better to be Bonded with. He'd always liked Kirheen and felt drawn to her like a moth to a flame. He doubted she realized it or would even accept his feelings if she did. For now just getting to spend each day with her was enough, even if her comments made it perfectly clear he was a fool for enjoying it.

Though he wished to remain in bed, his curiosity got the better of him and with a grunt he swung his legs onto the floor, favoring his wrist as he walked to the other room. It felt like he'd held his wrist to the sun. The skin was fiery and hot and he wondered how long it would feel that way. He pushed aside the blue curtain separating the rooms and stepped into a simple seating area. To his right were several cushioned wraith wood chairs forming a small semi-circle around a fireplace. It was empty now, the season still too warm for fires. The rest of the room was filled with a few large plants, and a couple light blue tapestries baring the symbol of the Allseer; a white eye with a jagged line through the center.

Kirheen was sitting in one of the cushioned chairs next to the fire place, peering into an intricately carved table he'd failed to notice at first glance. As he approached, he realized the center had been carved out and filled with water. Two colorful fish were at its center, swimming lazy circles around each other. Plopping down in the chair next to Kirheen startled them, sending them splashing away from each other. Kirheen looked up with a sigh, her chin cupped in her hands.

"Sorry," he said sheepishly. She shrugged, eyes wandering back to the fish. She was strangely quiet and he wondered just what was going on in that head of hers. He was about to ask when a knock at the front door cut him off. He rose quickly, crossing the expanse of the room in a few steps. He opened the door to see an older woman standing before him. She was tall and thin with dull gray hair pulled back into a meticulous bun. Her sharp green eyes regarded him over an upturned nose, her lips pulled into a tight line. He had to wonder if the woman had ever had a happy thought in her entire life.

"H-hello," Garild stammered, feeling uncomfortable under the weight of her gaze. "Can I help you?"

"For starters, you could get out of the way. And in the future, not reenacting a certain fainting spell in front of the whole Council would be preferable."

Garild blushed, his cheeks turning as red as an apple. He stepped out of the way, allowing the old woman to enter. She surveyed the room, eyes slowly inspecting every surface as if she were committing it to memory. As her gaze fell on Kirheen, her face seemed to melt into a frown that told them she was more than a little disgusted to be in the same room. Kirheen caught on to the look and she stared back menacingly, one brow arched high, an expression that was quite common when she saw a challenge to be had. Their eyes locked and Garild felt a chill run through him.

"And just who are you," Kirheen spat, twisted around in her chair so she could see.

"I could ask the same of you, but I find it unnecessary. You're ill manners speak for you, Kirheen. I was told my students would be a surprise. What an intriguing jest."

Kirheen huffed, a forced smile splaying across her face. "I'm glad you've heard of me. Saves me some effort."

"Still that flapping tongue of yours, girl. You may have earned a reputation around here, but it isn't one I respect. That is something you'd have to earn and right now, you're making a very poor case for yourself."

"My apologies," Kirheen said sweetly.

The woman ignored her. "Very well. Garild, go take a seat next to your companion."

He did as he was told, not wanting to test the woman's patience any further. He took his seat and watched as the woman passed around the chairs and tables to stand in front of them. He avoided eye contact, sinking back into his chair in hopes he would become less noticeable. He felt afraid to move, afraid to speak, as if a whisper might cause the room to explode.

"I'm glad someone can follow instructions. I suppose introductions are in order. My name is Herzin. So far, you've both been fortunate enough to have never stepped foot in my halls, but I'm sure you've heard stories. I am the Judge of Trials and now your instructor."

Garild felt himself drain of color. He'd heard about the Temple of Trials and none of it was good. For the Bonded that strayed from their given path, a trial was held to decide their punishment. Herzin alone held the keys to their fate and from what he had heard, her punishments wasn't always kind nor fair. He wasn't sure how much of it was truth and how much was grossly exaggerated, but the fact that she was now their instructor sent a chill of fear up his spine.

"We'll try to avoid getting into any trouble. We wouldn't want to see more of you than we have to," Kirheen snapped.

Herzin regarded her the way one would a bug they'd just squashed under their heel. "The feeling is quite mutual, dear. Do pray you never end up in my hall. I think your already dour opinion of me would sour quite quickly. Shooting down your insults is entertaining and all, but we have work to do. I need to explain a few things to you and I need your full attention. I assume that won't be a problem?"

Before Kirheen could shoot back with a remark, Garild spoke. "Of course," he said quickly. "No problem at all." Kirheen shot him an annoyed glance.

"Good. Now, I'm going to ask you some questions to get a grasp of your knowledge. Answer to your full extent. It will dictate the training you receive from here on out. First off, I'd like to hear your opinion on something. Garild, tell me what you know of your bond. What does it mean to be Bonded?"

All his life, he'd been told being Bonded was the greatest honor one could be given. To be granted such a connection with another was a beautiful and special thing, one to be cherished and respected. Deep within his heart, he truly believed that.

He also knew that their bond was meant to strengthen their powers; to help them learn and guide each other until they would be strong enough to face the Darkness. Though he believed in his bond so strongly, he found it hard to put to words such feelings, especially with Kirheen sitting next to him. For him, their bond meant a lot and though she didn't feel the same, he hoped there would come a time when her feelings would change. As long as he didn't give up on her, he knew she'd come around eventually.

"It's a great honor. It's the truest connection one can have with another person. It's quite a gift, being able to develop a connection so deep that you could know the heart and mind of another as well as you know your own. It is the best way to strengthen the powers we are blessed with." He felt himself blushing as he spoke, the words revealing what he truly felt in his heart. That feeling was quickly dashed against the rocks as Kirheen rolled her eyes, obviously at odds with his feelings on the subject.

"How very eloquent, Garild. It *is* a gift and one that should not be squandered." At this, Herzin cast a glance at Kirheen. "And what of you, Kirheen? Care to tell me how you feel about this subject?"

Kirheen sighed. "I don't believe it's a gift, so much as a curse. It allows our minds and hearts to be known by another, regardless of whether we desire such an intrusion. Using it to battle the Darkness is one thing, using our power to invade the minds of our friends is quite another."

"An...interesting perspective."

Garild felt his stomach drop. He really was a fool. "Kirheen, you can't really feel that way."

"And why not," she snapped. "Should you be allowed access to my thoughts and my heart simply because you desire it, because it is expected of me?"

He was at a loss for words. He couldn't believe she actually felt that way. Herzin spoke for him, calming the situation before it had a chance to escalate. "Strange that you two have been bound when you share such...different opinions on the matter. Perhaps you can find some common ground here. In ways, you are both right in your assessments. Our power, bestowed upon us by the Allseer, is a gift. To say otherwise is a slight against the Goddess herself, Kirheen. However, your bond, regardless of how you personally feel about it, is a means to an end. All of this training will lead you to one thing; battling the Darkness. But do tell me how you can expect to block out the power of the Darkness if you've never experienced the sensation? How would you know it was happening? You'd fall under that corruption without the training I am to provide you."

"There has to be others ways than this," Kirheen said.

"And we've tried them. This is the best method of strengthening your powers whether you like it or not. There is no argument to be had here. Either you learn to use your powers, or you spend the rest of your days toiling about and learning how to stitch."

Kirheen grumbled under her breath, crossing her arms over her chest protectively.

"I know you've both heard of the Darkness. Garild, please enlighten us on what that is?"

"The Darkness is a plague that swept through the lands beyond Sanctuary, destroying both the land and those that lived there, often turning them into violent husks. There used to be people like us but without the powers of the mind. They existed until the Darkness came and drove them all to madness. Only those blessed by the Allseer survived and fled North."

Herzin nodded. "Good. Do you have anything to add to that, Kirheen? What are your powers for?"

"Our powers are used to cleanse the Darkness. Our goal is to push back the corruption and reclaim the world that was taken from us."

"I hope speaking those words makes you realize the importance of our struggle, Kirheen. Without our powers, the Darkness would have taken this world long ago. You were both born with these powers and it is the only reason you survive. It is a heavy burden to bear, surely, but it is a responsibility that ensures our survival."

Kirheen sighed loudly, obviously bored by the history lesson. She had a tendency to disregard the dangers beyond their own bubble, believing it to be an exaggeration, something to spur them on the path of learning their powers. He wondered if the

Darkness frightened her at all, or if it really was just the thought of having another in her mind that scared her so.

"You can be bored of this if you want to, but you can either grow to fight the Darkness or you can become a testament to failure and spend the rest of your days aiding those that were more dedicated to the cause."

Something switched in Kirheen and a coldness seemed to grow in her stormy eyes. She locked her gaze onto her instructor. "I'll never be just a failure."

Herzin smirked. "Then you better stop acting like one."

Chapter 3

The first night in their new home left Kirheen feeling bitter. She listened to the gentle breathing of Garild across from her and wished she were anywhere but in her bed, stuck within Sanctuary. It wasn't possible, she *knew* that, but it didn't stop her from thinking it. If she hadn't felt completely trapped before, she certainly did now.

Their instructor hadn't helped matters. The Judge of Trials, feared by all, was a bumbling old woman with a chip on her shoulder. Kirheen didn't like her. There was something about the woman that felt wrong. She wasn't looking forward to spending her days training with her.

Morning came and they were delivered a meal of bread and dried meat. It was tasteless stuff, but Kirheen was used to that. Until the rest of the Bondless went through their Ritual, all meals were confined to their home.

A foul mood hovered over her like a cloud and it got worse the moment Herzin stepped through the door. She didn't want to train, didn't want to learn about her powers. She wasn't ready for this, to have her mind, the one safe place she had, defiled.

They took their seats in front of the fire and Herzin stepped before them, her air of pompous superiority radiating about her as it had the day prior. The fish swam in their home, slowly circling each other and Kirheen watched them intently, arms crossed.

"I hope you both had a good morning. Are you ready for your lesson today?"

Garild was in a fine mood and he nodded his head enthusiastically. Kirheen tried to ignore it, tried to ignore them both but his eagerness grated at her nerves. She just wanted to go back to bed, to be away from them both.

"Good," Herzin said, completely ignoring Kirheen. At least the feeling was mutual. "Today, we will talk about your gift and I'll provide a demonstration of the things you will be learning in the coming weeks. Tell me, do you both sense your powers? We've never had, nor allowed you to use them in the past, but they are there. Sometimes you've used them without trying. Garild?"

"I can sense something there, but I have to focus very hard. It's like it's just out of reach," Garild said.

Kirheen knew what he meant. She *knew* she had powers, had even attempted to tap into them before, but they always seemed a little beyond her grasp. Now, faced with having to use them, she found she didn't want to. How could she just be expected to give her thoughts away, to drop her walls and let someone in that she hadn't chosen? It wasn't fair and it wasn't right. Everything had been chosen for her. The people she grew up with, the clothes she wore, the food she ate, the path she was expected to take through life. Nothing was her own. The only thing she had was her mind and her heart and neither of those was she willing to give up.

"Kirheen, are you going to answer me," Herzin chided, looking at her expectantly.

"I feel the same as Garild. I feel it, out of reach."

"Nothing else?"

"No."

Herzin huffed. "Your powers are there, I assure you. It takes immense focus to use them. As we progress, you'll find yourselves feeling drained as you learn to hone and target your powers. Today, we will work on some very simple exercises, something to strengthen the bond with your power so you can find the use of it a bit easier."

Kirheen felt her palms begin to sweat, her anxiety getting the better of her. She wasn't ready for this intrusion. She couldn't just let them in. "I think I'd rather have madness," she whispered, instantly regretting her words. Herzin's eyes flickered to her, burning with malice.

"You *will* cooperate, girl. You don't have a choice. We're not doing anything today to harm your precious mind so calm yourself."

She felt the panic rising. "It doesn't matter. I won't do it. I won't allow either of you to just pull apart my mind and pick through it like a book you can just stick your nose into. You can keep your stupid powers. I don't want them."

Garild looked at her like she'd just punched him in the face. His jaw hit the floor, his eyes wide with surprise. Herzin crossed her arms, puffing herself up as she prepared to talk her down. She wasn't having any of it. Pushing herself up from her chair, she locked eyes with Herzin defiantly and then turned to leave. She was almost to the door when Herzin spoke.

"Kirheen, this display is cute but unnecessary. One more step and I'll make you regret your brashness. I have not excused you."

Kirheen realized Herzin probably wasn't used to people disobeying her, let alone a young woman, but she didn't care. Earning her ire wasn't exactly her plan, but she had to be free of them, to be out of the room before it all consumed her.

"I'll be excusing myself today, thank you. I want nothing to do with the Allseer, her powers and certainly nothing to do with you." She looked back over her shoulder to give Garild a half-hearted grin. She didn't want to do this to him, but she couldn't do what they wanted her to do. She couldn't allow it.

Herzin spoke, her voice thick with anger. There was an edge of warning, a hint of the consequences that would follow. "Kirheen...not...another...step."

It was too late to heed that warning. Kirheen reached for the door, her hand gripping the intricately carved door handle. It felt solid beneath her fingers, cold and smooth. As she went to turn it, the world shifted. A faint pressure blossomed in the center of her forehead, creeping outwards and gaining strength like the start of a bad headache.

Looking down, she watched the door handle melt, the glowing wraith wood oozing between her fingers and running down the back of her hand. She blinked, trying to comprehend what she was seeing. Pain followed the path of melted wood as it traveled down her arm, so intense she dropped to her knees. She reached out her other hand, placing it against the door as she tried to remain upright, but it had turned into a violent glowing pool. It pulled her close, covering her arms, her chest and finally her face.

Pain exploded through her body, spreading like a fire as it burned through her senses. In her mind, she could sense thousands of tiny black tendrils stretching out, poking and prodding, trying to find a weak point to pick apart. Each attempt felt like a needle stabbing into her flesh, like the strange white haired man stabbing her with inky blackness. Stab, stab, stab.

Suddenly the glowing hot fire that covered her shattered, just as the walls of her mind did the same. Out poured her thoughts, as powerful and overwhelming as a hurricane. She gasped for air, floundering about hopelessly in her own mind, searching for anything to repair the damage, to rebuild the walls, but there was nothing but doubt and sadness and an undeniable feeling that her life was not hers to control.

And then something appeared in the distance, bright and glowing like a jewel. It was an emerald, green and blazing. As it hovered closer, it took form and she realized it was an eye. A great hate filled emerald; the eyes of disapproval. It was Herzin, picking through her thoughts with clawed hands. Pick, pick, pick. "I warned you," she teased. "Warned you. I warned you."

"Get out," Kirheen gasped. "Get out of my head. Get out!" She curled into herself, pulling together her thoughts and wrapping them tightly against her body like a shield. "I don't want you here! Get out!"

The sensation continued, the hole grew bigger, the walls crumbling into the sea of her mind. She focused, breathing deep, tasting the sickly sweet copper taste of blood on her tongue. "GET OUT!"

With a scream, she threw her thoughts outward against the eyes, tearing through them with all the force she could muster. They widened and cracked, the emeralds shattering and filling the sea with green. She felt her own eyes open, those stormy eyes given to her by faces she could not remember. The pressure vanished and she collapsed against the floor, blood speckling the surface. She felt hands touching her face, heard her name whispered in the dark and then she was gone, sinking away into the only shelter she could find. Sleep took her quickly, embracing her in tranquil darkness. She welcomed it, letting her mind and body drift into oblivion.

Chapter 4

Tomias was thankful for a chance to stretch his legs, to journey about the village and not be cramped on the floor, needle in hand. It was his first week of Rituals and while putting on a show for the Union Master was amusing, it was also tiring. He was happy for a chance to get away. His twin, Fenir, walked at his side. His expression was somber, his eyes scanning the trees but he could feel tranquility radiating from him despite his frown. Their bond was strong, probably stronger than most in Sanctuary. It was both a blessing and a curse and he was forced to feel much of what his brother felt, whether he wanted to or not.

They had traveled South, away from the Temple of Union, meandering down the deserted path that led to the Circle of Rest. They didn't have a reason for going there, he simply wanted to walk and he'd let his feet carry him where they willed. He could see the giant wraith wood up ahead, towering over the circle of homes made for the Bonded. As they drew closer, he felt a strange sensation, an excess of power floating around them, crackling like the air before lightning strikes. Fenir glanced at him, tilting his head questioningly.

'*You feel that,*' he asked, forming the question with his mind and sending it out to Tomias.

Tomias nodded. "I do," he said aloud. "I don't like it. Something is wrong."

It was odd. The sensation was emanating from the home recently occupied by the Bonded they'd performed the ritual on the night before. Rumor had it Herzin had been tasked with teaching them. She should have been there now.

They increased their pace, stepping quickly towards the house. Fenir took the steps in a single stride with Tomias on his heels. The power was thick in the air, making his hair stand on end. His brother pushed the door open and nearly knocked over a brown haired boy he recognized from the ritual. What had his name been again?

It didn't matter. The smell of blood hit his senses and he instantly switched to the defensive. Fenir threw out a hand, catching the boy by the front of his robe and pulled him close. He looked terrified, his eyes squeezing shut as if he expected to be struck. He stammered out an explanation, words slipping out without control.

"I-I don't know what happened. They were arguing and Kirheen tried to leave and then...I don't know, something happened! Please, I didn't do it! I didn't do anything! I was trying to find help."

"Woah, slow down there! We're not blaming you yet. Fenir, let the poor boy go before he dies of fright!"

His twin grunted but released his grip. Tomias peered around them, taking in the scene. An ashen haired girl lay on the ground behind Garild's feet, blood splattered on the floor around her head. In the back an older woman, undoubtedly Herzin, lay in a similar state. He muttered a curse under his breath.

"You'll have to forgive my brother, he's far more suspicious than I. For looking so much alike you'd think we'd not differ so much in personality. And do forgive him, please, for he has not the tongue to ask for it himself. Quite a shame too, considering his ability to frighten children."

'Oh, will you shut up,' Fenir commanded angrily.

On a good day, Tomias found it hard to still his own tongue. Today was not a good day and with stress came an endless stream of words. He sometimes wondered if his brother hadn't chosen to be mute simply because he spoke enough for them both. "Ah, right. We have a situation to attend to. I'm Tomias. This silent, brooding companion of mine is my bond mate, Fenir. A pleasure! Now if you would kindly step aside, I must attend to this current crisis."

And what a crisis it was. Tomias was beginning to stitch it together. Someone had gotten out of hand and he had a sneaking suspicion of who that was. Fenir stepped to the side, pulling Garild with him so he'd have enough room to work. He knelt down next to the girl and rolled her over, wincing as he noticed the blood across her face, a result of a sudden bloody nose. He gently pried open an eyelid and looked closely. Her pupil was huge, dilated well beyond what they should have been. "Hmm, she's suffered quite a bit of trauma. All mental of course but she's having a physical reaction to it."

Garild looked terribly concerned. "What is that supposed to mean? Can't you help her?"

Tomias ignored him. "Oh, Herzin, you cruel old bat. Seems you bit off a bit more than you could chew this time, didn't you? Serves you right, using this much power against her."

"Wait! What do you mean? What did she do?"

"Hush. I've got to retrieve her. Unless you'd rather me not and then you can blame yourself when she doesn't wake up." He bent over the girl and focused his powers, forcing them out towards her. He gently prodded his way into her mind, slipping through the cracked surface of her walls with practiced ease.

"Kirheen, wake up." The words were faint, a distorted whisper that carried through her mind. With a flutter of her eyes, she woke up, pushing herself up into a sitting position. There was nothing around her but darkness, an endless night that seemed to go on forever. "Kirheen," the voice whispered again. She shrank back in fear, searching for those hateful emerald eyes but they were nowhere to be seen.

The pain that had been her prison was no more. She was now alone in the darkness. It was strangely peaceful, a quiet place, and she found herself wanting to drift off. *Sleep would be so nice*, she thought to herself.

"Don't fall asleep, Kirheen. You'll never wake if you do."

"Who are you," she questioned, squinting as she tried to find the source of the voice. "I can't see anything. There is nothing here."

"I'm a friend. Don't worry, I'll show you. Can you see me?"

She looked around again, but there were only shadows. "No. There's nothing."

"Look harder." Staring into the distance, she thought she could see a faint glow, but it was far off and she felt weak. For all she knew, it was just a trick. With all the strength she could muster, she stood, feeling a wave of nausea roll over her.

"Where am I? Why can't I see anything?"

"You're lost, Kirheen. Your mind has you trapped. You need to find a way out."

"My mind?"

"Yes. Now focus. Find a way."

"Alright, I'll try." Taking an uneasy step forward, she was suddenly blinded by a blue light shining just below her foot. It disappeared as soon as she stopped moving, and once more she was surrounded by night. *Odd*, she thought. She took another step forward and the blue light flashed again. "I see light whenever I walk."

"Do you trust it?"

Kirheen considered his words. She certainly didn't feel fear, not the way she'd felt when those terrible green eyes bore down on her. "I guess so."

"Then walk." And so she did. It felt as though her journey would never end. On and on the blue lights went until it felt as though her strength had been drained from her body. She trudged forward, slowing with every step.

"I'm so tired. I don't think I can make it. I thin--" Before she could finish her sentence, she stumbled forward. The darkness beneath her exploded into a burst of bright light and then she was falling. Big puffy clouds floated lazily around her, unaware of her panic as she tried hopelessly to grab on to anything that would stop her fall. Her hands slipped through rolling clouds, coming away slick with moisture. Far below her, she could see an ocean, bright and blue. She sped towards it, racing faster and faster, her heart feeling like it had lodged itself into her throat.

"Help me, I'm falling! I'm falling!"

"Trust yourself, Kirheen."

"I can't."

Just before she hit the water, a scream burst from her. The cold water filled her open mouth, freezing the scream in her throat and stopping her lungs. Her heart hammered a final frantic beat before it too stopped.

Garild watched as Kirheen awoke with a gasp, her eyes wild with panic. She thrashed under the arms of Tomias, digging at his arms with her nails. Tomias refused to let go despite the obvious pain he felt each time her nails caught his flesh. "Kirheen, stop struggling. You're going to be alright. Breath."

His voice was nearly drowned out by the sounds of Kirheen gulping for air. "I can't," she gasped. "I ca-can't breathe." Her nails found his hands and she clawed at his fingers, trying desperately to break his grip. Garild didn't understand why he didn't just let her go.

"Tomias, let go of her! She's awake now," he cried, voice thick with concern. He flung himself forward on to the ground next to Kirheen and reached for her. Tomias shot him a warning glare and his hand faltered.

"Don't you dare," Tomias said between gritted teeth. "Get out of the way. Now!" He turned his attention back to Kirheen, grabbing her arms and pinning them down. Her breathing had become more controlled and she'd stopped thrashing about. "Breathe, girl. If you go back to that place, you'll never return. Stay here with my voice. Right here. Good."

"I'm trying," she moaned, tears streaming down her cheeks. She sucked in air through her nose and released it through her mouth, calming herself.

"That's good. Again."

Garild stared helplessly. He wanted to do something to help her but he felt lost. Reaching out, he took hold of her hand and squeezed it gently. Suddenly he could feel it, the panic coursing through her veins, her racing heart, the ache of her lungs. All of the fear and the pain was his and he gasped as it overtook him. He heard Tomias shout, but through the fog he couldn't make out what he'd said. He struggled to separate himself from the pain, to hold it back but it was a violent rage, a tsunami of emotions that drowned him.

He felt hands digging into his arms and he was yanked backwards. His hand slipped out of Kirheen's and he found himself flat on his back, Fenir looming over him with a disapproving frown. His head pounded, though whether it was from hitting the floor or the wave of fear he'd just felt, he couldn't be sure. He pushed himself up slowly.

"This is the second time you've made a fool of yourself, Garild," Tomias chided. Kirheen lay by his side sound asleep, her face peaceful. "But, lucky for you, it's only your first day. You'll learn."

"I'm not so sure I want to learn anymore," Garild groaned, rubbing his forehead. "What happened?"

"It would require far more of an explanation then I can provide now, but put simply, Kirheen just entered your mind. In her current state, she couldn't quite control that."

Garild looked horrified. "Is that what it's like every time?"

"Oh! By the Allseer herself, no! Not in the slightest. If it were so, you really think anyone would let it happen? She merely transferred some of her feelings to you, her minds way of easing the pain she was feeling."

"So what I felt…"

"Those were her emotions, everything she was feeling at that moment. While normally I would scold you for making such a stupid mistake, it did allow me the chance to seal her mind so for that you have my thanks. How are you feeling?"

"My head feels like it's going to split apart. Is she going to be alright?"

Tomias smiled, though it didn't reach his eyes. He looked dreadfully exhausted, as if the use of his powers had aged him ten years. "Just fine. It might take her a few days to fully recover. Such a thing can be awfully tiring, especially when you aren't expecting it. She'll need lots of rest, so don't let her go running off seeking revenge just yet… or ever for that matter."

"What about Herzin?" He glanced behind him. Fenir had knelt down, scooping her up off the ground. She hung limp in his arms, in the same deep slumber as Kirheen. "Will she be okay?"

"Unfortunately, yes." Tomias scowled, his lips pulling down so far it was almost comical. "She'll be down for a few days, same as your bond mate. Let us all hope it is a longer recovery. I'm sure once she awakens, the whole of Sanctuary will feel her wrath. Come, we need to report to the Union Master. I don't imagine he'll be too happy about all this." Slipping his arms under Kirheen, he gently lifted her up, cradling her against his chest. Garild followed him out of the room and into their bedroom. "Pull back the covers."

He did as he was told, waiting until Kirheen was snuggled among the pillows before he tucked the blankets around her shoulders. She breathed softly, her face a mask of tranquility.

"Should I stay here?"

"I'd say so. If Nyson wishes to speak with you about this matter, I'm sure he'll come calling. Just stay here with Kirheen." He squeezed his shoulder reassuringly before trudging from the room. Garild doubted he was looking forward to reporting to the Union Master. It made him scared to think what would happen to them once he found out.

He sat on the edge of his bed, exhaustion sweeping over him. The pounding in his skull had subsided but he felt heavy, as if some great weight were pushing down on him. Perhaps it was how Tomias had felt. Lying back on the bed, he breathed deep, nestling his head against the pillows. It wasn't long before he too was resting peacefully, the events of the morning momentarily forgotten.

Chapter 5

The Union Master sat silent, his face a stone mask that shifted and changed with the fluttering of the candlelight. The sweet smell of cinnamon filled the air, giving warmth to the otherwise cold room. It did nothing, however, to warm his mood which cracked and splintered like ice shattering under ones foot. One wrong step was all it would take; a slight shift and some unlucky soul would fall into the frigid depths of his anger.

Today had not been the day for a situation like this. He already felt stretched, his mind so thin that it felt like it would snap at any moment. Before him, Herzin rested peacefully. She looked younger in such dim light, her long gray hair tumbling about her shoulders. It gave a hint of the woman she once was, before anger and pride had turned her into a weathered old crone. Nyson wondered if she knew, if she realized what the great green monster had done to her beauty. He doubted she cared. Beauty wasn't something Herzin fussed over, just as she hadn't thought to fuss over causing a near disaster.

The thought made him seethe, and he clenched his teeth tightly together, grinding them back and forth as he sneered down at her over the pointed tip of his nose. She wasn't entirely to blame.

He should have known, perhaps *did* know, that giving her power over a girl apt at challenging authority was a bad idea. He expected them to clash, but he hadn't expected them to try killing each other. He had hoped that Herzin would be able to rein her in, to fight fire with fire. Instead they'd both burned up, neither willing to back down. It had been foolish. Had he really expected anything less from the Judge of Trials?

She was a woman that spent her days deciding the fate of those who chose to break their bonds, those that chose selfishness over union. Whatever bit of sympathy she had, it had dried up long ago. He respected her for it. It was because of her that they could keep control. There were apt to be Bonded that slipped up and she was there to crack the whip. Her authority was absolute, the knife hidden behind his words.

She was known to be cruel, her punishments at times harsh, but without her he knew Sanctuary would be lost. She was the reason the youngest children told stories about being turned into emotionless husks, the very stories that kept many of the Bondless from doing anything stupid as they grew older, however exaggerated those stories were.

He respected her, but at the moment he also hated her.

She stirred, as if his thoughts had somehow roused her from her slumber. Her eyelids fluttered open, revealing emerald eyes dimmed by exhaustion. It took her a moment to gain her senses, and even longer before she met his piercing gaze. When she finally did, she said nothing, but her face was heavy with guilt. She took a deep breath before speaking, her words barely above a whisper, as if she feared awakening a sleeping beast.

"Nyson, I..."

"Silence," he hissed, leaning forward until his elbows rested on the bed, his fingers laced to support his chin. "You've disappointed me, Herzin."

"I'm sorry, Nyson. I can explain," she urged, holding the blankets firmly against her chest as she raised herself into a sitting position.

Nyson scoffed, annoyance flashing across his face like lightning. "I don't need you to explain anything. That job was already done for you. What I need you to do is make me understand. Make me understand how a woman far old enough to know better would try to break a child before she'd even shown her how to guard her own mind. Make me understand what would possess you to be so foolish that you'd damn near kill not just her, but yourself. Make me understand before I feel the need to finish the job and be done with you."

Not even the warm light from the candle could keep her face from turning a deathly white. She clutched the blankets tight, frail fingers digging deeply into the folds. She chewed on her lower lip, thoughts dancing in her eyes as she tried to formulate her next words, words she no doubt would choose carefully.

"I was trying to teach her a lesson, to teach her respect and authority. I didn't expect her to react so violently. I should have been more cautious and...more patient."

"You expect me to believe that is all it was? That you were trying to teach her a lesson? You don't set someone on fire and expect them to know how to put it out without teaching them first! Your haste and recklessness have shamed me, Herzin. You've made a mockery of me and it will not go unpunished."

Her green eyes were suddenly ablaze. "I've shamed you? I, the woman who has kept you in power all of these years. I, the woman who has done everything for the sake of this place! I shamed you? It shames me that you fail to see the reason for all of this."

Nyson bit back his anger. "You want to blame me for your brashness, now? That isn't wise."

"The girl is trouble. She has had far too much freedom, far too much free reign to act out and question the world around her."

"Oh, don't tell me this is what this is about! It's irrelevant."

"I'd say not. The girl is a spark and one that needs to be controlled. She's likely to burn the whole of Sanctuary down if we don't put her in her place now! Or should we just let her grow more dangerous? I have to admit, that seems more your style considering you let it happen before."

Nyson stood in a fury, his shadow looming ominously behind him like some dark force ready to consume the light. He couldn't believe she was so bold, to bring up the past in such a way. He only wished she'd realized those words were like throwing fire on an oil patch. "Watch your words, Herzin. I'm warning you."

She didn't relent. "But you did let it happen, did you not? When that bastard brother of yours spoke out, you did nothing.

You chose to back down while he tore apart the world your family so carefully built. *You* let him do it and we all paid the price!"

"You dare question my past decisions? We're still alive because of me, alive because I chose to let them create their own life instead of bringing Sanctuary down around our heads!"

Flinging the blankets away from herself, Herzin stood, stepping forward until she was mere inches from Nyson. She raised her chin defiantly, staring up at him through thick lashes. "Don't fool yourself. We're not alive, we haven't been for years. They took something from us and we'll never get it back. I'm not going to let it happen again. I can stop this from happening to others, from having others feel the pain that we felt. Do you know why I did what I did to Kirheen? I did what I did because all I see when I look into her pretty little face is the very man that betrayed us all, the man that stepped on everything we ever stood for in order to fulfill his own selfish desires. That bastard took everything and I am not going to let it happen again. I am not going to let her break our pride the way he did when he walked away with that whore you called a wife!"

Nyson lashed out like a snake, his fist connecting with her face with all the solidity of a hurled brick. She tumbled back against the bed, hand held to her face. He could see the shock and anger the blow caused and as her eyes turned back to him, he could see the loathing burning in those emerald depths. He bent down ever so slowly until he was level with her. He pulled her hand away from her face, seeing the bruise already forming on her cheek. His hand slid along her face, cupping her chin. He could feel her jaw tense beneath his touch. There was a void he was slipping into, a dark place where he fell at times like these.

"Herzin, if you ever speak of them again, I swear to you, it will be the last words that ever leave your lips. Do you understand me?"

She ignored him, her eyes fluttering away to a far corner of the room. A surge of anger and his hand slipped into her hair, pulling it hard and forcing her to turn her eyes towards him. Their eyes locked and she nodded meekly.

"Say it."

"I won't speak of them again," she said, her eyes never leaving his.

The anger was dissipating, fleeing as quickly as it came. He unlatched his hand from her hair, wiping his hand on his robes as if he were wiping away dirt. They were shaking now, a damned thing that always happened after an episode like this. He clenched them tightly at his sides, not wanting to show such weakness in front of her. "Tomias and Fenir will be taking over the training of Kirheen and Garild. You are no longer needed, nor welcome, to perform that task."

He turned away from her, catching a brief glance of her face flickering between hurt and anger, an endless struggle with no clear victor. He didn't like hurting her. Despite the actions caused by his anger, he did care for her. The Sanctuary that existed had spawned from both of their efforts. She was indispensable, he knew that, but she was also dangerous. He may have shared the responsibilities of leadership, and on occasion a bed, with the woman, but he didn't exactly trust her. If it came down to it, he was willing to break her, to control her mind as he'd done time and time again with others. She would learn to obey him... learn or be broken like the rest.

Chapter 6

For the first time, Kirheen had nothing to say. The people around her had faded into the background, becoming nothing but a ripple on the edge of her consciousness. She ran a small wooden spoon in lazy circles through oats that had long since gone cold and wondered how anyone found the stuff appealing. Many of the other Bonded had finished their meals and had set off to meet with their instructors. Only a few remained at the table, Garild among them.

It had been a week since her dreadful experience, and yet she still felt withdrawn and paranoid. She was acutely aware of her own personal space, of the walls in her mind. She checked them often, searching for cracks and holes that someone could squeeze through. Headaches were a frequent occurrence, painful and sudden, but Tomias assured her they'd go away with time.

Sleep was elusive. When she closed her eyes at night, she'd soon find herself slipping into terrible nightmares she found hard to wake from. She'd been given an assortment of foul tasting herbs to help but they'd been of little use. The dark circles under her eyes were evidence enough of that.

She had to admit, having new instructors was a welcome change. Tomias and Fenir were odd, to be sure, but it saved her from ever having to see Herzin again. She still couldn't believe what she'd done to her and she had no desire to have such a thing repeated. As far as she was concerned, nobody was getting in to her mind any time soon. They had their work cut out for them, that much was certain.

Fingers touched her hand and she jumped, causing far more of a ruckus then she'd intended. Her palm hit her spoon, sending it skittering across the table. The noise caught the attention of the few Bonded remaining in the room and they turned to stare. Kirheen sighed, turning her head to see who had disturbed her. Isa sat frozen, bright blue eyes wide, her hand pulled back near her face as if she'd been burned. Kirheen had grown up with Isa in the Temple of Growth. She was a kind, quiet girl but had a tendency to stick her nose into other people's business if she thought she could help.

"I-I'm sorry," she stuttered. "I was just seeing if you were alright. You haven't eaten anything today and I just…"

Kirheen grumbled, squeezing her eyes shut for a moment while she tried to bring herself back to reality. She didn't want to explain herself, didn't want to have to keep assuring people that she wasn't broken. With the curious faces of her fellow Bonded looming in her peripheral, she saw little choice in the matter. "I'm fine. I'm alright."

Isa brushed a strand of curly dark hair away from her face and exchanged a glance with her bond mate, a boy named Ian. "Are you sure? You really don't look like you're feeling good."

"I'm feeling fine," Kirheen said, forcing a smile. It made her face feel like it was made out of wax. "I just don't have much of an appetite today, that's all."

The girl stared at her, concern all but bursting from her big blue eyes. Ian shifted, clearing his throat as he prepared to speak. Kirheen let her eyes meet his, her breath catching in her throat. Like Isa, she had grown up with Ian. They'd always had a tense relationship, and it wasn't for lack of liking him. In fact, if she was honest with herself, it was because she liked him too much. She'd always kept her distance from him, always tried to avert eye contact and avoid conversation. It was too difficult to concentrate when he was around. When she'd pictured herself with a bond mate, it was always Ian she had imagined.

Like his bond mate, he had large, luminous eyes though they were a deep shade of green. Thick brown hair stuck out in an artful disarray that would have looked absolutely ridiculous on anyone else. Perhaps it was the air of confidence he gave off that allowed him to pull off not brushing his hair in the morning. Whatever it was, Kirheen had always found it intriguing.

"Are you certain, Kirheen? You haven't eaten breakfast the past three days." Peeking to either side, he leaned forward and spoke quietly. "Is it because of what happened? Because of what Herzin did to you?"

"Was it really as bad as people are saying," Isa piped in.

Kirheen fixed them both with a flat stare. It was incredibly difficult trying to go about your life and forget about being mentally attacked when that seemed to be all people wanted to talk about. She had a sudden desire to flee the room, to leave them behind without an answer. What good would that do? Sure, she might escape explaining herself but she'd be silently confirming what they all believed, that she was broken.

Kirheen sighed deeply, preparing a lie that she hoped would suffice. "Listen, both of you. What's done is done. It was just a simple accident and I'm fine. Me not eating these incredibly dull oats every morning has nothing to do with what happened. I don't like breakfast, plain and simple."

Several of the other Bonded that had been eaves dropping snapped their heads the other way as she scanned the table, whether out of disappointment or fear of being scolded she couldn't tell. They finished off the last of their meal, pretending like they hadn't just been waiting for some horrifying tale of mental torture.

Isa looked as if she'd been scolded by the Union Master himself, shuffling in her seat as she tried to contain her nervousness. She looked so innocent and unsure of herself that it made Kirheen feel horrible for snapping at them. Ian just gave her a look of uncertainty, lips pulled into a disapproving half smile, clearly not believing a single word she'd said. He didn't press the issue further and for that Kirheen was grateful.

Sliding his bowl out of the way, Ian rose from the table and waited for Isa to do the same. "Whatever ails you, Kirheen, I do hope you start feeling better," he said, his smile genuine this time.

"And I as well," Isa said, stacking her empty bowl with the others. She smiled and bowed to the both of them before shuffling out of the room, Ian at her side.

Kirheen bristled with irritation, her already bad mood reaching an abysmal low. To her right, she felt Garild shift nervously. "They are right, you know," he said softly, treading lightly into the conversation. His bowl was empty, pushed far in front of him. He'd been waiting for her, she realized. For some reason it made her even more annoyed.

Kirheen scoffed. "Not you too!"

"I'm just worried," he snapped back.

"Can we please just ignore the fact that I'm a complete and total wreck right now? It would be really nice for a change," she hissed, trying to stay quiet enough that the others wouldn't hear.

"I just want to make sure you're alright! I'm your bond mate, I'm pretty sure it's written somewhere that I have every right to worry about you!"

"Well…stop! I'm fine! Tomias already said I'd be just fine and that there is nothing to worry about!"

"Well, he also said that I need to keep an eye on you, to make sure you don't fall back into your own mind and it doesn't look like you're doing a very good job." He'd gotten bolder over the past week, perhaps a sign that her bad attitude was rubbing off on him. And to think he'd been so innocent.

"Can you return to the meek, quiet, do-whatever-I-say Garild for a bit? I think I'd like that."

He frowned but kept his mouth shut, at least about her current mental state. "Come on. We really should get going. We're going to be late and Tomias will never let us hear the end of it."

"There is no end to Tomias, ever. He never shuts up about anything," she said sarcastically. She rose from the table, stretching her arms over her head as she willed herself to do anything other than mope. It took far more effort than she wanted to admit.

She trudged after Garild, stepping out of the Temple of Gathering and into the bright morning light. She had to blink until her eyes adjusted. It was a brisk morning, the cold air seeping through the fabric of her robes, raising tiny bumps on her skin. She found it rather refreshing, a nice change from the stuffy air of the temple.

All around her, the trees shimmered in the sunlight, as if made of some fragile stone that would crack at the slightest touch. The pale leaves twisted and intertwined, a ghastly canopy that reminded her of the frost that would soon come to Sanctuary. Many of the leaves had begun to fall from the trees and they crunched beneath her boots as she walked. She could lose herself in such things, to just be outside among the beauty and far away from those that would try and control her.

The path to their dwelling was a simple one and it wound its way gently through the forest ahead of them. Wraith wood trees lined the path, spreading for miles in either direction. There was no fence, no border or barrier to keep any of them from wandering into the woods. Just miles and miles of trees and a fog of fear thick enough to keep people from leaving.

"Garild, do you ever wonder what is out there," she questioned softly, slowing to a halt. Her eyes looked out into the sea of trees, her heart filled with a longing she couldn't begin to describe.

Garild halted next to her. He gave an exasperated sigh and shook his head. "No. I don't."

"Really? You don't wonder at all?"

"What is there to wonder? We all know what is out there."

"And just what is that," she challenged, arms crossing over her chest.

Garild grimaced. "I really don't even like to think about it. All that's out there is an endless waste, filled with madness and death and probably a number of things that would eat us in seconds!"

"And you really think it's as bad as they say?"

"It's probably worse," Garild whispered, meeting her eyes. "I'm thankful for the life I have here. I don't need to wonder about what's out there. I really don't want to know."

Kirheen frowned. "Maybe so, but I'm still curious."

"When has that ever helped you?"

She thought for a moment, disappointed when she realized that it never had. Sanctuary didn't reward the curious, at least not in her case. "It hasn't yet, but only because I'm the only one that has a brain around here. Nobody else respects that."

"Uh-huh. Now can we get going? You may be curious about what sort of lecture we'll get from Tomias for being late, but I'm not."

With a hearty sigh, Kirheen let her gaze drift back to the path ahead of them. "Fine. Let's go."

They traveled for a time in silence, the only sound the rustling of leaves and the chirping of birds in the trees around them. The beauty of the world around her had been but a temporary reprieve from her thoughts and she soon drifted back to them.

It had been a long time since the Darkness had crept into the world. Could it really have been so bad? Could they really be the only ones left, the only people capable of holding back the madness that lurked outside the confines of their village? A large part of her would have given anything to know. The desire to simply leave it all behind, to step into that forest and never return, was strong. But there was a part of her too that feared what she would find. What if it was like they said; nothing but a dark and dreary world full of horrors she couldn't possibly face. What would she do then? She couldn't bear the thought of going so far only to come back. Part of her knew that even if she did come back, they wouldn't just welcome her back with open arms.

A thought, and one that she found all the more terrifying, was if they were wrong. Suppose she ventured out into the world only to find that everything she'd been told was only half truths. What if she found others, survivors living life on their own terms. If she found such people, she wondered if she'd be accepted among them, and how it would feel to have a life that she could call her own. Maybe they'd just be ordinary people, and they wouldn't have any stupid powers. Her thoughts would be safe, her heart protected. She could simply be who she wanted to be and there would be no one to hurt her or tell her otherwise.

She couldn't imagine the disappointment she'd feel if she ventured out and didn't find such a wonderful reality. It was the fear of disappointment that kept her from bounding off into the forest at that very moment, to leave Garild behind in the bubble he seemed to enjoy so much.

She glanced over at him as he walked along, lost in thoughts of his own, though she doubted they were quite so daring. A sudden curiosity sprung within her and without knowing how or why she felt compelled to, she pushed out with her mind, seeking purchase in his thoughts. There was resistance, like hitting a wall and a tingling sensation spread across her forehead. She frowned, disappointed.

She hadn't exactly been honest in her first meeting with Herzin. She had done a lot more than just sense her powers; she'd used them. Her fear of having her mind read had been a part of her childhood and she had taken the earliest of precautions to strengthen her mind against such intrusions. It had been a matter of trial and error, tugging at the edges of her powers until she began to grasp the concept. It was simple really, a matter of focus. Focus she could use now.

Trying again, she tried focusing more intently, honing in on Garild and that wall she'd felt. Perhaps there was a way to break through it, not in the way that Herzin had, but gently. She just needed to create a small hole that she could peer through, just enough to see what he was thinking about. Again, she felt the wall but this time she sensed a weakness, a spot that with enough force she was sure she could break through.

Garild raised his hand quickly, scratching the side of his face. It startled her and she gasped, snapping her focus away from him. She tried hard to keep a straight face, to avoid letting her guilt show. Garild glanced her way, but his attention returned to the path ahead of them.

She felt very stupid. Here she was, constantly complaining about others trying to read her thoughts and she'd just tried to do the same to Garild. She was suddenly overwhelmed by the thought that maybe it was her curiosity that was the curse and not her powers. Either way, she wouldn't try it again. Besides, what if she messed up? She didn't know what she was doing and for all she knew, the same thing that Herzin did to her she could easily do to another. She didn't wish that pain upon anyone.

Trying not to look as guilty as she felt, she turned her attention back to the road and followed Garild.

By the time they reached their home, Kirheen's head was throbbing. She could feel a tightness in her throat, a churning in her belly that made her glad she'd skipped out on breakfast. Garild led the way, Kirheen following sluggishly. She focused on her breathing, trying hard not to obey her bodies desire to heave up what little there was in her stomach. She just wanted to lie down, pull a blanket over her head and let the shattered fragments of her skull settle back into place. Had Tomias not been waiting in the doorway, she would have done just that, but the look on his face told her she wouldn't be doing anything without being scolded first.

"Well, if it isn't my two favorite students! What a pleasant surprise to see you both here. I'm glad I've finally been deemed worthy of your attention this morning," Tomias chided, voice dripping with sarcasm. He wore dark blue robes with silver trim, his white hair pulled back away from his face in a high tail. He leaned against the doorway, arms crossed over his chest. "I'd love to hear a good explanation for this one, either of you? An hour less of training for the one with the best excuse."

Garild grimaced. "We're very sorry, Tomias. We were talking to Ian and Isa and lost track of the time."

Kirheen rolled her eyes. "Oh please, we weren't really talking to them by choice. Apparently my personal problems are of great interest lately so I decided to waste the morning telling everyone about my tale of woe and eternal suffering."

Tomias raised a brow, obviously intrigued. "And how did they like such a tale?"

"Oh, they really enjoyed it. I took great care to get all the details just perfect. Nothing like a good tale of mental anguish at the hands of my former master to get people motivated first thing in the morning. It was such an intriguing tale I even forgot to eat." At the thought of food, she felt a sudden tremble in her throat and a wave of nausea rolled over her. She squeezed her eyes shut, taking a slow intake of breath.

There was a brief glance between Tomias and Garild. "Kirheen, are you feeling quite alright?" Tomias unfolded his arms and stepped over to her, taking her by the shoulders gently. She could only imagine what he saw; tired bloodshot eyes, dark circles, sweat on her brow. She was a mess. Raising her eyes, she gave a halfhearted smile. "Are you still not sleeping?"

"No," she admitted sheepishly. "Those herbs have done very little."

He frowned. "And your head aches?"

"I have one now."

He could see the pain in her eyes, however hard she tried to hide it. "Let's get you inside. I'll have them fetch Trista. We'll see if she can't figure out something else for you. We'll postpone training, for a while at least." He smiled a crooked smile that was all pity. "Looks like your excuse won today."

Fenir glanced over his shoulder as they entered the room, his dark eyes betraying a hint of anger. He was seated in one of the chairs next to the fireplace, his right arm draped casually over the back. Unlike his twin, his white hair was unbound and fell limp around his face.

One of the many things Garild had learned over the past week was that Fenir couldn't speak. When questioned, Tomias had merely stated that he'd been born that way. It didn't stop him much. Most of his communication was done mentally, though it was slight even at that. Just because he could communicate didn't mean he wanted to, and Garild rarely heard him. With the glare they were receiving, he was suddenly very happy for that fact.

Tomias led Kirheen to the chair next to Fenir and she plopped down without hesitation, letting her body sink deeply into the cushion. She squeezed her eyes shut, resting her head against the back.

He had noticed her exhaustion at breakfast, but now it was written plainly on her face. Everything about her seemed drained, her face lacking color and her body limp as if it had given up on moving any more for the time being. He wished there was something he could do for her, some way for him to comfort her and make the pain go away. She'd suffered enough.

Without a word, Fenir grunted, rising from his seat and taking several large strides to the door.

Tomias spoke. "If you would Garild, can you please go with Fenir and fetch our healer? She might need help carrying supplies."

Garild nodded. "Of course." Though he agreed readily, the thought of accompanying Fenir made his stomach twist into knots. The man terrified him. He swallowed nervously and followed Fenir out into the clearing.

Fenir trudged along ahead of him, the tall grass squishing flat beneath his boots. They crossed the clearing quickly, Garild struggling to keep up with his long strides. Along the path to the North, a small wraith wood house rested to the side, smoke curling from the chimney. There were strange smells drifting in the air, mint and butter leaf blossoms and a variety of other scents he could not name.

With a heavy hand, Fenir knocked loudly on the door. There was a crash from within the house, the sound of a heavy kettle hitting the floor. Garild heard someone curse from within and a moment later, a red headed woman opened the door, her freckled face streaked with black powder. She wore a simple dark green robe, a lighter green sash tied around her waist. Her long fiery hair was braided and draped over her shoulder, small leaves and twigs sticking to it where it had brushed against some earlier project.

"What do you want," she said. "I'm quite busy."

Garild hesitated, waiting for Fenir to answer for him. When Fenir peeked back over his shoulder in annoyance, Garild blushed, realizing his mistake. He cleared his throat. "Uh, Trista?"

"Yes? Get on with it," she huffed, wiping the back of her hand across her brow. She left a wide streak of black powder in its wake.

"Tomias sent us. He needs you to bring some supplies for Kirheen."

"The ashen haired girl I saw to before? What's wrong with her now," she questioned.

"She hasn't been feeling well. She hasn't slept in days, she won't eat and she keeps getting headaches. I'm worried."

"And the herbs I gave her?"

"They haven't been helping."

Trista made several clicking noises with her tongue, tugging idly at her bottom lip with a sooty hand. "Give me just a moment, I think--" A smell drifted from the open door, one that carried the scent of scorched plants. Trista bolted from the door, knocking over a bottle with her braid as she flipped around. It hit the floor and shattered, sending shards scattering in all directions. "Oh no, no, no! You weren't supposed to burn."

Fenir sighed, leaning against the side of the house while he waited. Garild stepped closer to the door and peeked inside, half expecting to be hit by something. The room was dimly lit, the window that would have let in natural light long since covered in soot. A wide table took up most the room, and it was covered in a variety of bottles, bowls, vials and herbs. Plants hung from the ceiling, soaked in pots of water and littered the floor wherever he looked. There was a small bed in the far corner of the room, though even that had an assortment of plants and scrolls covering its surface.

Trista was bent near the fireplace, trying to salvage the plants that had blacked in the bottom of a pan. She cursed and threw her spoon aside. "And here I thought it was going to be a good day."

"Is there, uh, anything I can help you with," Garild asked, peering into the room cautiously.

"Bring me that pouch of vials on the table. The leather one."

Garild grabbed the leather pouch of vials and brought it to her, stepping carefully through the room. He tiptoed around bottles and plants, trying not to crush anything, though it seemed an impossible task. Trista took the vials from him and scanned the room.

"Hmm, perhaps dream blossom? No, not nearly strong enough. Sleepers kiss should do the trick. Mix it with burnt fern? No, star nettle would be better. And wraith bark." She spoke quietly to herself as she danced through the room, picking up plants and tools along the way. It was a wonder she could find anything in that mess.

She shoved aside some earlier project, making room for the potion she planned on making. She took to crushing and mixing until she had three vials of a berry colored liquid that looked almost too thick to drink.

"I do believe that is it. Shall we?" She beckoned to the door and Garild stepped out. Fenir was standing at the bottom of the steps, arms crossed. As his eyes fell on Trista, the strangest thing happened. His expression softened, his shoulders slumped and he dropped his hands to his side.

"Sorry for the ill greeting, Fenir," Trista apologized as she approached him. "I was a bit distracted." A brief smile touched his lips. Garild was so taken back by his action that he did a double take, blinking several times to make sure he hadn't imagined it.

"Let's not keep them waiting any longer." She started down the trail, Fenir at her side. They walked in companionable silence, though occasionally she'd point out some plant and tell of its purpose to which Fenir would listen intently and stare at her as if she were some mystical plant herself. Garild glanced between them suspiciously.

As herbalist, Trista did not have a bond mate, not in the same sense that he and Kirheen were bonded. She was bonded with nature, her symbol being the broad leaf of the wraith wood trees. She knew nature better than anything and her purpose was to see to the health and well-being of all the Bonded. She was meant to be alone, never to have a companion.

In a way, Fenir held the same fate. As a twin born, he was bonded at the beginning of his life cycle to Tomias. They were two parts of a whole, capable of using their powers on each other long before either of them should have known how to.

It saddened him to realize that Fenir would never be anything more to Trista than a friend. It was obvious in the glances he gave her that he cared for her a great deal. Garild was sure, had the circumstances been different, the two would have been bond mates.

It wasn't long before they were back. They entered the house quietly, trying not to disturb Kirheen. Instead of Kirheen, it was Tomias they disturbed. He lifted his head off his chest quickly, blinking away sleep.

"Are we sleeping on the job now," Trista chided, a hand on her hip. Tomias stood and gave an exaggerated stretch, smile on his lips.

"I was merely pondering my morning, dear. I wouldn't dare sleep if it meant missing that flaming red hair of yours."

"You hate my red hair. And my freckles. You aren't fooling me."

"Those freckles seem to have mysteriously disappeared under some strange black veil. Is this some new herbalist magic?"

Trista rolled her eyes. "Oh, shut up and make yourself useful."

Garild stared at them, feeling utterly confused. If Tomias and Fenir were just one soul in two bodies, could it be they actually liked the same person? His world suddenly felt a lot more complicated.

"Where is Kirheen," he asked, glancing around the room. She wasn't in the chair he had left her in. "Is she okay?"

Tomias, straining to take his attention away from Trista, beckoned towards their bedroom. "She went to lie down. Thought a bed would probably be a bit more comfortable then a chair."

"Thanks." Garild turned away from them, crossing the small space to their room. He pushed the curtain aside gently, stepping in as quietly as possible. Kirheen lay on her bed, curled on her side. Her eyes were shut, her brows knit together in pain. Beads of sweat covered her forehead and she looked pale. At the sound of his footsteps, her eyes flickered open.

"Oh, Garild. It's you."

"Yeah, just me," he smiled down at her, stepping to the bed side. "Trista mixed up something for you. She'll be in soon. How are you feeling?"

"I feel like someone dropped a rock on me, so can we talk about something else," she pleaded, looking miserable.

"What do you want to talk about?"

"Anything."

"I saw Fenir smile," Garild said, trying hard to keep a straight face.

Kirheen snorted, a sharp laugh bursting from her. "That's funny! Untrue, but funny!"

"I'm serious! Trista made him smile. He is capable of doing so. I saw it, I swear to you!"

"I suppose if Tomias can smile then so could Fenir... but really, I cannot even imagine what that might look like on his smug face."

"Oh, about how it usually looks on mine," Tomias butted in, stepping into the room. He was trailed by Fenir and Trista, who held the three vials in her hand.

"Ah, my dear, Tomias wasn't lying. You really *don't* look well," Trista mused, stepping over to the bedside. After shooing Garild out of the way, she set two of the vials down on the table. The third she popped open and handed to Kirheen.

Kirheen pushed herself up and took the vial, staring at it with obvious distaste. She smelled the liquid, her nose crinkling. "What is this stuff? It smells horrible."

"It's really not as bad as it looks... or smells for that matter. It's really quite sweet. I promise you! Now let's take a look at you." She patted Kirheen on the leg and she sidled out of the way, allowing enough room for Trista to sit down on the side of the bed. "The fever and fatigue are quite noticeable. Feeling anything else?"

"I keep getting headaches. Right here between my eyes, like my skull is going to split in half."

"Ah, side effect of a near unbinding. Oops, I mean, well..." Tomias and Fenir suddenly shot her a look, one that warned she'd said a little too much.

Kirheen, not one to miss such a subtle shift in the conversation, looked interested. "What is an unbinding?"

"Something you'll learn about later. Much later! Please though, tell me anything else you feel."

Kirheen opened her mouth to press the question but decided she wasn't in top form for doing so. "I'm nauseous, if that makes any difference."

Trista smiled. "Glad you mentioned it!" She pulled a small folded piece of parchment from her robe. When she unwrapped it, Garild could see faint traces of a blue powder which she dumped into the vial in Kirheen's hand. "Without this, that little vial in your hand probably would have made that symptom worse. This should help!"

Kirheen stared at the vial as if it had been poisoned. "Do I really have to drink this?"

"Yes. And do it all in one gulp. It'll be easier that way. Uh, Tomias, perhaps some water to wash it all down?"

"Of course," he smiled, disappearing from the room.

Kirheen refused to take a single gulp of the mixture until he'd returned with water. Once it was within easy reach, she took a deep breath and lifted the vial to her lips, downing the contents in one sickeningly sweet gulp. Her mouth instantly puckered and she quickly handed back the vial, switching it for the cup of water. This too she downed quickly, savoring every drop as it washed away the horrid taste from her mouth. "Sweet was an understatement, Trista!"

"I'm sorry," she grinned. "I said it was sweet, I never said it was going to taste good!"

"So, what happens now," Kirheen asked with a frown.

"Now, my dear, you sleep. You'll take the next vial after you wake up and the other one in the morning," Trista said. "I warn you though, the mixture might make you hungry. Very hungry."

Kirheen rolled her eyes. "Oh great, just what I wanted."

Trista smiled and motioned for Fenir and Tomias to leave the room. She followed them out, taking the empty vial and cup with her. When they'd left, Garild turned his attention back to Kirheen. She was nestled in the pillows, her hands splayed over her stomach. "Feeling anything yet," he asked.

"I'm feeling a little sleepy," she said, stifling a yawn.

"Maybe you should close your eyes and get some rest."

She smirked. "Don't tell me what to do, Garild."

Garild watched as she fought off sleep, her eyelids drooping and her limbs relaxing. She was soon sleeping soundly. Garild smiled and reached down to tuck a stray piece of hair behind her ear. She smiled in her sleep and his heart fluttered at the sight. With a sigh, he left the room, letting Kirheen enjoy her last free day before their training would begin.

Chapter 7

"Are you going to eat that," Kirheen asked through a mouthful of food, pointing her spoon towards the bowl of soup Garild was eating. He gave her an odd look, spoon halfway to his lips. There wasn't much left in his bowl, but Kirheen eyed it hungrily. Ever since she'd awoken she'd been ravenous and had practically begged to go to the eating hall the second her feet had touched the floor.

Trista had warned him he might face an impending hunger unlike anything he'd ever seen, but he hadn't thought to take it quite so literally. She'd downed her soup, despite the heat of it making it all but inedible, in such haste that all the other Bonded looked at her as if she'd suddenly gone mad.

"I had kind of planned on it," he said, snaking his left arm around his soup bowl protectively.

Kirheen huffed. "I'm sorry, Garild. I'm just so hungry! I feel like I could eat ten bowls of this stuff!"

"You can have the rest of mine," Isa chirped from across the table. She passed the bowl over to Kirheen, the broth sloshing about in the bowl as she did. "I'm not all that hungry this morning!"

Kirheen barely managed to get a thank you in before her spoon was filled and diving towards her mouth. Isa smiled, though it seemed more from discomfort than happiness.

"Kirheen, are you feeling alright," she asked innocently. Ian nudged her, shaking his head as he watched Kirheen devour her meal. "On second thought, forget I asked."

Garild finished the rest of his soup quickly, trying to eat what he could before Kirheen finished the bowl she was working on. As she finished her meal she searched the table for any bowl left untouched, only to sulk when she found there was nothing left.

"How did your training go yesterday," Ian asked, trying to switch the focus away from Kirheen. At the topic of training, several of the other Bonded dared to scoot closer, though they still kept a healthy distance from Kirheen. She didn't seem to notice.

Garild frowned. "We actually haven't gotten to do much training yet. Things have been a bit... hectic lately. We're hoping to get some solid training in today."

Tegan, a freckle faced boy with mousy brown hair and a gap between his front teeth, looked confused. "You haven't trained much yet? You're really missing out."

"On what, exactly," Kirheen asked, peeking at the expanse of table in front of Tegan. She frowned at the lack of food in his bowl.

"Well, I don't know about the rest of you, but we've been playing games to help us learn about our power. We've had to think of a simple object and have our bond mate figure out what we're thinking. So far, I'm winning."

Irena, his bond mate, glared at him out of the corner of her icy blue eyes. She was stunningly beautiful, with peachy skin and hair the color of honey, but her demeanor left much to be desired. She spoke little, but when she did, it was terse and spiteful. She seemed to view the rest of the Bonded the way Herzin did, as if they were all beneath her.

Garild found it amusing that she'd been bonded with someone like Tegan. Having grown up with him, Garild knew Tegan was more interested in playing in the dirt and goofing off then he was at taking anything or anyone seriously. He was carefree and friendly where Irena was cold and distant. Garild almost felt sorry for him. He could only hope Irena wouldn't crush the kindness right out of him.

"Lying isn't becoming of you, Tegan. Why not tell them the truth? That you haven't been able to even use your powers yet."

The rest of the table shifted uncomfortably while Tegan just stared at the table, his cheeks tinged with red. "We need to leave. Harkin will be upset if we're late and I'm not going to disappoint him for your sake." She stood quietly, ignoring the rest of the Bonded as she stepped out of the room, head held high. Tegan stood quickly, trailing after her as he wiped at his eyes. "I'll see you all later," he sniffled, following after his bond mate.

"She's a tough one," Ian grunted.

"Ah, but her beauty is unquestionable," said Burk, smile on his face as he watched them leave. Burk was tall and muscular, easily the biggest of the boys and often times the most amusing. He was laid back, almost to the point of being lazy, but he was quick of wit and his jokes often had them all laughing.

His bond mate, Abby, rolled her eyes. "Beautiful and an absolute terror. I'm pretty sure she'd strike us all down if given the chance."

"Jealous," he chided, earning himself a punch in the arm. Abby wasn't exactly scrawny and her punch left Burk rubbing his arm, grimacing as he tried to make the pain stop. "Ow!"

"Oh, hush! You deserved that and you know it," she smirked. She was a perfect complement to Burk; kind, upbeat, and filled with enough wit to match Burk any day. It was easy to see why the two of them had been bonded.

"Let's go find Grant. I've an abuse to report," Burk chided, tugging on her braid as he walked by. She frowned in annoyance, chased after him and landed another punch on his arm.

"Make that two!"

"As much as I hate to admit it, we should probably get going too," Garild said, pushing himself up from his seat. The rest of the group nodded in agreement and slowly, the room cleared of people, Garild and Kirheen trailing behind. She was unusually quiet, watching the others ahead of them with inquisitive eyes.

"Everything okay," he asked gently, nudging her with his elbow.

"Oh. Yeah. I'm fine," she said, smiling sheepishly. "Feeling a tad sluggish."

"Might have something to do with all that food you just ate."

Warmth crept to her cheeks. "Can we just forget that happened? I don't know what came over me just then. Whatever Trista gave me really had some horrible side effects."

Garild chuckled. "It did. But at least you're feeling better. You don't look half as green as you did yesterday!"

"Well, that's a start."

"Are you feeling ready for training today?"

The smile slipped off her face as if he'd insulted her. Her brows furrowed and she shook her head. "I…don't know, Garild. After what happened, I just don't know if I'm willing to go through that again."

Garild frowned. "It's not going to be like that, you know? You really think Tomias and Fenir would do that to you?"

"Of course I don't. And I know that. I just…"

"I understand, Kirheen. You don't have to explain. Just promise me you'll try."

She met his eyes and he could see an overwhelming fear lurking in her gaze, an apprehension that words couldn't possibly take away. "I'll try."

Chapter 8

Tomias and Fenir were sitting on the steps outside their home, eyes locked in what appeared to be a silent debate. There was a discussion taking place in their minds that neither of them could comprehend. At the sound of their footsteps, Tomias glanced up wearily.

"Ah, a most welcome distraction. How are you both doing?"

"Better," Kirheen said. It was true, whatever Trista had given her seemed to be working. Despite her earlier episode of eating everything in sight, she was feeling well rested. She'd almost forgotten what that felt like. "I hope we aren't interrupting anything."

Tomias shot a glare out of the corner of his eye that Fenir ignored. "Not at all. Just having a pleasant discussion with my bond mate. I'm debating whether or not my life would be less complicated without him."

Fenir grunted.

"Fenir would like you all to know that he is mute. He cannot speak, but he can still hear! I find it rather hard to believe with how much he seems to miss my point during our most pleasant conversations."

Kirheen cleared her throat. "Should we leave you two to sort things out? I'm feeling a bit of tension here."

"Of course not! Come, gather round," he swept his arm out before him, gesturing to the empty space at the foot of the stairs.

"What are you two arguing about anyways," Kirheen asked, folding her arms across her chest.

"Let's just say, we have a difference of opinions when it comes to your training. I, for one, feel it's necessary to explain a few things to you first before we get started. Fenir, on the other hand, seems to think we should just jump right into things. That strategy seems to have worked so well for Herzin."

Kirheen winced. "Do we have any say in the matter?"

"I...suppose you could. We'll just let you two settle this."

Garild shrugged. "I'm fine either way. It might be good to go over a few things though. Considering we really haven't had any formal training up until this point, it couldn't hurt."

Kirheen nodded. "Just what I was thinking."

"I'm sorry, Fenir. It appears you've been outnumbered this time. You'll have to listen to me chatter away," Tomias said with a smile, obviously pleased with himself. Fenir huffed, shifting his attention elsewhere

"Your training with Herzin was cut rather short. Did you speak of anything you hadn't already heard?"

Kirheen shrugged. "We spoke briefly of our powers, of the Allseer and the Darkness. It was all very basic though but—"

"…You still have many questions. That much I know. I'll try and answer as much as I can, just promise to hear me out and not bombard me with your curiosity."

"I…suppose I can handle that."

"So, you know two of the major points. You at least have a basic understanding of what it is to have these powers. It's true, while your bond is powerful and unique, what is required of you once you've mastered your powers will be the most important thing to come from your union. It is with your powers that we hope to save the world, to bring it back from the Darkness."

"If it's all about strengthening our powers to defeat the Darkness, then why match us up," Garild asked.

"A valid question. Up until now, you've hardly used the power you have. With no training in the matter, it's hard to focus your power enough to use it for anything useful. But, even without training, some innate ability has shined through even in your youth. The Council has been able to see that through the years and matched you up not only by your personalities, but also by the initial strengths of your gifts. You are meant to work in tangent. Your strengths are their weaknesses, both in personality and in power. You've got to be able to overcome that, hence why you are paired. You help balance each other."

"So, what are our strengths? We've done so little with our powers, how can you tell," Kirheen asked.

"You've been using your powers a lot more than you think," Tomias said with a smile. "You know how many times you've successfully blocked me out over the past week?"

"You've been trying to read my mind?" She felt slightly betrayed by the intrusion. She hadn't expected Tomias to stoop to such a tactic.

"Not in the way you think," he said quickly, his hands rising in front of him as if to block her anger. "I've been scoping out your powers. If I have to teach you then I at least have to know what I'm dealing with."

"You should have told me," she said with a scowl. "I can't believe you!"

"That would have defeated the purpose, my dear. Simmer down. I wasn't trying to dig through your mind! I was trying to see how you would naturally react! This brings us to your question. You, Kirheen, have the innate power of blocking. You're able to feel someone entering your mind and react accordingly, even when you aren't aware of it."

"That's useful. Means I can keep my thoughts to myself without any unwanted intrusion," she snapped, making it clear she hadn't approved of his actions, no matter the explanation.

"In time and with proper training, yes, but right now if Fenir wanted to break into your mind, you'd have a hard time stopping him. His strength lies in breaking those barriers. Don't overestimate your own abilities. Against someone skilled, you'd crumble."

"Wouldn't Herzin be considered skilled," Garild asked.

"Yes, and she is, but she underestimated you; a dangerous mistake. She wasn't expecting you to reinforce the barriers of your mind and push her out and it cost her."

"If her strength is blocking, then what's mine? Attacking?"

Tomias frowned. "It seems the logical answer, but your power is far more subtle. You don't have the brute strength of Fenir. You don't just hammer down the walls and let yourself in. You, Garild, have the power of influence. You sneak into the mind and influence the emotions and thoughts of others without them even realizing you're there. As you become more experienced, you can shape the landscape of what they *see*."

Garild looked concerned. "I've been doing this all along?"

"At times. You feel emotions more than others. Your power latches on to those emotions and you tweak them, ever so slightly. Most people wouldn't even realize it was happening unless they were looking for it. You did it when you walked in here. You saw our tension and latched onto that, tried to change it."

"How could you tell?"

"Because it's my strength as well."

Garild and Kirheen fell silent, both piecing together what they'd learned. It was Kirheen that spoke first. "So, if we've been using our power without knowing, how do we get it under our control?"

Tomias leaned forward, propping up his chin with laced fingers. "Practice, my dear."

Kirheen looked down at the cards in her hand, trying to decipher the meaning of them. She held five cards, each one with a different symbol. Tomias sat to her right, holding a different set of cards, though instead of symbols they were numbered. She suspected Fenir and Garild held the same, but from her angle, she couldn't tell.

"The rules are quite simple. You are going to take turns figuring out which card your bond mate is holding. This isn't a guessing game. I want you both to try very hard to concentrate and use your powers to your advantage. I want you to *know* what the other person is holding," Tomias said, taking the cards from Kirheen. He shuffled them together, took the top card and flipped it for him and Kirheen to see. It was a symbol; two blue vertical lines with a circle between them.

"Start out gently. I want you to concentrate on your opponent, study them. Once your concentration is locked, you should feel a slight change, a gentle pressure here," he tapped between his eyes with a finger. "Don't let it alarm you. You're just feeling the natural resistance of their mind."

Kirheen looked at him uneasily, remembering the overwhelming pressure she'd felt when Herzin had entered her mind. The thought made her mouth go dry and she felt sweat on her palms. She wiped her hands on her robes, trying not to look as nervous as she felt.

"Kirheen, don't fret," Tomias said softly, reaching out to steady her hands. His touch was gentle and reassuring, his fingertips pressed softly against her skin. "It's not going to be like that."

"How do you know," she questioned.

He smiled. "Kirheen, we use these powers every day. You've *been* using them. Don't let that experience control you. I won't lie, this will strain you, but it won't hurt you. Not like that. Please trust me."

She studied him, searching for a lie hidden within his brown eyes, but she saw nothing. If there was a lie to be found, she couldn't see it. "I'll try."

"Then let's begin. Study your card and keep the symbol firmly in your mind. Once you've done that, we'll hide the card and begin." They took a moment to commit the card to memory and then shuffled it back into the deck.

"Think of their mind as a wall. Feel the resistance of it, feel it push back against you. But every wall has a weakness. Find it and you find a way in. Stay focused on the information you seek, avoid distraction and you'll be victorious. You may begin."

Garild glanced at her momentarily, uncertainty clouding his dark eyes. He fidgeted nervously, eyes scanning the room. *Distracted.* Taking a deep breath, she tried to reach out, feeling for the resistance she'd felt before. There was a slight vibration, a gentle tingle between her eyes but it wavered, faltering as she tried to push further. She frowned. *Well, that didn't work.*

It was clear he was unsure what to do, his focus wavering between her and Tomias. She sat quietly, studying him, her expression revealing nothing. She pushed again, this time with more strength. The vibration returned, but this time stronger. She could feel the pressure building, the thread connecting them pulling tight. And then she was there, against the walls guarding his mind.

It was an odd sensation, a feeling of floating outside of yourself. It made her feel dizzy. She closed her eyes, trying to block out anything that might distract her. She visualized the wall, millions of glimmering blue threads, tightly bound together. There was no weak point that she could see, and it seemed to stretch on forever, an endless wall holding back a tangled web of information.

Reaching forward, she touched one of the threads. It glowed brightly, sending ripples of light along the wall. She watched it dance across its surface for as far as she could see. After a moment, the light returned, glowing in the same thread she'd touched. The section of wall she stood in front of lit up, it's blue light blinding. She stumbled back, felt the vibration waver and suddenly she was back in her own mind. She gasped, eyes flying open as she tried to regain her sense of self.

"Are you alright," Tomias asked.

She took several unsteady breathes, looking bewildered. "Y-yeah, I'm fine. That...that is just a very odd sensation." Tomias smiled knowingly.

Garild was focused on her now. "You were just in my mind, weren't you? I could feel something, a slight shift."

"She was," Tomias confirmed. "Did you try blocking her?"

He shook his head. "No, I couldn't find her. It was all just noise and light."

"You'll need to focus harder. Envision your walls and find the source of the intrusion. You'll need to push her out or she's sure to break through. Be gentle about it though. And Kirheen, his natural defenses were enough to push you out. Push harder. Go ahead, you two. Try again."

This time it was Garild that pushed first. She could barely feel it, a slight tingle, like a fingertip traced across her skin. She closed her eyes, envisioned her walls and found him instantly. He stood before the threads, hands hovering over them uncertainly. He reached out, touching the wall gently. The wall shimmered, tendrils of light radiating out in all directions. There was an increase of pressure and a thread darkened, its glow fading. The darkness spread quickly, infecting the other threads around it. There was a loud snapping sound as one of the darkened tendrils frayed. It held for a moment before it gave way, leaving behind the smallest of gaps in the wall. Others followed in quick succession, a loud series of pops sending Kirheen into a panic.

Think, think, think. You're a natural blocker, so block him! She steadied herself, honing in on the gap quickly forming in the wall. She focused on the healthy threads, trying to pull them closer together to seal the gap but they wouldn't budge. As the gap widened, she felt a surge of fear. Her thoughts, her feelings, they were all she had and only a wall stood between them and Garild; A wall that was quickly disintegrating before her eyes.

Instead of fixating on the gap, she focused on the surrounding wall that remained. With a quick burst, she pushed against it, forcing it forward towards Garild. It reacted, glowing brighter, the threads coiling together in a strengthened bond. She pushed again and this time the wall bulged, the blue light intensifying until it was almost blinding. Garild recoiled, his hands covering his eyes. Though stunned, the gap in the wall still widened. She needed to remove him from her mind, but the only thing she could think to do was to force him out. Trying to keep a steady hold on her powers, she forced some of the threads forward, snaking them around Garild as he stood stunned. As gently as she could, she flung him backwards, feeling a wave of relief as the bond snapped, her mind suddenly her own again.

She turned her attention back to the wall, even as she heard Garild gasp, probably suffering the same sensation she had felt when she'd been pushed back. With the intruder gone, the darkening threads had ceased their advance and she was able to relax the wall, letting it sink back into its original shape. There was still the gap to contend with, an opening that couldn't possibly withstand another attack. She drew in a breath, and focused on the outside edges of the wall, trying to draw the power of them down into the breach. The outer edge of the wall dimmed, while the rim of the gap glowed with renewed strength. Slowly, new threads began to appear, weaving their way back and forth across the gap.

The process slowed after a time and her vitality with it. She felt tired, her energy draining with each new thread she formed. She found it hard to maintain her focus, and once, several threads broke before they could form, her power wavering too much to keep up.

As she started in on a new section, the entire wall flickered, the blue light becoming unstable. Something caught her eye and she found Tomias standing outside the wall, watching the process with concern.

"You've done well, Kirheen, but you're losing strength. Much more of this and you risk losing the whole wall. Once that happens, there won't be a force capable of stopping someone from getting in. Give it a rest."

"But I'm almost there. If I don't fix it, the next time he attacks, I won't be able to stop him."

He frowned. "If the whole wall is gone, will it matter? Leave it be and let your mind rest. We'll resume training once the breach is closed, but you need to let it repair on its own. Rushing it won't fix anything."

She hesitated, the sense of the gap filling her with unease. It was a weakness, an uncontrolled variable and she didn't like leaving it open to anyone. *Just a couple more threads.* She gave a final burst of power, forming several new threads at once. Immediately she regretted it. There was a loud crack, and a section of the wall crumbled, sending a cascade of blue sparks shooting into the air. The rest of the wall flickered, and she stood helpless, terrified that one wrong move would send the rest of it crumbling down.

Tomias shook his head. "You really aren't one to listen, are you? Very well." Holding up his hands, he pressed them gently against the air where her wall had crumbled. There was a sudden surge of power and the broken section of wall began to heal at an alarming rate. In a matter of minutes, it was as if the damage had never been done. The gap filled in, shimmering once more with icy blue light. She felt herself being pulled and then she was back in the room, blinking rapidly as she adjusted to the light.

Garild looked pale, his brow covered in sweat and his eyes wide.

"You look terrible," Kirheen said.

"I'm alright, Kirheen. Just feeling a little dizzy." He put his hands up, covering his face as he tried to keep the world from spinning. "You aren't looking so good yourself."

"I'm rather tired," she admitted. Exhausted was more the word she should have used. She felt absolutely spent, her eyes heavy and her thoughts sluggish. The thought of training another minute was almost unbearable.

"You both did very well," Tomias said with a friendly smile. "You're catching on quickly. Just like anything else, it'll take practice before you can use your powers without completely exhausting yourself every time. As you may have noticed Kirheen, some things such as blocking, take a surprising amount of energy. You need to learn to conserve your energy and work smarter."

"What happens if you push too hard," Kirheen asked, feeling guilty that she hadn't listened to Tomias. It was a weakness of hers, and while she could recognize that, controlling it was something else entirely.

"Depends on how far you push it. Exhaustion is just the start. You push beyond that and you risk losing your mind, unable to ever get the wall back as it should be. I've also heard of some falling into a deep sleep, never to awaken. Not gone from this world, but not really alive either." With that he reached out and flicked Kirheen hard on the cheek. Her hand flew up, and she gaped at him, eyes blazing with annoyance.

"What was that for," she hissed.

Tomias smirked. "That was for not listening to me. I get enough of that from Fenir. I don't need it from you too. Next time I tell you not to push yourself, please don't pretend that I don't know what I'm talking about and do it anyways. I've been using these powers a lot longer than you have."

She rubbed at her cheek. "Well, don't worry. I think I learned my lesson."

"I'm glad you've come to your senses. How are you feeling?"

"Terrible and slightly annoyed with you. I don't think I'll be able to move from this spot," she yawned, melting into her seat. "I feel like I spent my day running around the whole of Sanctuary. Repeatedly."

"To be expected. And you, Garild? Still feeling dizzy?"

He shook his head. "No, I'm alright now, just tired."

"You both have an hour. I'd recommend getting a good nap in before we resume our training. It'll be even harder next time, and I expect someone to win the game." He smirked. "No pressure."

Kirheen stifled another yawn. "What'll you two do?"

Tomias glared at his bond mate. "Oh, I'm sure we can find something else to argue about while we wait for you." Fenir grunted, shaking his head. He rose from his seat and stepped outside.

"We're off to a good start. See! He's already mad!" Tomias rose with a stretch, yawning loudly. "Take a nap you two, before you infect me with your exhaustion. I'll wake you in an hour."

Kirheen just waved her hand, too tired to speak any further. With the last bit of strength she could muster, she dragged herself to their room, flinging herself onto the bed. She didn't even bother to slip under the covers, the cloying fog of sleep already too thick to ignore. She heard Garild plop down on his bed, heard the door click shut as Tomias stepped outside and then she drifted off into a dreamless sleep.

Chapter 9

Tomias sighed heartily as he sank down on the steps next to Fenir. He ran his hands over his face, surprised to feel the prickle of hair on his normally clean shaven face. Had it really been so long? The week had flown by as he'd adapted his role to that of instructor. It had been quite a shift from his mundane duties, but he was starting to like it. "How do you think I'd look with a beard," he asked Fenir.

"*Ridiculous,*" Fenir scoffed.

"Really? I think I'd look rather dashing. I might just keep it."

"*Do as you wish. Just don't expect me to claim any relation to you.*"

"You always threaten me with that. A shame we look so similar. I don't think you can claim otherwise."

Fenir snorted, turning the conversation to other matters. "*How do you think they did?*"

"Quite well, actually. Now if only I can keep Kirheen's curiosity in check, I think we'll be okay." Truth was, he was surprised how quickly they had both caught on. It normally took much longer before they could enter each other's minds, let alone use their powers to start chipping away at each other. They'd done both, a sign that they had a decent feel for their powers. The late start to their training wouldn't be so detrimental after all. "In any case, Nyson will be happy."

I suppose so. He's pushing quite hard for results this time around. Could be dangerous."

It was true. The incident with Herzin had agitated Nyson and caused a delay in training, something that he deemed unacceptable. He was expecting to see results and he wanted to see them soon, especially when it came to Kirheen. Despite what Tomias had told her, she didn't have any predominant strengths. She wasn't a natural blocker; she was a natural at everything. And such a person could be shaped, molded and trained to be whatever you needed them to be. It was precisely why Nyson was so interested in her, and why he would push Tomias and Fenir to train them as quickly as possible, no matter the cost.

While Tomias respected Nyson, he wasn't about to go push them to the brink, especially not with Kirheen. She was too curious, too quick to find shortcuts and all too eager to take them. It was a dangerous situation to try and teach restraint to someone who had the potential to do so much more. He'd have to teach her control, before she accidentally hurt herself or others. If it meant taking longer with their training, then he was willing to face the consequences. He wouldn't risk it.

"You think he'll push for her to be on the Council," Fenir asked, face troubled.

Tomias frowned, his brow furrowed. "It seems likely, though I hate to think what would become of Garild if she is. Council status would dissolve their Bond, and unless Garild is strong enough, he'd spend the rest of his days making clothes and food for the rest of them. With how much Kirheen hates being Bonded, I'm sure she'd leap at the opportunity to be on her own if it were offered. She's smart though. Hopefully she'll figure out the truth sooner rather than later. Maybe it will convince her that being on the Council isn't all it's cracked up to be."

"What truth is that?"

"That Nyson doesn't want them for anything but their powers, however big of a show he puts on. He just wants people that can be effective against the Darkness, people he can shape and mold to fit where he needs them."

"If he asked, would you try to convince her? Do you think you even could?"

He shrugged. "Could I? Yes. Do I want to? No. I don't entirely care for the art of manipulation, despite the fact that I'm damn good at it. It just doesn't feel right, changing a mind like that. She's still a child and one that might be a little too headstrong to be part of the Council!"

Fenir grunted. *"Age is a funny thing here. She's older than she looks. I'd say she probably isn't too far behind us in age. Quit making it sound like we're old, brother."*

"Gah, I know! Sometimes I forget. Damn if I don't feel it though. I swear by next year I'll need a cane." They were only in their 23rd year, still young themselves. Having been Bonded since birth, their powers had come naturally to them. Following the incident that had cost Fenir his voice, their powers had grown exponentially. The constant need to communicate mentally had brought them closer, made them stronger. The accident had been both a blessing and a curse.

His mind drifted back to that day. They had been so young, two scrawny pale twins with powers they had yet to master. They had been attending a meeting with Nyson to discuss their future participation in the Council when an ashen haired woman had burst through the door, her face contorted in rage. She'd flung all she had at Nyson, every ounce of power mashed into one desperate blow. It was a true testament to the power of their leader that he had been able to divert the amount of power hurtling towards him. Unfortunately, it had cost Fenir. The dissipated energy had flung outwards away from Nyson, speeding in their direction. Fenir had pushed him away, saving him from a blast that surely would have killed him. Though he survived the blast, Fenir' voice did not. Something had shifted inside his head, blocking him from speaking and he'd never been the same.

The woman was exiled, set loose in a world overrun by the Darkness. The fear of watching her be hauled away, flailing while she howled like an animal was still something that haunted him at night.

"After all this time, brother? What's done is done."

Tomias huffed, shoulders sagging. "Sometimes I hate that you can read my thoughts. But, I do think of that moment, brother. I think I always will. What happened to you wasn't right and it wasn't fair."

"I don't regret what happened. If things had been any different it would just be me sitting here today. That blast would have killed you and you know it. Besides, being this way affords me certain… benefits."

"Like being able to scare children with a glance? I must admit, your infamous glare has become downright terrifying."

Fenir smiled, his eyes crinkling at the corners. It was a look he saw so rarely these days, and most of the time only when Trista was present. He'd always had an affinity for the bright eyed healer, a small spark of light in his dreary world. Tomias could understand the allure. She *was* beautiful, even when streaked with plant paste and smelling of skunk bloom. He even allowed himself harmless flirting, something his brother found entirely frustrating. Regardless, he knew that it was one person that Fenir truly treasured. It wasn't something he'd just take from him, even if the occasion arose.

As if manifesting from his thoughts, he watched as Trista made her way across the clearing. Her long red hair was loose around her shoulders, a rare and beautiful sight. Her face was bright and clear, free from the soot that had marred it before. She smiled sweetly as she approached. Fenir returned the smile, his features softening. He could feel the sudden rush of anticipation coming from his brother and he blocked it away, trying not to let it infect him.

"Good afternoon," Tomias called, giving a slight wave of his hand. "How are you faring on this fine day?"

She snorted, setting a basket down between them. "I, unlike you, have been positively busy this morning."

Tomias scoffed. "But you look so clean and fresh, very unlike the hard working lady we both love."

She rolled her eyes. "Oh, please. You're looking positively lazy. In fact," she bent down, inspecting his face. She grabbed his chin between finger and thumb, brushing over his stubble. "So much so, you've apparently completely given up on shaving."

He could feel a wave of jealousy washing over him. This too he tried to block out, but it seared against his walls like an inferno. "Hey, now! I happen to like the new look. I was thinking a nice beard would suit me just fine."

"You do that and Fenir will officially be more handsome than you," she joked, turning towards his brother. "And how are you today, Fenir?"

He shrugged, giving her his best crooked smile. It frustrated him that he couldn't speak to her. His thoughts remained locked away, unable to be shared. Trista, unlike everyone else around her, didn't have any special powers. She wasn't born with them. What she did have was an affinity for plants, the hands of a healer and a kind nature that earned her admiration from all that met her.

Despite not being able to communicate, she was always kind to Fenir. She never left him out of conversations, even if it meant sounding like she was talking to herself. Tomias tried to help when he could, but he always felt strange speaking for his brother, as if his words were something he wasn't quite meant to hear, let alone speak, especially not when it came to speaking to Trista.

"Is Kirheen feeling better," she asked, drawing him away from his thoughts.

"All back to her fiery self! She is…" He stopped suddenly, sniffing the air. "What in the name of the Allseer, Trista?" He turned towards the basket; a basket that had suddenly began to emit the most delicious of smells. She smiled, brushing her hair back behind her ear.

"Wraith blossom cakes," she said, bending down and opening the basket. She removed a white cloth from the top, revealing a pile of round golden cakes, their spongy middle speckled with blue. "Wraith blossom is a wonderful flower. It helps with mental clarity. I thought it might help with training today."

Tomias frowned. "You mean, I have to share?" He made to reach into the basket but she slapped his hand away.

Trista returned his frown. "I know how you are around stuff like this! Hands off until Garild and Kirheen have some."

"Fine, fine. Not like I wanted them anyways," he huffed. "I'll have you know, I promised them a whole hour of sleep so they could feel rejuvenated and prepared to take on another round of mind games. If I wake them now, they may just kill me."

Trista turned on him, hands on her hips. "I'm sure they wouldn't mind something to eat! With this kind of training they'll *always* be hungry!"

"Well, do *you* want to go wake them? If you truly insist, but I must warn you fair lady, it's a dark and dangerous place in there. I wouldn't want you to get hurt."

"Then Fenir will just have to accompany me on this most dangerous of quests," she turned, about sending Fenir into a panic. He whipped his hand back away from the edge of the basket, hoping she hadn't seen. If she had, she pretended not to. "Will you join me?"

She held out her arm and Fenir rose from the steps, linking his arm with hers. Before they slipped through the door, Fenir took the opportunity to sneer at his brother. Tomias merely chuckled, leaning back until he was sprawled out on the porch. The midday sun beat down on him, warding him against the chill that had slowly begun to creep into Sanctuary. Soon, the trees would be bare, leaving behind nothing but a glowing blanket of leaves. And once those faded, the trees would fall dark.

The winter months always seemed unusually dreary because of it. He took comfort in the glow of the trees, that icy blue light that seemed to mimic the moon itself. He always felt uneasy when the trees stopped shining, as if somehow they protected them from the Darkness beyond the walls. If even there was such a thing to protect them from.

It was a thought that often filtered into his mind, no matter how hard he tried to lock it away. There were so many secrets, so many things Nyson wasn't willing to tell. Sometimes he wondered if the Darkness really existed at all, or if it was just a tall tale, something to keep them within the confines of Sanctuary. He'd heard plenty of stories, sure, but he'd seen little to no evidence that there was anything outside the walls that would hurt them. Despite his doubt, it wasn't something he was willing to figure out himself. If the Darkness did exist, he didn't want to face it alone.

And certainly not in the dead of winter.

The click of the door disrupted his thoughts. He leaned his head back, watching as a very bedraggled Kirheen stumbled through the door. She was followed by Garild, his mouth stretched wide in a yawn.

Kirheen stopped a few steps away from him, looking down through bleary eyes. "What are you doing down there," she asked slowly.

"Just taking a moment to relax. Did either of you get any rest?"

Garild plopped down on the stairs, pouting as he rubbed at his eyes. "That didn't feel like an hour," he complained.

"And I know just who to blame for that," Tomias sighed, earning a cold stare from Trista as she stepped out the door. "But at least she has something to bribe you with."

"What smells so good," Kirheen asked, sniffing the air.

"That would be the bribe."

Trista rested her hand on Kirheen's back, urging her to sit down. She did so, taking a seat next to Garild. Satisfied, Trista opened the basket, the scent of the warm cakes wafting into the air. Tomias tried to ignore the rumble of his stomach as the smell hit him once again.

"Here is one for you," Trista smiled, handing Garild a cake. "Try not to eat it too quick."

He thanked her, taking the cake in his hand as if it were something delicate that would crumble if he moved too quickly. He sniffed at it and took a bite off the edge. "This is delicious," he exclaimed and then bit into the moist cake in earnest, finishing it off in two large bites.

Kirheen was handed one next, and she stared at it, taking it all in before she stuffed it in her mouth. She didn't even bother to savor it. "Thank you, Trista. That was really delicious!"

Trista beamed, her face triumphant. "I think that may be the first time anyone has complimented me on my cooking."

"These...these are really quite awful, Trista." She whipped around, hands on her hips. Tomias had taken a cake while her back was turned and he wiped away the crumbs with the back of his hand.

"See what I mean? Ungrateful"

Fenir shook his head. *"Please tell her I find her cooking to be the best in all of Sanctuary. I don't want her to think I don't appreciate such a fine gift."*

"*Oh, gag me,*" Tomias mentally huffed. "Fenir would like you to know he isn't the savage that I am and that he does appreciate your cooking."

"Well, that's kind of you. Thank you," she said, smiling warmly at Fenir. When she turned back to Tomias, her eyes were steely. "As for you, you'll be lucky if I bring you anything ever again."

"Ah, and what a loss that will be," Tomias frowned.

Kirheen and Garild were in a considerably better mood by the time they'd both devoured a few more cakes. No longer were they bleary eyed and hunched over from exhaustion. They looked alert, ready to take on another bout of training.

"Are you both feeling good enough to keep training," Tomias asked.

They took a moment to answer, taking the time to check their walls. "I'm ready," Garild said and Kirheen nodded.

Trista collected the empty basket. "Glad to see you are both feeling better. Good luck with your training today. Don't push them too hard," she warned, eyes flashing to Tomias.

"I won't," he assured her.

"Good." She smiled, spinning on her heels. She headed back across the clearing, Fenir watching her as she went. Tomias turned his attention back to his young pupils.

"Shall we try again?"

"Yes, we're ready," Kirheen said.

Kirheen scooted away from Garild, turning her body towards him so they were face to face. She was focused, her eyes alight with determination. Garild too seemed eager to try again, a small grin playing on his face.

Tomias handed each of them a card, shuffling it back into the deck once they'd memorized the new pattern. "You may begin."

Chapter 10

K irheen did not hesitate. The second the word was spoken, she closed her eyes, focusing on forming the link that would connect them. It was easier this time around; she could feel the pressure build and then snap, the invisible rope between them pulling tight. She stood before the blue threads of his mind, feeling confident that this time she would win.

She took a moment to check on her mind, staying alert for signs of Garild. There was nothing there. *He's on the defense*, she thought. She turned her head, inspecting the wall before her. It seemed to stretch on forever. It seemed pointless to just break straight through without knowing where she needed to be. She needed to find what she was after first. She took a deep breath and reached out, touching her hands to the wall. The threads vibrated against her fingers, sending tremors through her arms.

The humming vibration of the threads filled her ears, drowning out her thoughts. As she pushed on the threads before her, flashes of images filtered through her mind. They were nothing but blurs, a kaleidoscope of colors taking shape, only to melt together again before she could decipher the meaning of them. *Focus on the card, he's hiding it somewhere.*

She forced herself to push harder, to find meaning in the meaningless. The threads vibrated faster, the noise filling the spaces in her mind. And then she saw it, a bright flash of white, a card with a blur of color. She smiled to herself, victory within her grasp.

The thread that had revealed the card burned brighter, shooting off to her right, weaving in and out of the wall. She followed it for a time, stepping confidently towards the answer. After a time, she came upon a spot in the wall that was thicker than the rest, the threads closely coiled to prevent anyone from getting in. *Found you.*

Focusing the energy she had left, she forced her powers against the block, blackening the threads as she struggled to break through. They snapped loudly, sending a shower of blue sparks falling around her. As she pushed out with her powers, she could feel the energy draining, leeching out of her fingertips. She wouldn't lose to Garild, *couldn't* lose to him. Losing meant letting someone in to her mind, and she had already vowed not to let that happen.

The thought made her flick her attention back to her own mind, but as she did so, she felt the connection to Garild waver. She pushed back into his mind, feeling the connection reestablish itself. A wave of fatigue washed over her, her limbs feeling weighed down. She wasn't left with a choice. If she tried to guard her mind while attacking, she'd only wear herself out. Breathing deep, she pushed once more against his mind, blasting through the wall.

As the sparks settled, she could make out the card. Two thin green vertical lines and a yellow circle decorated the card, the image clear in her mind. "I found it," she exclaimed. She was giddy with excitement, her heart pounding wildly.

"Tell me what it is," Tomias said.

"Two vertical green lines and a yellow circle."

"Wrong."

The shock sent her back out of Garild's mind and into reality. Her jaw dropped and she looked at Tomias with an incredulous stare. "But it's right there! I can see it! Two green lines and a yellow circle."

Garild still had his eyes closed, his head dropped to his chest. There was a sickening realization that he was still in her mind. She felt her wall crumble, a sharp pain echoing where it shattered and then Garild was alert, staring at her triumphantly. "Two blue triangles with a red line beneath."

"No," Kirheen whispered. "No, you couldn't. I already saw your card."

Tomias smirked. "Was it his card? Maybe it was the card you wanted it to be? Or maybe he set it up that way to lure you away from the real answer so you'd let your guard down."

Kirheen gritted her teeth, trying to fight back her frustration. She could feel it bubbling beneath the surface, filling her words with acid. "How is that even possible? That had to be his card."

"But it wasn't his card. You fell into a trap, Kirheen, and the sooner you admit to it, the sooner you can realize your mistake. You went chasing after the first sign of victory and you left yourself open."

She wanted to fight back, to tell him he was wrong, but she knew it was pointless. Garild had bested her, whether she wanted to admit it or not. "I don't understand. How did he set that up so fast? I attacked right away!"

"I set it up before we'd begun. I knew you'd want to win, so I set it up to lead you away from the real answer. I'm sorry Kirheen," Garild said, his eyes filled with guilt.

Kirheen glared at him. "Is that even fair?"

"It is if you want to win," Tomias said, nodding. "You think everyone is going to play fair with you, Kirheen? Do you think everyone will follow rules? Did Herzin follow rules? Would the Darkness?"

Her anger got the best of her and tears stung her eyes. She ground her teeth, trying to keep them from spilling over. "No, they didn't. But I thought…"

"You thought that you could just bully your way into winning. You thought Garild was just going to break before you and that you'd be triumphant and everyone would sing you praise. It doesn't work that way, Kirheen. It won't work that way in training and it won't work that way out in the real world either. The Darkness will not just sit by and let you break it. It will find every weakness, every moment of doubt and exploit that, do you understand?"

"I don't want these powers," Kirheen said, lip quivering. "I don't want them and I don't want this responsibility. I don't want to worry about my mind like this."

"Kirheen."

She felt Tomias reach for her as she darted from the steps, felt his fingers brush against her arm. She wanted to run, wanted his arms to wrap around her and tell her she'd be okay, wanted to leave Sanctuary and let the Darkness swallow her whole. It was too much. It had always been too much. She wasn't meant for such powers and she raced for the one person she thought might be able to help her.

She collapsed on the steps of the quaint hut in the trees, the smell of willow bark and amber lily filling her nose. The noise must have alerted Trista for she was by her side a moment later, shushing her gently as she sobbed.

Kirheen sat cross legged, watching the crackling blue flames of burning wraith wood. The warmth of the fire was rejuvenating, calming her nerves and settling her spirit. Trista bustled around somewhere behind her, creating some concoction she promised would help her feel better.

Water bubbled loudly in the kettle that hung over the fire and Trista swooped in to retrieve it. There was the rush of water filling a mug and a moment later, Trista was pressing a warm cup into her hands. "Drink it. It'll help."

Kirheen nodded, lifting the cup to her lips gently. It was smooth and rich, tasting of berries and herbs. "Thank you," she whispered, basking in the warmth that spread through her.

"Of course." Trista seated herself on the floor next to Kirheen, careful to not spill the contents of the cup in her hand. She stayed silent for a time, watching the flames and sipping at her drink quietly. After she'd downed her cup, she set it aside and turned her attention to Kirheen, eyes filled with concern. "You want to tell me what this is all about," she asked.

Kirheen swallowed hard, feeling tears spring to her eyes at the question. The comfort of the drink and the fire had almost made her forget the reason she'd come in the first place. She set her cup aside, her stomach turning sour. "I'm sorry, Trista. I didn't know where to go."

Trista smiled sweetly. "I didn't say it was a problem, Kirheen. You're clearly upset though and your mental health is just as important as your physical, so start talking. Did something happen in your training? I told him to take it easy on you."

"No, I mean, sort of!" She shook her head, feeling flustered. It wasn't training itself that had upset her. Even Garild winning hadn't caused her grief. It was the meaning behind the training, the dawning realization that nothing would ever be the same for her. "Garild won."

Trista smiled, trying hard to mask her confusion. "Is that what upset you?"

"It isn't that. I don't know. I guess I'm fine with that." Although she wasn't about to admit it, she was actually proud of Garild. For being so timid, he'd done something bold and broken through her defenses before she even realized he was there. But he'd won in other ways. He'd broken through to her mind, seen her thoughts and fears. He'd seen everything she tried so hard to hide and she couldn't bear the thought of looking at him again, of knowing that he knew what she didn't want him to. "He was in my mind, Trista. I knew it was going to happen, I could feel it happening and I thought I could handle it."

Tears sprung to her eyes, unbidden and she wiped at her eyes with her sleeves, trying to gather enough breath to speak. "I can't handle knowing that they know everything, that they know every thought and feeling I have. I don't want them to know, I don't want them to see. I want those things to be mine." She struggled to get the rest of the words out before she burst into tears. Trista reached over, wrapping her arms around her tightly and rocking her gently.

"Oh, Kirheen. This life you lead is hard, I know."

"No you don't," Kirheen sobbed, instantly regretting she'd said it. "You don't have these powers. You couldn't know."

Trista nodded in agreement, a weary frown on her face. Kirheen suddenly felt guilty, as if she'd exposed something that Trista wasn't keen to reveal. "I'm sorry, Trista."

"Don't apologize. You're right. I don't have the same powers that you all do. But it isn't without trials. It's a lonely life to live, being surrounded by people different than you. It may be simpler, yes, but it isn't always easy. I have no bond mate, nobody to share my deepest feelings with and even if I could, I wouldn't be allowed such a thing. I can't even block others from seeing right through me. Everyone can read my mind and I couldn't stop them if I tried."

Kirheen untangled herself from Trista's arms, rubbing at her face with her sleeves. She winced as she did so, her eyes feeling raw and scratchy. "I didn't think anyone could read your mind? Without powers…"

"Ah, I wish it were so. The mind still exists with or without powers, Kirheen. And as long as it's there, people can know it. It isn't just our minds that speak our deepest thoughts. Our eyes, our lips, our tongues, the way we move and speak and act, those things speak just as loudly. Fenir and Tomias know me well and it isn't because they've been rooting around in my mind. They know my mind because it's part of who I am. It comes out in every action, every word. It isn't hard to know someone if you pay attention, and even knowing everything about them, a person can still surprise you."

Kirheen sat quiet, her hands grasped together tightly in her lap. She felt foolish as she listened to Trista. To be so wrapped up in herself that she failed to see she wasn't the only person suffering, it made her feel ashamed. "I'm sorry, I didn't realize…"

"I told you not to apologize. Never apologize for your feelings. I didn't tell you any of that to make you feel bad, Kirheen, but perhaps it will put things in perspective for you. Things aren't always as they seem. What bothers you now will probably seem like such a small matter later on that one day you'll look back on it and laugh that you ever thought it was a problem to begin with. Now, how about another cup of tea?"

Trista plucked the empty cup from her side, rising to fill them. A soft knock at the door caught both of their attention and then Tomias was there, peering around the room with dark eyes. He looked bashful, as if he fully expected a scolding from Trista. With her back turned, Kirheen couldn't see her face but she could certainly imagine it. It almost made her smile, but her lips strained with the effort and she let it fall from her face.

"What are you doing here," Trista questioned, carefully pouring water into each cup. She didn't even raise her head to look at him.

"I'm looking for a certain runaway. She's about this tall," he held up his hand to his chest, indicating her height. "Hair the color of a winter wraith wood, eyes the color of vengeance, mind as strong as…"

Kirheen snorted from behind the table. "Please tell me you aren't describing me."

"My, this table is new. Where did you find one that talks?"

Trista turned her head towards Kirheen, her lips curling into a smile. She handed her a cup of tea and offered the other to Tomias. He accepted it graciously and then tip toed around the table, plopping down on the floor next to Kirheen. She kept her eyes on the tea in her hand, feeling ashamed and too tired to explain herself. She closed her eyes, breathing deeply of the aromatic steam that rose in lazy tendrils.

"I'm sorry for what I said Kirheen," Tomias whispered, nudging her with his elbow. "I wasn't trying to hurt your feelings."

Kirheen shrugged, trying not to meet his eyes. She knew it was pointless hiding how she felt. Tomias always seemed to know what she was feeling, even when it wasn't written plainly on her face for him to see.

"I sometimes forget how great a burden it is that we carry. It's a lot to handle and I stepped out of line. I shouldn't have pushed you. I'm sorry." She could feel his eyes fixated on her, could feel the shame he projected her way. She quickly glanced at him and something about acknowledging his presence made her eyes fill with tears.

She huffed, setting her cup aside so she could wipe her eyes. "Uff, why can't I stop crying," she asked to no one in particular.

Trista laughed, sitting down next to Tomias. "That would be your age, I suspect."

"I suspect it's because you're a woman," Tomias chipped in, his hand rising to block the slap he already knew was coming.

Trista struck, hitting his awaiting hands, though her eyes shone with humor.

"Is Garild happy," Kirheen asked. She imagined he was quite pleased with his victory. It had been well earned and she knew she'd have to congratulate him properly. Running away hadn't exactly been the most celebratory thing she could have done and she was sure she'd robbed him of some of his excitement.

"He was until he realized how upset you were. I had to beg him to stay put so he wouldn't go running after you. Fenir blocking the door seemed to do the trick."

"Did he think it was his fault?"

"Probably to an extent. You're a competitive girl, Kirheen. He probably thinks he should have let you win."

"You don't know for sure? Aren't you always reading our minds?"

He looked at her seriously, brows knitting together. "Kirheen, just because I have powers doesn't mean I have to use them all the time. It doesn't mean I *want* to. Yes, from time to time I'll check to see how you're holding up, especially in training where a slip up could hurt you. As a general rule and greatly out of respect for another, I don't just go prancing around people's minds. None of us do. It's intrusive and you can learn plenty about a person without resorting to that."

"I... didn't realize that."

"There will be many things that come up that you don't know and that's okay. Just know that we really do have your best interest in mind. I won't push you to do things until you understand what that means. In the future, just don't run off in the middle of a lesson. It hurts my feelings."

"Oh, I'm sure," Kirheen laughed, rolling her eyes. Tomias shared her smile before standing. He yawned loudly, smoothing his robes as he did so. Turning to Trista, he lent her a hand and helped her up, then turned to Kirheen to do the same.

"Will you promise to trust me," he asked, hand extended. His dark eyes were unwavering. There was no trace of his usual humor to be found in his gaze. Despite her obvious mistrust of almost everyone, she really did like Tomias. She even liked Fenir, gruffness and all. Trista had listened openly and taken her in without question. And Garild, even though she didn't want to be bonded with him, really was a good friend.

Although it scared her to do so, she'd have to put her trust in others eventually, and Tomias seemed like a good place to start. With his help she'd strengthen her powers and learn how to block her mind effectively. If she could do that, she'd be able to rest easy at night, to not worry that her mind was being read or influenced. She'd know for sure that she was safe from such things, and to have that reassurance, she'd do anything.

She met his eyes, the flames casting the lines of his face with cold, blue light. Her hand connected with his and he pulled her to her feet.

"I promise."

Chapter 11

The weeks that followed brought a renewed sense of purpose for Kirheen. Training was no longer something to fear but a tool she could use to protect herself. The powers may have allowed others to enter her mind, but they also allowed her to block them from doing so, and that alone was worth the training.

They'd learned so much in such a short amount of time. This power that had been lurking over them their entire lives was finally starting to make sense, the picture becoming a little clearer day by day. Over the weeks, they'd both started to find their niche. Garild worked on subtlety, gently shifting the landscape of his opponents mind to move the game in his favor. He worked often with Tomias, learning various ways to manipulate and change thoughts, to shift reality just enough that he could trick and coerce even the most clever of opponents. It was an ability that terrified Kirheen and she dreaded the times she had to face Garild.

As for herself, Kirheen worked on blocking and there was none better to learn from then Fenir. He was a silent attacker, slipping in quietly and suddenly blasting with a wave of power that was astonishing. She had to quickly adapt to a variety of situations. His attacks were never straight forward and she learned to strengthen her whole mind, not just the parts that she thought would be attacked. It forced her to manage her powers accordingly, never exerting too much energy in one place and she always kept some reserved for the times when he really worked on breaking through.

Once they'd gotten a good grasp of their own powers, they shifted started training as a team. Some days it was Garild teamed with her, working together to try and take down their instructors. Other days she worked with Tomias, her blocking and attacking while he messed with their perspective on things. It was rigorous work and the training often left her feeling weak and exhausted. Garild too suffered under the effects of training, his otherwise optimistic mood stifled under the pressure. And they didn't seem to be the only ones.

The mood in the Temple of Gathering was somber, stories of training shared between them quietly. In the mornings, all were bleary eyed and exhausted and by their evening meals they seemed doubly so. Banter stayed at a minimum even out of the likes of Burk and Abby. Any other time it may have been cause for concern but at the moment, everyone welcomed the silence.

So wrapped up in training had they been that fall nearly passed them by. Towering wraith wood trees stood bare, jagged limbs twisting across the sky. The ground glowed with the remnants of leaves, and towards the evening they danced through the sky, blue sparks that faded into darkness. Days grew shorter and the evenings seemed to stretch on for eternity. Much of their training was done by the light of candles, and they soon added another layer to their robes and gloves to warm their hands. Trista often joined them at the end of the day, bringing with her spices that, when added to water, came alive with wonderful smells that lifted the spirit and warmed the bones.

It was on such an evening that the wraith wood trees fell dark. One would expect such a thing to happen loudly, like a great beast heaving a final sigh before drifting off to the hands of sleep. But there was no noise, no great telling that the trees were going dark. It happened swiftly, sweeping across the land, tree by tree losing its glow until the darkness seemed to be the only thing left. If one blinked, it would surely be missed and they'd be left wondering what had changed, why the light seemed so different and why the air seemed to have lost a bit of its magic.

A rare few could feel it.

As they sat around the hearth, blue flames crackling loudly, Tomias lifted his head. The conversation around him seemed to dull, Kirheen's laughter becoming a soft bell somewhere in the back of his mind. A feeling of dread pulled at his heart, forcing his stomach into knots. He felt his throat tighten, watched helplessly as his mug of cider slipped from his fingers and shattered on the floor. There was the inward rush of breath as everyone jumped.

All eyes were on him. He could feel them watching, could feel the stunned silence creep over them like a blanket. He stared down at the broken pieces of ceramic on the floor, glittering in the light of flames that were no longer an icy blue. Now they danced and swirled, a deadly tornado of red and yellow. Trista filled his vision a moment later, her hands warm on his face from the mug she'd been holding a moment earlier.

"The trees," she whispered, eyes filled with concern.

He reached up, grabbing her hands and pulling them away from his face. He held them tightly and she did not pull away. "Yes."

"They've gone dark," Kirheen said, eyes drifting to the window. The glow in the house was gone, the shadows darker and deeper. It felt like things lurked there, ready to crawl forth and steal them away.

"Come, you need to lay down for a bit," Trista goaded, shifting her weight to pull him to his feet. He felt weak, like his connection to the world had suddenly been severed. His brother grabbed his arm, taking some of the load off of Trista, and helped him into the next room. They shuffled in the dark, finally finding a bed to topple him on. He sunk into it gratefully and listened to the patter of footsteps as they left him in the dark.

Kirheen knelt on the floor next to Garild, carefully picking up large chunks of ceramic from the broken mug. She piled them in her hand, thinking back to the moment the trees had gone dark. It was an event that happened every year before the snow came to cover their little valley. She had never really noticed it before, not in the sense that she could feel a change. It was a normal changing of the landscape and before that moment it had never caught her attention.

This time was different. It was hard not to feel like the world had been smeared with a fine layer of grime. It wasn't enough to stop you from seeing it, but it was enough to taint it somehow, to distort your view of the world just enough that it bothered you.

Perhaps it was the newfound closeness she had with the powers residing within her that made her feel that way. When Trista and Fenir stepped back into the room, she asked about her instructor. "Is Tomias okay? What happened to him?"

Trista shrugged. "He'll be fine. He just needs to get some rest. We aren't entirely sure what happens to him when the trees go dark, but it happens every time. It's like he feels it happen, like someone just sucks the life out of him."

"You don't feel it, Fenir?"

He shook his head. Though he usually showed little emotion, she could tell he was worried. It was easy to forget that the two of them were connected in a way that she'd never understand. If such a thing were happening to Garild she would worry, but for someone like Fenir who was twin born, it was hard not to be hyper aware of the state of your bond mate.

"Do the trees actually have anything to do with our powers?"

Trista nodded. "Well, to an extent. We've long thought that our powers were stronger in this grove, that we are somehow tied to the trees. When they go dark, many claim to feel a slight dampening of their powers, but not nearly to the extent that Tomias feels it."

"It does feel different," Kirheen said. "Guess I never really noticed before."

"You're much more aware of your connection to your powers. It would make sense that you feel a change now where you didn't before. We should really let Tomias get some rest. Would you mind going over to see Grant? I'm sure he'd let you join his group for the evening."

Kirheen and Garild rose, making one final scan for broken pieces. "Very well, we'll head over there," Kirheen said, glancing towards her room. "Should we check back in a while?"

"I'll come fetch you when he's feeling better."

Garild nodded and the two stepped outside, eyes adjusting to the darkness that surrounded them. The lack of glow from the trees was eerie and made their skin crawl. Abby and Burk lived just to the left of them, a mere stone's throw away and they hurried across the distance, casting nervous glances as they went. It was easy to get lost in the darkness, to get lost in the fear of it.

They were relieved when they reached the steps of their house, and even more so when the warm glow of fire reached their eyes. Kirheen knocked quietly on the door and a moment later, Grant answered. He was tall and broad shouldered, dark of hair and fair skinned. He had bright blue eyes and a gruesome scar that ran across his right cheek and lip. It cut a path through his beard and he had the look of a man constantly scowling. No one knew where he'd gotten it and nobody dared to ask. His demeanor had a way of scaring people off.

"The moon whelps, is that you?"

Kirheen could only imagine he was referring to their symbols. "Yes, it's us. Trista sent us over."

Grant huffed and cast his gaze out into the darkness. "The trees, isn't it? Alright, get in here." He took a step back, letting Kirheen and Garild duck under his arm. He closed the door behind them. Abby and Burk whipped around from their seats next to the fire, craning to see who had come to visit so late. They both smiled when they realized it was them.

"Come join us," Burk said, raising a mug above his head. Abby smiled and raised her own mug. Kirheen and Garild made their way through the room and took up seats opposite each other.

"What brings you two here," Abby questioned.

Garild hesitated, unsure whether to tell or not. Kirheen was having the same struggle and both sighed with relief when Grant butted in. "That doesn't matter, girl. They are here now so treat them well." He brought them both a piping hot mug of tea. It was darker and less spiced then the tea Trista was prone to making, but it warmed them all the same.

Grant pulled up a chair from the other room, plopping it down next to Garild. He settled into it, the chair creaking as he did. "How goes the training?"

Kirheen shrugged. "Oh, I'm sure about the same as everyone else."

He snorted, amused. "No need to be modest, girl. Tell me, what are you specializing in?"

"Blocking, for the most part."

"Ah, that's suiting. Figured you'd pick up on that, especially after Herzin did you in."

At any other time, Kirheen may have found herself offended by his words, but after being asked about the event so many times, she'd grown numb to it. The mere mention of it didn't bother her the same way it had. She'd learned to block it out just like in her training.

"And you boy? You the pusher of the group?"

Garild smiled. "Not quite. I'm a manipulator."

Grant crossed his arms and sank bank in his chair. "Allseer be damned! Now that I didn't expect out of you. You've always been too quiet and polite. Didn't take you for the manipulative type."

"What about you two," Garild questioned, nodding to Burk and Abby.

"I think mine is pretty obvious," Burk grinned, playfully flexing his arm. Abby rolled her eyes.

"He's obviously a pusher. He's built like a bear, what else could he be? As for myself, I've kind of fallen split in between pushing and blocking."

"Is that pretty common," Kirheen asked.

Grant nodded. "It is. Not everyone has a predominant strength. Some people mesh their talents and use them in more unique ways than those that only focus on one. A blending of techniques allows a person to be less predictable."

"Couldn't anyone learn the techniques? Or are we stuck with what we've learned," Garild asked.

"You can learn as much as you're willing. Unfortunately, most people just stick with what they know. They'd rather limit themselves to what they are good at rather than face the humiliation of failing at something they aren't." He shifted his gaze to Burk whose smile wilted off his face faster than a flower in the heat of summer. "You know what I'm talking about, boy."

"I'll learn something else...eventually," Burk sighed, suddenly very interested in the bottom of his mug.

"You best be learning it before winter ends."

Abby frowned. "If it ever does. It's barely begun and I already wish it were over. I can't stand the cold."

Grant laughed, a gruff bark that sounded more condescending than amused. "You'll be too busy this winter with training to focus on how cold your toes are and too tired in the evenings to care."

"That sounds pleasant," Kirheen said, forcing a smile. "Why is it we are going to be training so hard this winter?"

"Because it's too damned cold to do anything else and these winter months will drag on like a bad case of the sniffles if we don't stay busy. Better to stay focused so we don't lose our edge. It's easy to lose sight of things once that chill sets in your bones."

"You're a cheery person, Grant," Kirheen noted, smiling.

"I try my best." He crossed his arms, leaning back into his seat.

"It's funny," Burk mused, blue eyes watching the fire dance. Everyone shifted their attention, watching him with curious eyes. "It's so easy to forget that these powers we use have a purpose. I mean, we learn them, but I forget that at the end of all of this, we'll be using these powers to protect people and save the world from the Darkness."

There was a collective nodding of the head from the group, a shared agreement. It was a thought that was always there in the back of their minds, dredged to the surface from time to time. It did feel strange, to have such responsibility and to so easily forget about it. Focusing on training was well and good, but there was a much larger picture, a darker picture that could taint everything they knew if they forgot about it. It was easy to pretend that Sanctuary was all that existed, that nothing else lay beyond the borders, but things did exist. It was a dark, twisted world out there and they would reclaim it. It was just a matter of time… time and power.

"Never forget your purpose for having these powers. If you know that someday you'll be beating back the Darkness with your gift, it makes wanting to learn it to the best of your ability that much easier," Grant said. "You've got to learn not only for your own sake, but for the sake of everyone around you. To fail is to watch Sanctuary fall."

"There are others out there now, fighting against it," Garild asked quietly.

"Of course there are. You aren't the first to be Bonded and you certainly won't be the last. Those that came before fight as we speak. They are keeping you safe. And those that aren't fighting are working hard to help keep you fed and clothed, so you better appreciate those that came before. We'd have fallen long ago if it weren't for them."

Kirheen opened her mouth to ask a question and a knock at the door stopped her. Trista poked her head in a moment later, her red hair bright in the light of the fire. "Sorry to interrupt, but I thought I might steal Kirheen and Garild back."

Grant nodded, leaning forward to take the mugs out of their hands. Kirheen thanked him for the tea.

"Probably won't see much of you this winter," said Abby sadly. "Take care of yourselves and train hard. We look forward to seeing what you've learned come Spring!"

"Will do," Garild smiled. "You two do the same."

"In fact, with two instructors, we expect you to know twice as much as we do by then," Burk teased. "Perhaps one of these days we'll be permitted to test our powers against each other."

"Sounds like a challenge," Kirheen smirked. "Think you could win?"

"You can save your challenges for later," said Grant. "It's late. Kirheen, Garild, it was nice talking with you both. Train hard and remember your purpose. The time to push back against the dark will come faster than you think."

With that, they followed Trista back outside. The night air was chilly and Kirheen watched her breath form tiny clouds in front of her face. "How is Tomias?"

"Tomias is fine," Trista said. "By tomorrow he'll be feeling like himself again."

"So, we should prepare for a lecture then, I take it?"

Trista laughed, leading them through the field. "Sounds about right."

With Tomias recovering, training would continue. The talk they'd had with the others had both inspired and terrified them. These powers weren't just for show. Someday, they would face the Darkness and use their strengths to heal the world. As they stepped into the warm glow of their house, they felt a new burden upon their shoulders. This was not the weight of trials and training, this was the weight of the world. Only time would tell if they could bear it.

Chapter 12

Winter crept into Sanctuary, devouring the light and leaving the day but a brief companion. The air grew cold and windy, and before long, snow was drifting in and blanketing the land in white. Light summer robes were traded for fur lined winter wear and cold bodies sought the rare warm glow of fire that now burned in a myriad of orange, yellow and red. And all around them, the wraith woods stood silent and dark, brooding beasts waiting to reawaken.

Training started in the first few hours of day light and stretched into the inky blackness of the evening. Meals were now taken within their houses and the Bonded saw very little of each other. With little to do otherwise, training consumed their every minute. They'd moved away from the basics of controlling their powers and now were learning new ways to manipulate the skills they already possessed. Where before Kirheen had seen a wall when using her powers against Garild, the view had now shifted and she saw what he wanted her to see.

At times it was a forest, filled with glowing wraith wood trees and alive with the sounds of bugs and birds. Sweet smelling flowers blossomed all around, luring her in with their fragrance.

Lush grass, tall and green, tickled her as she walked. The forest was designed to lower her guard, to make her feel safe and complacent, and it did a fine job. There were times where she'd lose her purpose and find herself wandering the forest aimlessly. Other times she'd come face to face with some wild creature that would chase and attack, forcing her back into the safety of her own mind.

It proved difficult for Kirheen, headstrong as she was. Her tendency to keep her eye on the goal left her open to manipulation and Garild did it well. So intent was she on the bigger picture that often times, she missed the little details. Subtle shifts in the forest went unnoticed and reality and the dream distorted into one until it was difficult to tell the two apart. The weeks went by slowly, leaving Kirheen feeling weak and defeated.

Recognizing this, Tomias worked on showing her how to seek out the traps, to move slowly and deliberately to her goal without leaving herself open or losing sight of what she was after. It was different from blocking. Blocking was the act of keeping someone out of your mind or deliberately cutting off their power. What he taught her was something else, a kind of counter manipulation that involved using their projections against them. When the creature would attack, she'd have to focus hard on the fact that it wasn't real. Then she'd shift her power and drive the creature to do her bidding, forcing it to seek out other traps and drive away other creatures that would seek to harm her. It was difficult at first, but eventually she could keep pace with Garild.

With their training came changes, both physical and mental. Over the cold winter months, they grew taller. Garild lost some of his boyish chubbiness, growing leaner, his jaw and muscles becoming more defined. As he'd grown more confident in his powers, so too had his confidence grown in everything else. He was still humble and obedient, but no longer was he so naive and pliable. Now he was the manipulator and that power gave him strength.

Kirheen blossomed, her tall, willowy figure giving way to the curves of a woman. As she learned control and patience, humiliation and defeat, she softened to the world. No longer did she fear her powers or the powers of others. She was confident enough to keep herself guarded and that comforted her. She'd learned a sense of humbleness that she hadn't known before and it showed. She smiled more willingly, communicated more openly and was friendlier with Garild than she'd ever been.

They grew closer, their friendship solidifying and strengthening their bond. Where before their teamwork had been clumsy, they now worked together, powers blending into a seamless mix that left Tomias and Fenir defeated more often than not.

On a chilly winter night, Nyson gathered them within the hollowed tree where they'd been bonded. A large fire burned in the center of the circle, and the Bonded crowded around it, basking in the warmth it provided. With them all gathered, Nyson announced a tournament to be held after the snow had thawed.

The tournament would pit the bonded against each other, testing their abilities to an extent they'd never been tested before. It would be an opportunity to learn, to grow and to show the Council all they'd learned during those winter months. And at the end of it, a grand celebration would be held to honor the Allseer herself.

The room exploded with electric energy that crackled and surged as the Bonded discussed it among themselves. A fire had been lit, the promise of competition bringing out a new sense of purpose for many of them.

The reign of winter came to an end, and green dominated the landscape as it thawed. Flowers bloomed, filling the air with fragrance and hearts soared with the sun as it rose, once more becoming the dominant force in the sky.

And on a dark, moonless night, the trees came alive with icy fire once again.

Chapter 13

"Wait, you never told me you told them," Tomias frowned, pressing his hands to the sides of his head. "When did this happen? This might just ruin everything." He flung his hands out, shaking them as if trying to rid himself of the disappointment he felt.

Kirheen shook her head, completely baffled at his concern. It had been casually brought up in conversation that they'd talked with Grant, Abby and Burk. She never dreamed it would turn into the rant they now faced. "It can't *really* be that big of a deal. They told us what they were learning! Besides, we told them at the beginning of winter, I highly doubt they remember."

"That is where you are wrong. Grant doesn't forget anything! He's a sly old fox. I bet he's been training to counter us all winter! And that, them telling you what they learned, it was probably a lie! Just because he looks like a bear, walks like a bear, and talks like a bear does not necessarily make Burk a bear. For all we know, he's actually a highly skilled manipulator and that won't bode well for anyone."

Garild sighed. "I think you may be taking this a little too seriously. Isn't this meant to be fun?"

Tomias spun on his heels and approached Garild, pointing his finger in his face. "Fun? Yes! But you think I spent all winter training you day in and day out to have you lose? Uh-uh! It's not happening, especially not to Grant."

"There are plenty of opponents we'll have to deal with. I don't think they are the only ones we need to worry about. Besides, we've learned a lot these past few months. Garild is more than competent when it comes to manipulating and I'd like to say that I've learned some interesting blocking variations. We could win this if we really nail down a strategy," Kirheen explained.

Tomias frowned, rubbing his chin. He'd kept his stubble, claiming he liked feeling different from his brother, but they all knew it was a thinly veiled attempt to annoy Fenir and Trista alike. So far, it had worked. "You're right. I don't mean to undermine your efforts. You've both gone above and beyond my expectations. This is just the first time we've had a tournament like this. It's exciting!"

"Can we not forget stressful," Garild added.

"Yes, it's been that too. You're both feeling confident?"

Garild nodded. "As Kirheen said, we've learned a lot. We manage to take you both down from time to time and you're far more skilled than we are."

"I was hoping you'd forget about that. You have grown a lot and I won't deny you have a level of finesse that we sometimes lack. Being almost the same person makes for a rather one sided perspective, wouldn't you say? Your teamwork is quite enviable.

With that said, we can't let our guards down. You'll be facing Bonded you've never faced before. You'll see variations of techniques that we couldn't possibly teach you, things that they learned from their instructors that we don't know. They all have an edge, an advantage, and they will use every bit of it to win."

"Does it really matter? It's not like we get anything out of this."

It was true. Aside from getting to show off to the Council, the only reward was a self-gratifying one, a chance to show the other Bonded that they were better. Perhaps it would push everyone to work harder and that was the goal, but Garild couldn't help but question the point of it all.

"There is no physical reward for your efforts, true. But it offers you a chance to impress the Council, a chance to show that you really have what it takes to face the Darkness in the coming years. Remember, not everyone goes off to fight the Darkness. Some of you will end up as workers, working hard to provide for the Bonded that come after you. Plus, bragging rights. Can't deny those. I, for one, would have a splendid time rubbing our victory into the faces of the other instructors."

Kirheen snorted. "Of course you would. How long do we have exactly until the Union Battle?"

"Three weeks. It's not a lot of time, but it's enough to get ourselves prepared."

"Will they be telling us who we're going to be up against," Garild asked. Details about the competition had been kept to a minimum. The only thing they knew was that they'd be using their skills to take down whoever they happened to go up against. Beyond that, they knew very little and it wasn't much help in keeping Tomias calm.

"I don't think we'll know until the day of the competition."

"So, let's use these three weeks to work out every possible scenario. There are only so many skill combinations we'll face. Between the four of us, we can at least practice facing what we have here at present," Kirheen argued.

"We have all the bases covered. Garild and myself as manipulators, you and Fenir both for blocking and Fenir again as a pusher. You've at least experienced all three. Not everyone will have that advantage and that will work in your favor."

"What would be the hardest for us to go up against?"

"Manipulators are by far the most difficult. There are so many ways to manipulate the mind of another that it can be difficult to counter. You've had a bit of practice with that, Kirheen, but not everyone will use that power the way Garild does. They do have a weak spot though, and that is where you will come in. Manipulators can only shift your attention, but when they are focused by a pusher, things can go wrong very quickly. You'll want to use that and also watch out for it. If you aren't keeping Garild's mind safe when you're attacked, you'll both lose. Remember that."

Kirheen sighed. "Well, this isn't stressful to think about or anything. What do you think, Garild? You think we can do this?"

Garild smiled, rubbing his hands together as he leaned forward. "As a matter of fact, I do."

"That's what I like to hear," Tomias smirked. He clapped them both on the shoulder and then took a seat between them, huddling close to further discuss the battle to come.

A week before the Bonded would see themselves pitted against each other, Nyson called for the Council to gather. They gathered in the Temple of Union, just as the sun began its slow descent in the sky. All of the instructors were present, as well as Herzin and Trista.

Tomias hated meetings. Such things required him to maintain a firm hold of his tongue, something he'd found near impossible when he'd joined the Council years ago. It had become easier, mostly because he spent the majority of the meetings conversing with Fenir in his head. It gave him the feeling that he was voicing his opinions without getting the scolding that usually came along with it.

Fenir grunted, eyeing the other instructors around him. *"Lot of bodies in this room. We're in for quite the competition."*

It was true. The Council had swelled in size over the years. There were eleven of them now, including themselves. And there would be more to come. Eventually they'd need a bigger space to conduct their business, but for now the glowing wraith wood tree sufficed.

"How do you think we'll do," Tomias questioned, casting a suspicious glance at Grant. He stood silent and stoic, blue eyes gazing off into space. His arms were crossed and his expression was grim, sign of a man that had better things to do. Things like practicing to best them in combat.

"We'd do better if you'd quit worrying. We might not even be against them."

"I am worrying too much, aren't I?"

"Yes. You need to stop. Kirheen and Garild are doing far better than we ever expected, so quit worrying. You're stressing me out."

"Sorry, sorry. I just…"

The conversation was cut short as Nyson entered the room. He looked calm, a rare expression on his haggard face. Most days the man looked like he was ready to snap, like he was a frayed rope being pulled too taut. All it would take was one good tug and the man would unravel. Today was different though. His usual frown had disappeared from his face, his eye shone, and the harsh wrinkles of his face seemed softer somehow, as if he'd suddenly reverted back to a version of himself that was ten years younger. It was almost unsettling.

Nyson took his place in the center of the circle. Never one to stand still, the set up afforded him the ability to move about the room and address whomever he wished face to face. "Thank you for joining me today," he spoke, sweeping his arms out as he turned a slow circle. "As you well know, the Battle of Union is almost upon us. Today I'd like to discuss details with you so we all know what to expect. For the battle itself, I will be splitting the Bonded into two groups. Each group will consist of eight students. These Bonded will face each other in pairs and try to secure their spot in the final competition." Nyson motioned for a servant and a moment later, a young woman arrived at his side, holding a bundle of scrolls. He took them from her and nodded approvingly before dismissing her. She wandered to the far corner of the room, face devoid of emotion.

"On these scrolls is a breakdown of the battles. We will be doing one battle at a time with Herzin and myself overseeing each. Please review your scroll as it is passed to you." The scrolls were passed around the circle and Tomias unraveled his, eyeing it curiously.

The scroll showed a breakdown of whom each pair of Bonded would be up against as well as the official rules for the battle. On the left hand side, he found his students names. A line connected them to the group they'd be battling and he sighed, nudging Fenir with his elbow.

"See, I knew I was worried for a reason." The first battle was against Abby and Burk, the very team he'd been agonizing over in the first place. *"If we go up against them first, this could end badly."*

Fenir shrugged. *"Doesn't look like we have a choice. No point whining about it now."*

Tomias let the scroll snap back together and looked around the room just as Grant finished reading his. He met Tomias' gaze and the deformed corner of his mouth rose in a smirk. Tomias looked away in disgust, but not before giving him his best glare.

"We're going to lose."

"Would you shut up? I didn't deal with those two all winter just to let them lose the first round."

"Right, shutting up now."

Nyson clapped his hands twice, bringing the attention back to himself. "These scrolls are yours to keep. While the breakdown of the battles is yours to review, please keep this information from your students. The matchups will remain a surprise for them. Please make sure to review the terms of the battles and discuss the rules with your students. Any Bonded found breaking the rules of the competition will be immediately disqualified and face disciplinary actions as decided by Herzin. This is a chance for your students to prove their worth, to prove they have what it takes to defend us against the Darkness. Do not let them disappoint." Nyson met the eyes of each instructor as he said this. "That will be all today. Please use this next week to practice. The Bonded, as well as yourselves, will have the day before the competition to rest. Use your time wisely."

As Nyson left, the Council trickled out after him, murmuring softly to each other. The sun had sunk low, leaving the world drenched in vibrant streaks of color and Tomias took a minute to soak it in before the ghastly blue glow of the trees dominated the night.

"It really would be a shame if this place fell to the Darkness," Tomias mused.

"It would," Fenir agreed. *"That's why we have to train them the best we can. They are our future."*

"When did you get to be so optimistic? You've been around Trista too much."

Fenir grunted, walking away from Tomias before the conversation could go further. With the brisk pace set by Fenir, the walk back was a short one. Kirheen and Garild were quietly discussing strategy, playing through possible scenarios as they sat across from each other next to the fire. They hardly looked up when they entered the room and Tomias felt his heart swell with pride. Perhaps he *was* being overly paranoid about the battle to come.

"Having fun," he asked his students, taking a seat in an open chair next to them. Fenir followed suit.

Kirheen smiled sweetly, but her smile faded once she saw the scroll in his hands. "Uh oh, what did you find out?"

"I found out all the boring rules you get to follow so you don't get disqualified and punished."

"And?"

"You're doomed."

Kirheen and Garild both sneered, showing their obvious distaste for his lack of enthusiasm.

Garild spoke first. "And why exactly do you say that?"

Tomias sighed. "Because as I feared, your first battle is against Burk and Abby. Need I remind you that they know all your dirty secrets?"

Fenir gave him an alarmed look. *"We aren't supposed to tell them!"*

"When have we ever followed the rules? It's more fun this way!"

Kirheen grumbled loudly. "Well, great. What does that mean for us?"

"It means you are starting this competition at a bit of a disadvantage. But fear not, I think I have a way to fix this."

"And how exactly do you plan to do that?"

"Lean forward my little doves and let me teach you the art of a well-placed lie!"

Chapter 14

I t was a day of rest for the Bonded, a day to recover from the bouts of training and enjoy a few hours of peace and quiet before the excitement of the battles kicked in. Kirheen and Garild lay in the grass, grown plush and green with the sudden onslaught of rain. They basked in the warm glow of the sun, breathing in the smell of the earth and watching the leaves twist and dance above them. The branches of the great tree above them broke the sky, making it look like a pane of shattered glass.

Many of the other Bonded did the same. All around them, they could hear the others talking, the air occasionally pierced with bright laughter. It wasn't long before Burk and Abby arrived, plopping down in the grass next to them. Kirheen sat up, smiling warmly at her soon to be competitors.

"Nice day, isn't it," Burk asked enthusiastically. He showed no signs of competitive glee, he just looked relaxed and happy. Abby sat by his side, plucking strands of grass out of the ground and twirling them between her fingers.

"It is," Garild agreed. "It's nice that they gave us a day to rest up before tomorrow."

Abby smiled. "It was kind of them. How are you feeling about tomorrow?"

Kirheen chimed in, trying not to sound too egotistical. "Oh, we've been practicing a lot. We're feeling pretty confident."

"Don't be so quick to say that, you're going up against us first!"

"Oh, that's right! I'm glad we're going up against a pusher and a blocker like ourselves. Means we'll be on pretty even ground."

Burk and Abby exchanged a look. It was quick, barely a flicker, but it was there.

"Well, we look forward to facing you both tomorrow," Burk said, pushing himself up. He towered over them, seemingly gaining height and girth day by day. He lent Abby a hand and pulled her to her feet with little effort. "May the strongest bond win."

Abby gave them a nod and the pair wondered off, probably seeking out Grant to tell him their advantage had crumbled. Kirheen didn't expect Grant to believe it, but if it even put a moment of doubt in their heads, it would help them when it came time to battle.

After a time, they grew tired of lazing about and went to seek out their next victims. Isa and Ian sat alone on the edge of the field, talking quietly. Big blue eyes filled with curiosity met them as they approached. "Mind if we join you," Kirheen asked sweetly.

Ian smiled, meeting her eyes. "Please do!" Kirheen felt a sudden flutter in her heart as their eyes locked. It took everything to look away and she silently cursed herself. *Stop that. This isn't the time to be feeling this way.*

They took a seat in the grass next to them and Kirheen took up a blade of grass, twirling it in her fingers as she tried to keep eye contact to a minimum. Garild gave her an odd look, tilting his head ever so slightly as he tried to piece together her sudden silence.

"How are you both feeling about tomorrow," Garild asked, trying to sound casual.

Isa shuddered. "Oh, I'm terrified. Ian says we can win, but we're up against Tegan and Irena first. I'm pretty sure Irena is going to tear us both apart." She sounded meek and terrified, wringing her hands together as she spoke of it.

Ian shook his head. He reached out and grabbed her shoulder softly. "Isa, you're one of the best blockers I know. Anything they throw at us, you'll be able to counter. There is no need to be afraid."

"Thank you, Ian. I appreciate it," she smiled. Though she relaxed some, her eyes were still filled with fear and she glanced across the clearing, searching for her opponents. They were nowhere to be found and she sighed with relief.

"You're a blocker too, huh," Garild questioned, trying to feign excitement. "So am I!"

"Oh, that's great. I really don't think it's very fitting. I feel like I should have been something else. I'm too timid for this. I think it would have been better to be a manipulator."

"You could always learn," Kirheen smiled, her eyes focused on Isa. "In fact, after the battles, I could teach you a few things!"

"You're a manipulator," Ian asked, eyes wide. "That does suit you. You're probably a force to be reckoned with."

"Oh, I'm not that good," Kirheen said, trying to force the heat from her cheeks. She wanted so badly to meet his eyes, to gaze at those green depths that so reminded her of the forest around them. Instead she smiled at the ground and felt like a complete and utter fool.

"You girls, always so modest," he said with a smile.

"What about you, Ian? What are you?"

"Oh, me? I'm a pusher. We make a pretty good team, Isa and I." Isa beamed at his words, smiling brightly. It was obvious by her body language that she was rather infatuated with her bond mate and it made Kirheen sick. She wanted to be where Isa was at that moment, to be sitting by his side close enough to feel the heat from his skin.

"He's really good," Isa said, breaking Kirheen away from her thoughts. She tried to keep her emotional turmoil from showing on her face as she responded.

"Any idea what you're up against tomorrow?"

Ian shrugged. "Not entirely sure. If I had to guess I'd say Irena is probably a manipulator. As for Tegan, I think he'll be lucky if even he knows that by tomorrow."

"That was certainly an odd pairing! It will be interesting to see how they do tomorrow. I'll be shocked if they can even bring themselves to work together," Garild said. "Well, Kirheen, you want to go find Vienna and Daris?"

"Yes, let's do that," Kirheen said, getting to her feet. She self-consciously smoothed her robes, keeping her eyes locked on Garild as she turned to leave. "Thanks for talking with us and good luck tomorrow!"

"It was good seeing you both! May the Allseer lend you her strength."

Kirheen walked away a bit quicker than she should have and Garild shot out his hand, locking it around her elbow and drawing her to a halt.

"Is there a problem," he questioned.

"N-no. Why," she asked, trying to look confused.

"You seem flustered. Did they say something wrong?"

"Oh, no. I guess I'm just nervous about the competition tomorrow. It's strange to look at these people as opponents, you know."

Garild smiled, dropping his hand from her elbow. "I can understand that. Just take a deep breath, okay? It'll all work itself out."

"I sure hope so," Kirheen sighed. "At least we're completely throwing them all off. If anyone talks to each other, they are going to have a hard time figuring out what we are ahead of time."

They found Vienna and Daris sitting on the steps of their home. They were an odd pair, seemingly content with the only company being each other. They often kept to themselves, taking meals in their quarters instead of joining the rest of them. Vienna glanced at them suspiciously as they approached and whispered something to her bond mate before they were in earshot.

Vienna was tall and graceful with short curly blonde hair and dark blue eyes that shone with intelligence. She was quiet and poised, wasting nothing with her actions. Everything with her was deliberate. Daris, though a bit more relaxed in his mannerisms, was much like Vienna. Tall and muscular, he was an intimidating force with dark hair, olive skin and eyes that were almost black. Unlike many of the other Bonded, the two openly showed affection for each other. Even now, their knees touched and their fingers were interlaced and the approach of others did nothing to deter their actions. It was hard to imagine doing such a thing with Garild. It made her uncomfortable.

"How can we help you," Daris spoke before either of them had the chance to.

"Oh, we we're just seeing how you both were feeling about the competition tomorrow."

"Fine," Vienna said tersely. "We'd rather not discuss the battles until after they are done."

Without another word, Vienna turned away from them, turning her attention back to Daris. He gave them a sly grin before turning back to his bond mate.

"Nice talking to you too," Kirheen muttered as they diverted in another direction. "They're really going overboard with the friendliness."

Garild grinned. "Yeah, they are certainly a little odd."

"Well, what do you say? Is our work here done?"

"I think so. We seemed to have surprised a few people with our trickery. Hopefully it will help tomorrow."

"I sure hope so."

They walked back in silence, enjoying the last few minutes of sunlight they could. Even though they knew the battles would happen come morning, it still felt strange. They'd spent so much time practicing, learning each other's strengths and weaknesses, learning the subtle shifts and changes of their minds... to think that they'd be facing the unknown was scary.

Tomias and Fenir were waiting for them when they returned to their home. Tomias had his hair pulled back away from his face and he lit up with a boyish grin as they entered. "So, how did our subtle manipulation go," he asked, barely able to contain his excitement.

"Better than expected," Kirheen informed him, plopping down in her favorite chair. Garild took up a spot next to her, finally able to relax now that they weren't lying to everyone they talked to.

"I just hope it helps," said Garild. "I didn't feel great about lying to everyone."

"Oh, but think of the reward for your efforts, Garild. Think about that! You've just thrown off all the enemy teams. You've probably got Burk and Abby second guessing everything at this very moment," Tomias beamed, grinning from ear to ear.

Fenir huffed, blowing his white hair away from his face.

"Oh, come on! It's exciting!"

They spent the rest of the evening practicing various scenarios, checking for weaknesses in their defense and making sure they would be prepared for what was to come. They went to bed feeling confident, ready to take on anything the world could throw at them.

It was a feeling that faded quickly.

Kirheen stared at the wall beyond her feet, her eyes following the wood grain, tiny glowing rivers weaving through the wraith wood planks. She'd been exhausted when she'd gone to bed. Weeks of training and scheming had taken its toll, but here in the dark, with the battles looming ever closer, she found it impossible to sleep. Her armor of confidence had cracked and now doubt and fear squirmed in, digging into her heart like worms.

When she did finally lapse into sleep, it was disrupted by nightmares. She moved slowly through a forest, eyes taking in her surroundings. It was autumn and the air swirled around her, leaving her skin covered in goose-flesh. Leaves crackled under her feet, sounding terrifyingly loud in contrast to the silent forest. Her breath left her in great billowing gusts that twisted and curled playfully.

Each step felt like her last. She could sense the traps around her, waiting for her foot to step off course. Eyes blinked at her from the shadows of foliage and she could hear breathing of creatures far more cunning than she. Looking through the twisting branches above, she saw Herzin staring down, her thin lips pulled into a cruel and knowing smile. Her eyes twinkled with delight, hungry to witness Kirheen fail.

She looked back to the forest floor, trying to ignore the eyes that hovered above her but her heart was hammering away with fear. Herzin was in her mind and this time, she wouldn't be so lucky. Now she wanted blood and Kirheen knew that this time, she would have it.

She came to a split in the path, one branching off to the west and the other winding to the east. They were identical, neither more worn than the other. Above her, Herzin cackled. "Choose wisely, little girl."

She stood for a time, silent and afraid, as still as a deer caught in the eyes of a predator. Her muscles ached from the stillness, her lungs burned. Leaves rustled behind her, spooking her into flight. She fled to the East, her feet carrying her as fast as they could. And Herzin laughed, and laughed, and laughed.

Through the trees, she thought she could see a clearing in the distance, a place of refuge. Hours seemed to pass before she finally burst through the edge of the forest, leaves swirling around her as she departed, trees stretching their limbs in an attempt to stop her.

Her breath came in ragged gasps and she glanced over her shoulder, fully expecting to find creatures in pursuit. The trees swayed, angered by her flight but she was safe for the moment.

When she turned back to the clearing, her heart froze. What had looked to be tall, green grass was a barren waste. The ground was cracked and darkened, splitting in great chasms that begged for moisture, despite the fact that the entire area was covered in thick, gelatinous goo. It was dark and putrid and clung to her bare feet, squished between her toes. Giant pools of darkness bubbled and spat and occasionally, a hand would burst from within, grasping desperately for freedom only to be pulled back and engulfed.

This was the future that awaited them, a land of darkness and chaos. In the distance, someone screamed, a terrifying sound that didn't seem human. She shuddered in fear, hugging herself as she crept across the land. The forest behind her had disappeared, leaving her in a rotting world with blackened eyes watching her from above.

Another scream pierced the air, this one closer and to her right. She shifted her direction, moving towards the scream. Perhaps she could help, to stop the pain that caused them to yell out in anguish. A man sat on the ground with his back to her, his head hanging in defeat. He rocked back and forth, muttering to himself as he did. He wore tattered robes so stained by the corruption that she could never tell what color they once were.

She approached cautiously, and as she did, she noticed another man lying in front of him, completely motionless. She crept closer, holding her breath, trying not to disturb the man. When she was finally close enough to touch him, she reached forward and gently touched his shoulder. He turned quick as a snake and latched on to her arms before she could react. His hands were slick with the corruption and it seemed to leak from his skin. The corners of blackened eyed oozed, trails of sludge looking like tears.

She tried to pull away in fear, but he held fast. There was a twisted sense of the familiar and she forced herself to look at her captor. Familiarity turned to horror as she realized she stared into the face of Tomias. She screamed, struggling frantically to get away from him. He forced her to the ground, pinning her hands next to her head.

"I didn't mean to," he wept, his inky black tears dripping onto her face. "I didn't want to. But now he's gone. Gone. Just like this world."

She looked towards the motionless man on the ground, his build so like Tomias, white hair stained with darkness. Her stomach twisted, a mixture of fear and anger. "You killed him!"

"I didn't want to. Couldn't have known. This… all your fault. Your fault. You wanted this world. You wanted this!" He raised his arm high above him, his fingers clenching into a fist. As he brought it down hard and fast, she whispered an apology.

"I'm sorry."

The blow broke the hold of the dream and she squirmed awake, frantically trying to move. It took her a moment to realize that someone held her down and she cried out. Tomias loomed over her. She saw his eyes dripping black and she struggled to free herself. He let go of her and she flung herself from the bed, scrabbling to the corner of the room.

He was on his knees in an instant, calmly speaking to her as if she were an injured bird. His brown eyes were filled with concern. Warm brown eyes, the color of caramel. Nothing like the inky blackness she'd seen in her dream.

"Kirheen, please. It's me. You were only dreaming. I'm not going to hurt you, okay?" He inched forward, his hand held out towards her. His white hair was unbound and it fell around his face like a halo of light. "Please let me help you."

The scuffle had awoken Garild and he stood, eyes droopy from sleep, watching from the far side of the room. "Is everyone okay," he asked, voice thick.

"Everything is fine, Garild. Just stay over there, please."

Garild cooperated, sitting on his bed without a word. Kirheen eyed Tomias suspiciously, still feeling the residual effects of the dream and curled herself tighter against the wall. "Kirheen, please."

He whispered gentle words to her, calming her and soothing her troubled soul. After what felt like hours, he wrapped a hand around her arm. "Kirheen, you're awake. You're alright."

A wave of emotion rocketed through her and she burst into tears. She felt his arms slide under her and he scooped her off the ground, cradling her close. He smelled clean and the warmth of him was a comfort she welcomed.

"Garild, stay here please. I need to speak with her alone for a moment."

She heard him protest but as Garild normally did, he slunk away from the confrontation, allowing Tomias to carry her from the room. They stepped into the living room and he carried her over to a chair next to the fire. She could see Fenir sitting in the edge of the light, his face half hidden in shadow. He watched them with inquisitive eyes, eyes that undeniably showed that he lived, that her nightmare hadn't been a reality.

Tomias gently sat down in one of the chairs, shifting so she was cradled more comfortably in his arms. She realized she was clinging to his arm tightly and she relaxed her grip, sighing as she tried to bring her tears to a halt.

She felt his chin rest on the top of her head and he chuckled softly. "Well, now that that is over, want to tell me what that was all about?"

Kirheen tried to laugh but it came out as a failed puff of air. "I'm sorry, Tomias. That dream, it felt so real."

"They often do for us," he said softly. "These powers aren't all they are cracked up to be. Mind telling me about your dream?"

She hesitated, trying to piece together what had happened. "It sounds so stupid now."

"I'm not going to judge you, Kirheen. I just want to hear. Maybe I can help."

Nodding meekly, she took a deep breath. "I... I was in a forest. It was a lot like the forest Garild likes to create when we're practicing. I knew there were traps and every step I took was loud, impossibly loud. When I looked above me, Herzin was there, watching me. She hated me, she wanted me dead. I could feel it." She waited for Tomias to comment but he said nothing, merely nodded. "I came to a split in the road and something scared me so I ran. I made it to a clearing and looked back at the forest, but when I turned back to the clearing it had changed. It was…horrifying. There was darkness everywhere. I can't even begin to explain it. Herzin was still watching me only her eyes were black, like she'd been corrupted. And then I found you and…and," she sighed, feeling the tears well up in her eyes again.

How could she tell him that she'd seen him hovering over the dead body of Fenir? How could she tell him that he had hurt him, hurt him bad enough that he'd lay so still, his life gone. She wouldn't do it, couldn't! "I saw you there and you were covered in the Darkness. It was coming out of your skin, your mouth, your eyes. You…you attacked me." She couldn't hold it back any longer and she cried, burrowing her head under his chin. He shushed her, rocking her gently.

"And then you woke up. Kirheen, I'm sorry if I frightened you. That must have been so confusing. I heard you thrashing around in your sleep and came to check on you. I didn't realize…I shouldn't have tried to wake you so suddenly."

"It's not your fault. It was just a stupid dream."

"Was there anything else you saw?"

Death…And Fenir, so cold and broken. "No. That was it. Is that really what it's like? Is the Darkness really so terrible?"

Tomias nodded. "Kirheen, I've yet to witness the Darkness with my own eyes. The Allseer has seen fit to bless me with that much. I have, however, heard many stories and it is much as you described it."

"How can we face such a thing?"

"We do what we can, Kirheen. It's a sacrifice, but if we are to stay safe, it is one that has to be made. Tell me, are you worried about tomorrow?"

She saw no point in lying. "Yes."

"Your dream seemed to indicate so. Kirheen, do not fret. You are strong and smart and we'll be standing by to keep anything bad from happening. You'll be letting people into your mind, but you know how to block them now, you know how to turn their manipulations against them. Don't forget that. You're going to do fine."

"What about Herzin?"

Tomias sighed. "It's true, she'll be watching in on the whole thing which means she'll be in your mind as well, but she'd be a fool to pull anything in front of Nyson. He wasn't exactly thrilled with her earlier antics, if you couldn't tell. And as I said, we'll be there to protect you."

Fenir nodded, sharing a rare smile with her. It was such an odd thing to see on his face that she found herself smiling too. "Thank you both." Now calmed, she felt suddenly self-conscious, her body pressed so close against Tomias. In the moment it had been comforting, but now it just felt strange. She squirmed and he loosened his grip, allowing her to untangle herself and stand. "I'm sorry about all this. I think I'm going to head back to bed."

"Don't apologize," Tomias demanded. He stood and stretched, giving her a warm smile as he lowered his arms back to his sides. "You are more than welcome to stay up with us. I'm loath to admit it, but it's hard to sleep for us too."

Kirheen smiled. "Thank you, but I should probably get what sleep I can before tomorrow."

"True enough."

She turned to leave and she felt his hand slide around her arm, halting her. "Kirheen, you're going to do fine tomorrow. I promise."

His brown eyes were steady, filled with an unspoken truth. She nodded and his hand fell away. "Thank you again. I'll see you both in the morning." She walked away, stepping back into the darkness of her room. Garild stirred as she entered.

"Are you okay," he asked, sitting up in bed. She could barely see his outline in the light of the moon. "I was worried."

"Sorry to worry you, Garild. I'm fine. It was just a bad dream, you can sleep now."

"Do you want to talk about it?"

She sighed. "I'd rather not. I'm just going to try and go back to sleep."

"We're going to do great tomorrow," Garild said softly.

"I sure hope so," Kirheen whispered, slipping beneath the covers. She listened to the world around her for a time, listened to Garild as his breathing deepened and he sunk back into a dreamless sleep, listened to the creaking of the house, the trees rustling as the wind caressed them. She thought of the battles that would occur come morning and she found the fear that she'd felt was dissipating. Tomias had said he'd keep her safe and she trusted his word. She trusted Garild to stand strong in the battles, knew in her heart that her own strength would help them both. The battles were new and frightening but she felt a sense of excitement as well. Whatever struggles they faced, they'd make it through. She was ready.

Chapter 15

Tomias leaned over Kirheen, hand hovering in the air between them. He felt horrible about waking her. With the night she'd had, it seemed cruel to rouse her from a peaceful slumber. The battles weren't going to wait for them and as such he was forced to choose cruelty. Losing a battle was one thing; disqualification for being late was quite another.

With a deep breath, he reached down and gently shook her shoulder, half expecting her to go leaping from the bed in fright. Instead, her eyes flickered open and she blinked at him sleepily, her storm colored eyes patched with red. The skin around them was puffy, a direct result of many shed tears. "Rise and shine my little blocking master! Your talents are required."

Once her brain was able to comprehend his words, she rolled over onto her stomach, pulling her pillow over her head with a groan. She clenched it tightly over her ears and he had to strain to make out the mumbles from beneath the pillow. "Can't I just sleep a little longer?"

If only… Tomias reached down, plucking the pillow away from her grasping hands. "I'm afraid not. I already let you sleep far longer than I should have. You need to be up and ready in ten minutes or the battles are going to start without you."

"Ugh, fine." Kirheen rolled over with a groan, throwing her blanket over the side of the bed. Garild was already shifting in his bed and he sat up, brown hair sticking out in all directions.

"Is it already time?"

Tomias grinned. "It is, indeed. You best be up and ready soon. Hurry up!"

This was met with an elaborate sigh from both of his students. He left the grumbling duo to the task of getting ready and joined his twin in the front room. Fenir sat in a chair by the fireplace, slowly devouring an apple as he stared at the forest outside. He barely shifted as Tomias sat down.

"*You think they're ready for this,*" Fenir asked, biting into his apple.

"*Guess we'll find out soon enough. I can't tell who is more nervous about all of this. Me or them?*"

"*Is that even a question? If you desire clarification, I can provide. You are more nervous by far. They aren't even out of bed yet.*"

As if on cue, Garild stumbled from his room, hands fumbling at the silver sash around his waist. He was wearing a new robe, dark blue with their symbol emblazoned on the back. Though he'd made an attempt to smooth his hair, it was obvious he'd just rolled out of bed.

"How are you feeling, Garild?"

Garild, finally content with his sash, looked up and shrugged. "I don't know... I'm nervous. It's just a competition and I know it doesn't mean anything but I can't help but let it get to me. We've put a lot into this and...I want to win. Hard to believe huh?"

"A little competitive spirit is good, Garild. Use it. And trust me, you aren't the only nervous one around here. Apple?" Tomias held a basket of apples out to him and he shook his head quickly, choosing instead to sit down. "You won't get another chance to eat, you know?"

"I know. Just the thought of eating right now..."

Kirheen bustled into the room, deftly tying her sash as she hustled towards them. She gave Tomias a curt nod before snatching an apple from the basket and planting herself in a seat next to Garild. Tomias shrugged, setting the basket back on the floor next to his brother.

"And how are we feeling this morning, Kirheen?"

Her teeth were parted, apple almost to her lips. She glared at him over the top of her apple and then lowered it, shuffling it in her hands. "I just want to get this over with."

"Nervous?"

"Yes? No? I'm excited to use my powers in earnest against an unfamiliar opponent. I'm not so delighted about that unfamiliar being in my head. It's one thing to have any of you in there, but to have someone else... Uck, just thinking about it is making my stomach hurt."

Tomias frowned. "It's going to be difficult. You're going to be pushing yourselves to the brink today but I know you'll do great. This nervousness we're all feeling is a good feeling. It means you know you can lose and that will keep you cautious. Walk in with an attitude and you'll fall the hardest. Just remember that."

They both nodded, falling into a moment of silence before a knock at the door caught their attention. Trista bounded through the door, radiating levels of cheer not felt by the rest of them. "Good morning!" She sauntered into the room carrying a covered basket and earned the interest of everyone in the room.

"What did you bring us today," Tomias asked though his nose picked up the scent of wraith blossom cakes as he asked the question. "Ah, my favorite."

"And fortunately for everyone else, none of them are for you," she chided, stopping next to his brother. She set the basket in his lap, allowing him to open it and look at the contents.

Fenir snorted. *"Told you she holds a grudge."*

"Yeah, yeah. Shut up. My dearest, darling Trista. What would it take to be put back in your good graces?"

Trista rolled her eyes. "You were never in my good graces, you know that. I'm not sure why you'd start trying now."

"Because I'm hungry," he said with a grin. Her green eyes were amused and she motioned for Fenir to hand him a cake.

"At least you're honest. Only let him have one for now. The rest of you get to eat until your content and he can have the crumbs."

"Thank you, dear lady. You are too kind," he said with a mock bow. He took the cake from his brother, giving it a light squeeze and relishing in the spongy texture. It was gone far quicker than he'd hoped and he watched as Fenir handed out the rest, leaving only a few at the bottom of the basket. He eyed them hungrily but Trista strategically positioned herself between him and the cakes.

"Grudge was an understatement."

"Maybe you should be nicer."

"Pfft, never!"

Despite their earlier hesitation to eat, Kirheen and Garild were down to the last of their cakes and they look satisfied and content. "I think we'll be disqualified for being so well fed ahead of time. Do you ever get in trouble for this, Trista?"

Trista shrugged and handed him the last of the cakes. "The good thing about not having powers is nobody really pays attention to what I do. I get left to my own devices unless something is needed. My obvious favoritism of this group hasn't been noticed...yet." She leaned against the back of the chair Fenir was sitting in and began toying with his hair absentmindedly. Tomias was hit with a surge of emotion he wasn't expecting and he dropped the cake he'd been raising to his mouth. He plucked the crumbs from his robe and glared at his brother, though he was too happy to notice. A couple deep breaths and he was back in control and Trista was none the wiser.

"Thank the Allseer for that," Garild said gratefully, leaning back in his chair. "Not sure how we'd make it without the extra food you keep bringing us."

"I don't think he's kidding either. Our Garild here is a growing boy and goes through more food then you could believe," Tomias said with a grin. Garild looked away, cheeks red with embarrassment. "Oh, don't be like that. It's perfectly normal."

A deep hum filled the air around them, reverberating through the room before disappearing a moment later. The noise repeated two more times before he realized it was the sound of a horn. It was time.

"Well, would you listen to that? I do believe it's time."

Kirheen and Garild exchanged nervous glances.

"You're both going to do great. Let us hope the Allseer is on our side today. Let's show them what we're made of."

Chapter 16

The Temple of Gathering had been cleared, the tables and chairs removed leaving a long hall alive with excited murmurs. The Bonded stood to either side of the hall, clustered together in nervous bundles. Kirheen swallowed hard, eyes drifting across those standing next to and across from her. This was it. This is what they had been training so hard for.

Waiting was unbearable. At the front of the hall she could see the instructors, looking about as wound up as their students. She caught Tomias' eyes and he gave her a reassuring smile. Even Fenir, normally so proficient at ignoring them, took a moment to bow his head.

Herzin stood at the back of the room, watching them like a hawk. Her posture was rigid, her face devoid of a smile as she scanned over them. When her eyes drifted to the side of the room Kirheen occupied, she looked away quickly, not wanting to meet those hateful emeralds the old woman called eyes.

Garild was a mouse at her side, standing slightly behind her shoulder as he surveyed the hall. She could hear the shuffling of his hands twisting together nervously and it set her on edge. She gritted her teeth together, trying to block the urge to whip around and force his hands apart.

The group of instructors parted, clearing a path for the Union Master. He stepped confidently towards the back of the room where Herzin stood, a scroll in hand. The two took a moment to deliberate about the contents and then he turned towards them. The room fell silent, all eyes glued to the man that held the key to the start of the battles.

"I apologize for the delay. I know this is a time of great anxiety for you all and I'm sorry to delay the ease of such. Thank you for being patient. The Union Battle is the first of its kind and we're very excited to see the results of all your hard work. You've all grown so much these winter months. It is an honor to be able to stand before you all and know that the future of our kind rests in your hands.

The rules of this battle have been explained to you by your instructors. We stand firmly by the rules we've established for this. Anyone found breaking these rules will face punishment befitting the crime. Do not bring shame to your Bond. With that said, let us announce our first battle."

The room grew still, not a lung drawing breath while the seconds ticked by agonizingly slow. "Vienna and Daris, please step forward."

There was a collective woosh of air as everyone resumed breathing. Vienna looked to Daris and smirked, her eyes revealing secrets that only her bond mate could understand. They wore dark red robes, their symbol that of a wolf standing on the top of a cliff, a full moon hovering behind it. She took his hand, locking her fingers within his, and crossed from the side of the room opposite Kirheen to stand before the Union Master. They stood tall and proud, fearsome predators waiting for their prey.

"Tyrin and Bell, please step forward."

Bell jumped when their names were called, her brows knitting together in frustration. She brought her hands to her lips, shaking her head in disbelief. Her bond mate, Tyrin, stroked her long blonde hair and whispered softly in her ear. She gathered her courage and allowed Tyrin to lead her to the front of the room. Blue robes clashed with red, their symbol that of two gentle feather fish forming a circle. A meal for a wolf.

"You will have 20 minutes to figure out the card held by your opponent. Any battle going beyond the 20 minutes will have the victor decided based on the skill shown. Please, turn your backs to one another and Herzin will come by with a card."

They did as they were told and Herzin drew a deck of cards, similar to the ones they had used in practice so long ago. She drew a card off the top of the deck and showed it to Vienna and Daris. They nodded, stowing the image away. Bell and Tyrin were next and they too memorized their card.

The two groups took up a position opposite of each other. Bell and Tyrin opted to sit on the floor, legs crossed under them but Vienna and Daris remained standing, their fingers interlaced. The contrast was startling. Where Vienna and Daris looked absolutely sure of themselves, Tyrin and Bell looked as though they'd already lost. Kirheen was glad she wasn't in their position.

"Let the battle begin."

As she was taught, Kirheen let her mind drift, floating out to latch on to the mental struggle happening on the other end of the room. It had taken quite a bit of practice learning how to be a spectator without actually entering the mind of another. She was glad to have learned it though so she could see the battles as they took place.

Kirheen had never been close enough to either group to pick up on their particular skills. At first, nothing happened between them. The connection remained at a standstill with neither party vying for dominance. There was a slight glimmer and then her vision was filled with a beautiful moonlit field, tall grass swaying in a gentle breeze. The moon was large in the sky above, much larger than she'd ever seen it look before. It was a beautiful sight to behold and she was saddened by the arrival of Bell and Tyrin at the edge of the field, drawing her attention away from the moon.

Shifting her gaze, she could see an object floating on the opposite side of the field. It was thin and rectangular and she realized it was Vienna and Daris' card. *"Intentional bait,"* Garild commented in her mind. She almost jumped, not expecting his voice with her attention so focused on the battle.

"Geez, a little warning next time would be great," she chided. *"It sure seems like bait though. Quite the bold move."*

"This is Vienna and Daris we're talking about."

"True."

Bell pointed towards the card, whispering to Tyrin as she did. They entered the field cautiously, their steps light, eyes alert for signs of traps. Each step through the tall grass set Kirheen on edge. Anything could lurk in the shadows, could be stalking them and watching with hungry eyes. As they passed through the field unharmed, they became less cautious, their steps a little bolder. It was just what Vienna was wanting. At that moment, a large hawk dove from the sky above, claws extended towards its target. It latched on to the back of Bells head, claws digging into her hair. She screamed, flailing about wildly trying to get the bird out of her hair. Each attempt led to the bird pecking and soon her pale blonde hair was streaked with blood.

Tyrin shifted gears, gathering strength and pushing strongly against the illusion. It shattered, breaking apart into dust that was blown away with the wind. Bell lay on the ground sobbing, holding her bloodied hands in front of her face.

"Bell, it's not real. Come on." Tyrin knelt down next to her, trying to coax her back to her feet. It took several precious minutes but the rest of the illusion shattered and Bell regained control of herself once more, no longer feeling the phantom pain that had been there a moment before.

They strategized for a moment before moving on, creeping through the tall grass with far more caution in light of the attack. It wasn't enough. The grass took on an unnatural sway behind them and Kirheen gasped when she spotted Daris, tailing them with delicate steps. His movements were slow and deliberate as he hunted his prey, his steps mimicking theirs as he pushed his way through the field.

A hawk screeched in the night sky but Tyrin was prepared. He pushed against the illusion and it was at that moment that Daris moved against him. Before the energy Tyrin had created could dissipate, he blocked it, turning it back on its creator with ease. The force knocked Tyrin hard enough to break his concentration and the link was broken, effectively taking him out of the match. Bell was left alone, and by the look on her face, she was terrified of the thought. Daris had circled around and now stood before her, his sweat slicked skin glowing in the moonlight. His expression was smug, his eyes as black as the night.

"You should yield, girl," Daris said smoothly, creeping closer to her. She shook her head, her blonde hair swirling in the breeze.

"I won't," she said but her lip quivered as he approached.

"You're out here all alone, with no one to protect you now. What do you hope to accomplish? You're nothing without your bond mate."

It was sickening watching him toy with her mind. It made Kirheen angry.

"*You think she'll yield?*"

"*I don't know that she has a choice,*" Kirheen said, feeling the fear that radiated in the air around Bell. "*She's too scared.*"

Daris smirked, pushing against her lightly. She took the blow, falling back a few steps. "You want the card, you'll have to go get it. It's so far away and your just one girl. You think you can make it before I tear you apart?"

Daris struck out again with his powers, a teasing blow that forced her back. He struck out again but this time, she redirected the blow, adding a burst of her own power that he hadn't been expecting. It hit him hard, throwing him back onto the ground with a satisfying thud. She leapt over him, running through the grass as fast as her legs would take her. It was her only hope, to reach the card before Vienna could catch her.

Her breath came out in great gasps as she frantically wove through the field, strands of grass lashing against her face and hands as she ran. At one point a root came ripping out of the ground but she jumped, barely clearing it.

She was almost to the card, could see the blank back of it bobbing in the horizon. Her legs carried her ever forward, over obstacles and traps, each one deftly deflected or dodged. Kirheen could scarcely believe when she burst through into the clearing where the card rested, her face sweaty but triumphant. She reached up, hand grasping the edge of the card when two wolves burst from the field, eyes glowing and menacing.

"Did you really think it would be so easy," Vienna said, her voice coming from the smaller of the two wolves. It was massive, it's earthy brown fur sleek and glistening. The other wolf was even bigger and black as the sky above. It was a deadly shadow, eyes red, fangs dripping with anticipation.

"You should have yielded," he growled, padding forward.

Bell took a deep breath, turning her attention back to the card. She tore at the edge, flipped it around and gasped. It was blank.The growls grew louder behind her, the snapping of fangs filling her with fear. There was no time to yield. The wolves descended upon her and as their fangs sunk into her flesh, her concentration broke and she came back to reality with a scream, startling everyone in the room.

Tyrin reached over, wrapped his arms around her and pulled her close. He held her until the fear dissipated, casting a venomous glare at Vienna and Daris.

"The winner of this round is Vienna and Daris," Nyson called, his face emotionless. There were a few scattered cheers, but for the most part, everyone was far too shook up to celebrate the victory. Any of them could be next and with what they'd just seen, Kirheen was no longer sure they wanted to be. They'd seen one of their fellow Bonded toyed with, torn apart and spat out, a fate they now all faced.

"That was brutal," Garild whispered, watching Bell and Tyrin as they sulked from the room. Their instructor, Verin, fell into step with them, anger clouding his face. "It didn't even seem like that had a chance."

"Brutal may have been an understatement, Garild. This…this isn't good."

"That was a wonderful first battle. I hope all of you were paying close attention. Your battle could be next. Use this time to take notes and learn what you can from the things you've just witnessed. In these battles, knowledge is power," Nyson explained. While his words broke the tension in the room, it did nothing to ease the feeling of dread that crept up her spine, filling her with doubt and making her considering fleeing. Her legs tingled, urging her to run.

"Stay calm, girl. You're further along than Bell and Tyrin. You're better equipped for this. Stay focused," Fenir said, an edge of warning in his voice. *"Don't you even think about running out of here. I will drag you back."*

"Alright, alright," she said sheepishly. A sharp nudge from Garild and she turned back to the front of the room where Nyson was about to announce the next battle. Her heart plummeted into her stomach, and she reached out, grabbing his hand. He squeezed it tightly.

"Isa and Ian, please step forward."

Isa let out a little gasp, her hands flying to her mouth. She glanced around, uncertain whether it was their name that was called. Ian gave her a nod and they stepped to the center of the room. While Isa positively bounced with excitement, Ian remained cool and calm, his arms crossed over his chest while he waited for the next set of names. Kirheen let out a relieved sigh and dropped her hand from Garild's, feeling a wave of embarrassment that she'd felt the need to hold it at all.

"Irena and Tegan, please step forward."

Irena marched to the center of the room, Tegan slogging along behind her. From the look of it, the two had already been squabbling. Irena wouldn't even acknowledge her bond mate, her arms folded over her chest and her lips firmly set. He looked like a mouse next to her with his frail frame and he fidgeted, casting uncomfortable glances at those staring at them.

The teams received their cards and both opted to sit for the battle. Irena eyed her opponents with obvious distaste and Ian returned her expression, wrinkling his nose as if he smelled something bad. The reaction from Irena almost made Kirheen giggle.

Nyson called for the battle to start and Kirheen let her mind drift, feeling the rippling tension between the two teams. She latched on to that tension, focusing until the battlefield came into view. From the start, it was hard to tell whether there was a manipulator present. The battle was reminiscent of earlier days when all she saw was a wall. As their powers had advanced, so too had their surroundings. It was odd to see it stripped back to something so basic.

The formidable wall was tall and gray, surface worn smooth. Green patches of moss clung to the surface, creating bursts of color that contrasted starkly with the otherwise bland surroundings. Tegan and Irena appeared before the wall, taking stock of their surroundings. Tegan looked frightened, his shoulders hunched as he swayed his head from side to side, watching for anything that might jump out at them. After the last battle they all witnessed, Kirheen couldn't blame him.

Irena didn't seem phased in the slightest. She approached the wall confidently, hand rising to press flat against the wall. She closed her eyes and lowered her head and the wall rippled around her fingertips. After a moment, she stepped back, pointing to the left. "We need to head that way," she said, her voice icy. She stepped past Tegan, bumping him with her shoulder as she moved past. It seemed she planned on winning the battle with or without his help. He slinked behind her, head bowed. Had he been a dog, his tail would have been tucked between his legs as he sulked.

They traveled for a time, Irena checking for traps as they moved. The wall changed very little, maintaining the smooth, moss covered surface before they came upon a change so subtle that it was almost unnoticeable. A small section of the wall curved inwards, thinner than the rest of the wall around it. A weak spot.

"Tegan, if you think you can handle it, break through here."

Tegan nodded, stepping up to the wall. He shook his thin arms, trying to relax himself enough to focus on the task at hand. He held a hand out in front of him and closed his eyes, applying force to the wall. As he attacked, Irena focused on the same part of the wall. As the wall crumbled, there was a slight shimmer in the air and the wall reappeared, courtesy of Irena. It was an illusion, made to mimic the wall that had been. To the person being attacked, it would seem like the wall was still there, allowing them to enter without being noticed.

They stepped through and found themselves in a land of rolling hills and trees. In the distance, a card floated above the hill before them and standing in front of it was Ian. Isa was nowhere to be seen. Irena glanced around, her expression masked. If she was concerned, she did a good job hiding it. Tegan stood slightly behind her, peering around her shoulder at their opponent.

Ian smirked, waving at them from across the clearing. "Are you going to come take this card or do I need to bring it to you?"

Irena grimaced in disgust, hissing through her teeth as she glared at Ian. She drew in her power and then placed her hands on the ground. Thin vines burst from the grass around Ian's feet and wrapped around his legs, effectively pinning him in place. His eyes widened in surprise but he didn't let it break his concentration.

"Tegan, now!"

Tegan nodded, running around her and towards Ian, building his power as he went. When he was close enough, he flung his power forward with all the strength he could muster, knowing for sure the force would kick Ian out of the match. He smiled as the power blasted forth but it left his face as soon as his power hit an invisible wall, rebounding the energy and knocking him off of his feet. The force was enough to roll past him and it hit Irena, forcing her back.

"Tegan! What was that, you fool!?"

"It wasn't my fault! You didn't sense it either!"

Though still tangled, Ian laughed. "Really should have checked that first," he chided.

Irena was furious. "Guess I need to do this myself." She stood, stomping across the clearing and approaching the invisible wall. Before she could reach it, she collided with another wall. It was so unexpected that she stumbled backwards, losing her footing and hitting the ground with a thump. The wall had moved and she was none too happy about it. Ian couldn't help himself and he threw his head back, laughing heartily.

"Oh, that was priceless," he laughed, wiping tears from his eyes.

"You'll pay for that!"

"Give it your best shot!"

She stood, glaring at the space she'd collided with. She directed a burst of power towards the wall but before she could fully release it, there was a loud scraping sound from behind her, like rocks sliding down a hillside. She turned, her anger melting into fear as she watched the wall behind them getting closer. Her attention diverted, Ian pushed against the outer wall, driving Tegan towards her.

They stood between the two walls, frantically searching for a way out. The illusion she had created had been destroyed, the hole in the wall restored. It would take too much to break through it again and breaking through the invisible wall would mean facing Ian. Their options were limited.

"Break the invisible wall, Tegan," Irena demanded.

Tegan shook his head. "It's over, Irena. We've lost this one. We're going to be crushed!"

"Quit being a sniveling brat and break down that wall! Now!"

"And what do you plan to do after that," he questioned. "Ian isn't completely helpless there and Isa still has plenty of energy left. We're done."

Irena stepped forward, her hand reaching out to grasp the front of his robe. She pulled him close, crystal eyes alive with fury. "This isn't over. You break that wall and you do it now."

Tegan looked at her with sad eyes and shook his head. "We forfeit," he said loudly. Irena was about to hit him when he broke focus, leaving her behind as the walls pressed closer. She hissed, glaring at Isa floating over the wall creeping ever closer.

"This isn't over," she threatened and she too broke focus. The room shimmered back into view and everyone stared forward, watching Irena in shock. Irena looked straight ahead, her eyes distant. Tegan looked at the floor, shame and sadness making him seem even smaller than usual. She rose quietly, bowing once to her opponents before walking away. Tegan rose and chased after her, reaching out and grabbing her sleeve with an apology on his lips. She spun around and lashed out, the flat of her palm connecting with his face with a snap. It was a sharp, painful sound and Tegan staggered back, holding a hand to his face.

"You're a fool, Tegan," she spat, turning on her heels and fleeing the room. Her instructor Harkin followed her out, grumbling to himself as he went. Tegan stood silent, hand still pressed to his cheek, his brown eyes welling with tears. "I'm sorry," he whispered to the space where Irena had stood.

Isa had risen from her spot on the floor and she approached him kindly, wrapping her arm around his shoulders and pulling him close. She coaxed him over to the side of the room, staying with him as Ian accepted their victory.

The Union Master leaned over and whispered to Herzin. She gave a curt nod and marched across the hall, stepping outside to presumably deal with Irena. Such a display was apt to get her punished. Kirheen couldn't help but feel bad for Tegan. He really wasn't cut out for such things. He was too timid, his heart too soft to use his powers in such a way. She'd never understand why they'd bonded them together. Doing so had made a breeding ground for conflict and it affected all aspects of their relationship.

"The winner of this battle is Isa and Ian. Congratulations to you both," Nyson said, his voice lacking any cheer. "Please take the next five minutes to prepare before the next battle. I hope I don't have to remind you that your bond is paramount to winning these battles. If you turn against each other, your hopes of winning are diminished greatly. You cannot do this alone. Let this be a lesson to you."

Nyson stepped towards the front door, patting Ian on the shoulder kindly as he passed. The conversation in the room instantly turned to the battle they'd just witnessed and speculative words were exchanged, though quietly enough to not upset Tegan. Tomias and Fenir took the moment to weave their way towards them.

"These have been rough," Tomias sighed, rubbing the stubble on his chin. He looked down at Kirheen, giving her a half-hearted smile. "I suppose watching these hasn't exactly helped you feel any better about what's to come."

"Not exactly," Kirheen admitted, frowning as she looked over to Burk and Abby. They stood on the far side of the room, lounging against the wall comfortably. When Burk caught her eye, he lifted a hand and waved. There were only a few groups left, the chance for their names to be called greater than ever. "I thought I was nervous before but…"

"Don't fret. I've been watching the battles closely. You're far more cohesive than what I've been seeing. You and Garild work well together. Abby and Burk shouldn't give you much trouble."

"You sound so sure," Kirheen grimaced.

"Oh, I'm not. Doesn't mean I can't pretend."

"That's reassuring," Garild said. "I'm getting more nervous by the minute."

Fenir was eyeing their opponents. "*He's right. I wouldn't be too worried.*"

"Way to bash the other Bonded," Kirheen chided. Fenir smirked and turned his attention back to them.

"*You're both going to do fine. Enjoy the next few minutes while you can. I think you're up next.*"

Kirheen went to punch his arm playfully and he jumped back out of the way, walking away to take his place among the other instructors. Kirheen shook her head as he did, smiling to herself.

"Good luck to you both. Remember, work together and you can take down anyone you face next."

"Thank you, Tomias." She watched him walk away, feeling her stomach twist anxiously as his comforting presence faded away. She turned back to Garild, shrugging uncertainly. "You ready for this?"

"I think so. I mean, what could possibly go wrong," he laughed nervously.

"Yeah," she agreed, trying to smile despite the knot that had developed in her throat. "What could go wrong?"

Chapter 17

"Kirheen and Garild, please step forward." Garild locked eyes with Kirheen as the realization of what was happening crashed over them. She shrugged her shoulders, masking her nerves but he could see it all below the surface. Her eyes lost their luster, a sign she was retreating into the safety of her mind.

Win or lose was all they could do now. He felt sick, his stomach churning, sweat beading on his brow. He wiped it away with his sleeve, licking at his salt tinged lips nervously. He followed Kirheen across the room, his feet dragging across the floor, the full scrutiny of the other Bonded pelting his back as he went.

He kept his eyes on Kirheen, on the graceful curve of her neck, now visible with her hair pulled back away from her face. She glanced over her shoulder, making sure he was still following and he nodded. They came to a halt in front of Nyson and Herzin and waited for the names they knew would be called. Kirheen purposely kept her eyes down, not wanting to cast them upon Herzin. He couldn't blame her for that. He had a hard time looking at her himself. Seeing her filled him with an uncharacteristic rage. He'd never forgive her for making Kirheen feel so vulnerable…so helpless.

"Abby and Burk, please step forward."

And there it was. Even knowing ahead of time, it was still hard to hear their names called. Burk and Abby looked excited, all smiles and bouncing steps as they took their place next to them. Their robes were a dark sage green, their symbol emblazoned on the back in cream. They shared the symbol of a beautiful stag standing in a forest of wraith wood trees, long blades of grass around its feet. Burk leaned over, nudging Garild lightly.

"We look forward to facing you both. This will be fun!" Burk smiled, his grin nearly consuming his face. They truly were happy about the pairing, and he could only guess it was because they knew what to expect. Garild tried to return the smile but found he didn't possess the strength.

Kirheen shifted uncomfortably. *"Did it really have to be them? Tomias has me so worried about this matchup...I could punch him right about now."*

"Well, if we're lucky, we've thrown them off a bit. If not, I guess we're in for a good fight."

"I suppose. Go after them fast. Let's play on our territory."

Garild had planned on it all along. If he was lucky, neither of them would be a manipulator and he could shape the field to their advantage. Being able to fight on familiar ground would make it an easy battle if everything went according to plan.

"The battle may begin when you're ready."

Burk and Abby took a moment to get settled and then nodded, alerting them that they were ready. "Good luck to you both," Abby said, flashing them a quick smile before closing her eyes and bowing her head forward.

Garild did the same, closing his eyes and focusing his power to conjure his illusion. He pushed against them, grabbing Burk and Abby and pulling them into the forest he'd created. It worked flawlessly and he sighed with relief.

"Oh ho, so you were bluffing," Burk laughed, surveying the forest that materialized around them. "Thought we might have been going crazy when you said you were something else. Tricksters, both of you."

"That was clever," Abby chimed in, sticking close to her bond mate. They moved cautiously, taking small steps and watching their surroundings with sharp eyes. "A forest may not have been your best choice. This is what we've been training in for weeks."

As if to prove her point, she deftly avoided the traps that had been laid for them, side skirting around a covered pit and avoiding a bundle of vines intended to reach out and pin them in place. Garild hadn't expected her to see through his traps so well. He needed a distraction.

Burk stepped forward, a branch cracking loudly under his feet. At that moment, a flock of birds burst from the trees, flying over head with a flurry of wings and screeches. It startled them both and just as he had hoped, Abby took a cautious step back, planting her foot right on a trap. Her foot flew out from under her and she was hoisted up, suspended in the air high above Burk. She spun helplessly, looking around for a way out. "Burk, you're going to have to conjure something to get me down or I'm stuck here."

Burk shook his head. "I'd love to get you down, dear, but I have a feeling that trap was on purpose. In fact, if I had to guess," he paused, pushing out with his powers towards a nearby bush. Kirheen jumped backwards, narrowly avoiding the blast. As she landed, she looked up, glaring at her opponent. "I'd say Kirheen was waiting to ambush me. Nice try!"

From the pocket of her robe Kirheen drew a card. She showed the blank back to Burk, smiling as she dashed off into the trees. Burk cursed, glancing up to his bond mate and then back to the path Kirheen had cut through the trees.

Abby shouted from above. "You so much as think about it and I will personally beat you over the head with this branch I'm hanging from. You get me down and we both go after her."

"Alright, alright." Burk concentrated, forcing his own illusion into existence. A small dagger appeared in Abby's hands and she reached up quickly, cutting at the rope. It gave way with a sharp snap and she fell, hitting the ground with a thump. The air was forced from her lungs and she sat for a moment trying to catch her breath. Burk coaxed her to her feet, brushing leaves and dirt from her robes as she rose. The fall had shattered the illusion and the dagger had disappeared. "So, guess we need to be more careful."

"Apparently," Abby coughed, pushing her braid back over her shoulder. She closed her eyes, letting her powers flow outwards until she picked up on Kirheen. "She's not that far away. Let's get her."

They were far more cautious in their approach and the few traps Garild laid for them were avoided or deflected entirely. They were no longer playing around. *"Be careful, Kirheen. They are coming for you."*

"I sense them. I'll be careful."

Kirheen skidded into a clearing, a flurry of leaves rising as she came to a halt. *"I'm going to set the trap, Garild."* She bent down, placing the card on the ground in front of her. She placed her hands to either side of the card and let her powers trickle from her fingers. There was a burst of light and then a tree began to form around the card. It sprang upwards, the card pulled and twisted into the bark of the tree until it sat nestled within the glowing, translucent bark. It would give them valuable time to defend if either of their opponents tried to get to it.

Nodding her approval, Kirheen ran into the trees, remaining close to the trap but out of sight. She projected her powers outwards, hoping to attract the attention of her opponents. Abby and Burk took the bait and a moment later, they burst into the clearing.

"Now that is an odd looking tree, isn't it," Abby asked, taking a moment to catch her breath. She had her hands resting on her hips and she peered up at the tree, eyes squinting. Burk took stock of the clearing, making sure they were alone and then he too looked up.

"It is odd."

"And obviously a trap."

"Why do you say that," Burk questioned. Before she answered he saw it, the card sitting in the center of the tree high above them. "Ah. A bit inconvenient, I'd say. Well, get to choppin' Abby!"

Abby rolled her eyes, crossing her arms over her chest. "Well, what do you say? Trap?"

"Seems a bit obvious. Then again, considering the work it would take to get to it, it could be the real thing."

"Or it could be a trap."

"Or, yes, it could be a trap. You sense her?"

Abby nodded, tilting her head to the right. "She's close. I can feel her power."

Burk glanced over his shoulder. "We've got two options. Go after the card here or go after Kirheen. So, the tree. Trap or no trap?"

"I've got a bad feeling about this. This feels like a trap. It's too…there. I don't trust it."

"I'm thinking that's exactly what she wants us to think."

"This isn't helping," Abby sighed. "Try to break it."

Burk grunted, stepping up to the tree. He placed his hands on the cool bark, feeling the smoothness of it beneath his fingertips. He pressed against the tree and grinned with satisfaction as the tree fractured, splintering and cracking with terrifying ferocity. He stepped back and waited for the card to fall.

At that moment, Kirheen burst through the trees, catching
Burk off guard and pushing him to the side. He fell, landing on a
patch of ground that gave way beneath him. He very quickly found
himself in a dark pit, cut off from the battle above.

Kirheen rebounded back just in time, narrowly missing a
powerful blast from Abby. They circled each other, both watching,
muscles tense and ready for action. Abby chanced a glance towards
the card that lay nearby and Kirheen smiled. "You're on your own
Abby! You really want to go for it?"

Abby pushed forward, shooting a blast of power at Kirheen.
Kirheen threw up her hands, blocking the power and diverting it to
either side, but there was enough force behind it to push her back
despite her efforts.

"So, you're the pusher," Kirheen noted with a smile. "And
here I thought Burk was the muscle of your little duo."

Another blast rolled towards her and this one Kirheen flung
back at her, pushing the blast back with an added burst of her own.
Abby rolled to the side, narrowly missing the blow and flung a
smaller one at Kirheen. She side stepped easily and went to fling
herself forward when a hand wrapped around her leg and pulled
hard. She flailed her arms wildly, desperately trying to remain
upright. It was too late to recover and she tumbled back, falling
back into the pit designed to hold Burk.

She hit the ground hard and the force of her fall was almost
enough to break her concentration. She steadied her focus, patching
up her walls as best she could. Staggering to her feet, she readied

herself for a hit, glancing up quickly to see how she'd found herself in such a predicament.

"Kirheen, he's a manipulator! Be careful!"

Burk smiled as he climbed up over the edge of the pit using a ladder he'd conjured. He shattered his creation as soon as he was clear, turning back to wave at Kirheen. She glared up at him as he stalked away from the edge, presumably to pick up the card that lay at the top. Abby gave him a high five and together they approached the card.

"Well, that wasn't so bad," Abby said, bending down to pick it up. She flipped it over and Kirheen heard her bristle with anger. "Burk, she still has the card!"

Flinging himself around, he leaped back towards the pit and was about to jump back in when he realized Kirheen was nowhere to be found. "She's gone, Abby."

Abby looked over the lip of the pit, her face falling into a frown. "I can't sense her either. We better get to finding her, now."

"I'll make that easy for you," Kirheen said from behind them and she pushed forward with all she had left. The blast hit them both, sending them flying into the pit. The fall broke Abby, forcing her out of the match and nearly did the same to her bond mate.

He lay at the bottom of the pit, looking up at the trees above. "That was clever, Kirheen. Real clever. And painful. Thank you for that."

"You give up, Burk," she asked with a smile, staring down at him from over the edge.

"Oh, I don't know. I think I'll sit here a while. It's quite nice down here, actually."

Garild approached the pit, no longer in danger. He glanced over the edge and Burk waved at him casually. "Never took you for a manipulator," Garild said. "That nearly won you the match."

"Yes, it was *so* close. But here I am, doomed to rest in this pit forever." He sighed, propping himself up with an elbow. "I suppose there is nothing left to do but the inevitable. We…I forfeit."

Garild pushed them from his mind, shattering the illusionary forest. He felt exhaustion wash over him, coating every inch of his being in fatigue. Despite it, he managed to feel an immense sense of joy and he looked at Kirheen with a look of utter disbelief.

"Kirheen and Garild, you have won this battle."

Her face lit up, a mirror of the dumbfounded joy he felt, and she lurched towards him, wrapping him in her arms excitedly. Garild returned her hug, feeling elated at the closeness. A grin broke across his face and despite his best effort, he couldn't make it go away. They'd actually won!

"Alright you two. I suppose you've earned some praise. That was very well played," Burk said, clapping him on the shoulder. "You both did well."

"Thank you, Burk! You gave us quite the challenge."

"Not enough of one, I'm afraid," Abby said with a smile. She was quickly blocked out of view by Tomias and Fenir and Garild let himself be ushered from the room, the cheers of the other Bonded waning as they stepped outside. Having won their battle, they were free to rest until the next match, something Garild wasn't apt to deny, despite his excitement.

As his excitement left him, the full weight of his exhaustion hit like a ton of bricks. His shoulders slumped and his eyes grew heavy, muscles relaxing until they felt heavy and lifeless. Kirheen too seemed to be feeling the after effects of using so much power in such a short amount of time. Her eyes fluttered rapidly, as if she could somehow blink away the tiredness she felt.

"That was close, but incredibly well played. I find myself feeling quite proud," Tomias said, his excitement bubbling just below the surface. His eyes twinkled and Garild could only imagine he was already scheming to rub their victory in Grants face the first chance he got.

"Don't get too comfortable. You'll be up again soon." Three pairs of eyes narrowed and bore into Fenir with the force of a meteor slamming into a planet. He waved a hand in the air, brushing off their glares like he was swatting away flies and turned away from them.

"I feel completely drained. How are we supposed to keep up this kind of momentum," Kirheen asked, rubbing her temples in slow circles.

Tomias sighed. "I won't lie. It's going to be tough, but your training this winter is going to help. We worked as hard as we did so you'd have the stamina to last through these battles."

"I hope you're right," Kirheen grumbled. "If anyone needs me, I'll be resting over there."

"I think I'll join her," Garild muttered, unsure whether the words had even left his mouth properly. His tongue felt thick and clumsy, too big for the space it occupied. He'd thought to catch up with Kirheen but she seemed so far away. When he did finally reach his destination, he crumbled to his knees, turning himself to rest his back on the smooth, cool bark of a wraith wood tree. Kirheen was already situated, her head reclined back and her eyes closed.

"*Good work today*," Garild said, letting his thoughts drift out to her. The wind rustled the leaves above them, tiny whispers of sound that lulled him into a more relaxed state.

"*Same to you. I'm glad you're on my team.*"

He smiled, letting her words fill him with warmth. Before winter, he'd thought himself such a fool. He didn't think Kirheen could ever come to care about him or see him as an equal, but over those cold, bitter months she'd changed. While he still doubted she felt the same way he did, it didn't seem like such an abstract possibility anymore. There was hope for them and despite his own desires, he was willing to wait. For now, just sharing a friendship was enough.

They rested for a time, silent and comfortable, letting the fatigue slip from their bodies. Walls were mended, weak spots bolstered for the battle to come. A part of Garild wished he were back in the temple watching the other battles. He wanted to learn from them, to watch them make mistakes and adapt to new situations. That knowledge would be a powerful aide in the next battle. His body and mind demanded rest through and he was weary to ignore such urgings.

The realization that he'd fallen asleep in earnest didn't come until Tomias woke him. He smiled apologetically and reached down a hand to help him up. "How long was I out," Garild asked, looking around. Kirheen stood to the side, awake but quiet. Her eyes were cast to the temple and his stomach turned sour. "Oh."

"Afraid so," Tomias said. "It's almost time for your next battle."

The nervous energy he'd come to be well acquainted with surged as he followed them back to the Temple of Gathering. As they entered the room, the other Bonded burst into cheers.

"Celene and Aeirn, you have won the battle."

They beamed, obviously delighted by their victory. They shook hands with their opponents, Carter and Fiona and both parties faded back into the crowd. Kirheen and Garild rejoined the rest of the Bonded, standing slightly back from the crowd as if it would prevent them from being called next.

"That concludes our first round of battles. You have five minutes before we start the next set of matches. Please be ready," Nyson said. He waved at them dismissively and the room exploded with conversation. Strategies were discussed, victories and losses fussed over, debates arising about the power of manipulators. All of this swirled around Garild. It filled the air around him but he heard little of it and participated even less.

Kirheen seemed to be in a similar mood, keeping her distance from the others and not slipping into the conversation. He reached over and grabbed the soft fabric of her robe.

"You ready for the next match," he asked.

"Yes, I guess so," she said, but her face seemed troubled. She frowned, choosing to confide in him rather than hide her feelings. "I am ready, I just… I feel more nervous this time. Our first round wasn't exactly easy. It can only become more difficult from here, right?"

"I suppose you're right," he said softly, searching the room and picking out the remaining competition. There were in for a tough fight, regardless of who they ended up against.

The break they'd been granted was gone before they could process its existence. Nyson took his place back at the end of the room and the room settled into silence. All eyes watched the Union Master and Garild felt the hair rise on his arms. When Nyson spoke, the words settled into his heart like they'd been pounded into him with a hammer.

"Kirheen, Garild, Ian and Isa, please step forward."

Chapter 18

Kirheen kept her eyes cast down towards the floor, trying to avoid the green eyed distraction standing across from her. Now was not the time to be caught up in silly feelings, not the time to feel her heart fluttering in her chest or her breath catching in her throat.

There was also the very real terror that if things fell apart during the battle, her mind would be open for Ian to pick through. There would be nothing stopping him from learning the truth, nothing hiding the answer that he seemed to seek with his eyes.

"Good luck," Ian said and she merely nodded, choosing instead to focus her eyes on Isa who seemed just as nervous as she was, though for entirely different reasons.

"Same strategy as before," Garild asked her.

It took her longer than it should have to formulate a response. *"Yes. Get in before they have a chance to do anything. One of them is a manipulator. Let's not take any chances."*

The match started with a power struggle, Garild locking energy with one of their opponents as he sought control. He feigned a dip in power and then burst forward, effectively pulling Isa and Ian into his illusion. They appeared in a clearing, watching the trees around them with cautious eyes. Garild had chosen to use the forest again, though he'd changed it from the last battle.

Isa looked upset. "I'm sorry, Ian. I tried."

"Don't apologize! He's strong. We're in for quite a fight."

Instead of dashing off into the forest, the pair opted to set up a fortress at their location. Kirheen watched from the nearby trees as Isa conjured up a wall around them and together they fortified it to a surprising degree. There would be no getting to them physically.

A moment later, Kirheen felt a twinge of pain as someone began an assault on her senses. She hadn't been expecting it and the next blast of power sent her to her knees, the world around her a blur of greens and blues as it spun. She flung up her defense as best she could and squeezed her eyes closed while she waited for the moment to pass. When she opened her eyes, she was staring at the canopy of trees above her.

"Isa is going for individual attacks and somehow she is doing it from afar. Watch your defenses. We're going to need to end this quick."

"Got it!"

Kirheen gathered herself up off the ground and turned back towards the clearing. The fortress was still there, but without a way to see through it, there was no telling whether they were in it. She didn't know how long she had been down. It had felt like seconds, but time was funny in illusions. Turning away, she gasped as she came face to face with Ian.

It was sheer instinct that saved her.

She managed a thin shield just as a blast of power hit hard. It was enough to shatter her defense, but not enough to take her out of the match. Her shoulder smacked painfully against a tree as she was flung back. The shield had deflected some of the energy back on Ian and he had been knocked onto his back. Kirheen used the time to stagger forward, fully intent on taking him out of the match.

Ian raised a hand in front of him. "Kirheen, please don't. I think I'm hurt."

Something in his voice stopped her in her tracks, something in his green gaze that pleaded for mercy. She locked eyes with him and found herself unable to look away. She saw Isa step through the trees a moment too late. There was nothing she could do as a wave of power rolled her way, the force of it whipping up leaves and dirt like a tornado.

A great wall of dirt rose to her left, blocking her from the impact. It was still enough to crumble the wall but it gave her time to retreat. Garild stood at the edge of the trees, ready for another attack. Isa and Ian stood a few feet away and they eyed each other, both groups tense and at the ready.

"You almost fell for that, Kirheen. I'm surprised," Ian said.

Kirheen felt herself blush. "I knew Garild was there! I was trying to throw you off."

"Is that so? You seemed mighty concerned."

"Keep him talking," Garild said.

"Oh, the concern wasn't for you. It was entirely for myself."

"You're a terrible liar."

"But I'm such a great distraction!"

At that moment, a dozen snakes appeared beneath the feet of Ian and Isa, hissing and slithering around their ankles. Isa screamed, her big blue eyes wide with panic. Unable to stay still, she stepped back, her foot digging into one of the slithering menaces. It responded in kind, lashing out and fixing it's fangs into her calf. It was too much for her to handle and she quickly dropped her concentration, taking her out of the match. Ian, though looking a bit unnerved, managed to keep his focus. "Well, that was humiliating."

Kirheen smiled. "Care to forfeit?"

"Not just yet," he said and flung a burst of power towards his feet. The illusion shattered, the snakes breaking apart into dust. He used the force of the blast to fling himself backwards and launched a wave of energy towards Garild before Kirheen could react.

The blow took him in the shoulder, spinning him around before he collided with the ground. Ian darted off into the trees, intent on drawing out his defeat. Kirheen took off after him, ignoring the leaves and branches that scratched against her skin as she darted through the forest.

Ultimately, it was his haste that cost him the match. In his attempt to flee, Ian had stepped into a trap. He swung in the air high above her, twirling from a rope around his ankle.

"Now do you forfeit," Kirheen asked with a smile.

He scoffed. "Of course not! I can still beat you from up here."

"I'm so very intimidated. Come on, I'll let you make the first move."

Ian sent out a blast of power towards her but it wavered as it got closer, breaking apart before it made contact. The movement had caused the rope he dangled from to spin wildly and Ian groaned, immediately regretting his action. "Alright, I forfeit."

The link between them dissolved and they opened their eyes to a room erupting with cheers and shouts. Isa looked completely embarrassed, her cheeks tinged red. "Did it have to be snakes?"

Garild laughed. "What would you have preferred? A bear?"

"I'd take anything over those! Uck!"

"Kirheen and Garild, you have won this round," Nyson called from the back of the room. Garild was grinning ear to ear and she couldn't help but join him. With two battles under their belt, it was finally starting to feel like training was paying off.

"You two did well. It was a good fight," Ian said. "Kirheen made a great distraction. That was clever of you, Garild."

Garild merely nodded, eyeing Ian suspiciously. Ian and Isa bowed, stepping away from the center of the room to reclaim their spot among the others.

Kirheen laughed nervously as they stepped away. When she turned to Garild, she was surprised to see an annoyed look on his face. "What's your problem?"

Garild shrugged. "It's just... I don't know. I get an odd feeling from him sometimes. The way he looks at you..."

Kirheen prickled with irritation. "Quit being paranoid. You don't know anything," she snapped and walked away, leaving her bond mate behind to puzzle over her reaction. Tomias and Fenir were waiting for them at the far side of the room. As she came within reach, Tomias grabbed her by the shoulders and pulled her into a hug.

"Again! My students dazzle with their talent! Look upon them, for they are mighty!"

Kirheen rolled her eyes. "You're too much, Tomias! You're going to jinx us before the next match."

"Next and final! You've only one round to go! How are you feeling?"

"Better than before, but still exhausted."

"I need a nap," Garild announced as he joined them.

"I'm afraid you won't have much time for that. You'll be up again soon!"

As if on cue, the next match was called. "Vienna, Daris, Celene and Aeirn. Please step forward."

"This should be interesting," Garild said.

And it was. The match lasted all of five minutes before a clear victor was called.

"Vienna and Daris, you have won the match."

Kirheen watched them turn towards each other, watched Vienna smirk, her blue eyes cold and calculating. Her blood turned to ice as Daris turned his head to look over his shoulder. His dark eyes found hers and he smiled. Glistening teeth, blood lust in his eyes, the smile of a wolf ready to kill.

Chapter 19

Kirheen tried to look calm, but those hungry eyes had unnerved her. Even now her hands shook, her legs feeling like limp noodles as she crossed the room. The other battles had been difficult, but she hadn't felt fear, not like she felt it now. It infected everything, creeping over her skin like ivy suffocating a tree.

Her opponents would be standing for the battle, sneering down at them from great heights while they cowered on the floor. She wanted to match them, wanted to show them that she could be strong too but the wobbling in her knees told her it wasn't about to happen. *"I'm going to need to sit for this battle,"* she informed Garild.

He gave a quick nod, wiping his hands on his robe as he did. They positioned themselves on the floor, trying not to feel self-conscious under the scrutiny of Vienna and Daris. The seconds ticked by painfully slow until Nyson called for the battle to begin.

Before she even had a chance to think, she was struck by a force so powerful it felt like she'd been picked up and slammed against a wall. She jumped to defense, trying to push back against the attack. She could feel Garild losing his grip on the situation and then they were pulled into an illusion. It wasn't one of theirs.

"Allseer be damned," Garild cursed. "I'm sorry, Kirheen. I couldn't hold the illusion under that much pressure."

"It's fine. We just need to be very, very careful."

Vienna and Daris had opted to use the field again. It had earned them victory in two battles so far, each time ending in a brutal assault by way of giant fluffy monstrosities. Kirheen wasn't about to lose in such a way.

The tall field grasses rustled, looking like shimmering glass strands in the moonlight. Far ahead the card floated, shining brightly. "We're not going to go for that. We both know it isn't real."

"I thought as much. You think one of them has it."

She nodded. "Yes. We know they both know what it looks like. I'll hammer it out of their heads if I have to."

"Let's do this."

Kirheen led the way, opting to walk along the perimeter of the field rather than through it. It stretched on for a long time, but Kirheen didn't mind. They weren't even after the card. "*Get ready to split.*" At the count of three, Kirheen broke away from Garild and went diving into the tall grass. As she did, Garild began releasing small bursts of power, not enough to drain him but enough to light him up like a beacon for anyone nearby.

It worked flawlessly. Crouching down, Kirheen watched as Daris crept through the grass to her right, dagger gleaming in his hands. His movements were slow and controlled and he was completely focused on Garild. He hovered just on the edge of the field and Kirheen worked her way closer. He was pinned on either side and she held her breath, trying to still the frantic beating of her heart.

"Now!"

Garild whirled, flinging a wide arc of power forward into the grass. Daris hopped back, giving away his position and Kirheen lashed out, flinging another arc of power his way. It hit him in the back, knocking him off his feet. His face connected with the ground and then he shattered like glass. "Illusion," Kirheen shouted frantically. The words had barely slipped from her lips when Daris came crashing through the grass in wolf form. He slammed into Kirheen, knocking her onto her back. Teeth snapped the air in front of her face and Kirheen tried to fend him off, her hands gripping tightly on the fur around his neck while his claws dug tracks into her shoulders.

Under different circumstances, she might have laughed at how outmatched they were in terms of strength. She was a girl, strong of mind but weak of flesh and he was a wolf rippling with muscles she could feel beneath the layers of fur. She was quickly losing the battle against him and her focus was slipping. Sucking in her breath, she flung out with all she had, letting the power rip from body. It slammed into Daris, tossing him through the air like a rag doll. He hit the ground with a yelp and rose a moment later, growling and snapping his teeth at her. Such a use of power would have been considered incredibly wasteful, but at the moment Kirheen didn't really care.

Now standing, Kirheen and Daris circled each other. She tried to ignore the burning, bloody lines arcing across the front of her. She could feel warmth sliding over her skin beneath her robes, trickling over her belly and down her legs. The mere sight of the blood seemed to work Daris into a frenzy and he lurched forward, his powerful stride bringing him close. He made to knock her down again when a swath of field erupted into flame between them and burst out towards Daris. The heat was incredible and she staggered away from it, holding a hand up to block out the light. There was a yelp of pain from the wolf and a moment later, Kirheen felt the energy surrounding Daris dissipate.

"I got him," Garild said. *"I'm heading over to you."*

Kirheen watched the flames die down before her and waited for her bond mate. There was a soft rustle of grass behind her and she opened her mouth to greet Garild. A hand slipped around her neck and the cool touch of a dagger caressed her throat. "Ah, Vienna. I was wondering where you were." *Stupid, stupid… You let your guard down.*

"Shut up, Kirheen. One wrong move and I open your throat."

"Mad about Daris? He had it coming."

The dagger pressed against her throat and she felt a sting as the blade nicked her flesh. Garild stepped into view, his eyes going wide as he surveyed the scene. "Garild, forfeit now or I end this on my terms."

"Don't listen to her. Don't you dare. You hit us both if you have to but take her out."

"I know."

Garild held up a hand. "Please, Vienna. Let's be rational here. It's two against one."

Vienna snorted. "Is that what this looks like to you? Two against one? There isn't anything you can do."

Garild went to step forward and stopped, halting mid-step at an angle that looked entirely uncomfortable. He looked up in shock, his face strained.

"Garild?"

"She...she did something to me. Kirheen, I can't move."

"You see, Garild, you couldn't do anything if you wanted to. In fact..." Her hand slipped away from Kirheen and she stepped around her casually. Kirheen made to hit her but found she couldn't move. It felt like she'd suddenly turned to stone and no matter how hard she tried, she couldn't force her body to move. They were done for. "I could take either of you out right now. Or I could toy with you. I could drag this out for the rest of the time until your begging for mercy."

"Garild...no matter what she does, you stay focused. None of this is real. Stay here. Do not let her win."

"I'll do my best," he said but as Vienna crept close with the dagger, his face paled. She slashed at him and Garild gasped as the dagger cut across his chest. Kirheen winced, looking away as blood welled up on his skin.

Another slash. And then another.

"Kirheen, I'm slipping."

"Don't! Damn it, I have an idea! Cling on with all you have and be ready to attack!" As Vienna dove forward with the dagger, Kirheen yelled. "Hey, Vienna! A shame I didn't get to do this to Daris! I would have had fun cutting him to ribbons. A beast like him deserves to be put down."

The hand holding the dagger stopped in the air, the tipped pressed against Garild. She turned her head slowly, locking eyes with Kirheen. "Do not speak of him."

"He's probably pretty humiliated right now, isn't he? He was probably hoping for another five minute battle, huh? I guess in a way, he got it, he just wasn't the victor this time."

Vienna was furious. She whirled around, stepping towards Kirheen with the dagger held in a white knuckle grip. She raised it high, preparing to slam it down on Kirheen. With a smile, Kirheen broke her focus, taking herself out of the match. She opened her eyes to reality and turned towards her bond mate. Garild had his head bowed forward, his chin resting on his chest. "Forgive me for this," she whispered. *"And for the love of the Allseer, stay focused."* She flung her fist forward and hit Garild in the side of the face with enough force to knock him to the floor.

Garild felt physical pain as something hit him in the side of the face. At first he thought it was something Vienna had done, but she still had her back turned. The blow disoriented him as he tried to sort reality from the illusion. He reached up to touch his face and froze, staring at his own hand hovering in the air before him. *My hand...I can move!*

As Vienna turned, he forced all the energy he had left at her mind, taking out her defense in a single, unexpected blow. "Green dot, two yellow lines," he shouted and then broke his link from the battle. When he opened his eyes, he was sprawled on the floor, his jaw on fire from where something had connected with his face. He sat up slowly, reorienting himself to the room. Vienna and Daris stood over him and from their dour expressions, he could tell what was about to happen.

"Congratulations Kirheen and Garild. Victory is yours," Nyson said and the Bonded went wild. Cheers and shouts reverberated off the walls and he looked towards Kirheen in disbelief. She was rubbing her knuckles and he had a moment of realization that the object that had connected with his face had actually been her fist.

"Ki-Kirheen? Did we just... is this real?"

Kirheen smiled at him and that smiled turned into a laugh. "I think we did."

He was overwhelmed. He reached forward, pulling her into a tight embrace. They stayed that way until they were swarmed by the other Bonded and pulled apart. They mingled for a time, hovering in a cloud of excitement and adrenaline as they chatted with the others. Vienna and Daris, humiliated by their defeat, marched from the room, anger following in their wake like a swarm of bees.

Eventually, Tomias and Fenir made their way over.

"By the Allseer, if that wasn't the most exciting thing I've ever seen. I'm so filled with pride I think I might burst," Tomias said, grabbing each of them in an arm and squeezing them. "That was an excellent battle. You'll have to tell me how you knew how to break her power, Kirheen. We never went over that."

"You're right," Kirheen said, her eyes hinting at some inner turmoil. "We didn't talk about it. What was that? And why did we never discuss this in training? That could have cost us the match!"

Tomias met her eyes. "And I apologize for that. I didn't think... We'll talk about it soon, just not here."

Garild was confused by the exchange and glanced between them. "What are you talking about?"

"Later, Garild. Later. You two enjoy your victory right now. We can discuss details another time." With that they turned and drifted from the room. When he turned towards Kirheen he watched her eyes following them, her brows furrowed in frustration. He was about to ask her what she was feeling when he was pulled away by Burk and tossed among the others, a dozen different voices vying to talk about their victory.

"It's rare. It's not something we talk about often because it isn't something we see. To be honest, aside from Nyson, I don't know many with that power."

Kirheen sat in front of the fire, chewing on a piece of bread while she listened to Tomias explain what had happened in their last battle. It had been such a terrifying feeling. One minute she'd been in control and the next, she hadn't been able to move or use her powers. It had been like someone had gone in and cut her brain from her body. No matter how much she told her body to do something, it wouldn't respond. She never wanted to experience it ever again.

"It was terrifying. And Nyson has this power?"

Tomias nodded. "Yes, he does. As far as I know, he doesn't use it. It's a bit of a touchy subject. People don't exactly like the idea of that level of control. As you said, it's terrifying if you aren't expecting it."

"Is there a way to break through that, aside from punching your bond mate in the face?"

Garild sat to her left, his fingers idly massaging his jaw where she'd hit him. It was already starting to color, a great purple and yellow patchwork of bruises. "Please," he said. "I could do without her punching me ever again."

Tomias sighed. "I wish I had better news, but I honestly don't have a clue. What you did in the battle, hitting him outside the illusion, it was almost like hitting the reset switch. It allowed his body to recognize what was happening and break through it. But would that work every time? Would someone more experienced be able to prevent that from happening? We don't know."

Kirheen stared at the fire, mulling over his words as she watched the flames dance. As much as she hated the thought, she almost wished she were friends with Vienna. She could ask her about her powers, about how they worked. Not knowing made her feel vulnerable. It was something she didn't know how to face and until she did, she didn't think she'd be able to rest easy.

It opened the door for more questions. If this was a branch of power that existed that she hadn't even known about, what else could exist? What other powers lurked out there waiting to overwhelm her? It was a sobering thought and she spent the rest of the evening in solemn silence, her mind trying to piece together a puzzle that wasn't yet making sense.

Chapter 20

The coming days were a flurry of activity with workers from
the eastern villages bustling to and fro as they prepared for
the festivity to come. The workers, men and woman found unfit to
battle the Darkness, moved with a focused manner, their gazes
never wandering from the task at hand. They rarely spoke to each
other, their heads bowed over this or that as they prepared for the
feast.

Kirheen watched all of this as she meandered through
Sanctuary, finally feeling well enough to leave her room. The
battles had been rough, taking a toll far greater than she'd ever
experienced. Despite the days spent in bed, she couldn't have been
happier. Against all odds, they had won, earning the respect of the
Council, Bonded and instructors alike. It was a good feeling,
powerful even, and she delighted in the peace it had brought to her
heart.

The celebration was to take place the following night, as the
sun sank low in the sky. Food and drink and merriment had been
promised until the wee hours of the morning and she looked
forward to such revels.

She passed the next day quietly, choosing to keep to her bed
as she flipped through a worn book Trista had given her. Its cream
colored pages were cluttered with drawings and information about
various plants found in the region. She came to rest on a page with
a short, dark blue mushroom covered in inky black spots. It was

found in dank, dark places and was incredibly dangerous to humans if consumed. Such information was interesting, but completely and utterly useless to her. She closed the book, tucking it away beneath her bed.

Several hours before the festival was to begin, Kirheen made her way to the little hut that Trista called home. She'd promised to help her tidy her hair for the festival and Kirheen looked forward to the change. Most days she wore her hair pulled back away from her face in a loose tail or wore down but unkempt. It had grown terribly long the past few months and she found it harder to care for, the wispy strands tangling and knotting despite her efforts, which were few if she were to be honest.

Kirheen knocked softly on the door of the hut and Trista appeared a moment later. She smiled warmly and ushered her inside. The room seemed foreign, so devoid of vials and bottles and burnt plant matter that she almost laughed. Everything had been tucked away neatly, leaving a room that you could actually step through without fear of breaking your neck. The smell of cinnamon filled the small space, creating a sense of warmth that drew Kirheen in.

"What brought this on? Expecting company," she asked, raising a brow.

"Ah, is it that obvious," Trista asked, her cheeks turning a shade of pink that was much too obvious on her pale skin.

"Is there a certain white haired man paying you a visit later?"

Her green eyes grew wide, her lips parting in shock. "Beg your pardon? I—he.."

"Oh please," Kirheen said with a roll of her eyes. "I'm not stupid!"

It was pretty obvious the two had feelings for each other, and though unable to communicate, they shared a bond not so unlike the one seen in the Bonded around them. Kirheen had suspected it went beyond the flirting they seemed to do on occasion, though this was the first time she'd seen fit to voice that. She imagined such a thing was frowned upon greatly, but she found herself caring little for the rules and stipulations laid forth by the Union Master. If they cared for each other, she saw very little reason why they shouldn't be together.

"I know you aren't stupid, Kirheen. I just…"

"Trista, it's okay. You don't need to explain. I'm just messing with you."

Trista huffed, hands on her hips and her lips pulled into a frown of disapproval. She procured a chair from the far side of the room, and sat it in the empty space next to her bed. Kirheen sat down willingly, letting her tangled hair down. Trista ran her hands over it disapprovingly.

"This won't do. You've just won the battles and you look like it. We're to celebrate the Allseer tonight and we can't have you looking like this. You'll need to bathe if we're to do anything with this hair of yours."

Kirheen grinned sheepishly. "I'm sorry. I've been trying to keep it neat, but it's getting so long, I'm finding it hard to do."

"Well, we'll worry about that later. Come on, off to the baths with us."

They left the hut behind, weaving through the trees towards the direction of the baths. The baths were actually a set of hot springs that bubbled out of the ground just a short walk from the village. Set in a craggy nook, the multiple springs were blocked off from each other, one for the girls and the other for the boys, separated by a crude wooden fence. It wasn't much, but it did the job.

At the edge of the pool, Kirheen stripped out of her robe, feeling slightly self-conscious in front of Trista. Trista was tall and lean, her skin pale and freckled and smooth. She was self-assured, confident in her body in a way Kirheen had yet to learn.

Trista sank into the pool, relaxing into the hot water. She rested her head against the rocks behind her, her red hair spreading out like a fan. Kirheen shimmied out of her undergarments, wrapping her arms about herself as if that would hide her naked skin. She tip toed into the water, sucking in a breath as the heat kissed her. It took her a moment to adjust but then she melted into the pool, feeling the stress of the past few days dissipate.

They soaked for a time in silence, eyes closed while they listened to the sounds of the wilderness around them. Trista raised her head, opening her eyes to look at Kirheen. "I know it was already mentioned yesterday, but congratulations. You did very well. Your bond has grown strong."

"You think so?"

"I do. You and Garild have grown much closer." There was a momentary pause, before Trista spoke again. "Would you permit me a personal question?"

Kirheen hesitated, fearing the question before it could even be asked. "I suppose."

"I, I'm not sure how to ask this, but would you say your bond is of a romantic nature," Trista asked cautiously.

Kirheen fell silent, her thoughts scrambling together into a confusing mess. In a way, Trista was right. Their bond *had* grown stronger. They'd grown closer as friends, finding comfort and strength in each other's presence .Their harsh training over the winter months had brought them closer than she could have imagined, had forced her to trust him completely with her thoughts and her feelings. Growth had brought out a physical charm in Garild that had been lacking before and it hadn't gone entirely unnoticed. But for all of those things, Kirheen couldn't see Garild as more than just a close friend.

Relationships were an odd thing in Sanctuary. Love was something Kirheen knew very little about. How much of that was taught? How much just simply existed? It was obvious that they Bonded young men and woman together for a purpose. She'd known from a young age that eventually she'd be expected to bear a child with her bond mate, though what that entailed held little meaning to her. It was clear to her that they were Bonded together not just for their powers but also for their personalities. The intention was for them to fall in love. How could a bond get any stronger than that? Wouldn't you fight to protect the things you loved, no matter the cost?

Whatever the concept of love meant to her, she could not say that she felt such feelings towards Garild. It was hard to her to grasp what that would feel like, what it would mean. She did feel things from time to time. Sometimes the sight of Ian would set her heart a flutter, her skin would grow hot and she'd feel a longing deep within her. She tried her hardest to hide those feelings. Somehow it felt wrong. It made her feel ashamed that someone she wasn't supposed to have a connection with could make her feel such a way when her own bond mate didn't.

Trista smiled as if reading her thoughts. "For all we teach you, it seems the whims of the heart get left untaught. I only asked because I'm curious how much you know of such things. You're a young woman and matters of the heart are bound to become a problem sooner or later. You don't love Garild, do you?"

Kirheen frowned. "I... "

"Speak freely. This will stay between us."

"I don't. I never have. I care about him and I trust him, but I can't say that I love him. I wouldn't even know it if I did. I think about things sometimes, how it would feel to hold his hand or to stare into his eyes...and I feel nothing."

And there it was… The truth she'd tried so hard to hide and it was spilling out of her, as real and tangible as the water bubbling around her. Trista studied her, her expression guarded. *What must she think of me…*

She was supposed to be happy about her bond. Love was something that was just supposed to happen to them. It would reach in and grab her heart and her soul and make her see something in Garild that she was missing. But it wasn't happening, it hadn't happened, and Kirheen feared it never would. Could she pretend? Or would doing so kill something inside of her that she was trying so hard to protect? It was all so complicated.

"You'll learn in time. I just want you to be aware, you're going to go through changes, both physical and mental, and I want you to be prepared for them. I know you've already experienced some of these changes, but be mindful. Your body will do things you don't expect, will *want* things you can't have and you need to be prepared to fight those temptations. For better or worse, you are Bonded to Garild and even if you yearn for something or someone else, you can never break that Bond. Do you understand?"

Something about her words brought Ian to mind. Tousled brown hair and eyes the color of the forest, warm and welcoming and smelling of spices. Something she could never have… "I understand," she said, breaking the image from her mind. She'd have to lock away her feelings for Ian. Lock them away or be pulled under by them. She wasn't sure it was a battle she was willing to fight or if she even *could* fight it. Trista nodded, accepting her answer. She pulled herself from the pool, allowing the water to drip from her body. She dried herself with a length of fluffy cloth and then left one on the edge of the pool for Kirheen.

Kirheen pulled herself from the water, grabbing the towel and wrapping it around her body. She dried herself quickly and slipped back into her robes. She followed Trista to her hut, trying to fight away the feelings of melancholy dripping into her soul. A veil of silence fell over her as they entered the hut and she took a seat without a word, letting Trista get to work.

Trista didn't seem perturbed by her silence in the least. If anything, she seemed to willingly give Kirheen distance, to let her work through her thoughts without interruption. A small basket was pulled off a shelf and Trista took to brushing her hair. She was gentle but firm, working through the tangles of her ashen hair until it was smooth.

As her hair was left to dry, Trista took to applying strange things to her face. Kirheen was unfamiliar with makeup, having never been exposed to it before. She stared cautiously at the strange jar Trista held, its contents dark red and creamy. Seeing her confusion, Trista laughed. "This is just for your lips. It will add a bit of color." She ran her finger in the cream and tilted Kirheen's head up towards her. She pressed her finger against her lip, dragging it back and forth until they were coated in the red substance. "Rub your lips together like this," Trista demonstrated. Kirheen did as she was told, her lips feeling odd coated in that unfamiliar substance. Next came a dark, chalky substance that

Trista ran along the line of her lashes. Trying to hold still enough for her to do it was nearly impossible, but she did her best, allowing Trista to have her fun.

"Do I even get to see what I look like," Kirheen asked.

"Of course, but only after I do something with your hair! You're looking beautiful!"

Trista went back to work on her hair, loosely braiding her hair on either side and pinning it in the back with a beautiful bronze clip crafted to look like a butterfly. When she had completed her masterpiece, she procured a small mirror, something that Kirheen saw very little of in Sanctuary. She handed her the polished surface and Kirheen held it up, her jaw dropping at the changes she saw reflected back at her.

It had been a while since she'd looked in a mirror. She'd been so consumed by training and the stress of the battles that her personal appearance had been left by the wayside. But now, she looked at a young woman. Her cheeks had smoothed, revealing a set of high cheek bones. Her upper eyelids were artfully lined and the dark contrast made her gray eyes look brighter. The tinge of color on her lips contrasted with her pale, smooth skin and hair and she took a moment to admire herself in the mirror. She looked clean and fresh and happy. Lowering the mirror, she smiled up at Trista.

"Thank you, Trista. I look beautiful!"

Trista grabbed the mirror, safely tucking it away. "You always have! We just made it more obvious. You feel ready to be in the spotlight tonight?"

Kirheen shrugged. "I suppose so. It'll be nice to celebrate and relax for once instead of stressing over battles. I think I'll enjoy myself."

"Good," Trista said with a smile. "Be careful changing into fresh robes later. Don't mess up your hair! Oh! Before I forget—" She rummaged through a basket, pulling small bottles out and sniffing the contents of each. Settling on one, she handed it to Kirheen. The bottle was small and the liquid within clear. When she opened the top, the smell of vanilla wafted into the air. "Put a little of that on after you've changed. Just a little dab here and there will help you smell nice for the evening."

Kirheen rolled her eyes but hugged Trista, thanking her for all of her help. When she returned to her own home, the room fell silent as she walked through the door. Tomas, Fenir and Garild all stared at her, wide eyed and fascinated. She raised an eyebrow, confused by the look on their faces.

"Why, Kirheen, you look positively stunning," Tomias exclaimed, breaking the silence.

Garild nodded in agreement and Fenir gifted her with one of his rare smiles.

Kirheen felt herself blush. "Um, thank you. It's really nothing," she stammered, brushing a stray piece of hair behind her ear. She was thankful when they turned their attention away and she could slip into her room. Once there, she rid herself of her old robes, careful to not mess up her hair and slipped a clean robe over her head. Unlike their customary robes emblazoned with their symbol, this robe was dark gray with a vibrant white eye on the back, the symbol of the Allseer. She tied a sash around her waist and stepped back into the sitting room.

Garild had already changed into his robe and his brown hair had been smoothed back away from his face. He gave her the same dumbfounded grin he'd given her when she'd entered earlier and she huffed. "I don't look that different," she protested.

The grin dropped from his face. "You look really beautiful," he said awkwardly.

She thought about arguing but found the effort daunting.

"Thank you," she said. "You look good too."

Tomias and Fenir were both prepared for the festivities, dressed in black robes with the symbol of the Allseer in white. Tomias had his hair pulled back into a half tail and he'd even shaved his face. It made him look far younger. She often forgot the twins weren't much older than she. Fenir wore his hair straight as he always did, not bothering to do much else with it. She suspected she wouldn't be seeing much of him at the festival considering there was a certain lady friend awaiting his company.

"Well, are we all ready," Tomias asked, rubbing his hands together. "I'm starving and I hear there is food."

They left as a group, winding their way to the Temple of Gathering. The sun had begun its slow descent in the sky and soon the world would come alive briefly with color. There was already a group gathered at the steps of the temple, Bonded and instructors alike. They mingled, chatting amongst themselves happily. As they arrived, Burk waved from above the crowd.

"Hey, hey! If it isn't our champions," he called over the crowd and everyone turned their attention towards them. A wave of cheers rolled through the onlookers and they parted to let them mingle at the front of the group. It was odd being so accepted now. It almost felt as if she belonged. Isa and Ian were at the front and as Kirheen stepped out from behind Burk, Isa flung herself at her, giving her a quick hug. "Oooh, you two did amazing yesterday! We're quite jealous of your talents," Isa chirped.

Recovered from the initial startle, Kirheen smiled. "Oh, it was nothing really. You all gave us quite the challenge."

Ian snorted. "Don't discredit your victory, Kir. You both won because you were skilled. You deserve the victory and all the praise that comes with it."

Kirheen melted at the sound of his voice and she met his eyes, smiling widely. His green eyes were calm and tranquil, his body language relaxed. His brown hair was smoothed back, the stubble that usually covered his face shaven for the event. It showed off his strong jaw and her eyes went to his lips. She realized she was staring and broke her eye contact quickly, before anyone else could notice. She glanced at Garild nervously and found him chatting with Isa, neither of them aware of the moment they'd just had.

Ian stepped to her side, bending down slightly so she was forced to meet his gaze. "You really were amazing out there. The way you handled the unexpected was something else." He gave her a warm smile and Kirheen felt her heart flutter.

"Thank you, Ian," she said, trying to keep her voice steady. *Stupid, stupid girl. Just don't look at him. Look away.*

She pried her eyes away, turning towards Garild and Isa. She was about to speak when Nyson appeared at the top of the steps. He looked tired, dark circles under his eyes making him look older and worn thin. She imagined the battles had taken their toll on him as well, the constant supervision throughout the entirety of the battle exhausting. He scanned the crowd, his eyes searching over them to see if all were in attendance. Satisfied, he spoke.

"Welcome everyone. Tonight, we celebrate our savior, the woman responsible for blessing us with the gift we all share. Our powers, gifted to us by the Allseer herself, were granted to us to we may stand firm against the Darkness that rages outside the borders of our land. It is because of her, and the sacrifices of those that have come before you that we remain safe. You've all shown great talent, the battles a testament to the strength you all possess. I'm proud of you all and I feel safe knowing that one day, it will be this group protecting us. Tonight, I want you to celebrate these powers. I want you to celebrate the Allseer with all the love in your hearts. I want you to congratulate our winners for their victory was well earned and they have shown you all the level of skill I want you to aspire to. In the temple, refreshments have been prepared for you all. Eat, drink and celebrate with your fellow Bonded. You all deserve this night!"

Stepping to the side, Nyson swung his arms towards the doors. Two servants pulled them open, revealing the long interior of the Temple, now decorated for the night. The left hand side was filled with rows of tables, all piled high with a variety of food and drinks. The center of the room was left empty, a place for them to mingle. To the right, several seating areas had been arranged. Marble tables sat in the center of each seating area, center carved out and filled with crackling wraith wood. The blue flames glowed and spat, sending shimmering blue sparks into the air. The large fire place at the end of the hall was roaring, filling the room with warmth.

Having won the battles, Kirheen and Garild were permitted to enter first. Their rise up the steps was followed by cheers and Garild gave them all a quick wave over his shoulder. Inside, the room smelt of so many scents Kirheen couldn't place her finger on just one. The tables were overflowing with food, many of which she'd never seen before. The dessert table looked particularly appealing, loaded with small cakes and cookies in every color imaginable.

They were each given a plate and set loose. So much food was there that Kirheen had a hard time even comprehending it all and she spent far longer than was necessary looking over the various options. When she'd finally chosen, her plate was overflowing with food and she took up a seat on the far side of the room. Garild joined her and they ate happily, commenting on some of the more unfamiliar dishes. Neither could remember a time when they'd had anything so delicious.

The rest of the Bonded had filed into the hall and they too loaded up with food. Ian and Isa joined them at their table, grinning from ear to ear.

"Isn't this something," Ian said, pushing around chunks of meat in a sauce the color of cherries. "Can't say I've ever seen so much food in one place. This should happen more often!"

They nodded their agreement, everyone too enthralled with the food to say much. They ate, occasionally getting up to grab a particular favorite. Kirheen found some small chocolate cakes filled with a gooey reddish sauce that were absolutely divine and she got up more than once to pile extra on her plate.

The room was alive with energy, everyone talking and laughing and genuinely enjoying their present company. Even the instructors seemed to be enjoying themselves. After a time, they all took to mingling, joining the crowd in the center of the room. Trista took to playing the lute, her pleasant voice carrying through the room. Burk and Abby started dancing to the tune and soon others had joined them. Kirheen avoided that particular activity like the plague. Dancing had never really been her thing.

Her shoulder was jostled lightly as someone stepped up next to her. She turned her head, her breath catching in her throat as she took in Ian in all of his glory. His eyes wandered over the people dancing and then she had his attention, the full weight of his gaze settling over her.

"Don't agree with dancing," he asked kindly, smiling at her.

She took a shaky breath, trying to calm her nerves. "Ah, no I'm afraid not."

"I've never been much for dancing either." He took a sip of the drink in his hand and the smell of apples and cinnamon carried her way.

"This is quite the event," she said, feeling absolutely ridiculous. Why did talking to him have to be so hard? Why did the words have to get caught in her throat, blocked by the weight of all her secrets?

Ian nodded. If he was fazed by her lack of finesse during their conversations, he did a great job hiding it. "It sure is something. It's nice to be able to spend time with everyone." The next words came out as a sigh, as if his words simply spilled out with his breath. "Especially you."

Kirheen looked over at him, eyes wide and lips parted. Had she heard him correctly? She rearranged her facial features, hoping he hadn't noticed her momentary shock and carried on as if she hadn't heard. Ian said nothing further, but his eyes searched the crowd and landed on Isa. She was currently dancing, locked arm in arm with Burk as they twirled in circles, laughing. Her curly raven hair bounced with each twist and turn, bobbing around with the rhythm of her feet.

"Do you ever think they get the bonding ritual wrong," Ian asked, his eyes never leaving Isa. He looked almost sad as he asked the question, as if by asking he was admitting to the doubt he felt.

Kirheen hesitated, hoping she wasn't reading too far into things. It was entirely possible he was just asking for reasons that had nothing to do with either of their feelings. At least part of her wanted to believe that. *Make this easier for me, please.* "I've always thought it a possibility. Why do you ask?"

He shook his head. "I don't know. I understand the intention of the bonding is that you eventually fall in love with your bond mate, right? Our personalities and traits were so matched that any other outcome shouldn't exist. But, what if they get it wrong? What if you aren't bonded with someone you love?"

Kirheen whirled, her head filling with so many thoughts at once she felt like she might faint. So he thought of these things too? It shouldn't have surprised her. One of the things she'd always liked about Ian was his way of questioning things. He thirsted for knowledge the same way she did, wanted answers to questions that shouldn't be asked.

She gathered her courage and spoke. "I've wondered these things myself," she said softly. Ian looked at her, his eyes curious. He turned his body towards her and took a step closer until she was breathing in the smell of spices from his drink.

"Do you… like Garild? No, forgive me. That isn't quite the word. Would you say you… love him?"

Again, that question. "I…" She wanted to lie, to say that she did love Garild, to end this game and get out while she still had a chance. The lie almost slipped off her tongue but it felt wrong. She couldn't let this moment pass. To hint at the truth was too great of a temptation. "I don't love him."

Ian looked serious as he took in her words. It was as if he already knew the answer. He sat his cup down on the table behind him. "Will you walk with me? I think I could use some fresh air."

Alone with Ian? She could feel the blood flowing through her veins, could feel the slight heat of her cheeks and the slow pace of her breathing. Her eyes wandered through the crowd. Garild was in a corner of the room, talking with Carter and Tegan, his attention entirely devoted to the conversation at hand. She nodded her head, weaving through the crowd with Ian.

It had cooled significantly outside and she shivered slightly, feeling the warmth of the room disappear behind them. The clearing in front of the temple was almost devoid of people. The only movement came from a couple servants but they were busy focusing on the jobs they'd been assigned. They paid little mind to the two Bonded wandering the road in the dark.

The moon was unusually bright and the trees seemed to glow brighter because of it. Despite the hour, it was still easy to see. They wandered the path in silence, listening to the chirping of crickets. Halfway between the Temple of Gathering and the Temple of Trials, Ian stopped.

"You ever feel like doing something rebellious?"

The question caught her off guard and she raised a brow. "What did you have in mind?"

He laughed softly. "There's a little clearing I slip away to from time to time when I get the chance. I bet it looks beautiful right now. Care to see it?"

No. Just turn back. You know what will happen. "I'd love to."

He seemed almost relieved as she said it, as if he'd been expecting her to reject him. He smiled, reaching out and taking her hand in his. The feel of his skin against her sent a shock up her arm and she met his eyes. His hand, so much larger than her own, enveloped hers in warmth. It made her feel safe and she melted into that warmth, letting it ease the guilt she felt at his touch. He smiled mischievously and pulled her off the trail.

She followed willingly, her curiosity drowning any protest. Tall grass whipped against her arms as they darted through the underbrush, slowing only to bypass the occasional rock or fallen tree. At one point, they startled a deer and Kirheen jumped, clinging to Ian. He laughed, wrapping his arm around her protectively. Once the fear had passed, she burst into giggles, adrenaline dredging up girlish jitters she so seldom felt.

At that point they walked hand in hand and eventually entered a beautiful moonlit clearing. The grass was tinged blue in the light of the moon and it swayed back and forth with the gentle breeze. The motion and sound was almost hypnotic. He led her a little further and then plopped down on the ground. Kirheen looked down at him, eyes curious. "What are we doing?"

"I wanted to watch the stars," he smiled. He laid back, his fingers laced behind his head. Kirheen joined him, making herself comfortable in the grass, as comfortable as she could be being so close to Ian. She tried not to think about the bugs that crawled on the ground beneath and around her. Even more so, she tried not to think about how close they lay, tried not to think about the heat radiating from him or the smell of cinnamon and apple that still clung to his breath. She turned her attention to the sky above and it was momentarily consumed by the beauty of the moon. Thousands of stars twinkled overhead and she felt her breath escaped in a rush.

"It's so beautiful," she whispered.

"It is," Ian sighed but his tone implied it wasn't the sky he spoke of. He rolled onto his side, watching Kirheen with his luminous eyes. Feeling his gaze, she rolled towards him. His face was stern and serious and he reached out hesitantly and brushed a strand of hair out of her face, tucking it gently behind her ear. His fingers lingered a moment longer than they should have. "Kirheen, I think they got it all wrong. I don't love Isa. I care about her, I respect her, but I don't feel with Isa the way I feel every time I'm around you."

Kirheen was stunned, her mouth gaping open but words failed her. His confession so mirrored her own and she found herself feeling foolish that she'd doubted it all along. All this time, he'd had feelings for her too. She sat up, suddenly feeling sick to her stomach. To hear him actually say it unknotted something in her, something she'd kept locked up and hidden. Years of pent up feelings were now free to be expressed and the feeling nearly brought her to tears.

Ian gripped her shoulder and when she met his gaze his eyes were sorrowful. He looked on the verge of breaking, as if his entire sense of self hung on her response. He was waiting for the validation he'd just given her, clinging to a fragile hope that still had a chance of slipping through his fingers. "I'm so sorry, Kir. I shouldn't have ever confessed this to you. It was foolish. I just thought that maybe…"

Kirheen couldn't help herself. She laughed, a great shaky thing that forced its way from her belly and filled the air around them before fading away into the night. Despite his fear, Ian smiled. "It wasn't foolish. It never was, Ian. I feel the same way. I'm sorry… this just came as a shock. I feel like I can hardly breathe."

His face shifted through a myriad of emotions before it settled on pure, unadulterated joy. He sidled closer to her, his green eyes searching hers for the truth. "You really mean it? All of it?"

"I do."

You're Bonded…

And then he was there, his hands cupping her face. He leaned forward, bringing his lips to her ear. She shivered at the touch and he whispered softly. "Then please allow me this. Just this once."

Chapter 21

Garild had never had such fun. In all his youth, he'd never experienced the elated joy that good food and good conversation could bring. Mingling with friends had brought a sense of peace to his soul that seemed to have been missing over the long winter months. He felt whole again.

He could hardly contain his cheer and he went seeking the one person with whom he wanted to share it with. He fully expected to find her tucked away in a corner, possibly hording a number of small chocolate cakes while trying to avoid the dancing and conversation she cared little for. But she wasn't there. Garild realized with thundering disappointment that she wasn't in the room at all. She was gone.

And so was Ian.

His happiness was a glass ball of emotion that someone had picked up and hurled against the floor. It shattered and out spilled a swirling glob of confusion and anger. He tried not to jump to conclusions, tried not to let that thought filter through his brain, but he'd seen the way they looked at each other. He couldn't have been imagining the awkward way in which they stood near each other, or how their eyes would meet in conversation only to flitter away again before either of them could notice the other staring.

He closed his eyes, focusing hard on his missing bond mate. Instead of a general sense of her direction, he was hit with a pulsating wave of conflicting emotions. It was tumultuous, like a waterfall of emotion crashing over his head. There was fear and longing and shame all pulling at his heart, each emotion tugging a separate string until he felt like he'd come unraveled.

He struggled to separate himself from the emotions. They'd hit like a freight train, barreling through his defenses. He tried to move towards the door but his legs felt laden with an unbearable amount of weight, a weight that threatened to drag him into a pit of despair he would never leave. Staggering, he made his way towards the door. If only he could get outside, maybe he'd be able to breath.

But he couldn't make it. It was too much. He was fighting a battle he couldn't win and he didn't want to feel anymore. He just wanted to block off his mind and to do that he needed help. This wasn't something he could do alone.

The woman swimming in his vision regarded him with a cold stare as he approached.

"Please help me," Garild begged. His legs slid out from under him and he found himself at her feet.

"What is it, boy? Speak," the woman demanded.

And so he did.

And so Herzin listened.

Just this once.

Just once.

Ian slid his lips away from her ear, kissing a line across her cheek until he found his way to her mouth. When his lips pressed against her own, the world seemed to spin. His lips were warm and soft and the taste of apples was sweet on his tongue. Nobody could teach such perfection. This was natural, meant to be.

Even if you yearn...

You are Bonded.

Finding her willing, his kisses grew more passionate, his hands roaming from her face. His strong hands pressed against her shoulders, pushing her back into the grass and he followed her down, his lips never leaving hers. The feel of his body pressed against her own was almost too much to bear, the feel of the blood rushing through her veins, the beating of her heart making her feel out of control.

This can't be a mistake.

A hand wandered down her body, pressing against her side and traveling to her hip. His fingers dug into her flesh and she gasped. Fingers danced down her thigh, coming to rest behind her knee. He pulled her closer and she felt herself slip, anticipation drowning out her senses like a drug. She let her own hands travel, feeling the firmness of his chest, the strength of his shoulders. Her fingers found the sash of his robe and she undid the knot, slipping it off of his waist. She reached up to push back his robes when she felt the first whisper of warning, a slight tingle of pain echoing softly in her mind.

It was ignored in favor of the lips nestled against her neck.

A whisper turned into an inferno and she found herself flowing with anger, an unwarranted aggression bursting out of her. She pushed Ian away from her, trying to shake away the anger but it clung to her, sticky syrup coating her synapses in red.

Ian looked angry himself, his face a mask of hurt and confusion. And then he went rigid. He fell to the side, his hands gripping the sides of his head. A cry forced itself out of his throat and he rolled back and forth on the ground. Kirheen sat up quickly, terrified that she had caused the pain he now felt. She scrambled on hands and knees towards him, only to be stopped by an intense bolt of pain that struck her mind like a bolt of lightning.

Her ears began to ring, a gentle chime that rose into a horrifying cacophony of sound. She felt something warm drip from her nose and she raised a hand to her face, panicking as her fingertips came away bloody. *No, no, no... Please, not this. Please...*She made a desperate attempt to block her mind but it was much too late. The pain ripped through her, cutting through her defenses like they were made of butter.

There was yelling from across the field and a familiar voice cut through the fog of pain.

"Stop, please! You're hurting them! You've got to stop!"

Another wave of pain sent her doubling over and she heaved into the grass, feeling her stomach spasm painfully. And then it was her whole body, shaking violently and completely out of her control.

This is how it ends...

A broken bond...

Payment for my folly...

Everything faded but the pain. She lay in the grass, her body twitching violently. It seemed like hours before the pain finally stopped but her mind was gone. It wandered in that dark space again, alone and afraid. And this time, she didn't think it would ever return.

Chapter 22

In the early hours of the day, Tomias had promised a final attempt. *This is it,* he'd told himself. *After this you'll rest.* But he hadn't rested. Exhaustion hovered over him, and each attempt brought him further and further into its grasp. He wouldn't give up… no matter what it cost him. And so after every failed attempt, he remade his promise, knowing full well he'd never follow through with it.

He pushed forward, gently prodding Kirheen's mind. He desperately tried to find a way through the wreckage that had been left behind, past the pain and fear to the place where she hid. So far, his attempts had been fruitless. She remained in a deep slumber, her mind lost to him once again.

She was lucky to even be alive. Herzin hadn't been merciful when she'd found them in the field, doing what young people do best. Whether it was the nature of the crime itself or the fact that it involved Kirheen, it had made the old crone nearly insane with rage. It had taken Nyson himself to subdue her and he was none too happy about it.

Word had spread like wildfire and rumors with it. Bonded and instructors alike were confined to their homes until word was received from the Union Master. That meant Tomias was stuck in a home with two broken students, one on her death bed and the other lost in a land of his own misery.

Upon arriving, Garild had plunked down before the empty fire place and he hadn't moved since. He stared off into space, his eyes glossy and distant. He hadn't spoken a word and he refused to eat. It seemed a miracle that he even allowed himself to breath. Tomias couldn't exactly blame him. He'd been betrayed in the worst way possible. Unfortunately, his choice of confidant had nearly cost Kirheen her life.

It pained him to look at her. The soft flesh around her eyes was terribly swollen and bruised, her nose a network of broken vessels. There was a welt on the side of her face from where she'd hit the ground in violent spasms and her lip was broken and bloody. The outside appearance was bad enough, but it was the internal damage that worried him. Trista had done a thorough evaluation and had declared that while the outside damage would heal, the internal damage could very well kill her and there was little she could do to help.

On occasion, she'd spasm wildly and Tomias would hold her down, keeping her as still as he could to prevent her from hurting herself more. These moments filled him with terror and each spasm he expected to be her last.

He'd been by her side for two days, watching and waiting. Most of his sleep was done in the chair he'd dragged to her bedside and his waking moments were spent trying to crack through her walls. If he could just get in, even the slightest bit, he might be able to talk to her, to wrestle her away from the darkness that gripped her. He prodded gently at her walls and was met with a wave of resistance that pushed him back until he could no longer withstand the pressure. He broke the contact and lowered his head into his hands, trying to keep his headache at bay.

"*You need to stop*," Fenir said, his tone carefully measured. Tomias didn't even have to lift his head to know he stood in the doorway, arms crossed over his chest. "*She's not likely to make it, mind or no mind. The sooner we all accept that the better.*"

Tomias prickled with frustration. He ground his teeth together, trying to keep his anger from leaking into his words. It really wasn't his fault. He was being logical, something Tomias was most certainly not. "*I can't just give up on her, Fenir. If I had paid closer attention, maybe I could have stopped this. I just...*"

"*This isn't your fault, brother. Regret will change nothing. You need rest or pretty soon you'll be joining her. Go lay down. I know this is important to you. I'll keep trying.*"

"Be gentle with her," he said aloud and his twin nodded. His bones creaked and his muscles protested as he slowly rose to his feet. Too long sitting had aged him. He could feel every ache of body and mind as he made his way to the other bed. Lacking the energy to even pull back the covers, he let himself fall forward into the pillows, his arms sprawled off to either side of the bed. He kept his face turned away from Kirheen, hoping to block her from his mind, but when he closed his eyes, it was her broken face that filled his dreams.

He awoke hours later, though he felt no more rested then he had when he'd gone to bed. He sat up, expecting to find his brother watching him from across the room. Instead, it was Garild that greeted him. He stared down at Kirheen, his expression blank. When he heard Tomias move, he raised his head, his brown eyes dull and tinged with red. He said nothing, just stared for a moment before lowering his gaze. "Why did she do it," he asked to no one in particular. "We are…we were Bonded."

Tomias sighed, swinging his legs over the side of the bed. The poor boy was a wreck, his face contorted with a strange mix of grief, fear and anger. The anger was a dull thing, glowing like coals beneath his other emotions. "Garild, I'm so sorry. I know this hurts."

"We were Bonded, Tomias. Does that mean nothing," Garild asked, his eyes filling with tears. "Did it really mean so little to her?"

He wasn't ready to deal with this. How could he even begin to explain to Garild the complexity of something as strange and wild as love? How could he make him see that it was their very nature that drove them to such things? "I can't speak for her. What she did…it was wrong. I hope when she wakes she is able to give you the answers you seek. "

Garild wiped at his eyes, his hands shaking. "It's been days…is she even going to wake up?"

"I honestly don't know. I'm doing everything I can to bring her through this. I can only hope it will be enough."

"Please bring her back. I may hate her right now but...but I can't bear to lose her. I can't..." He leaned forward, taking hold of her hand. He raised it to his lips and kissed her finger tips softly, as if he feared breaking her. Something slipped from him then, the last of his hope draining out with his tears. "There's to be a trial, you know? Nyson himself is going to judge them..."

Tomias couldn't suppress the shiver that ran through him. He must have been sleeping when they'd made the announcement. If Nyson was overseeing the trial, things could only be worse than he'd feared. "We'll figure this all out... I'll do whatever I can to protect you both."

Garild nodded and shambled out of the room, as lively as a corpse. Tomias was no better as he crossed the short distance separating himself from Kirheen. He reached down a hand, resting his palm on her forehead. *So cold...* Her skin was dreadfully pale, so devoid of color that she seemed to be made of ash instead of flesh. The only sign that she still lived came from the steady rise and fall of her chest. He shook his head. What more could he possibly do for her? It would take more than his powers to pull her from the shattered center of her mind.

And even if she did wake, there was the trial to deal with and Nyson would not take her crime lightly. She'd be punished, likely stripped of her bond and exiled. Tomias couldn't let that happen. He had failed to notice the turmoil brewing around him, had failed to divert Kirheen down a better path and if he didn't do anything, she was going to pay the price for his ignorance. It was his responsibility.

And so he slipped from the window, landing in the grass with a huff. The movement sent shocks through his tired muscles and he leaned against the wall of the house until the spasms passed. The sun shone brightly above him, stinging eyes that had spent days in a dreary room. He had to squint until they adjusted to the light and then he set out on the path that would lead him to Nyson.

His home had taken root between the space occupied by the Bonded to the South and their instructors to the North. Nestled in a grove of ancient wraith wood trees, it was a small home for a man of such importance. Tomias didn't even bother to knock when he reached the front door. He simply walked in, his current mood providing a level of indifference when it came to following formalities.

Tomias had never thought to question what his dwelling might look like. Seeing it now, he realized it was just what he would expect from a man like Nyson. The room was wide, open and scarcely furnished. Every stick of furniture had a purpose and there was no room left over for frivolous things such as décor.

Nyson sat behind an ornately carved wraith wood table, a piece of faded parchment gripped between his fingers. His slate blue eyes wandered from the paper in his hand and settled on Tomias with a look of mild annoyance. Annoyed he may have been but he seemed hardly surprised to see him there. "You seem to have left your manners on the other side of the door," he said dryly. He nodded towards the empty chair across from him, his lips pulled into a disapproving frown. "Have a seat."

Tomias approached wearily, never letting his gaze wander away from Nyson. He settled into the chair stiffly, his muscles rigid. "I--"

"I'm no fool, Tomias," Nyson said, cutting him off before he could speak. "I know why you've come. Care for a drink?"

"Only if I can find the answers I need at the bottom of the glass."

Nyson smirked, though there was nothing friendly in the gesture. He let the paper in his hands settle on the desk and Tomias had to resist the urge to look at it. "It always comes to that. Questions need answers and it seems human nature to seek them out. I've been fighting against this very nature for years."

Tomias took a deep breath, settling himself before rage could hijack his words. "Don't you dare dance around this. I don't care about your struggles, Nyson. I just want to know what is going to happen to my students?"

"Kirheen and Ian have committed a terrible crime. This is an incredibly delicate matter and one that could have consequences for all that exist here. I can't just slap them on the wrist for this. You don't get off easy for breaking your bond."

"You think I don't know what they've done? I fully understand the implications of this. I do. But I need to know so I can prepare myself for what's to come. I can't just keep walking in the dark like this. What is going to happen to my students," he asked again, enunciated each word forcefully.

Nyson leaned back in his chair with a heavy sigh, his intertwined hands resting in his lap. He regarded Tomias with a level gaze and he took his time picking him apart, measuring his worth drop by drop. A game of chess in his head, Tomias just one of the pieces. He was evaluating the risk and he would be found worthy of it or he would not.

"Garild and Isa will be sent off to the work camps," Nyson said plainly.

The words were a punch to the gut. Tomias could scarcely believe what he'd just heard. "You're...sending them away? Two perfectly capable students that could assist greatly against the Darkness and you're just going to throw them away?"

Nyson grimaced. "This is not punishment for them. I'm fully aware of their capabilities. I take no joy in sending them away but they have just been betrayed in the worst way possible. This is a pain that will hinder them in all aspects of their lives. They need time to rest and heal. Once they've had that, I will reconsider their position. In the meantime, this is the way things must be."

Tomias had seen many of the workers over the years. They appeared in the village from time to time, helping with a variety of tasks throughout Sanctuary. They had always seemed so frail to him, so distant. They lived and breathed but it was like someone had shut off the lights upstairs. There sole purpose became work. They did a great service for them all, but at what cost? "I've seen the workers from the camps. If I'm to be honest, punishment is exactly what this seems like. They all seem like they are dragging themselves around, overworked, underfed and desperately in need of a good laugh."

Nyson let out an exasperated sigh. "If you speak of the workers from the past few days, then yes. They are in need of a break. They just worked very hard to help celebrate the victory of your students. One of which turned around and rewarded their hard work with a slap in the face." he said dryly. "Despite what you think, the workers are treated well. They are housed and fed just as they are here."

"You talk about them like they aren't even people, Nyson!"

"I speak of them as a group. I'm well aware they are individual people and they get treated as such. You seem to be letting suspicion cloud your memory."

Tomias put his argument aside, the fate of Kirheen still up in the air. He didn't have time to argue with Nyson. He needed to get an answer. He needed to let it settle in his soul so he'd know what to do next. When he asked the question, he dropped a wall over his heart, trying to keep his emotions at bay. "What'll become of Kirheen and Ian? What about them?"

"Ian's condition is declining. I had Trista look over him this morning. She does not expect him to make it more than a few days. The extent of his injuries are more than his body can handle."

"And so he dies, just like that. Herzin goes off the deep end but that alright 'cause he was going to suffer consequences anyways. Death might as well be the answer."

There was a subtle shift in the Union Masters face, a slight dampening of the light in his eyes that was quickly replaced by anger. "Still your tongue, boy. I know what she did and don't think for a second she won't be punished for her actions. When the time is right, I will deal with her. In the meantime, I don't need you starting a crusade. We've enough trouble as it is."

"I think that is exactly what we need. This is the second time her hatred has gotten out of hand and this time its cost lives! Do you really believe this is okay?"

Nyson grimaced. "I am greatly upset over this matter, but the punishment of the criminals must come first. Herzin will be dealt with."

"Kirheen broke her bond, she did something foolish. What Herzin did was practically murder them both and she's out there running loose while my student knocks on deaths door." The floodgates of his anger had been drawn back and the words poured out of him like acid, scalding everything they touched. He was out of line, he knew that much, but he didn't seem able to stop once the words started to flow.

Nyson took note. "Your tone is becoming entirely disagreeable. I understand you're upset but I am not the person to be pushing right now. Watch your tongue, Tomias, or have it removed."

Tomias gritted his teeth and gave a curt nod. Nyson took the moment to reach for a pitcher of water and poured himself some into a ceramic mug. He sipped from it slowly, giving Tomias the chance to calm down. Sure that he'd gotten his anger under wraps, Nyson continued.

"Kirheen is a special case. The details of her punishment are...complicated. Your students displayed remarkable talent in battle, Kirheen in particular. She can think on her feet, she's determined and has shown a wide range of skills I could find useful. I *need* someone like that on the Council. Ordinarily her crime would be met with a lifetime of work or even exile, but I find myself leaning towards leniency if certain conditions are met."

"And what are those conditions?"

"Kirheen agrees to join the Council and dissolve her bond. I would expect a public apology for her actions and a vow of loyalty. If she will submit to my will, I will forgive her crime and allow Garild and Isa to join up with the armies in the East when they feel ready."

He'd known all along that Kirheen was being groomed for the Council. He expected this day to come sooner or later, but after everything that happened, it shocked him that Nyson would still push for such an outcome. Tomias shook his head in disgust. "You know that wouldn't happen. Kirheen may not love Garild, but she wouldn't dissolve her bond just to serve you."

"She would if it meant their lives. Guilt makes one do all manner of irrational things. And I expect your help with pushing along this outcome."

"My student was just brought to the edges of death and had her mind bashed in for no crime other than being young and stupid. And now you want me to lie to her, to convince her that unless she joins the Council her friends will be exiled or worse? That's what you want me to do for you? I don't understand you."

"There is much you don't understand. You're barely more than a child yourself and you've hardly got the world figured out, much as you think otherwise. I can't expect you to understand the reasons for the things I do, but I can expect that you'll follow orders. For her sake and the sake of the others, I suggest you try."

There were daggers hiding in his words, lurking at the edges and waiting for him to slip. If his loyalty faltered now, he knew that the daggers would cease to be metaphorical. They'd become real and one night he'd find one sticking out of his throat.

Despite the very real threat of death, he needed to know the truth. He'd spent so long in the dark, willingly wearing a mask so he wouldn't be consumed by all his questions. They'd been kept at bay, locked away and constantly distracted. He couldn't do it anymore. The questions were becoming hard to ignore. They danced at the edge of his vision, laughing at his blindness, his reluctance to see the truth.

He refused to be blind any longer. "You're right. There is so much I don't know...so much I don't understand. I've been on the

Council for years and I've always accepted that I'd never have all the answers, that I'd never have all the cards in my hand. Up until today I've been pretty happy *not* knowing everything. I haven't wanted your burden. But I ignore the things I see anymore, Nyson. I can't will myself to be blind.

You know, I've never stepped foot outside of Sanctuary. I've never seen the village where the workers live. I've never faced the Darkness, never seen those sent away come back. We've grown up on a tale of a tainted world beyond our borders and I'm starting to feel like we're jumping at ghosts. I've lost a lot being loyal to you all these years. My brother lost a lot. I can't keep being loyal to secrets. I can't keep sealing my questions away and expecting to not burst apart at the seams. So please, enlighten me. Make me understand. You give me those answers and I'll give you my life. I'll give you Kirheen. Make this worth the sacrifice."

Only after he'd stopped speaking did he realize he was leaning halfway across the table, his hands balled into fists on the desk. He was shaking, his arms quivering like branches in the wind. Nyson smirked but the thoughts dancing behind his eyes were unreadable. "You've fire in you, boy. Best temper it now before it grows too powerful…before it consumes."

Tomias sank back into his chair, feeling the weight of his promise settling over his shoulders. If Nyson chose to confide his secrets, if he chose to give him the answer he so desperately needed, it would change everything. The Union Master sat quiet, mulling over his thoughts as if he were slowly chewing a piece of steak.

They were all just pawns, moved piece by piece into position. But what was the game? And the question that dug at him the most; who were they playing against?

"This world is complicated and dangerous beyond measure. If I have withheld information from you, it has been solely to protect and preserve all I have worked for. I value those that have helped me keep it safe throughout the years, you and your brother included. The time was coming when the veil would be pulled back, when answers would come to the light, but with recent events, things have become muddled. Things will have to settle before I can show you the card up my sleeve."

"But---"

Nyson glared, cutting his protest short. "*But*, I can see when withholding information works against me. I can see when it starts to develop a rift. You are part of my Council and therefore part of a much bigger plan, a plan that you've yet to know. I can't expect you to be loyal if you don't have the information you need. You're intelligent and that intelligence demands you seek answers. I know you won't stop until you have them."

He stood then, crossing the room and procuring a locked box from one of several book cases. It was inconspicuous, made of smooth wraith wood and glowing brightly. He set it on the table between them, his expression grim. Reaching into his robe, he withdrew a small, delicate key and held it out. Tomias simply stared at the key dangling before his eyes.

"I'm offering you answers, Tomias, but the choice is yours. Once you choose to take this key…"

"I can't stuff the answers back in the box. I know…" *Choose wisely.*

The key was cold to the touch but it warmed quickly in his hand. He leaned forward, letting the key slide into the lock. It unlatched with a pop and the sound set his heart to beating frantically. *Once you know the truth…*

His hands settled on the sides of the lid and he lifted it slowly, afraid of what might jump out. Much to his surprise, the only thing within the box was a pile of dusty scrolls. They looked old and frail and he looked to Nyson for approval before reaching in and taking one out.

He unraveled it slowly, the paper crackling loudly as he did. It was a map, worn and faded, but a map none the less. It took him a moment to take it all in and even longer to realize it wasn't a map of their little valley. "This is…"

"This is the world beyond the mountains. This is what exists beyond Sanctuary." He knelt forward, weathered finger pointing to a small valley to the northern corner of the map. "This is Sanctuary, this little patch right here. This is where our kind fled when the Darkness consumed the rest of the world."

Sanctuary took up such a small portion of the map in his hands. It was hard to imagine the rest of the world was corrupted, fallen to an ancient evil he couldn't begin to comprehend. "And the rest of this belongs to the Darkness…"

Nyson simply nodded his head. Tomias let the scroll snap back together and pulled out another. It was a faded piece of art, showing impossibly tall buildings stretching far into the sky as if they were trees. Smaller buildings surrounded these towers, spreading off into all directions. This must have been a picture from before, from a time when humans hadn't huddled in a valley, chipping away at the Darkness one bit at a time.

So many people...gone. All of them corrupted. Broken. Turned to husks.

He shook his head and let the scroll settle back into the box. Only one remained and he grabbed it carefully. It was more worn than the others, as if it had been taken out and looked over time and time again. The center of the scroll was taken up by a sketch of an old man. He was rough looking, with wild eyes and a long bushy beard. His face was sharp, carved from stone and brought to life on paper.

The rest of the scroll was confusing. The top of it requested information about the man and his whereabouts and listed crimes he had committed, the primary of these relating to something called black magic and the use thereof. There were also charges for manipulation of a public official, coercion, and attempted murder. The bottom of the scroll announced that he had been last seen fleeing to the North and others had followed in his wake. There was a reward offered for his capture, dead or alive.

"What is this," Tomias asked, not understanding what he held. "Who is this?"

"That would be my great grandfather, Elis, the founder of Sanctuary," Nyson said. "A great man with a grand vision that earned him the scorn of those not gifted with powers. He was forced North, to the safety of a land seemingly made for his kind. And others followed. They formed Sanctuary, formed this land so we could be safe from the darkness gathering out in the world. Safe so that we could one day strike back at those that drove us here in the first place."

Those that drove us here...

"No..." Tomias looked again at the scroll in his hands. He knew it was real, knew it to be a tangible thing. He could smell the age of it, could feel the roughness against his fingertips. Stains from another time and place scarred the page. A place that still existed. "No, no, no."

Scared for so many years, words and stories used to trick the mind into fearing the unknown. They'd been lied to all along. Kept in line, bred for a purpose, bred to fight against a corruption beyond their land, a *human* corruption. They'd been jumping at shadows on the wall all along.

"Who else knows about this," Tomias demanded. His fingers had lost their grip on the scroll and it rolled back together, making him jump. "Who?"

"Only a select few." His voice was stern. "I intend to keep it that way. We aren't ready to face this. We get closer every cycle, but we need more time, more strength. If everything dissolves before then it will all be for nothing. You see? Now do you understand? Tomias?"

"Y-yes, I understand," he sputtered. *Get yourself under control.* "I need air. I need to be outside." *Make me understand. You give me those answers and I'll give you my life. I'll give you Kirheen. Make this worth the sacrifice.* He rose from his chair, staggering to the door on legs that seemed to sway beneath him. The world was new and foreign and moving under his feet, spinning at impossible speeds and he couldn't keep up.

Nyson stopped him at the door. "Tomias. This is a lot to take in, but I expect this to stay as it is. You've opened that box and you can't put it back. It goes no further. You offered me your life, your loyalty. If these words slip from your lips, if I hear them whispered in the wind, it is your life I will take."

"Of course... My life is yours." He bowed deeply to the Union Master before slipping out the front door. He felt sick, bile burning in his throat as it rose from the depths of his churning stomach. He could feel eyes watching him until he disappeared around a bend in the path. He tried to remain calm, tried to keep his thoughts filled with loyal intentions. However, he could not still the beating of his heart, the nervous twitch of his right hand. He could not stop the sweat from beading on his brow or keep the saliva from fleeing his mouth. All were signs of the guilt and anger and shock he felt. Nothing could hide such things.

He stood with his hands pressed against the door of Trista's home, too afraid to knock. His breath came in great gasps and when the door disappeared beneath his fingers he thought it might leave him altogether. Trista guided him inside and forced him to sit in a chair she'd provided. She filled his blurry vision a moment later, taking his hands in her own. "Tomias. I need you to answer me. Tell me she lives? By the Allseer, please tell me she lives!"

He hadn't even been aware she'd been talking. The words seemed fuzzy and distant, taking shape one syllable at a time until his brain could decipher it all. Did she live? *Kirheen...*

"She lives," he sputtered. "But she isn't safe."

"What...happened? Tell me." Her hands grabbed his face, pulling him closer until he had no choice but to look into her green eyes. "Speak."

"They aren't safe here anymore. They've never been safe."

"Who isn't safe? Damn it, Tomias, what are you talking about?"

"I'm sorry, Trista. It's all clicking into place... I can't even focus."

Trista shook her head. "You're tired. You need rest. I don't know what's happened to you, but you aren't making sense."

He grabbed her wrists, pulled her close until her face was mere inches from his own. She looked frightened and he knew that if he didn't convince her within the next few moments, she was likely to beat him over the head with a frying pan. "I spoke with Nyson tonight. I went by myself, I needed to find out what would happen to my students. I *needed* to know. He gave me a key to a box…and Allseer be damned… It isn't real. It's never been real. The Darkness, the war… none of it's real."

Trista looked like he'd just reached out and slapped her across the face. Her eyes narrowed, her mouth dropped open and she pulled out of his grasp. "Did Fenir hit your head? What is wrong with you? You've gone absolutely mad."

"It *is* mad. Why do you think I'm an absolute disaster right now?"

"You can't be serious!"

"I've never been more serious. Trista, I'm signing my life away by telling you this. And when I tell my brother…when I tell Kirheen… and Garild, I'll be sealing my fate. But I can't let Nyson keep hiding behind this…this…lie. I can't let this go on another minute."

She'd stopped walking and turned towards him, her hand rising to cover her mouth. "Allseer…you are serious. No…that can't be. I've seen…"

"We never have, Trista. We never have because it doesn't exist."

"The Darkness…"

"It isn't real."

Chapter 23

A scream, haunting in the sorrow it carried, reverberated through the Circle of Rest. When Tomias heard it, when he recognized that sound, it sent chills up his arms. He peered out the window, watching as Isa was dragged from her home by Burk and Grant. Her feet flailed as she tried to break away from their grip, her scream filled with enough grief that it no longer sounded human.

Such a thing could only mean one thing; Ian had passed.

Official word spread soon after. He'd died of a sickness, the lie swallowed by all, but whispers of the truth existed none the less. People knew the truth but none were willing to openly call the Union Master out on his lie. Not a soul was willing to accuse Herzin for the crime she'd committed. No one was willing to say that she was a murderer.

Kirheen still remained a thrall of her own mind. Her seizures had become less frequent, her rest more peaceful, but her mind was still guarded, an impenetrable wall that he couldn't find a way through no matter how hard he tried.

Feeling defeated he reached out towards her, wrapping her hand in his own. He stroked it with his thumb as if to comfort her, but the truth was he was only comforting himself. This was it. One final attempt to break through her mind. If he failed now, he wasn't sure he'd be able to live with the guilt.

They were running out of time and the trial was to take place the next morning. He either broke through now or lost all hope of saving his students. Trista sat in a chair at the far side of the room, visibly upset by the events of the past few days. She stared out the window solemnly, flipping a small vial of liquid end over end, the purple substance within sloshing back and forth as she did. Fenir stood at her side, sullen and angry.

"Trista, it's time."

Her eyes snapped to his, her hand stopping and closing around the vial. Standing, she approached the bed side and tilted Kirheen's face towards her. Tomias gently lifted her up, holding her while Trista dumped the contents of the vial in her mouth and forced her to swallow it. It was a massive dose of a mind altering plant, meant to break open the mind and make using powers easier. It was highly frowned upon.

It was also their last hope. Trista stepped back, letting the bottle slip from her fingers. It fell to the floor with a small clink and she sat back on the bed opposite them, resting her elbows on her knees. She would wait and watch, though there would be little she could do if things went wrong. Tomias dug in his pocket and procured his own vial, making sure to sit down before downing the contents.

"Careful, brother. Make sure you come back to us."

"I will."

"Well, here goes nothing." A sickly sweet taste coated his tongue. The effects were almost immediate. He suddenly felt very drowsy and his eyes rolled back. The last thing he remembered was sliding off the chair onto the floor. When he opened his eyes, he was no longer in the world he knew.

He stood at the edge of a forest, a clearing laid out before him. The clearing was green and lush and the breeze whispering through the trees pushed him forward. He went willingly, enjoying the feel of the sunshine and the grass tickling his bare feet. A few paces ahead of him, a girl lay in the grass on her side, her back to him. Her hair was long and ashen and it splayed out behind her like a waterfall. He smiled as he realized it was Kirheen. He ran towards her, swooping down to surprise her. He grabbed her shoulder and rolled her towards him and the illusion shattered.

Her eyes were frozen in terror and black goo dripped down her face as if they were tears. Her mouth was open and wide, her teeth stained black. As he pulled his hands away in terror, black strings attached to his hand, forming a bond between him and Kirheen. The grass around them melted away, leaving behind hard, unforgiving earth that was scorched black. Pools of black tar bubbled around them, making disgusting slurping noises as bubbles popped at the surface. The air was filled with terrified screams and he wanted so badly to drown them all out. He stood, stumbling back away from Kirheen. Finding his feet, he shambled off into the distance, hoping to reach the other side of the clearing. The tree line had disappeared and any avenue of escape was lost to him.

There were more bodies along the way and each one he turned over was Kirheen. He saw her everywhere. The body half lying in a pool of sludge was Kirheen. The body torn and ravaged shared her storm colored eyes. Everywhere was ashen hair and pale skin tainted and corrupted by the Darkness.

When he was finally ready to give up, he saw something alive and moving up ahead. Like the corpses he had seen, this one too shared the ashen hair of Kirheen, but she was so frail and thin, rocking back and forth in front of another corpse he couldn't yet see. Before he could reach her, she turned towards him. Her boney finger reached out, pointed at him accusingly. "You killed him," she croaked. "This is all your fault! All of this... You did this." She moaned, inky tears tracing lines down her pale skin. She wailed as he approached and her rocking resumed.

On the ground before her was a pale figure, lean and tall and masculine. He had white hair, his dark eyes open and alive with accusations despite the fact that he was very much dead. For a moment, Tomias thought it himself, imagined it was his corpse lying there. But there was something different about the face, something off. And then he realized it was his twin, Fenir. A dagger had been plunged through his heart and the veins around the wound had turned black.

Collapsing to his knees, he went to grab his twin and he fell apart in his hands, his body melting away into the black sludge that coated everything. He began to cry, all hope leaving his body. He curled up in the spot where his brother had been, letting all feeling bleed from his body.

He wasn't sure how long he stayed that way. Time passed slowly in such a place. Seconds felt like hours, hours like days. He was awoken by a gentle touch and when he opened his eyes, Kirheen stood over him. She was wearing blindingly white robes, the edges stained with black. Despite the corruption around her, she looked clean and unsoiled.

"What are you doing there," she asked, genuinely curious. He blinked, thinking her a mirage, some sort of strange apparition that would disappear if he moved too quickly. She remained where she was, arms crossed over her chest. "You don't belong here."

Tomias laughed in disbelief, pulling himself up out of the sludge. "You don't know how happy I am to see you. You're alive!"

"I never died," she said, tilting her head to the side, an eyebrow raised at the curiosity of his statement. "Why are you here? You need to leave. You shouldn't be here."

"I came to find you, to help you escape this place. You're trapped in your mind. We need to get you out."

Kirheen looked at him as if he'd been bludgeoned over the head and lost all his sense. "We can't leave! There isn't anywhere to go. The Darkness is here and we must push it back. We're all that's left. If we don't do something, if the corruption anchors itself here, all will be lost. I need your help!"

Trapped in her own mind, she'd completely lost sense of what was real and what was her dream. In her mind, she really was fighting the Darkness. She was simply doing what they'd always trained her to do. Only the Darkness wasn't real. He'd didn't have much hope of convincing Kirheen of that fact, not when all of her senses were telling her that what she was seeing was real.

"Kirheen, everyone is in terrible danger. All of those left need you to return. You need to get back to Sanctuary. If you stay here, they'll all die."

Her expression shifted to one of concern. "But I can't leave this place. Not yet. There is so much to do, so much..." She began to wander off, as if pulled by some call he could not hear. Before she got too far, he reached forward, grabbing her arm gently. He left a black stain on her robe.

She looked at him over her shoulder, her eyes angry. "I have to get back to my work."

"And that work...it isn't here," he said calmly, meeting her eyes. "Look around you, Kir. Look closely. Does any of this look real to you? Does any of this feel right? You aren't meant to be here. You need to wake up. Come back with me and help me save your friends. They need you!"

She considered his words, turning away from him to scan the horizon. She tilted her head again, questioning that which surrounded her. "You are real, aren't you? I've been trapped here so long. I forget...."

"You can be free now. All you need to do is wake up."

"I can be free of this place? I can leave the Darkness?"

"Yes."

She nodded and closed her eyes. Suddenly the ground gave way beneath their feet and he was startled awake, gasping for air as he sat upright. Trista leapt back from him, giving him space while he reoriented to his surroundings. He was drenched in sweat, his robes soaked through. He staggered to his feet, using the chair to aid him. Wavering, he stumbled towards the bed, towards Kirheen. He watched her face intently, waiting for any sign of movement. Breath held, heart hammering away, he sat in anticipation. There was a flutter of eyelids and her gray eyes met his. He cried, bending down and pulling her into a hug. She hesitated at first, her expression one of complete and utter confusion. Despite the oddity of the situation, she returned the hug, patting him on the back. Breaking away from the hug, he held her shoulders and pushed her back away from him.

She was a bit more beat up than she'd appeared to him in the dream, but she was there none the less. Real and alive and tangible. "You're alive," he sputtered and he couldn't help but grin from ear to ear.

Her laugh was a soft, pained thing. The action hurt her but she allowed it to happen none the less. She smiled and then said softly, "I never died."

Chapter 24

Garild was angry, a sensation that was entirely new and foreign to him. His entire life he had been calm, following the rules and instructions he'd been told without the slightest resistance. He'd never felt anything like it, a spark so hot it burned holes in his heart. He could think of nothing else but the anger. Didn't want to think of anything else.

Tomias had explained everything to him and the world he'd known had been flipped upside down. He'd believed in nothing but lies. His powers meant nothing, his bond meant nothing, his faith in their cause... all lies. And what could he do about it? Running away wasn't an option he even wanted to entertain, despite Tomias' assurance that the plan was for them to do just that if it came down to it. He found he didn't want to. He didn't want to run from this. If being forced to work away his days was what he would have to do, then he was willing to submit to such a thing. Pretending the lie still existed was better than what he was currently feeling.

In the other room, Tomias and Trista were preparing to wake Kirheen. She'd been trapped in her own head, so damaged and broken that many believed she'd never return again. She may have been alive, but stuck in such a state wasn't really living. For her sake, he hoped they succeeded, but he didn't plan on being around if they did.

A servant came for him in the early hours of the morning. He was alone in the front room, the others occupied with the task at hand. It was easy to slip out the front door, easy to disappear without having to say goodbye. He took one final look at their home, feeling a deep sense of sadness and loss settling over his soul. The world he'd known was slipping through his fingers. Everything he'd ever wanted rested in that house and now he was leaving it behind.

The servant that led him was a middle aged woman. Her auburn hair was cut to her shoulders and she wore a simple white robe. She didn't speak a word as they made their way towards the Temple of Trials. She didn't seem to show any emotions at all.

As he studied her, he began to think of all the other servants he'd seen over the years. He'd always thought them so dedicated, so focused on their work that they could hardly be disturbed. Looking at this woman now, he began to see how odd they were. These were supposed to be people like them, people that weren't powerful enough for whatever Nyson had planned. They were still supposed to act like people and yet it was almost as if they were nothing more than husks, bumbling about from task to task with little regard for anything else.

"Are you alright," he asked the woman.

She didn't falter in her steps, didn't even seem to register that he'd spoken. She just kept moving, keeping the same steady gait she'd used since they'd left his home. He asked her again, louder this time. Again he was greeted with silence. It wasn't as if she were simply ignoring him. There was no suppression of her facial expressions, no hardness of her gaze to say she'd been told not to talk to him. He simply didn't exist in her world. It made him uncomfortable, as if the person he walked alongside wasn't entirely human.

They passed under the great wraith wood tree forming the Temple of Union. It loomed over him, casting spidery shadows across his face. It was where he'd undergone the Ritual of Union, where he'd felt his heart flutter when he'd learned he was to be bonded with Kirheen. It was strange to think it held no meaning anymore. It felt like a life time ago, a part of his life becoming nothing but a fuzzy memory.

He'd been lucky to never have set foot in the Temple of Trials. The dedication he'd shown throughout his youth had kept him far away from the doors that stood before him now. The temple sat on the northern end of the village, a long singular building much like the hall they ate at every day. Though it had no physical differences from that familiar hall, the mere sight of it filled him with an unexplained dread.

The servant pushed open a door and ushered him through. The temple had high ceilings and was well lit by rows of windows that ran the length of the hall. It was simply furnished, with a row of chairs set to the left hand side of the room and a raised platform in the back. On this raised platform sat a long table and sitting behind that table was the Union Master himself. Herzin sat to his right, her green eyes critical.

It was only when he met her eyes that he felt the first flicker of fear catch fire in his heart. He'd seen her power, knew the damage she could cause. He only hoped his cooperation would save him the pain Kirheen had endured.

As the servant led him to a chair on the left hand side of the room, he realized one of those chairs was already occupied. He'd missed her at first glance, so small and fragile she looked. It was as if a touch would shatter her. Isa glanced up at him, her raven hair lackluster and her blue eyes ringed in red. He could envision himself swimming in those eyes, drowning in the pools of pain that they held. She looked away, curling further into herself.

They called her name first. She rose from her seat, eyes glued to the floor. She seemed to limp more than walk to her destination, her arms wrapped about herself as she trudged her way before those that would judge her. It hurt to look at her, to see her falling apart at the seams. There was nothing he could do, no comfort he could offer to make things better.

Nyson leaned forward, his elbows propped on the table. "Isa, I regret that things have come to this point. You have suffered greatly these past few days and it hurts me to see you suffer so. The crime of your bond mate has been felt throughout all of Sanctuary, and his passing has shaken us all. As such, we would like to extend to you a chance to rest, a chance to work and heal away from this place. We want to give you a chance to let your mind heal so you can finally face the Darkness. Do you accept our offer?"

There was a sinking feeling in his stomach at the mention of the Darkness. It was one thing to know the Darkness wasn't real and quite another to hear it lied about so convincingly. On any other occasion, he probably would have petitioned, but what could he do now? He'd committed to this, lie or no lie.

Isa nodded her head, accepting the terms of their agreement. It was only when Herzin rose and walked down the steps that she showed any hesitation. Herzin stood before her, looking down at her with an expression of genuine sadness. Something changed in Isa, a flicker of emotion rippling the pools of grief in her eyes. She raised her head, meeting the gaze of the Judge of Trials. "Murderer. This is your fault." The words left her as if she were simply stating a fact. There was no anger in her words, no malice. Grief had consumed those emotions, left her an empty shell.

Herzin simply looked down at her, lips pulled taunt. She reached forward her hands, placing her palms flat against the sides of her head. Isa didn't move, didn't react. She simply let her gaze drop down to her feet. There was a sudden feeling in the air, that slight crackle right before lightning strikes and then Isa dropped to the ground like a sack of grain. He gasped, hands gripping the side of the chair. Had she killed her? His heart began to hammer in his chest, a drum beat of terror.

"Isa," he called across the room, his concern for her life forcing her name from his lips.

After several seconds, Isa rose from the floor. If he'd thought she looked emotionless before, he had been wrong. There was nothing left of her now, her eyes glazed over and empty. There was no emotion in her face, no personality in her movements. Anything that even hinted at the girl she once was had vanished, stripped away from her in a second. She bowed obediently to Herzin and began to walk out of the room.

A husk just like the servant that had led him there. Without thinking he darted across the room and grabbed Isa by the elbow. He spun her around but she hardly reacted to the motion. Her blank eyes just looked through him. "Isa, are you okay?"

Nothing. There wasn't even the barest flicker of recognition in her eyes. Something had happened in that moment when Herzin had touched her. Something she'd done had made her like the workers he'd seen before. She'd taken away her light and if his hunch was correct, Isa hadn't been the first to fall victim to her power.

"Allseer…What did you do to her," he questioned, whipping around to face Herzin.

Herzin had the gall to smile. "I've merely helped ease her mind. She's gone through so much these past few weeks and now she can heal without being assaulted by her emotions. She can work through this without having to face grief. What was done to her was wrong, Garild. She shouldn't have to suffer for the mistake of her bond mate."

"You took her away. Everything that made her Isa is gone! What did you do to her? This...this isn't right! It's like she's dead!"

"I assure you, Garild, she isn't dead. Isa is still very much alive. I've only blocked her mind for a time. We're helping you." She took a cautious step towards him and he wrapped his arm around Isa, dragging her back a step with him.

He'd thought he'd been prepared for this. He thought he was ready to leave everything behind. He'd committed to this moment, committed to the anger and frustration and the desire to see it end. He thought once they sent him away he'd be able to work through his emotions, to be able to heal. He hadn't expected them to strip him of his emotions in order to make that happen.

It was a fate worse than death.

He didn't want this.

He wanted to live.

"Garild," Nyson called as he rose from his seat. "This change will not hurt you. You need not fear this. The pain that Kirheen has caused you is more than this. That pain will settle into your soul. It will linger and fester. Your bond was broken, your trust betrayed. We simply wish to ease your mind, to allow you the chance to heal so you can face the Darkness. We still need you in this. Will you please accept this gift?" His voice was fluid and calm, luring him into a false sense of security. *Lies.*

He wanted so badly to believe Nyson, to believe that this was just a temporary reprieve. But it wasn't. It never had been. The workers were enough proof of that. And he'd been lying to them all.

His entire life had been dedicated to this man, to this spider. He'd spun a web and he had them all trapped like flies. *Poisonous words. All a lie.*

"No. I don't want this," he whispered.

"Speak up, boy."

Garild looked towards the Union Master, at the man he'd trusted. "I don't want this," he shouted, his voice echoing in the room.

Nyson narrowed his eyes. "You don't have a choice."

In that moment Herzin dove towards him, her hand outstretched. He flung a blast of power towards her, halting her advance while he spun away from her, dragging Isa along with him towards the door. Halfway there, she dug her heels into the ground and stopped, vacant eyes pointed towards the floor. "Isa! We have to go! Come on!"

She wouldn't budge and he was wasting time trying to force her. He went to move, to launch himself towards freedom when he realized that he couldn't move either. He was frozen in place, just like he'd been in the battles. *Nyson…*

Herzin approached him, the friendly mask she'd worn melted away to reveal the annoyance beneath. He'd taken her "gift" and shoved it back in her face. He'd denied her words, denied her power and now he'd pay the price.

There was nothing he could do, no way to fight his way out of this. He closed his eyes, waiting for the pressure he knew would come. *Kirheen…I'm so sorry.*

The cool touch of hands on his face, a change in the air...
And then chaos.

Chapter 25

I an was dead. The Darkness was a lie. Her head spun, her heart aching in a way she never thought possible. A flurry of emotion lashed at her, pulling her thoughts and feelings in so many directions that she felt ill. Everything she thought she knew about the world was shattering around her like one of their illusions.

Tomias sat on the bed in front of her, disheveled and covered in sweat. Strands of white hair stuck to his forehead and there were dark circles under his eye, a testament to the long nights spent trying to save her. Trista and Fenir stood at the far side of the room, watching her with sad eyes. They too showed signs of long nights and lack of hope. Without them, Kirheen would have been lost in that place, locked in an eternal struggle against...a lie. She shuddered at the thought, wrapping her arms around her knees.

Tomias reached out a hand and placed it gently on her arm. It was strange how reassuring his touch could be at times like these. "Kir, I know this is a lot to take in. Are you alright," he asked, leaning forward. She looked into his eyes and as much as she tried to hide it, she knew he saw the truth. She was crumbling, breaking away under the weight of reality. It was too much. Tears stung her eyes and he slid closer, nudging her legs out of the way so he could pull her close. "I'm sorry," he whispered against her hair. "I'm so sorry. Please forgive me. If I had known…"

"This is all because of me. I was so stupid and now… now Ian is dead," she cried, clutching tightly to his robes. "What is going to happen to us? What are we going to do?"

Tomias sighed. "Nyson wants you on the Council. I can only piece together so much but he wants to use us as fodder against an outside enemy, a *real* enemy. The Darkness might not be real but in his head the threat is just as bad. Kirheen, if I let this truth come out, I'm putting all of our lives at stake. But I also can't sit by and just let this play out. He's dangling your lives from a string and I won't let him do that to my students. I think our only option is to flee from here."

Kirheen pulled back away from him, drying her eyes with her sleeve. The thought never crossed her mind that they might just run from this. It didn't seem like a possibility. There was too much at stake and so little they knew. The Darkness might not be real but there was still danger out in the beyond. "Flee? Where would we go? We don't exactly know what's out there!"

"I don't know, Kirheen. I'm not even sure it's safe for us out there. If Sanctuary was founded because our kind was in danger than there is no telling what is beyond those mountains. We'd be running into the unknown. Unless everyone agreed to leave, this could get chaotic fast."

"Not everyone would agree to leave, even if they knew. You know that. Not just that, but there has to be others loyal to Nyson!"

"I know, I know. That's the problem. It would become a power struggle and it would be the students caught in the middle. Nothing about this is going to be easy. If we could slip out a few people without tipping off Nyson, we could find out what is beyond and maybe we could get help. If we all try to leave, this is going to turn into a battle and one I'm not sure we've enough numbers on our side to win."

"But who would go? How can we possibly make that choice?"

He frowned, his lips cinched together as if he were afraid of the words that might come out. Kirheen tried to meet his gaze but his eyes drifted to the bed. Was it guilt she saw on his face? Hesitation? Trista stepped to the edge of the bed, expression dour. "Right now, only you and Garild know about this and as such, you're at risk. If we can sneak you out of here, Nyson will have no choice but to claim you were both sent away. If he told everyone the truth about your whereabouts, he'd be exposing the lie for what it is and he won't do that. He's worked much too hard to let that slip over two students."

She felt her jaw drop before the pain of those words registered. She glanced between Tomias and Trista hoping desperately that one of them would save her from the whirlpool of emotions she was being sucked down into. "No..."

"Kirheen..."

"No! You can't just send me away! I can't leave like this. This was all my fault and I need to help fix it!"

Trista threw her hands up. "What choice do we have? You want to risk starting a damned war with Nyson? Is that what you want? Think of how many casualties there will be if that happens. We don't have the numbers on our side, Kirheen. We pick this fight and we all lose. At least if you flee there may be a chance."

"This can't be the only way. Tomias, tell me there is another way!"

He raised his eyes to look at her, a flicker of sadness flashing through them like a spark. It disappeared as quickly as it came and his demeanor changed. His jaw was rigid, his eyes flat. "There isn't. We have to get you both out of here. If it means keeping you both safe, then we're willing to play along with Nyson. We're willing to make that sacrifice. Now you need to do the same."

She felt like she'd been punched. This was her mentor, her friend. He was asking her to leave them all behind, to leave them there while she went off in search of help that might not exist. "You can't ask me to do this. I can't just leave everyone...I can't leave without...without you."

His hardened expression melted, revealing the conflicting emotions beneath. "You can and you will, Kirheen. I need you to do this for me. For all of us. We're living under the thumb of a mad man. If someone learns of this on the outside, maybe they'll help. Please do this for me..."

She didn't think she could feel any more pain, but there it was. She hugged herself, trying to keep from falling apart. With a shaky breath, she gave her answer. "I'll do my part. Does Garild know what you intend to do? Does he know?" She hadn't seen Garild since the celebration and she wasn't entirely sure she wanted to. Her actions had probably devastated his entire world. He'd be angry. As much as she wanted to shy away from it, she needed to face that anger and try to apologize. It might not fix anything but if she could patch his heart, even a little, she would.

The mention of his name brought a concerned expression to every face in the room. Tomias looked briefly at the window, at the slants of light pouring through and filling the room with a warm glow. Trista followed his gaze and her eyes went wide. "The trial!"

Fenir was already moving towards the other room. He returned a moment later, shaking his head.

"Damn it," Tomias spat, standing from the bed.

"What is going on," Kirheen choked.

Tomias rubbed at his forehead. "The trial for Garild and Isa is supposed to happen this morning. Supposed to be happening now! For all I know, they could already be there. We've no time to plan. Trista, get the supplies together as we discussed. Kirheen, Fenir, we're going to have to get Garild out of there."

"Won't this start the very conflict we were trying to avoid?"

"Yes, damn it! Unless someone has something really clever, I don't think we're getting out of this one peacefully. Come on, we need to move."

Days spent sitting in bed had taken their toll on Kirheen. Too quick a movement and pain would shoot through her skull and her eyes would grow fuzzy. Her muscles ached and her lungs burned as she tried to keep pace with the long strides of her mentors. There was no time for rest, no time to stop and catch her breath. Despite her discomfort, she was driven by a need to protect. She'd save Garild. She owed him that much. She just hoped they weren't too late.

At the edge of the Temple of Trials, they stopped, all three feeling a strange excess of power in the air around them. It made her hair stand on end. "What is that?"

Fenir grunted. "I don't like this."

"We need to get him out, now," Tomias demanded, approaching the steps with confident strides. Kirheen stayed on his heels, trying to scramble together enough focus to be of any use if it came down to a fight. Tomias flung the doors open and they launched into the room.

It was a strange sight. In the center of the room, Garild and Isa stood rigid, as if they'd both frozen mid step. The only movement came from Herzin and she stood in front of Garild, her hands pressed to either side of his face. At the sound of the door, she looked over, green eyes blazing.

Kirheen didn't even hesitate. She knew the damage Herzin could cause and she wasn't about to let Garild be her next victim. Prepared for the mental anguish that would follow, she flung out a blast of power, hammering it against Herzin's mind with as much force as she could muster. The blast hit home, sending her staggering back away from Garild.

The backlash was immense and it forced Kirheen to her knees. Her body and mind weren't prepared to handle that much power. She was still too weak. Fenir stepped to her side, reaching down and pulling her to her feet with little effort. He reached into the pocket of his robe and drew out a vial filled with a fiery red liquid.

Tomias looked alarmed. "Is that what I think---" He didn't have time to finish. The vial was chucked across the room where it landed near Nyson. There was a high pitched whistling and then the vial exploded, sending plumes of red smoke to every corner of the room. The temple became a foggy dream world, her vision painted red by the smoke in the air. All sense of direction was lost and she would have stumbled if it weren't for Fenir still holding onto her sleeve. He tugged her back towards what she hoped was the exit, tendrils of red smoke curling around them like a cloak.

There was shouting behind her and then she was pulled out into the daylight, coughing and wheezing as she went. Tomias flew out of the red cloud a moment later, hauling Garild along with him. "Go, go, go!"

They continued running until they were out of sight and then Fenir pulled them into the trees. Then and only then did they slow their pace. All of them were breathing hard, the strange red cloud having filled their lungs with its potency.

"We don't have much time," Tomias said, bent over with his hands on his knees. "Garild, are you alright?"

Garild looked stricken by fear, his face pale and eyes distant. He took a moment to gather himself. "I'm...I'm alright. But...Herzin... she did something in there, something to Isa. We were never going to the work camps of our own free will. She was just going to break our minds and make us slaves."

Tomias and Fenir exchanged a glance. "What are you talking about, Garild?"

"She said she was just going to help us, to shut off our minds for a while so we could recover. All she did was touch Isa and it was like she sucked the life out of her, made her just like the workers. No, Allseer, they can't all be that way..."

"They are all that way and I'm a fool for not seeing it sooner. Allseer, damn them both. This is unforgiveable! She's been unbinding them and a second later and you would have joined them."

There was a familiarity to that word, a question she'd tucked away and forgotten about long ago. Hearing it again brought it back to the forefront of her mind. "You mentioned that before, back when Herzin attacked me. What is it?"

Tomias glanced through the trees nervously. "Listen, unbinding is normally something naturally occurring. It's a breaking of the mind often caused by severe stress or damage. It doesn't kill you but it leaves you as good as dead. When Herzin attacked you, I always thought it was just the force of the attack that nearly did you in. I never thought..."

"She is doing this...unbinding intentionally?"

"She *can* do it intentionally which is precisely the problem! I don't know how, but she's been breaking their minds and I can only assume it's so they are easier to control. Can't exactly have a rebellion if half your subjects can't even think for themselves."

There was a shout from far away. It carried through the trees, reverberating off the glowing behemoths like icy warnings. "We're out of time. I can only hope Trista has your things together. We're going to need help now more than ever."

"You can't seriously still think this is a good idea! If Herzin is really doing this then we all need to escape!"

Tomias shook his head. "And what of all those people who've already been broken? How do you intend to take them with us? I refuse to leave them behind. We can't do this alone, Kir. We can't. Now you both need to go. We'll hold them off as long we can, but you won't get much of a head start."

Kirheen didn't like the tone of his voice. There was a sense of finality in his gaze, in the rigid set of his jaw. She could have sworn she heard his heart shatter as they made eye contact. It was a wordless goodbye, silent and dreadful.

"Tomias, you can't…"

"Take care of each other," he said and then he turned, Fenir on his heels. They crashed through the underbrush, rushing off in the opposite direction to lure away those pursuing them. They were buying them time and even though it broke her heart to even think about it, she couldn't let their sacrifice be in vain.

We'll come back for you…

Kirheen turned, urging Garild to keep running. The activity of the morning was starting to catch up with her but she couldn't bring herself to slow down, not with so much at stake. She slowed near Trista's hut, approaching from the back so they wouldn't be seen off the main trail. She pounded lightly on the back window, hoping the only recipient of the noise would be Trista herself.

Trista appeared around the corner a moment later, carrying two overly full packs. She glanced between them. "Where are Tomias and Fenir," she all but demanded.

"They stayed behind to buy us some time," Kirheen explained, feeling a wave of guilt. If anything happened to them, it would be on her head and she knew Trista would never forgive her. Truth be told, she'd probably never forgive herself. Trista nodded sadly, giving one of the bags to Kirheen and one to Garild. She'd sewn straps onto each bag, to make it easier to carry.

"I stuffed what I could in there. There are some basic medical supplies, blankets, extra clothing, water and food. There isn't much there, so make it last as long as you can." She remained stoic as she prattled off her list. When she was done, her eyes became glossy and she leapt forward, giving Kirheen a quick, motherly hug. "You two stay safe. Whatever you do, whatever you find out there, stay together. Now go!"

She gave Garild a quick hug, pressing her lips close to his ear to whisper something Kirheen couldn't hear. She shooed them off into the trees, pushing against their packs to get them started and then they were off, bolting through the trees with the wind whipping through their hair.

Kirheen didn't look back, didn't glance over her shoulder. She couldn't afford to let herself think it might be the last time she ever saw home. There was too much at stake, too many people depending on their success. She wouldn't fail them.

Chapter 26

The sun was making its slow descent in the sky when Kirheen called for them to stop. She could no longer keep up the pace they'd set, her body too fatigued to keep pushing through underbrush and weaving around trees. She was terribly thirsty, her lips dry and cracking, every muscle protesting the stop as much as it had the running. Sinking to the ground, she tried to stay alert and listen for any sounds of pursuit but the only thing she could hear was the rush of her blood flowing through her veins.

Satisfied that they were at least momentarily safe, she dug into the pack Trista had given her. Just as she'd promised, there was a bundle of basic supplies, hastily gathered and thrown in a heap at the bottom. She picked through it, sighing with relief when her fingers wrapped around a liquid filled jug. The stopper came loose with a pop and she took a cautious sip, feeling the weight of the jug lighten. There was so little there and no way to know how long their journey would take. The thought of running out of water terrified her.

As for food, there was a pack of dried meats and a few wraith blossom cakes, kept safe in a small container Trista had tucked them in. She picked at one of them, hoping the restorative quality of the wraith blossom would help ease her fatigue. Garild ate too, chewing slowly on a piece of meat. She could feel his gaze wander over her from time to time. When he turned back to his food she lifted her head, allowing herself to take in his appearance for the first time since they'd fled. He was a mess. Her eyes followed the curve of his cheek and down to the frown of his lips. When his brown eyes rose to meet hers, she quickly looked away.

When they were done eating and the food and water was packed, he spoke.

"Thank you," he mumbled.

"For what?"

"For saving me. A second more and I would...I would have been nothing."

He'd almost been unbound, his mind stripped from him. It didn't entirely make sense to her. She didn't understand how it worked and even worse, had no way to defend against it.   "What exactly did she do?"

He shook his head, obviously dreading the memory that came with the retelling. "I don't know. She just reached out, touched Isa and suddenly it was like she was a different person. Everything about her was...gone. I can't explain it. It was as if she sucked out her soul..."

Kirheen frowned. "I'm glad we made it in time. Garild, I'm so sorry, I –"

He held up a hand, cutting her off. "I don't want to hear it right now. Please. We can talk about all of this later. Let's just keep moving."

She'd been wanting to apologize, to try and make things right. The rejection hurt and for the next few hours, she spoke little. With no sense of what lay ahead, gauging their progress was impossible. The scenery changed little as they made their way, nothing but an endless expanse of wraith wood trees and thick underbrush. It would be an easy place to get lost and she had little desire to do so. She kept watch of the sun through the trees overhead, keeping track of the direction it sank in the sky.

As the sky darkened, fear crept into her heart and questions began to plague her mind. What if they ran out of food? Water? What would they do? For all she knew, nothing lay beyond but more forest. She'd never been put in a position like this before. She didn't know how to hunt. She was suddenly very grateful for the little interest she'd shown in Trista's books. Picking out edible plants wouldn't be too much of a problem, but if they didn't encounter enough...

Hunger. Starvation. Exhaustion. Thirst. Death.

She tried to shake the thought but it clung to the back of her mind, scratching at the surface. There had to be something out there. If there wasn't, their entire mission would be for naught. They walked as long as they could by the light of the trees, but once darkness had fully descended, it was too easy to get turned around. They found a nook tucked away in the roots of a wraith wood tree and it was there that they camped for the night.

Despite the obvious indifference Garild showed her, they slept close together that night, both afraid and unsure of the darkness around them. Neither slept well, the unfamiliar sounds of the forest lending itself to paranoia. Kirheen longed for conversation, but there was none to be found from Garild. Her companion stayed quiet, mulling over his thoughts. Kirheen did the same.

This had been all her fault. Everyone would be hurt, *had* been hurt because of her actions. She had been selfish and foolish and it had cost Ian and Isa their lives. She felt a burning shame, a wound that festered and throbbed the more she thought of it. There was no choice left. She had to make things right or everyone she knew and cared for would disappear. And without them, would life even be worth living?

The morning was overcast and cool, the sky plump with gray clouds. Rain was the last thing she wanted. With little shelter to speak of, the thought of running in wet clothes was enough to make her grimace. Garilds mood had grown as gloomy as the sky above them. He focused on the task ahead, barely sparing her a glance. They ate and drank in silence, the void between them growing.

Eventually it became too much and she lurched to a stop. Garild looked back at her, annoyed that they were stopping again. Kirheen took a moment to catch her breath and readied herself for the words she had to speak. She looked at her bond mate. The stress of the past few days seemed to have aged him. His eyes were bloodshot and weepy, his skin dirt streaked. His brown hair was messy and caked to skin now tinged pink from the constant exposure to the sun. Flat eyes, lips tight, brows knitted in frustration.

Kirheen took a deep breath and then willed herself to speak. "Garild, I'm sorry."

Garild frowned. "Kirheen, I told you I didn't want to hear it. I still don't."

"I know you don't want to! I know you are angry! You've every right to be. But right now, I can't handle all of this coming from you. I just need you to talk, to speak to me. I need something to fill my head other than all of this guilt. I need my friend!"

His expression shifted from one of indifference to one of anger. "You want me to drown out your guilt? Would that make things better? You brought this upon all of us. Isa and Ian are dead because of you. And guess what? Our instructors are probably next and they'll be dead too! All of Sanctuary is paying for your mess all because I wasn't good enough for you!"

The words hit like a slap to the face, triggering her anger. She was furious, her blood boiling. "How can you say that? Garild, none of that matters now! It was all a lie! Everything! Our Bond is a lie! The Darkness is a lie! I made a mistake, Garild. I did. I can't exactly just go back and change things, can I? Right now, I am trying to make this right. I can't keep up a charade knowing that everything around me isn't real. I need to find out what is real though and right now I know that despite everything that has happened, I still count you as my friend, a friend I very desperately need right now."

Garild looked hurt. "It was never just a lie for me, Kirheen. It never was. This was my life and despite the fact that it was a lie, this life wasn't horrible. Here we are, running through a forest with no idea what we'll find. There may be nothing out there and this will all be pointless. Or maybe we'll find someone but how are we supposed to get anyone to help us? You've taken everything from me, Kirheen. Everything I loved and wanted, you've stripped it away. I can't just forgive you for that. I'll help you fix this Kirheen because I owe you my life, but I can't be your friend. Don't expect that of me right now. I can't do it."

Kirheen slumped, her shoulders drooping, eyes casting down to the forest floor. She turned away from him silent and broken and continued walking. She wanted so badly to cry but found herself far too tired to let it happen. She felt more alone than she ever had. There was nobody there to console her, nobody to tell her it would all be okay. She wished more than anything that Tomias was walking beside her. He'd tell her it would be okay and right then she needed the lie.

Misery and guilt plagued her sleep. The days wore on and her thoughts were all consuming. The sun rose and fell, a cycle with no end. Food rations grew thin and each day she grew hungrier, eating less and less until there was nothing to eat except for what she could forage. Water was refilled once at a small stream they passed, but even that was downed fast, leaving them with little to keep them going. The forest seemed to stretch on forever, though there were subtle changes to the landscape. The ground, once a dense green underbrush, had thinned. It was more rocky and uneven here and the trees seemed to have grown further apart, becoming sparser.

Eventually, the wraith wood trees were joined by a variety of others that Kirheen had never seen. One tree in particular had smooth bark and towered above them, broad leaves green and lush. There were skinny trees with speckled bark and large coned shaped trees with strange needles. Kirheen found herself avoiding these ones, finding the needles painful to run into.

The days grew warmer and their progress seemed to slow, the humidity sapping them of their strength and desire to travel. They rested for a time in the shade, sipping at their water. Garild twisted a stick into the ground angrily, making a hole as he did.

"You okay," Kirheen asked. She tried to push her anger aside and instead focus on their survival, on keeping them in check both mentally and physically. It was the least she could do.

He didn't raise his eyes, just kept on looking at the hole he was creating in the ground. "This is how it's going to end, isn't it? Here in this stupid forest..."

Kirheen didn't want to think about it. They were out of food and the water was almost gone. A few more days of this and they wouldn't have the energy or strength to travel. They'd wither away and die, their bodies picked apart by wild animals, their bones lost and forgotten until they became dust. "I don't know, Garild. We've got to be near something."

"You don't know that."

"I don't... I just..."

Garild scoffed, throwing the stick down in front of him. He stood up, stalking a few paces away into the woods, his posture stiff and rigid.

"Where are you going," Kirheen asked, concerned.

"Nowhere," he yelled angrily. "There isn't anywhere to go! We're stuck here, Kirheen! We're just going to die in the woods. Are you happy now?"

"You know what," she said angrily, rising to her feet. All promises of keeping her anger in check went up like a match. She marched into the woods after him, cracking the stick he'd thrown on the ground with a loud snap. "I've had about enough of your attitude! You don't think I hurt too? You don't think I feel defeated? I do, Garild! I know you're mad but this isn't helping!"

"Nothing is going to help! There..is...nothing...out...here," he yelled at her, throwing his arms out to the side. He stepped back, his foot catching on a tree root. It sent him stumbling and he tumbled back on the ground. There was an audible hiss, a flash of movement and Garild yelped, pushing himself up and away from the spot he'd been as fast as he could. Something low to the ground slithered away hurriedly.

Garild held his hand up high, frantically eyeing the ground around his feet. Kirheen looked up in alarm. There was blood running down the side of his hand and she rushed forward, pulling his hand towards her. There were two small puncture wounds near his pinky and blood oozed from them. The skin around the marks was already swelling and the skin was red and hot.

"Are you alright," she asked, still holding his hand.

He pulled away from her, tucking his hand firmly against his chest. "I'm fine," he said, but his pain could be seen in the set of his jaw, the quick frantic movement of his eyes. Kirheen had read about snakes, had even seen one a time or two. She knew that many of them were completely harmless, but a select few carried powerful venom that moved through the body, causing all sorts of foul side effects in a human. Whether there was venom now coursing through his veins was yet to be seen, but Kirheen knew they'd know soon enough.

If his reaction to it was bad enough, they'd need an herbalist. Kirheen swept her gaze over the surrounding forest, suddenly feeling very helpless. If something happened to Garild, if he succumbed to poison on her foolish mission to get them help, she'd never be able to live with herself.

Garild walked ahead of her, still bristling with anger. She followed him, quiet as a mouse. She didn't want to rouse his anger any more, didn't want his venom infested blood quickened. A few miles further and Kirheen could see sweat rising on his neck, could see his movements slow and waver. She crept to his side, offered her arm and he refused it with a shake of his head.

"Garild, please. You're looking terrible. Let me see your hand," she pleaded, trying to get him to cooperate. He winced as she darted her hand forward. His skin was so hot it almost startled her out of her grip and she gasped, turning his hand over so she could get a better look. His fingers were swollen, far beyond anything she'd ever seen. The edge of the bite marks were crusty and red and a cloudy liquid oozed from them at her touch. He was clammy, skin and robes slick with sweat. When she raised her eyes, he looked away, expression one of shame and pain. "Garild, this...this isn't good."

"I know," he whispered. "We can't stop though. We need to keep going."

"We're stopping for just a few moments," she said, her tone halting any further argument. She swung the pack from her shoulder, following it to the ground. She dug through, finding the small amount of medical supplies Trista had packed. Her hope had been that they wouldn't need them. It pained her to be wrong. She cleaned the wound as best she could, slathering some foul smelling green paste over the bites. She wrapped it in clean cloth, gently tying it so not to hurt him. Part of her knew it was going to do little for him. Without proper treatment, it could be hours or days before he succumbed to the poison.

They set off again, setting a slower pace than before. Neither of them wanted to slow down, but in the state Garild was in, there wasn't much else to be done. The ground grew even rockier and they found themselves wobbling over giant boulders, each step more precarious than the last. Kirheen watched Garild closely, afraid that a misstep would send him to the ground and cause further injury.

Towards the evening, hunger set in. Kirheen felt sick, her stomach a roiling pit of acid. With little to settle it, she had no choice but to try and ignore the feeling. Garild seemed to be having an easier time ignoring his hunger, his mind completely absorbed by the symptoms he was experiencing from the bite. As darkness overtook them, they chose the only flat spot they could find, setting down their packs and laying down to sleep.

Despite the heat, Garild shivered the entire night, his teeth chittering loudly. Even after she'd piled her blanket on top of his, he continued to shake. Kirheen couldn't sleep through the unknown and she stayed by his side, brushing his damp hair out of his face with soft strokes. Every now and then, she'd help him down some water and he drank greedily, as if it was the last water he'd ever have.

Come morning, Kirheen roused him from his slumber. His fever had eased in the middle of the night, but his hand was still incredibly swollen and the skin around the wound had started to take on a shade of gray terrifyingly devoid of life.

As he cracked open his eyes, he searched for the bottle of water with his good hand, patting at the blanket covering him trying to find it. There was only one good swig left and Kirheen almost didn't give it to him. With a sigh, she handed him the last of their water and said a small prayer as he finished it off. Whether the Allseer was real or not, she was the only thing that would see them through this. It would take a miracle for them to survive more than a few days. Without water, all hope was lost.

Kirheen packed up their things and helped Garild to his feet. He was wobbly and unsure of his footing. "I'm sorry," he said softly. "I'm really dizzy."

"I know," Kirheen said. "I'll help you walk, okay? Just stay close to me."

Whatever fight had been left in him had fled during the night. He struggled with his pack for a moment and then they set off. He leaned against Kirheen as he walked, but his steps were slow and sluggish and by noon, he was putting so much pressure on her shoulder that they had to stop. She helped him to the ground to rest.

He sank back against the rock behind him, nursing his injured hand against his chest. His forehead was once again covered in sweat and his breathing was abnormal, each breath too long and ragged. After a time, he raised his head, seeking her eyes with his. For a moment he said nothing, watching her with an expression that spoke of the pain and defeat he felt.

"Kirheen, I don't think I can go much further," he said.

Something about the verbal confirmation of what she already knew filled her with dread. Her eyes filled with tears and she nodded her head, unable to speak. It took her a moment to recover and she hid her face in the meantime, trying to keep Garild from seeing the fear in her eyes.

Wiping away the tears, she took a great shuddering breath and rose. "Can you try to make it just a little further?"

Garild grimaced. "I'll try."

He allowed her to help him back to his feet. Kirheen took both packs, struggling to balance them both and also help him walk. It took a few moments to get settled before they could walk more than a few steps at a time. They pressed on through the day, though their previous pace was abandoned for one much slower. The ground continued to grow uneven and it was a terrifying experience keeping Garild steady through it all.

As the sun fell in the sky once more, Garild took a turn for the worst. Mid step, he stopped and turned away from her quickly, heaving what little was in his stomach onto the rocks next to him. He dry heaved for several moments, struggling to breath as his stomach spasmed. When he recovered, Kirheen cleaned his face with one of her tattered robes and helped him back up. "I can't go on," he cried into her shoulder, his weight now a familiar and reassuring burden.

"Just a little further," she coaxed. "Please, just a little further."

She knew it was hopeless, knew that she'd soon find herself alone. Without Garild, there was nothing left for her to do but slowly wither away. Hunger and thirst would do away with her and she'd soon join Garild, bonded in death as they had been in life.

The sky blazed in a fiery reign of orange and yellow. She could see the clouds clearly now, the trees now so sparse that their surroundings were clear. A mountain rose before them, rocky and barren. The sight filled Kirheen with defeat. Even without Garild,

Kirheen had so little energy left. There would be no possible way
for her to make it over the mountain.

A few more steps and Garild crashed to his knees, yanking
her down with him. She stumbled as she was pulled and scraped her
knees on the rocks beneath her. Gritting her teeth, she recovered,
trying to keep Garild level as she did so. She unhooked his arm
from around her shoulder and lowered him down. He shook
uncontrollably, his face a mask of tormented pain.

"Garild, come on. Are you okay?"

He sunk down in the rocks without a reply, shivering as if it
were snow bearing down on him and not the heat of the sun. He
burned with fever; she could feel the heat radiating from his skin as
if it were alive with fire. She pulled at his arm, trying to get him
back on his feet but he couldn't move. This was it, the moment that
she had been dreading. The venom had done its job and now she'd
be left alone.

She tried to get him back on his feet, pulling his arm
roughly. He groaned loudly, his arm heavy and useless. She
dropped it in defeat, sinking down next to him. Hunger and defeat
ate at her like worms on a corpse and there next to the friend she'd
betrayed, the friend that lay dying because of her, she cried.

Great sobs wracked at her body, her shoulders shuddering
with the force of her cries. She didn't want this, didn't want the
death of her friend or the death of Ian on her hands. There was
nothing more she desired than to return to the way things had been
before.

Anger quickly replaced her grief and she stood, racing across the rocks towards the slope of the mountain. She picked up a rock as she went, throwing it into the distance with all the strength she could muster. The rock crashed against others, the sound echoing loudly in her ears.

She took one step too far and the ground took a sudden dive. She rolled forward, sliding down the slope in a flurry of robes and dust and pebbles. She earned a few new scrapes and nearly broke her finger on a rock as she fell. It throbbed angrily. She may have paid it more attention if it weren't for the great stone face staring down at her.

It was a great round piece of stone, the edges smooth. It had been delicately carved with the face of a woman, her hair billowing around her in thin, wispy tendrils. Her smooth cheeks were puffed, her lips forming an 'O' as if she were blowing the very wind through the trees.

Blue glowing eyes, staring into her soul. There was a familiar feeling, a searching, tendrils prodding the walls of her mind. A voice spoke then, low and soft and feminine.

"Ah, a visitor. It has been so long since your kind has ventured through my halls. You are of the mind…If I'm not mistaken?"

Kirheen blinked, trying to clear her mind. Surely she'd hit her head on the way down. The statue didn't move but where else could a voice be coming from? She staggered to her feet, dusting off her robes.

"Fear not, your head is intact. Perhaps an introduction will still your trembling, girl. I am Akra, guardian of the Whispering Woods. Only those with the power of the mind are free to wander this place."

"What do you mean this place," Kirheen asked aloud, feeling foolish.

"The caves behind my face, they whisper secrets...so many secrets."

"Where do the caves lead? Do they go beyond the mountain?"

"They lead to the land beyond, but that place is dark and corrupt. Hunted you are and many more like you...swaying with the breeze. Picked apart."

The face wasn't making sense to Kirheen but neither was the situation she now found herself facing. Perhaps thirst and hunger had driven her mad.

"The main chamber is open to you, child. What lies beyond, only your mind can say."

There was a scraping of stone on stone, a jagged crunch that shook through her bones. The great circular slab of rock rolled aside and a blast of cool, damp air blasted her face from the cave beyond. She could taste water on her lips, could feel it in the breeze that carried past her. She stepped into a cool, misty cave alive with sparks of blue light. The room was large, stretching far and wide.

Up on a ledge, the massive tangled roots of a wraith wood tree could be seen. They curled and twisted about the room, lending a soft glowing light that scrapped at the darkness. The rest of the tree, the biggest she'd ever seen, broke through the roof of the cave. Where it went, she'd probably never know, but she could only imagine it stretched far and wide through the mountainside.

The sensation of moisture in the air and on her skin grew stronger. Stepping further into the room, she gasped. Beneath the ledge that housed the great tree, water trickled from the cave walls, forming a large circular pool at its base. The water was cool and fresh and churned and swirled, blue and clean and crisp. Her feet carried her faster than she could believe and a moment later she was on her knees before the water, dipping her hands in and splashing her face with wild abandon.

The water kissed her skin, washing away the dirt of travel, easing the pain of scrapes and bruises. Her parched lips lavished in the feel of it as she brought a cupped handful of water to her lips. She didn't think she'd felt anything so wonderful. She lay for a time next to the pool, her hand in the water. She was lost in her discovery, lost in the blue twinkling lights of the cave, the gentle glow of the tree.

Her thoughts drifted back to reality, to what lay back outside the cave. Feeling renewed, she rose from the cave floor and ventured back out. Darkness would overtake the world soon and Kirheen had to somehow get Garild inside before that happened. She rushed back to where she'd left him and her heart sank when she found him. He had pushed himself up to a sitting position in her absence. One of the empty water containers lay close to his open hand. His eyes were closed, his expression troubled, chin tucked against his chest.

Kirheen ran forward, chest tight with fear. She bent down next to him, reached a hand towards his face. She quivered, her fingers shaking as they touched him. He lurched awake, grabbing her wrist with his good hand. Gasping with fright, the realization dawned on her that he was still alive. It was a slight thing, he looked awful, but he was alive. She didn't know whether to laugh or cry and the sound that came out was a mix of both. She choked and sputtered and wrapped her arms around his neck. He protested, trying to push her away with his good hand.

When she released her grip, Garild was looking at her with bleary eyes. "What happened," he coughed, keeping his injured hand close to his chest.

"I found something," Kirheen said with a bright smile. "You just need to make it a little further."

Garild looked pained but he allowed Kirheen to help him to his feet. She gathered up their packs, making sure to retrieve the empty water jug. Stars twinkled overhead as they made their way over the rocky terrain, using the fading light of the sky to help guide them. When they made it to the entrance of the cave, Garild perked up. Just as Kirheen had, he could sense the water and it awoke a primal thirst.

She guided him to edge of the pool, helped him down to his knees before it. He cried out with surprise as his fingers found the cool edge of the water, and then he cried in earnest when he brought that water to his lips. He drank and kept drinking until Kirheen raised a hand to stop him. Water dripped from his chin and for the first time since she'd betrayed him, he smiled.

Chapter 27

They slept that night in the cave, the sound of trickling water lulling them to sleep. Hunger was still on their minds, but the water had satiated them for the time being. They slept soundly, momentarily protected from the elements in their blue sanctuary.

Kirheen woke first, feeling refreshed for the first time in days. She was hungry, but she filled herself with water, trying to push the need for food to the back of her mind. The darkness of the room seemed more absolute, the bright sparks of blue looking like stars on a night sky. She peered towards the entrance of the cave, fighting down a wave of panic as she realized the stone face had rolled back to its original position, blocking them from leaving. The only way through was to keep moving through the cave.

She roused Garild from his sleep. He awoke slowly, his eyes following the blue specks of light hovering around him.

"How are you feeling," she asked.

"I'm okay. My hand is numb but I'm feeling a bit better. I think I'll be okay."

He drank water from the pool, scooping the water to his lips with his good hand. He seemed more alert, the effects of the venom having subsided for the time being. She hoped it meant an improvement in his condition. She didn't want to be left alone in this.

Kirheen walked the edge of the cave, searching for another path that would take them through. She found one on the left corner of the room, a small, jagged pathway in the wall that was small enough that they'd have to side step their way through. She gathered up their packs, keeping a hold of both so Garild wouldn't have the burden of the weight.

"I'm okay," he protested, reaching for one of the packs.

"Let's not chance it, Garild," Kirheen said firmly, swinging away from him so he couldn't grab the pack. He opened his mouth but shut it abruptly, choosing instead to narrow his eyes. Kirheen led him to the path she'd found and slung the packs off her back, holding one to either side as she side stepped through the narrow pass. The craggy surface of the cave walls scratched at her skin and clothing but she was through a moment later.

The next room was darker than the one before and Kirheen had to squint to make out the surroundings. The walls were slick with moisture and they glistened in the sporadic blue light. Roots of the great wraith wood tree could be seen weaving through the floor to their right, the soft glow lending a bit of sight to the otherwise dark cave. There was a deeper spot of darkness in the far corner of room, a place where the light seemed to be devoured. Kirheen led Garild towards it, carefully stepping over rocks and roots alike.

Another narrow passage led them to an even darker part of the cave, one filled with a strange buzzing. It was a low, steady sound and soon Kirheen found it plucking at her nerves, driving irritation up from her pool of stifled emotions.

"Allseer, what is that sound," Garild said, his hands rising to cover his ears.

"I don't know," Kirheen said. "I don't think I want to know. Let's try to find the next room."

It was a struggle to see her surroundings. The glow of the tree wasn't there to guide them and the steady hum of the noise echoing off the walls was distracting. She couldn't get a sense of direction without the sounds around her. She felt along the wall to her left, letting her fingers touch the surface of the cave. Walking forward slowly, she stepped out, feeling with her feet and hands to find where they needed to go. Garild remained behind her, pacing back and forth as he tried to ignore that all-consuming humming.

A few more paces and her fingers slid into something sticky. She pulled her hand away with a gasp, shaking it to get rid of whatever foul substance clung to it. She couldn't make out what it was and the humming continued to fill her head, continued to pick at her nerves, skeletal fingers strumming on the strings of her sanity.

She rubbed the goo onto her robe, not bothering to care about the state of it. It was filthy anyways and she could only reason that something else added to it wasn't going to do much to harm her appearance. As she moved forward, her eyes kept fluttering to her hand. Her throat tightened, a feeling of dread sweeping through her. And the buzzing… it was a terrible sound. Another step and she stopped and raised her hand in front of her face. The tar like substance was still on her finger tips but it was moving, slowly crawling towards her wrist in twisting black tendrils. It was dark, so terribly dark. Black as night, corrupted. *It doesn't exist.*

"Kirheen," Garild called, but she could barely hear him over the sound reverberating through her skull, through the fog of fear that surrounded her, thick and heavy as a blanket.

It's not real… The Darkness isn't real.

She tried desperately to reign in her fear, to still her nerves, but her thoughts spiraled out from her, scattering into the dark. She swore she could hear them hit the ground, tumbling away from her into the unseen corners of the cave. The Darkness was moving. It was now halfway up her arm and no matter how much she wiped away it kept crawling, like vines taking over a tree. She staggered back in the dark towards Garild.

She could hear him speaking but she couldn't make out his words. Her legs gave out to the fear, driving her to the ground. Garild was at her side a moment later, his hand grabbing her arm. His eyes went wide as his own hand came away dark, dripping with the darkness that had tainted her skin.

"No, no, no, no. This can't be real," he whispered.

His panic ignited hers and they both huddled in the dark, feeling the strange creeping sensation work across their skin. The buzzing grew louder and another sensation entered the fray, a strange prickling in her head. It was a familiar feeling, one she'd felt before, as if someone were trying to break through her mind. Dripping black hands flung aside pieces of her mind, digging through as it searched for the fear, that deep primal fear that made all the hairs stand up on her body.

She squeezed her eyes shut and flung up her defenses, paying no mind to the amount of power she used. Grasping out, she extended her power to shield Garild as well. The buzzing in the room stopped, the ink on their skin shattering away before their eyes.

Kirheen sighed in relief, rolling onto her side and letting the smooth cold stone beneath her cheek calm her. It took several minutes before her heart calmed enough for her to stagger to her feet. She knelt down in the dark, grabbing Garild by the arm and helping him to his feet.

"Allseer what…what was that?"

"There is someone in this cave, Garild. Or maybe something. The door… it talked earlier. It pressed into my mind as if it were alive, as if it had our powers. I thought I was imagining things, but I'm starting to think it was real. It had to be real."

"That…doesn't seem possible," he said.

"I know, but I'm telling you the truth. I don't think we're supposed to be here. Let's move. I want to get out of here as quick as we can." Kirheen shielded herself with her mind, forcing her powers out and over Garild. "I'm going to need your help. This thing isn't going to stop attacking our defenses and we're both too weak to do it alone. Hold on to the packs. I need you close to block out this thing... whatever it is."

She readjusted the packs on her back and waited for Garild to latch on to them. When she felt the weight of his hands and the added resistance in her mind, she crept forward. With little choice, she placed her hand back on the slick surface of the cave, shuddering as her hand touched the wet walls. Though the buzzing had stopped, she could still feel the pressure in her mind, a steady strum of energy forcing itself against their walls.

When her hand found empty space, she nearly fell over into the gap in the wall. She recovered quickly, steadying herself so she wouldn't pull Garild down with her. Entering the next part of the cave was like entering a dense fog. There was a power there, something dark and dangerous that made her hair stand on end. The force against her mind strengthened and the buzzing could be heard once again, though not as loud.

She was filled with an intense need to be rid of the cave, to be back in the sunlight, away from the buzzing that threatened to burst through her walls. She hurried forward, stepping as quickly through the dim light of the cave as she could without falling. The last thing she wanted to do was get them killed in her haste.

Her foot struck something hard and she watched a faintly glowing object clatter across the slick surface of the cave. It was long and white and her eyes grew wide with terror as she realized what it was. She reached back, grabbing Garild by the hand and pulling him along quicker.

"What is it," he asked and then his breath left him. There were other bones littered over the cave floor and several whole skeletons could be seen leaning against the cave wall. It was obvious many of them were old, long since cleaned of the flesh that had once covered them.

There were multiple points of pressure in her mind and she reinforced the wall. If that thing got in... she didn't want to think about the results of such an intrusion. She stepped over the bones, shuddering at the thought that they might soon be joining them.

She found the next weaving corridor and pulled them through, ignoring the pain that flared up as the cave wall scraped her face. She caught a flash of movement from her right and flung herself forward, breaking her grasp from Garild just as a man dove through the space where she'd been standing.

As the man turned back around, she could see how terrifyingly thin he was. The dirt streaked clothing that clung to his bony frame was tattered and stained. His cheeks were gaunt and covered in long, thin scratches, the bones protruding out with more emphasis than they should. She could see madness in his eyes, an urgent violence that flung itself against her senses. He gave a sickening smile, showing a row of blackened teeth, a few of which were broken or missing entirely.

He let loose a sound that wasn't entirely human and flung himself at Kirheen. The weight of the packs kept her from keeping her footing on the slick surface and she was pulled down to the ground by the man. The ground behind them must have sloped because before she knew it, she was rolling down an embankment, the fingers of her captor digging painfully into her arms as they fell. She landed on her back, the contents of the pack poking against her spine. Her breath left her in a rush and she gasped for air, though each attempt sent shooting pain through her sides. The man was above her and he quickly found her hands, pinning them at her side. His face was inches from her own, his foul breath filling the air around her.

"You can't get out," he laughed. "The buzzing will keep you here. You can't leave. You can't. You're trapped. Stay. Stay. Stay here with us."

"Get…off…me," she struggled. Despite the look of him, he was freakishly strong and he kept her pinned easily.

"No! No! The darkness will take us all. The darkness will find us, even here. You can't leave. No. You can't leave. Never. Stay with the buzzing. It'll protect you!"

The fall had shattered her concentration and she could hear the buzzing louder than ever, cutting through her skull like it was butter. The smell of the man's breath, the sound in her ears, it was almost enough to drive her crazy. She pushed hard against him, trying to free herself before he pulled her into madness with him.

As the pressure in her skull grew stronger, the figure above her changed. No longer was the man a stranger. Now it was Tomias, his eyes and teeth dripping with black goo. His white hair was streaked with black and it tickled her face as he leaned close. "Stop struggling, Kir. This is what is meant to happen. This is how it ends."

"No! It isn't real," she screamed, flailing wildly. She could feel her walls begin to crack, could feel the buzzing oozing into every fiber of her being. There was a feeling of fading, of being pulled into a comforting pool of water. She was about to let herself go when there was a loud crack above her. The illusion shattered and the skeletal man slumped to the side, eye wide with surprise.

Garild stood in front of her, hand holding a rock that was now slick with blood. He closed his eyes, stretching his mind out to protect her. The buzzing retreated and she pushed herself up off the ground quickly. Garild dropped the rock and ran to her side, grabbing her hand tightly.

"Are you okay," he asked, brown eyes wide. "Did he hurt you?"

Kirheen shook her head. "I'm okay, Garild." It was a lie. She didn't feel okay and she suspected she wouldn't until they were free of the cave. She regathered her strength and patched up her mind, helping to keep the noise at bay. "We've got to get out of here. Now!"

"Not going to argue that," Garild said.

The slope had led them to the entry way of another room filled with light like the first one they'd entered. Kirheen had thought that first room was welcoming, but the illusion of it had been shattered and she now saw the truth of the cave. Across the room from them, another round door glowed in the far wall. As they approached, Kirheen could make out the same delicately carved face of the first door, the one that had spoken and called itself Akra. As if sensing her thoughts, the eyes began to glow blue.

"Ah, children of the mind. You've survived your trials. I am pleased," the door whispered, and her voice was genuinely excited. Garild looked to Kirheen, his eyebrows high.

"*I told you,*" Kirheen said, keeping her eyes on the door before them. "You seem surprised we made it through."

Akra was silent for a moment. "Many of your kind have passed through my halls unscathed, but there have been those that chose to let go. They've stayed here where it is safe. Protected by the buzzing. As for those unlike you... they've never left this place. They aren't welcome here. Not like you. They are vultures. Hunters. Despicable."

"What do you mean, unlike us?"

Akra scoffed, the sound echoing through the cave. "Empty minds and corrupt hearts. They aren't like you. They cannot feel, cannot hear, cannot see or share. They are empty, empty...Husks. Unworthy of power. You'll find many beyond here. Turn back before they corrupt you too."

Kirheen shook her head. "We're not staying another minute here," she said firmly. "Open the way for us."

"Are you certain? The world is unlike what you've grown accustomed to. The place beyond isn't safe for you. Swinging...picked clean. Hunters. Don't go," Akra sighed, her voice husky and seductive, like that of a lover whispering secrets into her ear.

"Open the door, Akra," Kirheen demanded, trying to keep her resolve. Her words were toying with her mind, killing her desire to flee.

"I warned you," she sighed. The blue glow of her eyes faded and the door rolled to the side with a loud grinding whine. Day light filtered through the cave, forcing them to both squint as they crawled out of the cave. The sun was high in the sky overhead and it was a welcomed change from the chilly air of the cave. As soon as she reached level ground, Kirheen swung the packs from her shoulder and lay down, letting the sun warm her face.

Her ribs ached from her encounter with the mad man, her body covered in scratches and ugly purple and yellow bruises, but at the moment she didn't care. Garild had sunk down next to her and he pulled a pack close, digging through. His face turned into a frown as he did, his hand coming up with a cracked water jug.

He tossed it aside and pulled the other pack to him. Luckily, that jug had survived and he took a few cautious sips of the water before handing it to her. She pushed herself up on her elbows and tipped some water into her mouth. It was refreshing but part of her was disgusted knowing it had come from that cave. She handed it back, unable to stand the thought.

"We'll have to make it last," Kirheen said. "I'm not sure we're going to find any place to refill it." She stood up, hugging her ribs as she did. The land around them was similar to what it had been on the other side, though it was entirely devoid of wraith wood trees. The rocky landscape went on for a time before dipping down into a lush forest that she could see far ahead. "We better get moving while it's still light. Are you feeling okay?"

"Well enough for now," Garild said. "Let's just get away from this place."

Kirheen couldn't have agreed more.

Chapter 28

It came to a point that everything began to look like food to Kirheen. Her stomach rumbled, her legs sluggishly carrying her body forward as she watched the world around her with hungry eyes. She couldn't remember how long it had been since they'd left the cave. They'd found water in a stream, a stream they now followed, but food wasn't readily available. It wasn't as if they could hunt and every squirrel that passed she had to watch scamper off with drool pooling in her mouth.

Garild was faring even worse. His condition combined with a lack of food had left him exhausted and fevered. They stopped often, giving Garild a chance to catch his breath before setting off. His hand was looking worse by the day, the skin colorless and peeling away from the bites. She'd tried to clean it, but it didn't seem to help.

When Kirheen saw a wooden structure far in the distance, she had to stop herself from running towards it. Surely hunger had driven her to imagine it and thinking so, she raised her hands to her eyes and rubbed at them. When she lowered them again, her heart began to hammer in her chest. There was something there and just slightly beyond it she could barely make out the tops of other houses. She reached over and tugged on Garild's sleeve.

"Do you see that," she asked, pointing in the direction of the structure.

Garild squinted. A moment later his eyes went wide and his jaw dropped. "Is that…"

"A village."

"I don't…Have we…"

"Garild, I think we've found help." She realized at that moment that tears had sprung to life in her eyes and she wiped away at them with a dirty hand. A village meant food, shelter, warmth. They'd gone a while without such comforts and the thought of having them back again filled her with happiness. But there was a devastating realization that seeing that village confirmed what she'd been told, that the Darkness wasn't real, that it had never been and the childhood she had known had been nothing but a lie. She realized that outside that cave, she knew nothing of the world beyond. It sobered the drunken happiness she'd felt and she found herself frightened. "Garild, I think I should go alone."

"Why is that," he asked, inclining his head towards her.

"Because we don't know what to expect. Just let me go see what is there and I'll come back for you."

"And what if you don't?"

She winced. "I'll come back, Garild. We've made it this far, I'm not leaving you behind now."

"Just come back," he said. His mood had darkened and he took the packs from Kirheen, laying them on the ground next to the stream. He sunk down next to them, his eyes wandering to the forest. He didn't watch her leave but she could feel his doubt follow her, clinging to her back with desperate hands.

As the distance between her and the village dwindled, she began to hear noises drifting towards her, could smell baking bread and the curls of wood smoke hovering lazily over the town. There was another smell though, something closer. It was sickly sweet, like meat left to rot in the sun. As she passed through a thicket of trees, she found the source of the smell.

Three bodies swung from a post at the edge of the village, a rope holding them around their necks. Two of them were male and a third was a female. They were in various states of dress, one of the males being completely devoid of clothing. His pale skin was covered in crisscrossing bloody red lines and the fingers of his left hand were all missing save for his thumb. The woman was missing an eye and her clothes were scorched. Her hair had been burnt and what little remained stuck out from her scalp in a disarray of frizzy locks. The third man had a dagger through his chest. All three had a bloody 'X' carved into their foreheads.

The sight made Kirheen gag and she turned away, using a tree to steady herself. She could feel the corpses at her back, their fingers reaching towards her pleading for mercy. She would have fled to Garild had she not had an overwhelming need to be in the village.

Forcing herself to move, she stepped around the bodies, giving them a wide berth. She could feel their lifeless eyes follow her and she shivered as she passed. She took a path in between two buildings and found a road alive with people. Giant wooden carts pulled by large muscular beasts rolled up and down the street, many of the carts laden with supplies. Weaving between them were people going about their daily business.

Doors along the street were flung open and people went in and out of the buildings at their leisure, some coming out with baskets of supplies. A woman to her left walked by with a basket of fresh bread and Kirheen watched her wander by, her eyes intently fixated on the bread. She felt her stomach twist into knots and she had to stop herself from bowling over the woman and stealing the contents of her basket.

Nobody paid her any attention as they passed. They were focused on their duties and they scurried past without a glance. The few that did notice her simply sneered down at her as if she were dirt, worse than dirt. And she supposed in her current state, she was. Her robes were torn, bloodied and streaked with dirt and she imagined her hair and face didn't look much better.

She looked up and down the street, trying to find something familiar, something that could help them. She found it in the form of a small, rickety wooden house just a few doors down. Though hungry as she was, Garild getting help for his hand was the first thing on her mind.

She stepped into the street, trying to dodge past the carts that wheeled by while avoiding running into anyone on the street. She failed miserably and a man shoved her roughly to the side and yelled something about filthy beggars over his shoulder. She caught the hand rail of a set of stairs and she steadied herself, glaring back over her shoulder at the man that had shoved her.

Nobody around her stopped to ask if she was okay and she found herself feeling very out of place. Hurrying along, she slipped into the small building she'd seen, relishing in the quiet the front room offered. The room was dark and cramped. The walls were of a dark wood and the floors were covered in faded rugs of gold and red. A set of stairs sat off to the right and the left hand wall was covered in rows of shelves with a variety of bottles and tinctures. Two chairs sat by the window to her right and in front of her was a large wooden desk.

Behind it stood a tall man, dressed in the same odd manner as those outside. He had a thick head of gray hair and a moustache hovering over lips that were pulled down in obvious distaste. His bright blue eyes watched her closely. "Is there something I can help you with," he said, but his voice didn't sound friendly.

As Kirheen went to speak, she realized how strange it felt to talk to someone other than Garild. She felt her palms grow clammy and her voice broke as she spoke. She had to clear her throat before the words would come out. "I have a friend…he's hurt. He was bit by something, some kind of snake but…"

The man raised a hand and shook his head. "I don't mean to stop your tale of woe, but let me get straight to the point. I don't cater to beggars. If you don't have the money to pay for my services then please leave."

Money? The word was foreign to her. From what she could gather, he was asking her for something in return for his help, but she'd never heard of what he asked for. "Money," she asked. "I... what is it?"

The man clucked his tongue against his teeth in disapproval. "I'd laugh if I hadn't heard it before. Just because you've never seen a copper piece in your life doesn't mean you can come in here and demand services without paying. Now, if you'll follow me, I'll escort you out." He moved past her, swinging the door open and sweeping his arm out towards the street. "That's it, girl. Get out of here." His blue eyes bore into her own and she saw he was in no mood to argue.

The second her foot was out the door, the man slammed it shut behind her with enough force to rattle her teeth. She turned back, fixing him with a glare before stepping back into the street. She was so distraught by his treatment that she nearly got herself run over by a cart. One of the great beasts whinnied, breaking her out of her cloud of anger. She dove forward, narrowly missing being crushed. The driver of the cart spit at her as he passed and she looked at the bubbling pool of saliva on the ground next to her hand with disgust. Suddenly the cave didn't seem so bad.

Leaving Garild behind was the best thing she could have done. There wasn't a friendly face to be seen in the crowds around her. How was she supposed to find help in such a place?

As she went to take a step forward a hand latched onto her right shoulder, strong fingers digging in painfully to the hollow above her collar bone. Lips moved next to her ear, the voice low and gritty and edged with warning. "For the love of the Lightbringer herself, stop using your powers."

Kirheen whipped her head to the side to see who the voice belonged to. The man at her side was tall and thin and there was something very familiar about him. He had startlingly blue eyes under wild grey brows that were pulled together in concern. He had a strong, curved nose and a bushy beard that filled in his otherwise thin face. He had but a crown of grey hair left on his otherwise bald head. He looked down at her with a flash of anger.

"Are you trying to get yourself killed? A seeker finds you here and you might as well go find the nearest cliff to fling yourself off of."

"I don't know..."

"Guard your mind, girl."

Kirheen realized she had been using her powers to keep a pin point on Garild. She'd been afraid of getting lost and so she'd latched on to his mind before she'd left him. She quickly dropped the link and threw up her guard. The man next to her scoffed. "That'll have to do, I suppose. Follow me."

He began walking but Kirheen planted her feet. He whipped around angrily but she held her ground. "I don't even know who you are and you want me to just go with you?"

He looked from side to side, giving a small grin to a woman walking by as if everything was just fine. When she passed he leaned forward and grabbed her shoulder, speaking so only she could hear his voice. "Listen to me, I'll explain everything until I'm blue in the face, but not here. We need to get out of here before we both end up strung up like those bodies on the edge of town. Got it?"

Kirheen opened her mouth to argue but thought better of it. This was the closest she'd come to finding help and she wasn't going to let the opportunity pass. She couldn't leave Garild behind though. "I have a friend in the woods. He's injured. I came here to find help and I'm not leaving without him."

The man looked surprised. "A friend?" He was quiet for a moment as he mused over her words. "Can you get him here?"

"I think so."

"Then go fetch him and meet me at the edge of town." He pointed to the place he'd be. "Don't use or speak about your powers, understood?"

She nodded and he released his grip on her shoulder. She rubbed at the spot where his fingers had been, giving him an annoyed glare. "I'll meet up with you soon," she said and he nodded, grabbing the leather straps of the strange beast behind him and pulling it forward. It sidled past her, hauling packs to either side of its long body. Glancing around, she took the first opening she could find and slipped between two buildings. She could only hope Garild was where she'd left him.

Chapter 29

Garild glanced up as Kirheen approached his face inquisitive. She could see the hunger in his eyes and his gaze wandered to her hands. Finding them empty, he frowned. "Did you not find anything?"

It was hard to explain what she'd seen, to explain the way she'd been treated. "There is a whole village full of people and nobody willing to help. I did find someone though that seems very interested in us and our powers. He said he'd help us out if we meet him at the edge of town."

"And you trust him?"

Kirheen felt no hesitation in her reply. "I do. Allseer help me, I don't know why, but I do. Just...don't use your powers until we're well away from here, Garild. I get the feeling our powers would get us in trouble in this place."

Kirheen helped Garild gather up their packs. Perhaps with something in their possession, people would stop thinking she was out to steal from them. Kirheen guided Garild to the outskirts of the village, taking care to avoid the dead bodies she'd found earlier. She didn't want him to see that.

"This...this isn't what I expected," Garild said as they slipped through an alley way. "Everything is so different."

"If you think they look different, think how we must look," Kirheen grumbled, catching the eye of a man passing by. He took one look at her ragged clothes and grimaced, quickening his pace. Her eye caught the large spotted creature the man had been leading and she hurried across the street with Garild, dodging people and carts alike.

The man stepped into view and seeing Kirheen, he motioned her over. He glanced over the crowds again before addressing them. He took a quick look at Garild, hovering his gaze on his injured hand. "We need to get out of town. If we get stopped along the way, just say you are my niece and nephew. You don't look anything alike but it'll have to do."

"I...don't know what that means, but we'll do it if it means you'll help us."

The man huffed. "I'll do what I can for you, but let's get to a less eventful area. I promise to explain more when we're safe. The name is Therin."

"I'm Kirheen and this is Garild. It's a pleasure to see a friendly face."

There was a scream from up the road that caught all of their attention. Just a few doors down, a young girl was hauled out of a building by two men. She screamed, her legs flailing as she tried to break free. She was pushed down in the dirt while a circle of people gathered about, curiosity drawing them in like moths to a flame.

"This little bitch is one of them. One of those cursed ones," said one of the men, circling her like a hawk. The other man held her down by the back of her neck, pushing her face into the dirt. She shuddered, tears leaving tracks in her dust covered face.

"Sharon," yelled an older heavy set man as he weaved his way through the crowd, hands pushing aside people frantically. Before he broke through the edge of the crowd, he was grabbed by two men. He fought against them but a punch to the gut from a man in the circle stopped him. He slumped to his knees. When he recovered his breath, he met the eyes of the man who'd punched him. "Clive, you've got it wrong! She isn't one of them. You leave her alone. Leave my girl alone!"

"You hear that," Clive barked. "He thinks she isn't cursed. He thinks she's just normal. Well, isn't that what they all say." The man worked the crowd, raising his hands with emphasis, stalking around the edges of the circle while he whipped them into a frenzy. He drew a dagger from his belt and stepped towards the man who'd tried to stop them.

Kirheen took a cautious step forward, hands clenched into fists, but Therin reached out and stopped her. "We can't get involved with this, girl. You show your face and you're as good as dead. We need to move."

But she couldn't move, she couldn't drag her eyes away from what she was seeing. She was watching death creep along the edges of the circle and she couldn't look away. The girl on the ground, seeing the man draw a dagger, squirmed beneath the grip of the man above her. She pleaded for them to stop, pleaded for them to not hurt the man. They didn't listen.

Clive drove the dagger into the man's stomach and the girl screamed. There was a ripple in the air around her and then the man holding her was thrown back into the crowd, pushed away by a wild blast of uncontrolled power. "You see! Cursed! The girl is a monster! She strikes out against our savior. Her power comes from the unholy one herself."

The girl cried, holding her hands over her face. The crowd was like a pack of rabid dogs crowding around her. They screamed and yelled and spit on her, jostling each other to get closer. "You know what we do to those that worship the Allseer?"

"Kill her," yelled a woman from the crowd! "Beat her to death!"

A chorus of cheers rose from the crowd and Kirheen covered her mouth with her hand. She was too shocked by what she was seeing. They couldn't actually mean to hurt her. Garild was at her side and he gripped her arm tightly. She could feel him shaking.

"I like that idea," said Clive, taking a long heavy piece of wood handed to him by a bystander. He gripped it in both hands, testing its weight as he made a mock swing. The girl recoiled, shuffling to the edge of the crowd but someone kicked her in the back, sending her back into the center of the circle.

It was like someone had unleashed a wild animal. Clive struck her, the blow earning a fervent cheer from the crowd. And then he continued to strike her over and over again, smiling as he did. The crowd was laughing as the young girl was beaten to a bloody pulp in front of them.

When Clive had finished, he stood and hoisted the bloodied club over his head. He flashed the crowd a wicked grin and proceeded to drag the body towards the other unfortunate souls that had been found by him and his pack of wolves. They'd hang her as a warning.

Kirheen stumbled to the side, dry heaving into the bushes. Even when she closed her eyes she could still see his white teeth, shining bright in a mask of blood. Therin was gentle as he grabbed her, helping her back to her feet. "This is why," he whispered. "This is why they can't know. They can never know."

Chapter 30

The trip out of the village was a somber one. Kirheen and Garild walked in silence, listening to the clip clop of hooves as they made their way out onto the main road. A war between hunger and disgust fought for dominance in her stomach and once they were out of the village a ways, Kirheen spoke up.

"Could you spare a bite to eat? I'm not so sure I'm hungry anymore, but I need something."

Therin walked in front of them, holding the reigns as he guided his great beast along. He looked back at her over his shoulder, seemed to scrutinize her and then drew the beast to a stop. "You both are just skin and bones, aren't you? How long has it been?"

Kirheen shrugged. "I honestly can't say. Time has been...funny where we've been."

"I see." He flipped open a wide leather pouch hanging from the side of the horse and from it drew something out from a paper bag. It was a loaf of bread, its top golden and buttery. It was soft and still warm, the smell alone making Kirheen's mouth water. He split the loaf in two, handing half to each of them. "Eat slowly. If it's been as long as you say, you'll make yourself sick if you force that down too fast."

Therin pulled himself up onto the strange beast he led, sliding himself into some leather contraption that acted as a seat. Kirheen eyed it curiously and tentatively reached out with her free hand to touch the beast. The fur was bristly and rough and she nearly jumped out of her skin when it twitched beneath her hand.

The road out of the town was wide and rough, the ground made uneven by a patchwork of cart tracks. As they got further away, the amount of people grew to a trickle until they turned off another, smaller road. They only passed a few people and those gave a friendly wave to Therin as they traveled by.

They walked in silence, too absorbed with the food in their hands to say anything. Despite the warning, they ate faster than they should have, scarfing down bites of bread as fast as they could chew the one that came before it. It was a meager meal, but food was food. When she was through, Kirheen wiped the crumbs from her mouth and looked to Garild.

While the food may have eased his hunger it did little for his current condition. He looked pale, sweat beading his forehead. When she reached out to touch his hand, she found he once more burned with fever. "Are you okay?"

Garild shrugged. "I'll be alright. I just need rest," he said, but he slid his hand out of sight, away from her prying eyes. She hoped that wherever Therin was taking them there would be a healer to help Garild.

The road broke free of the trees after a time and the land before them was all rolling hills and swaying golden grass. The sun was starting to sink in the sky, the heat of the day dissipating as it did. They came upon a village, much smaller than the one from before. There was only a single road dotted with shops that were closing up for the evening.

A few of the shopkeepers looked at Kirheen and Garild with curious gazes, casting questioning looks to Therin. He merely waved them off, continuing through town. The landscape was dotted with houses, quaint little things built of sturdy wood. Many had small gardens teeming with vegetables and flowers. Therin led them to one of these small homes, set further away from the others. A larger building was set to the side and he led his creature to this building.

Swinging off the saddle, he landed with a thump. He started working on the packs, unloading them from the animal with practiced ease. He piled them at his feet and then led the beast into the building. While he was busy, a woman came busting out of the front door of the house. She was short and sturdy, her long gray hair pulled back in a messy bun. She huffed down the steps and pulled up just short of them. She surveyed them with dark brown eyes that were alive with agitation and curiosity.

"You were supposed to be back hours ago," she called towards the barn. "I've been worried. And what are these you brought back with you? I told you to get bread, not children!"

Therin smiled as he made his way back towards them. He ignored the woman's complaints and pulled her close, wrapping his arms around her. "I'm sorry. This has been an…interesting day to say the least. And these aren't just children, Leann. If my suspicions are correct, they come from the North."

Leann gasped, her hand flying to cover her mouth. "You jest."

"I wouldn't jest about something like this."

The woman looked upon them with renewed interest and she shuffled forward, grabbing at Kirheen's left hand before she could say otherwise. The woman flung back her sleeve, revealing the beautiful tattoo that seemed to have been put there so long ago. Tears sprung to her eyes and she pulled Kirheen into a hug.

Kirheen laughed nervously, patting the woman on the back as she looked at Therin, one eyebrow raised. He smiled in such a way that she knew it was only a matter of time before they would find out more. The woman released her and stepped over to Garild.

He too was forced into a hug but Leann pulled away quickly. "Boy, you are burning with fever. Let's get you both inside."

While Therin finished hauling in the packs, Leann led them into their home. The front room was small and cozy. There were a set of cushioned chairs in front of a fireplace to the right and to the left was a rectangular table lined with chairs. The room was lit with small bronze lamps that glowed softly. The room smelled of spices and Kirheen could hear something bubbling away in the next room. Despite the bread she'd eaten, she was still starving.

Leann coaxed them to the table and made them sit while she helped Therin unload the supplies. Kirheen smiled when she overheard her ask about the bread. A few moments passed and she came bustling back into the room with two steaming bowls. She set them down on the table with a smile.

Kirheen inspected the food before her. It was a soup of some kind, a delicate blend of chicken and rice and vegetables. It smelled amazing and little curls of steam rose from the bowl, warming her face. Therin set a bowl opposite Kirheen and sat himself at the table. Leann joined them last, settling in a chair next to Therin.

As if sensing her questions, Therin nodded to the food. "Eat first, then we'll talk."

She frowned but took to eating her meal. Once she started eating she could barely stop. She had nearly finished her soup when she looked to Garild. He was trying to spoon soup into his mouth with his non-dominant hand and failing. The spoon shook badly as he brought it to his mouth and he stared at it, brows knit in frustration.

"Garild, do you want me to help you," Kirheen asked cautiously.

He dropped the spoon back into his bowl and sunk back in his seat. It wasn't just his hand shaking, his whole body shook. Kirheen pushed back her chair and leaned towards him, raising a hand to press it against his brow. He felt as if his skin were made of fire. "Garild?"

Leann raised her head, studying him with concern. She pushed back her chair, stepping around the table to be closer. "What happened to him? Is he ill?"

Kirheen frowned. "He was bit by a snake on our way here. I cleaned the wound but I didn't have supplies. I don't know if he was poisoned or not. Garild?"

He closed his eyes, gritting his teeth as he fought against a wave of pain. Leann reached down, grabbed his hand gently and pulled back the bandage. "Therin, can you go ask for Carra. This needs seeing to right away. Dear, help me get him to the back room please."

Kirheen rose from her chair and slid her shoulder under Garild's arm, helping him from the table. They led him past the kitchen and into a small side room. The room had a small cot against the far wall but looked to otherwise be used for storage. They lowered Garild down onto the cot and Leann fetched a lantern and a blanket and draped it over him. She pulled back the edge of his bandage and gasped. A smell like rotting meat followed and she lowered his bandage back down carefully. "How long has he been like this?"

Kirheen shook her head. "I don't know. Time has been...funny."

Leann nodded her head knowingly. Footsteps sounded in the hallway and a moment later a young woman poked her head into the room, surveying them with bright blue eyes. She was tall and lean, with curly brown hair that was pinned back away from her face. "Leann, is everything alright? What's happened?" Her eyes drifted to Garild and Kirheen. "Who are your visitors?"

"I'll explain that later dear. This young man was bit by a snake. I fear the wound is terribly infected."

"Let me through," Carra demanded, stepping between them. She sunk down next to Garild, her hand touching his forehead. "Fetch me water and a rag, we need to bring his fever down." Leann turned to get it but Therin was already on the way. He returned, handing it over to Leann. She sat the bowl down and Carra dipped the rag, wringed it out and set it upon his brow.

She reached for his bandaged hand and set to unwrapping it. Garild moaned and tried to pull his hand back but she held it firm. Her face grew pale as she examined the wound. His hand was a terrible thing to behold. The wound had blackened and the skin around it was devoid of color. The skin was cracked and peeling away from the bites and vivid red veins snaked up his wrist.

"Oh no," Kirheen whispered. "Is there anything you can do?"

Carra looked up at her with sad eyes. "We can save him, yes, but this hand... there isn't anything I can do about this. If I don't remove his hand, the infection will kill him... I'm sorry."

Kirheen felt something crack inside her, felt the entirety of her guilt and anger spilling over. She sank to the floor and cried while a stranger she'd just met wrapped her in her arms and whispered comforts in her ear.

Chapter 31

G arild was drugged and the amputation was performed. Kirheen had asked to sit in the hallway but Leann had forced her outside claiming she didn't need to hear or see what would happen. She didn't need those memories. Kirheen wondered if she knew how right she was.

They sat out on the porch, the gentle glow of a lantern between them. Therin joined them, handing a steaming mug of tea to Kirheen. She sipped at it gingerly, decided it was too hot and set it to the side. Leann was the first to speak.

"Kirheen, I am so sorry for this. It sounds like things have already been tough enough for you on your journey here."

"This is all my fault," Kirheen said, resting her head in her hands. "I forced all of this and now Garild is paying the price."

"This is the price of change, Kirheen. It is high but it is often necessary," Therin said softly, taking a seat next to her. "It is a price I know well. It's been years since anyone has come through the cave there in the mountains and yet here you both are. I didn't think I'd be alive to see it."

Kirheen raised her head. "You speak as if you know what lies beyond?"

Leann smiled a sad smile. "We do. Before we came to live here…we were Bonded. Sanctuary was our home." She flipped over her left hand so her palm was facing the sky. Kirheen saw for the first time a puckered patch of skin on her wrist, and in that scar she could barely make out the faded remnants of a tattoo.

The words hit Kirheen like a ton of bricks. She was equal parts incredulous and angry. "You're kidding me. You've known this whole time what has been happening there? You've known and done nothing?"

Therin and Leann exchanged a troubled glance. "Kirheen, it's been years since we left Sanctuary behind. It had a purpose then, but I didn't want that life. I didn't want a life lived for revenge," Therin said.

Leann shook her head. "I think it might be best if you explain the world you grew up in. Much has changed, both here and in Sanctuary. I'd like to know what we left behind."

And so Kirheen told them everything. She spoke of her childhood, raised communally and taught to fear the world outside. She told them of the ritual that bound her and Garild, told them of her fear of her powers, of letting someone in her mind. Herzin and her anger, the lies her whole world had been built on, her betrayal and having to leave behind her friends in order to save them. By the end, she was shaking, so filled with anger she could barely contain it. "And you left us to that!"

When she regained her composure she saw that Leann was crying and Therin was dreadfully pale, even with the warm glow of the lantern. "This…this is not what I wanted to hear," Therin said, leaning forward to rest his elbows on his knees. He rubbed at his face, sighing deeply as he did. "I am so sorry. If I had known my brother would fall to such madness, if I had known he would go to such lengths… I would have never let him continue on."

Kirheen's breath caught in her throat. She felt a flutter in her heart. "What are you saying?"

"Nyson and I are blood brothers. We're related. Heh, you probably don't even know the word. I guess you really have no concept of what it means to be a family. It was our grandfather that founded Sanctuary, our grandfather that first led our kind through the caves and found a safe haven for our kind."

Leann took over the story, her voice bringing to life a tale Kirheen had never heard. "There was a time when our powers were considered a gift. We were considered blessed by Riel the Lightbringer herself. The Allseer, as you call her. We had the power to heal and change the world around us, but some began to see it as a threat. Those without powers had always been uneasy around our kind, but it came to a boiling point when the Zekaren Royal Family took the throne. They decreed that our powers were an abomination. They worked the land into a frenzied blood lust and then they began hunting us. Our kind were tortured, murdered in the streets, chained and burned for all to see. At the height of the massacre, his grandfather gathered a group of individuals wanting to start a new life and followed old tales that hinted at a place to the

North, a place where our powers originated. They made it through the caves and Sanctuary was formed."

"It was a hard life for them at first, but slowly they began to grow as did their desire for revenge. A large group, his grandfather included, wanted to cultivate our powers. They wanted to shape them for the future so that they could one day strike back against those that had nearly wiped them out. That philosophy took root and it slowly began to shape itself into the world that you grew up knowing. When we came of age, we were Bonded by their father. I was Bonded to Nyson, a man I did not love and forced into a life I did not desire. And Therin was Bonded to Herzin, a woman he did not wish to spend his life with. The truth was, we were in love with each other. Always had been."

"And there were those that desired freedom as well. There were those that didn't want powers, that didn't want to spend their whole lives waiting for bloodshed that they had no desire to see. And so we gathered those willing to rebel and we left Sanctuary behind. We've found a freedom here that you have never known, but I fear you have all paid the price for it."

Kirheen sat quietly, taking in the overwhelming amount of information she'd just heard. It was shocking to hear how her childhood had been shaped by events years before her time. A twisted desire for revenge and the pain of a broken bond had shaped Nyson into the cruel man he'd become. The lies he'd told to keep them close, his desperate bids for control, the cruelty Herzin had showed her at the first spark of her own rebelliousness, it all was starting to make sense. The reasons were there in front of her, she need only grasp them to understand the entirety of her life. This had been a struggle that had gone on long before she had existed, but it was a struggle she intended to end.

"Nyson has gone mad," Kirheen said. "I can't let him keep doing what he's doing. He's taken things even further, taking those unable to be part of his elite council and stripping them of their powers, breaking their minds and using his powers to control them. He's turned my friends into husks and kept us all locked away in a safe little cage so he could accomplish the task his elders set him on. I came here to seek help and I fully intend to return to Sanctuary and stop him."

Leann looked alarmed. "You want to go back?"

"What choice do I have, Leann? I left behind the only people in my life I've ever cared about. I left them behind with a promise that I'd come back and save them. I don't intend to go back on that promise. I don't intent to just leave them to suffer for my mistakes. What Herzin is doing to people, I can't let that happen to those I left behind."

Therin whispered softly. "She's been unbinding them…Allseer help us, I never thought it would come to that."

"Unbinding. What is it exactly?"

"It's a branch of power not very often seen amongst our kind. It's a strategic breaking of the mind. Before we left, it was only ever used against those that abused their powers. It's an unstable power though. A wrong move while performing the unbinding can permanently break a mind and the only mercy left for those is a swift death."

"Can it be reversed? If you can unbind someone couldn't you reverse that process?"

Therin sighed. "In some cases, yes, but it has risks of its own and requires a delicate use of our power. Again, a wrong move and you break their mind beyond use. While you may be able to bring someone back, they aren't always the same person they were before the unbinding. The longer the mind stays in that state, the worse the deterioration. I'd say it isn't worth the risk most of the time."

"They've been unbinding so many people. I've always wondered where the adults go after the birthing age, but I think I know now. Allseer, I feel sick. This isn't right what they are doing. They need to be stopped."

"And you think this can be done," Leann asked, reaching forward to touch Kirheen lightly on the knee.

Kirheen turned towards her, all the pain and rage she felt burning in her eyes. "It must."

Chapter 32

Kirheen was by his side when her bond mate finally woke from his slumber. He looked confused, his eyes searching the small room, picking apart the dusty shelves and linen sacks until they came to rest on the bandaged stump that had once been his hand. There was a moment of disbelief, his mouth falling open as he looked for what should have been there.

The pain of the wound and the realization seemed to hit him at the same time. His eyes filled with angry tears as the fingers of his good hand crawled over the bandages, trying desperately to feel what had been taken from him. It took everything Kirheen had not to look away when his eyes finally met hers.

"What did they do," he asked, pawing the blanket away from him. "Kirheen, what happened to me?"

Kirheen tried to push him back down on the bed but he struggled against her, the full brunt of his anger driving his strength. "Don't touch me," he growled. "Tell me what happened now!"

"Garild, your hand was infected. That snake that bit you…it was too late. If they hadn't taken your hand you would…you would have died. I'm sorry..."

"Maybe that would have been better," he yelled. Kirheen winced at the words and stood, taking a few steps back from his bed to avoid his flailing arms. There was nothing she could do for him, she knew that. No matter how guilt ridden she was, it wasn't going to bring his hand back. There was nothing left to be done for Garild, but she could help save the others. She had earned his anger and she would deal with it in time, but she had other matters to focus on.

"I'm leaving in the next couple days," she stated, trying to keep her voice level. "Therin and Leann have agreed to help me."

"I'm going with you," Garild said suddenly, a look of mild panic crossing his face. He swung his legs off the bed. "You can't do this without me."

"I can and I will. You need to heal and you can't do that by going with us. You need to stay here and rest and come to terms with what has happened."

"You caused this! If it wasn't for you, I'd still have my hand! We'd still be back in Sanctuary and none of this would have ever been a problem!"

Kirheen squeezed her eyes shut and bit her tongue, hoping pain would still the words that so desperately were trying to push their way past her lips. She met his eyes one last time, her expression unreadable. His face was all torment and grief, anger and defeat. "I'm sorry, Garild. I hope to see you again soon. Keep us in your thoughts."

She turned away from him then and quickly slipped out of the room. She lowered the bar over the door as she closed it, keeping Garild locked inside. The healer had demanded that he stay behind, that he get rest, even if it meant locking him away until they could depart. She'd promised to look after him, promised to keep him safe. It felt strange to be leaving that job to another.

Kirheen jumped as Garild began to pound on the door behind her. "Kirheen? Kirheen! Don't leave me in here! Don't leave me like this! Please! Please!"

Grinding her teeth, she forced herself down the hallway and out the front door, trying to keep the tears from spilling down her cheeks. It was all wrong. It shouldn't have happened like this. He hadn't deserved what happened to him and he didn't deserve her abandoning him in a time of need. If there had been another way...

But they were out of time. Her attention was demanded back in Sanctuary and there were dozens of others that needed her. Garild would have to wait.

Leann was waiting for her on the steps outside. Night had fallen and the air outside was cool, the moon big and bright overhead. The long grasses of the plain swayed in the breeze and they seemed to glow in the light of moon. It reminded her of Sanctuary, the place that until recently she'd considered home.

She sat down with a sigh, rubbing her hands over her face, agitated by the events unraveling around her. Leann let her have a moment before speaking. "He'll forgive you someday. It may not be as soon as you'd like, but he'll come around. Time heals all things."

"How I wish that were true. If I could just plant myself here and let time settle what's happening back home, I'd happily oblige."

Leann let out a soft chuckle. "Alright, well it may not fix *everything* but in this matter, it is the only thing that will help. He has been traumatized, Kirheen. It will take time before he is himself again. Just be his friend and he'll come back to you."

"I can't even see that far ahead. Every part of me is consumed with what must be done. I can't even be certain I'll return from this. There is so much to do... I don't know if I can handle this."

"You made it all the way here with not much but the clothes on your back. You stood by your friend during his suffering, stood by him through his hatred. You had the courage and the strength to leave Sanctuary, to do what you had to do in order to have even the possibility of saving the rest of them. You are a wonderful young woman, and now you have the backing of all of us here to right our wrongs. Don't doubt our success, Kirheen. Don't doubt your ability to pull this off. You made it this far, you can make it a bit further."

"Thank you so much, Leann. I don't know what would have happened to us if Therin hadn't noticed me that day. You've taken us in without question and shown us incredible kindness. I'll never be able to repay you for this."

"If we succeed, it'll be payment enough."

Kirheen smiled. "I suppose so."

"He's calling the meeting tomorrow. Not everyone is likely to join your cause, but these are good men and woman. Many of them will be willing to take up arms. You were right when you said we left you to that fate. The least we can do is free you from it."

"A rebellion," Kirheen huffed. "Who would have thought." She turned her gaze to the moon overhead, its icy blue glow so like the wraith wood trees of Sanctuary. She'd be back amongst them in a few days, back to free her friends from the bonds of Nyson. She only hoped she wasn't too late.

Chapter 33

"You're asking a lot from us, Therin," said a portly man to the far side of the room. He had a thick mustache and eyebrows and his cheeks were as red as tomatoes. He was one of the few standing in the room and his muscular arms were folded over his chest. "My father journeyed here with you to escape from Sanctuary, so we could be free of it once and for all. He wanted us to be safe, to be able to have a family, to love freely…you're asking us to throw that away."

Therin watched the crowd gathered in his barn carefully, taking his time as his gaze traveled from face to face. In reality he *was* asking a lot from them. He was asking them to leave obscurity, to use their powers once more, to own up to the mistake of their past and possibly lose their freedom forever. It was a heavy price he asked.

He spoke firm but gentle, trying to rile the emotions in the room in his favor without bringing them to anger. "I know I ask much from you, Zith. I ask much of you all. It is regrettable, but it is necessary. When I started the rebellion that freed us from Sanctuary, I was young and foolish. I'm a man grown old now. The days of thinking only of myself and my wants are far behind me. When we fled, I didn't think of the children that remained. I didn't think of the consequences they would suffer as a result of our actions.

My brother, my own flesh and blood, has made these children to suffer. Their entire lives have been spent believing that there was nothing beyond the walls of Sanctuary. They believed that was the only life they'd live. An entire generation has been stripped of freedom and once their purpose is done, they've been forced to undergo the unbinding, forced to become mere shells of themselves in order to serve the Bonded after them. How is this any life for these children to live? How can we live a life free without thinking of those we left behind? These children didn't ask for this. These children didn't ask to be left behind. They didn't have a choice. I say it's about time we gave them one."

His words carried through the room, rippling over the crowd like a forceful wave. The large man named Zith looked for an ally in the crowd and found himself wanting. He took a seat with a huff, his cheeks still tinged red from anger and what was now suspected to be a bit of embarrassment.

Therin let the words sink in, let it settle into the hearts of the men and woman that surrounded him. Once he was satisfied, he continued on. "I know I ask a lot. I ask you to leave your families, to possibly expose yourselves as bearers of the powers you try so hard to hide. But I ask this of you because I believe you can make a difference. I believe you can change the future for these children. So, I ask now, who will stand with us?"

The first to rise was an elderly woman with leathery skin and blue, sunken eyes. She smiled as she rose, raising a hand for all to see. "Therin, in my youth I joined under your leadership to win our freedom. I am prepared to follow you again, wherever this leads. I pledge myself to this cause."

The man next to her rose as well, raising his hand high. "And I pledge myself as well."

There was a chorus of noise as more rose, offering the pledge that would unite them under a single cause. In the end, even Zith committed to their rebellion. Therin smiled, feeling the familiar weight of leadership and responsibility on his shoulders. It was a fearsome burden to bear but one that filled him with a childish excitement all the same. It had taken strength and courage to leave Sanctuary all those years ago, and now he'd go back to reclaim it, to face his brother after all these years and put an end to his madness.

Chapter 34

Though many had offered their help in reclaiming Sanctuary, they'd been forced to keep their numbers small. The decree of the Royal Family still carried and the noose was only ever so far from those with powers, waiting and taunting them to come out of hiding. Ultimately, they settled on a small party of eight, Therin and Kirheen included.

Leann stayed behind to care for Garild, though Kirheen could see in her eyes that she hated to do so. She packed their supplies with care, making sure to stock it well with food and water and bid them farewell in the early hours of the morning. Garild was nowhere to be seen. In her mind, Kirheen had thought he would have at least come out of hiding to see her off. It pained her that he didn't, but she remembered Leann's words, that time would fix the rift between them. She could only hope she was right.

They gathered their packs and took to the road in pairs, leaving at set intervals as to not draw suspicion. The last thing they needed was to be stopped by a Zekaren sympathizer and turned over to a patrol. Once the road was clear, they split off into the woods, heading towards the cave that even now sent tremors of anxiety through her body. She could only hope Akra would be more excited to see them than she was to see her.

She was absolutely delighted to have so many visitors. The journey back through the cave turned out to be far less perilous with more people and a light to guide the way. They used their powers in turn, guarding each other from the whispers that filled the cave, luring them towards madness. If a stone picture could pout, Akra would have done so at their departure.

They rested out of eyesight of the cave door, settling down with their packs to eat and drink. Back on this side of the mountains, Kirheen found that food was the last thing she wanted. She nibbled at a piece of dried meat all the while pacing back and forth. A man in the group named Erick watched, his green eyes following her back and forth. He was younger than the others and had never lived in Sanctuary. He'd pledged his service all the same claiming he didn't want to miss out on the action.

"Kirheen, you should rest. We've a long day ahead of us," he said, trying to lure her back to their circle. The rest of the group looked up from their meals, all eyes falling on her. She felt embarrassed until she remembered that for them, this was a return trip they'd never planned on. They were probably just as nervous as she was, they just hid it better. Her frantic pacing was probably jangling their nerves more than anything.

With a sigh she joined them in their circle, taking a seat next to Therin. He gave her a reassuring pat on the shoulder. An older woman across from her, her brown hair streaked with gray, pushed a piece of cinnamon bread into her hands. Kirheen struggled to remember her name. Celene?

"It's Sarah," the woman said, giving her an amused grin. The rest of the group laughed and Kirheen focused intently on the bread in her hand. "You can guard your mind now. There isn't a soul willing to cross through those mountains that doesn't have powers."

Without willing it to do so, her mind dredged up an image of that poor girl, broken and bloody in the street. And that smile… Kirheen brought up her guard, pushing away the image. It was like wrapping herself in a favorite blanket.

They finished eating and packed up, finally setting out on the road at a pace that was all too slow for Kirheen. They wound their way west for a time, setting a steady pace through the trees that towered over them. Their flight had been nothing but a blur before, an endless flurry of blue and green as they'd fled. It was strange to see it all now with open eyes, retracing that frantic trail through the woods.

After a time, Therin called for the group to halt and turned to Kirheen. "You said that they've been unbinding the adults and those without adequate power, correct?"

Kirheen nodded, unsure why he asked. "Around our 21st year in the cycle, we enter the Birthing Age. I don't know much about it, but when that time comes, those people just disappear. "

"We're going to divert from here to the North. I'm curious about something. It isn't too far out of our way and knowing the answer may make things easier… for all of us."

"What do you hope to find," Kirheen asked.

"You'll see."

They changed directions and Therin led them through the forest. It was obvious he knew the place like the back of his hand. Kirheen imagined he'd probably learned as much as he could about the forest before leading his fellow Bonded out of it. Dark fell before they reached their destination and they were forced to sleep among the trees. But Kirheen could feel the nervous energy around her and she knew that night that she wasn't the only one unable to fall asleep.

They rose with the sun, quietly packed up their things and were off again without a word. They came upon a stream after a few miles and were forced to slog through it, the cold water feeling like thousands of tiny needles upon her skin. And then Kirheen saw it, a village up ahead. At first she thought it the small cluster of homes shared by the Bonded, but she realized that there were far more than just the few that they dwelled in. She could see rows and rows of long, narrow buildings with peaked roofs.

"What is this," Kirheen asked, unable to raise her voice above a whisper.

"This was our original village. This was what Sanctuary used to be. In time, it became used for farming and crafting, hosting all the supplies we needed from year to year while we moved our homes just a little further away. And now…"

"This is where they go. They don't go to fight the Darkness because the Darkness isn't real. They come here to work until what? Until they grow old?" She could see movement now, dozens of people of various ages bustling about. She was too far away to see their eyes but she knew if she could she'd see nothing there. Everything that made them who they were would be gone.

"I always knew Nyson was powerful. He had been gifted with the ability to control, to lead, but to use it like this. He must be stretched terribly thin to be controlling all of these people at once. The amount of power required to do something like this… it's hard to believe he's capable of it."

They crept closer, staying out of sight of those working. Kirheen could make out faces now and her heart dropped when she saw someone familiar. Isa, once so cheerful and bright eyed, bumbled around the village, carrying a basket of vegetables in her hands. Her black hair was dull and lackluster, her skin sallow, robes dirty. Her eyes were dead and vacant and she stared off into space, looking at nothing in particular. Even when she tripped and the basket spilled its contents across the ground, she showed no emotion. She simply stooped to pick them up and hurried along as if nothing had happened.

Kirheen felt a surge of anger as she watched. She wanted to charge into that village, wanted to rip them free from the bonds that held them. Therin had warned her of the pain this would cause, the pain of seeing these people and being unable to help them. Even if she had the ability to fix their minds, there was always a chance they'd still be broken. And what then?

"I can't believe he has done this. This is unthinkable," said Sarah. She stared across the clearing, her eyes filled with spite.

"This is too much. We need to end this, for their sake, before he does this to anyone ever again."

There was a mumbling wave of agreement from the rest of them. She saw hands grip tighter at weapons, their body language changing as they prepared for the battle to come. Anger swept through them like a noxious cloud. If they hadn't had a reason to take down Nyson before, they certainly had one now.

When they finally turned away from the village, the pace they set was much quicker. They had purpose now and Kirheen could see it in every angered step.

Along the way, Therin gathered information from her, piecing together what she told him like a puzzle. "We want to keep casualties to a minimum. If we can take people without hurting them, we will. Nyson has probably forced many under his control. If we can break them of that link, we can keep things from becoming a blood bath. Are there any completely dedicated to Nyson?"

Kirheen thought about each group carefully, trying to sift through what she knew of all of the people she'd grown up around. "There will be some loyal to Nyson, but it's a relatively small group that I can think of. I'm afraid of what he may have done after we left."

Therin frowned. "Those that didn't openly commit to him have probably been unbound and put under his control. It's easier that way and with how many people he's already taken, it's the only way he could keep control without everything falling apart."

She thought of Tomias and Fenir, Burk, Abby... It was possible their minds were no longer their own. The thought filled her with disgust. She could only hope they had fought back, that they had kept Nyson at bay long enough for help to arrive.

"If we can keep him busy with small skirmishes, keep him focused on controlling the battlefield around him, wouldn't it be easy to ambush him?"

"It would and it's what I intend to do. If we can spread ourselves through the village and create chaos, he'll be forced to split his attention. It'll make him incredibly vulnerable and we can use that to our advantage."

Kirheen continued to divulge information to him about the Bonded, sharing their strengths and weaknesses. She spoke at length of the instructors and their loyalties. They discussed strategy and timing, and it almost felt like she was back preparing for the battles. Only this time, it was real and now death was on the line. She tried not to think about that as the Circle of Rest came into view.

Chapter 35

The Circle stood as it always had, a ring of wraith wood houses with their symbols emblazoned on the door. She caught sight of her own home and her heart sank. It felt so long ago and now she was back, feeling like a stranger in her own home. After the battle, she'd probably never see it again. She hadn't expected that thought to make her so sad. Despite her feelings, it was a beautiful place and she knew deep down she'd miss it.

The wraith wood tree in the center of the circle towered above them, casting web like shadows over their position. All was still.

"I don't like this," Kirheen whispered.

Therin nodded gravely. "Neither do I. He must be expecting us." He turned towards the rest of the group. "We're going to carry out as we planned. Split off into groups of two and head for the circle you've been assigned. If it's clear, head for the Temple of Trials. It's the most likely spot we'll face resistance. And everyone," he paused, meeting their eyes one by one. "Thank you for this."

They broke apart into their groups. Therin and Kirheen made their way to the center of the village, moving quickly but cautiously. Therin carried a bow in his hands and he gripped it tightly as he ran. Weapons weren't a common thing in Sanctuary as far as she knew, but there were many secrets in Sanctuary. It wouldn't surprise her to face them now. Therin had given her a dagger for the journey and though she didn't intend to use it, it was a comfort to have it close.

She held it in her hands now, feeling the weight of it. Her muscles were taut, her jaw locked, ears open for any noise that would give away an enemy. They encountered very little as they made their way along the dusty roads.

As they rounded the bend, Kirheen caught sight of a familiar hut and forced them to stop. "This is where Trista lives. The healer," she explained, catching her breath. There was a body lying at the foot of the steps, and she could see an arrow sticking out of the man's back. Dozens of broken glass fragments lay near him and there were patches of scorched earth around the hut. They approached cautiously, Therin holding his bow at the ready. When they neared the body, Therin flipped him over with his boot. It was Verin, former instructor of Bell and Tyrin. His eyes were wide with shock, as if he hadn't been expecting the arrow that had taken him in the back.

Kirheen shuddered and forced herself up the steps, feeling the eyes of the dead man follow her. Her palms were sweaty as she pressed them against the door of the hut. Therin raised his bow and whispered three counts under his breath. At the third, Kirheen flung open the door and ducked. Trista stood on the other side, bow in hand.

Neither let their arrows fly and there was a look of confused shock on Trista's face. Kirheen quickly rose to her feet, stepping between them. "Don't shoot, either of you. Please! Trista! Are you alright? Are you yourself?"

The bow quivered in her hands, her green eyes suddenly shiny with tears. The weapon clattered to the floor and she flung herself forward, wrapping her arms around Kirheen tightly. "Is it really you," Trista cried into her hair. "Please tell me you're real. Please don't just be an illusion."

"This is real, Trista. I'm back," Kirheen said, hugging the healer tightly. She pulled away, looking her up and down. She had seen a struggle, that much was certain. The right sleeve of her robe had been torn away and her upper arm was bandaged. There was a burn mark on her right cheek and her hair, while braided, was a mess. She looked exhausted and considering the events that had happened, she could see why.

Trista pulled her into the hut and Therin followed them in quickly. She scanned the road and satisfied that they were safe for the moment, she pulled the door shut. As Kirheen turned, she was surprised to see Burk sitting on Trista's bed, a bandaged leg propped up on a chair. He tried to sit up and winced.

"Burk! Are you okay," Kirheen asked, setting her dagger down on the table next to her.

He gave her a dismissive wave. "I'm fine. A little beat up but no worse off than the last time I got beat up. I get kind of used to these things being Bonded with Abby. Girl knows how to punch."

Kirheen smiled. "I can imagine. Where is she?"

Burk shook his head, all humor faded from his expression. "I don't know. She was right behind me when we were attacked. We split up. I saw her run into the trees and I haven't seen her since. Damn it, she better be okay. I couldn't live with myself if...if..."

Kirheen reached out her hand and took his own, giving it a reassuring squeeze. "Burk, she's a strong girl. She'll be okay."

"I think you've got some explaining to do," Trista said. When Kirheen turned, she was leaning against the door, arms crossed. A bow and quiver was propped up against the door next to her, ready and waiting.

We don't have time for this...

"Trista, I'd love to explain all of this but we're running out of time. What is the situation like around here?"

Trista frowned. "After you left, things went chaotic real fast. The Council was called together and I don't suspect the meeting went so well. Herzin was let off the leash and the first people she turned against were those near her. Apparently, with Tomias and Fenir turning against him, everyone was suspect. Most of the instructors have undergone the unbinding and are running around like puppets on a string. They've been apprehending anyone they come across and taking them back to Herzin. I think Nyson intends for all of them to go through the unbinding until things settle. I've been keeping them away with a few tricks of my own, but they've been getting clever."

Burk snorted. "Verin tried to use me to get Trista out. The man had gone mad. He damn near cut my leg off and then told me to get Trista to help me so she'd come outside. Instead he earned himself an arrow in the back."

"And there have been others. Some of the other Bonded have been through the unbinding. They've crept close but there is nothing I can do for them. I've been driving them away with vials of fire clove. I refuse to hurt any of them. They didn't ask for this."

Kirheen was prickly with anger and she surrounding herself with it like needle sharp quills. "This has to stop. Nyson is completely out of control."

"Who is this," Trista asked, tilting her head towards Therin. "This is...uh..."

Therin stepped forward, offering his hand. "My name is Therin. I am... Nyson's brother."

Trista's mouth fell open, her green eyes regarding him with both suspicion and awe. "You...you're his brother? This is the truth," she asked, eyes darting to Kirheen for confirmation.

Kirheen nodded. "As I said, there is a lot to explain and not a lot of time to do it. Where are Fenir and Tomias?"

Trista shook her head. "I don't know. Last I saw they were both pulled into the Temple of Trials. It isn't where they were unbinding people. I don't know what's happening. I'm... scared for them."

"We're going to get them back, Trista."

"I expect no less. I just hope..."

"Trista, I know. I hope so too."

Trista suddenly lit up. "I can come with you, you know. I can fight too."

Kirheen shook her head. "And who would look after Burk? If I find anyone, I'll need someplace safe to send them. You're as good a bet as any. I need you to stay here and guard them. Keep everyone safe."

She nodded, her expression grave. "Please bring them back…"

"I'll do everything I can," Kirheen said gravely and then she and Therin left, stepping back out into the dusty road. The path was still clear, no resistance in sight. They continued up the road towards the Temple of Union. She could see the shattered wraith wood tree high above them, standing out from the rest of the surroundings.

As they neared, they branched off the path, creeping through the trees until they could scout out the entrance. There were two instructors standing guard in front of the tree. One of them was Velga, previously the instructor of Isa and Ian. It was sickening to see. To twist her into a mindless husk after she'd lost both of her students was unthinkable.

Kirheen couldn't help but feel guilty as she looked over her. The old woman had gone through a lot and most of that pain had been a direct cause of Kirheen. She wouldn't be surprised if the woman hated her for what she'd done and part of her believed she deserved it. If it hadn't been for her, Ian would still be alive and Isa wouldn't be broken.

There was another instructor standing next to her named Isaac, though she didn't know him well. As small as Sanctuary was, she didn't know everyone. She only hoped he hadn't suffered because of her actions.

There was a crack of a branch to her right and then a wave of shimmering blue power manifested in her sight, crashing towards her through the trees. She forced herself into her mind quickly and blocked what she could, disrupting the amount of power. *Uh oh, too slow!* Despite her effort, the blast hit her hard and she flew back into Therin with enough force to send him to the ground.

"You alright," Therin called, untangling herself from her and rising to his feet. He hoisted her up by the back of her robes, keeping her steady while she recovered.

"I'm alright," Kirheen huffed.

"I fear I'm a little rusty when it comes to this, Kirheen. Be prepared to block on my behalf."

"Will do!"

The culprit of the attack was Daris and he hovered in her peripheral, his blank eyes watching her. His usual bravado was gone from his mannerisms and it made him seem smaller somehow, less dangerous. There would be no wolfish grin, no glimmering white teeth ready to cut her open. Just power against power.

The noise had caught the attention of the two instructors guarding the building. They raised their heads in unison, scanning the trees for the source. Velga locked her gaze on their location and shot forward.

"This isn't good," Kirheen said through clenched teeth. "Not good at all."

"No. No it isn't," Therin agreed, raising his bow. They put themselves back to back and prayed to the Allseer that the next few minutes wouldn't end in a blood bath.

Chapter 36

S arah crept into the clearing, careful not to break any twigs beneath her feet. She held a dagger firmly in her hands as she moved through the underbrush, Erick close behind her. There was a scuffle up ahead, Bonded against Bonded.

One group was still in control of themselves. There were three of them; a girl, a boy and an older man that could only be an instructor. Forming a crude circle around them were several of the Bonded that were clearly being controlled. There was far too much expression in their movements, too much intelligence in their eyes. They weren't unbound, but they were being controlled none the less.

The instructor was wounded, a hand held to his side as he stumbled back behind his students. The Bonded formed a protective barrier, blocking him from those that meant them harm. A girl stood at the forefront, beautiful and stoic. Her honey colored hair swayed around her as she stood firm, waiting for an attack from the others.

"Tegan, stop this. I know you can hear me. Stop this now," she called to the boy in front of her. He hesitated for a moment, head tilting as he processed the sound of his own name. The brief moment of expression slipped away and his mouth went slack.

And then she saw the dagger in his hands, the silver dripping with wet blood. At that moment, Sarah burst from the underbrush, sending her own dagger up into the air and pushing it forward with a burst of power. The blade sunk into the kids left shoulder and he cried out in pain, his link from Nyson broken. The other controlled Bonded behind him, one a girl with braided auburn hair, turned and attacked. Despite the advantage of their numbers, Erick blocked them easily, pushing back against them hard enough to break the link. They came to, disoriented but in control of their bodies once more.

The girl she'd saved dropped to her knees next to the boy she'd hit with the dagger. He was a small, mousy thing and his breath came in ragged gasps. He was obviously in pain and the girl looked at his wound, her eyes dancing with anger. "Why did you do that," the girl burst out at Sarah.

"He would have killed you," Sarah said softly, kneeling down next to them. "He wasn't himself. Nyson had him controlled."

"I could have gotten through to him, I could have." She looked down at the boy, caressing his pained features with her fingers. "Tegan, it's okay. I'm right here."

Sarah inspected the wound. The dagger had bit deep and pulling it back out was going to hurt worse than the injury itself. It would heal in time and with care, he'd have full function of his shoulder. "He'll live, girl. I'll help you tend to the wounded."

"We don't need your help! We've never even seen you before! Who are you," the girl snapped.

Sarah smiled. "My name is Sarah. We're with Kirheen. She's come back and we're going to help her stop Nyson."

There was a gruff bark of laughter from behind the honey haired girl. The wounded instructor was chuckling, his hand still holding his bloodied side. He was a large man, bearded save for where a scar arced across his lips "Oh, this is too good. She leaves us all to die and now she's back to save us all. I'll be damned but I think the little shit might be able to pull it off. Allseer, help us. Irena, let them help. We need all we can get."

Irena nodded grudgingly, allowing Sarah to take hold of the dagger in his shoulder.

"Hold him, this is going to hurt."

"I didn't think I would care this much," she whispered, taking hold of his shoulder gently. "I didn't think I cared, Tegan. But I do... I do care."

Fending off three opponents being controlled by one person turned out to be a lot easier than Kirheen had expected. Daris lay on the ground before her, knocked out from a blow she'd landed. Misdirection seemed to be the key to keeping them at bay. They weren't as quick on their feet, their movements sluggish and predictable. Kirheen imagined a single person under control would be a pretty fair match, but Nyson was cracking, his powers spread too thin.

There was a hum of power behind her and she turned, extending her block and diverting the blow away from Therin. It was successful and she flung the power back on her opponent, knocking Isaac back against the tree behind him. He rose, showing no sign of pain, not the slightest bit of hesitation.

"They'll keep fighting until they are dead or exhausted, Kirheen. They can't feel anything unless we really cause some damage."

Kirheen gritted her teeth. She didn't want to hurt them. They were unwilling bystanders, caught in the crossfire of their struggle. "Let's get close, try to knock them out."

"We can try," he said, keeping his bow at the ready.

Kirheen flung an illusion at Isaac, the hawk spreading its wings wide as it dove for his face. Velga took the bait, shifting her power to shatter the illusion. At that moment, Kirheen swopped in with a real burst of power, flinging it towards her. It struck her hard, forcing her off balance. Therin used the distraction to swing himself behind her. He cracked her over the head hard with his bow and she crumpled to the ground. He wasted no time and turned quickly, using the momentum to drive his fist into Isaac's stomach as he turned towards him. He crumpled forward and a quick hit to the head left him lying next to his partner.

They were both breathing hard by the time the battle was won. Therin was leaned forward, his hands resting on his knees as he regained his breath. "Oh dear, I'm getting much too old for this."

"You're keeping up quite well for an old man," Kirheen teased, giving him a devilish grin.

"Hmph."

Something was pulling at Kirheen, a steady buzz of power radiating from the temple. She felt her skin rise in tiny bumps over her arms and she rubbed at them, trying to hold back the chill that had moved over her body. There were only two people with that kind of power.

"Tell me I'm not the only one that feels that."

Therin frowned. "You aren't. That's a lot of power radiating from in there. You ready for this?"

Kirheen nodded but she felt panic taking over, the thought of facing either of them causing her to quiver. Herzin had almost killed her twice and Nyson was as dangerous as they could get. This was a turning point and Kirheen couldn't help but think of all the things that could possibly go wrong the minute they stepped through those temple doors.

Therin stepped towards the Temple, readying an arrow as he went. He wasn't taking chances. Kirheen was close at his heels but she stopped as a voice called out to her. It was a voice she'd been longing to hear since she'd left Sanctuary and it flooded over her senses, calming her.

Turning to her right, she could see someone lying in the dirt far ahead. White hair, brown eyes pleading her to come close. And blood, so much blood. He reached towards her with a slick red hand. "Kirheen, please help me."

"Tomias! Oh, Allseer. I have to help him." Her legs moved without thought, carrying her towards him without hesitation. There was a shout from behind her but it was lost to the wind rushing past her ears. There was only Tomias and an overwhelming desperation to save his life.

Chapter 37

S he'd been right behind him, hovering near his right shoulder
when he heard her take a sharp intake of breath. Therin froze,
muscles tight as he waited for the attack he was sure was coming.
Instead, he heard Kirheen peel away, her feet kicking up dust as she
ran. There was something muttered under her breath but he
couldn't make out the words.

"Kirheen," he hissed but the words were lost to her. He
watched her run, ashen hair billowing behind her. There was
desperation in that run but for the life of him, he couldn't tell what
she was running towards. "Damn it, girl."

He was now left with a dilemma. The power in the temple
hummed, low and powerful like the beat of a war drum. If he left to
chase after Kirheen, his chance would slip away. The girl was
powerful. He could only hope she was strong enough for whatever
pulled her away, at least until he could deal with his past.

The task at hand and the consequences that it had spawned
were his to bear. He took a cautious step through the door set in the
giant wraith wood tree, an arrow notched and ready. The room was
dim, only the soft glow of candles and filtered daylight providing
vision in the room.

She stood at the center of it, tall and proud, her green eyes studying him. She was so much older than he remembered. She was still beautiful but there was a harshness about her now, a weathering that stripped her of what she once was. Her hair was as gray as his own, flowing around her shoulders in soft waves that hid a hardened heart.

Those emerald eyes were staring at him not with the malice he expected but with a broken, desperate look. It was the look of someone seeing a ghost of the past. He was dredging up feelings in her she had probably long thought buried. But they never were. Feelings like that never truly faded away. They stayed hidden for a time, tucked away in spaces they'd tried so desperately to forget.

"It is you, isn't it" she said softly, her voice barely filling the space around her. "I can't believe it. You said…"

He relaxed his arm, allowing the bow to droop towards the floor. She had no weapon save her mind and she looked fragile, her hands clutched in front of her. Though he dropped his guard physically, he took a moment to strengthen his mind. "I said I'd never return. I meant to hold true to that."

"And yet you're here, you're standing before me. Unless this is some cruel trick of the mind…"

Therin scowled. "A cruelty you would know much about. Herzin, I don't understand, how could you use your powers like this? How could you do this to…to children?"

She recoiled from the sound of him speaking her name, her eyes squeezing shut. "I never wanted things to be this way. I never wanted any of this. I only ever wanted you. I only ever wanted our Bond. But you...you..."

"I left. I left Sanctuary so that we could be free. You were given a choice and you chose this."

Herzin grew tense, her green eyes ablaze. "What choice was that? To follow you into exile? To watch you dawdle over...over her! You didn't want freedom for some grand purpose. You wanted freedom so you could have the woman you lusted after. You broke our bond and you left me without a thought. You took everything from me, Therin."

Therin was taken back to a dark night before the rebellion. He had told Herzin everything, poured out to her his thoughts and feelings. He'd wanted her to have answers, to know the reasons so she wouldn't spend her waking hours wondering why she hadn't been good enough. He'd left her crying and heart broken. All those years, events rippling through time. To be standing before her now, in front of the woman he'd broken...

Perhaps it wasn't too late to fix his mistakes. "I'm sorry for what I did to you, Herzin. I tried so hard to help you understand, but that pain is something you can't understand. It must have hurt so much and I'm sorry. I wish I could have chosen who I loved, but you can't change the yearnings of a heart. I couldn't commit my heart to you when it had always belonged to another."

She was crying now, tears leaving streaks down her dusty face. She raised her hands to hide her shame, her shoulders slumped. Therin let the bow clatter to the ground and stepped towards her, arms spread wide.

"Can you ever forgive me for what I've done? For what I allowed to happen to this place?"

Herzin lowered her hands, her eyes showing genuine remorse as she met his gaze. "You were always forgiven, Therin. All this time I've wanted nothing more than to tell you...I never blamed you. Not once."

Therin stepped forward, wrapping his arms around the weeping woman he'd been bound to so long ago. She collapsed against him, her head resting heavy against his shoulder. They remained like that for a time, basking in the memories of old. So many feelings, so much pain in his heart and that old wound was finally knitting itself shut. He'd been forgiven.

There was a sound behind him, a sound like a piece of rope being pulled too tight, fraying from the pressure. He reacted on instinct, flinging himself to the side as an arrow went whizzing past him. He could feel the rush of air on his arm from its passing. There was a stomach churning thud as it connected with Herzin and she staggered back, eyes wide. The arrow had struck home, directly in her heart. Something thin and metallic slipped from her fingers, clinking as it hit the ground.

A dagger.

She'd intended to kill him all along.

The woman that had loosed the arrow was the red headed healer named Trista. She lowered the bow with a satisfied smirk while he looked on in disbelief. "I've always wanted to do that."

Therin was shaken. He'd been such a fool to believe her. She'd used that old wound against him, used it to manipulate his feelings and she'd done it flawlessly. Still, it saddened him that it had ended that way. More death, more blood on his hands. Would it ever end? "I suppose I should thank you for that."

Trista shrugged. "I'm just glad you moved."

"How'd you know I would?"

She smiled, green eyes mischievous. "Honestly? I didn't. I was hoping those old ears of yours worked. Had you not reacted, you probably would have been a dead man either way."

Therin looked down at the dagger, feeling his stomach flip flop as he did. He knelt on the ground next to Herzin, looking over the woman he had been meant to love. Years of bitter anger and this was the result. He let his fingers flutter over her eyelids and wept for a woman that had caused so much pain. Trista left him alone, stepping outside to give him a moment to himself. When he'd said his goodbyes, he stepped outside.

"Thank you," he said. "Thank you for giving me a moment to myself."

Trista gave him a sad smile. "Of course. For what it's worth, I'm sorry it ended this way."

"As am I, but this was the path she chose and the consequences of her actions are her own. This was the price that had to be paid."

Trista nodded, her gaze wandering the area around them. "Where is Kirheen," she asked, concern clouding her features.

Therin cursed, turning towards the direction she'd ran. "She took off on her own and for reasons I can't fathom. It was follow Kirheen or end Herzin and I couldn't allow this opportunity to slip. Who knows what she has gotten herself into? We need to hurry!" They took off after her, setting a pace as fast as his old bones could handle. And all the while he could feel it, events rippling outwards, like the dust stirred by his feet with every step.

Chapter 38

"Kirheen, help me!" The metallic smell of blood filled her nose as she got closer to Tomias. He rose to his feet as she approached and slowly began to limp away. "Wait, Tomias! Let me help you," she called but he kept walking, leaving a trail of bloody foot prints in his wake. "Damn it."

She raced after him, frantically trying to catch up. No matter how fast she ran, he always seemed to be just a few steps ahead. He slipped through a door up ahead, leaving a bright red handprint on the glowing surface. She realized that they stood at the Temple of Trials and her brain reeled. Why was she there, standing by herself?

The thought slipped away as quick as it came, breaking into a fragmented after thought like a crushed piece of glass. She followed into the temple. The center of the room was heavily shadowed, a great behemoth stretching the length of the room, clawing its way towards her. It was a great contrast to the bright sunlight bursting through the windows on either side of the room. At the deepest point of shadow, a man sat. Hawkish eyes watched her enter, regarding her with disdain.

Nyson.

To either side of him stood a pair of familiar faces. Tomias looked up as she entered, his eyes filled with pain. His face was a patchwork of purple and yellow bruises. The corner of his lip was bloody and one eye looked painfully swollen. Fenir kept his eyes to the ground. He looked better off than his twin, but his gaze never wandered from the floor.

There was a thought wriggling in her brain, twisting and churning just below the surface. The Tomias she'd followed into the room was nowhere to be seen. He was beaten, surely, but the dying man she'd seen lying in the road didn't exist. He'd never existed to begin with. She nearly stopped breathing when the realization hit her.

"You led me here," Kirheen said, glaring up at Nyson as he sat safe on his perch.

"It was easy enough," he said smugly, barely moving. "You may be strong, girl, but you're still just a pup. Your powers have only just developed. Imagine what they could be, given time and proper training." His words dripped with seduction, as if he were offering her all the secrets the world had to offer. It was disgusting.

She snorted, crossing her arms over her chest. "Yeah, thanks, but I think I've had it with you and your powers."

Nyson huffed, leaning forward so his elbows rested on his knees. "Did you see the world outside, Kirheen? Did you get a taste of the barbarism that happens to our kind, what happens simply because we exist?"

Her mind wandered back to those swinging bodies, swaying in the wind, the creak of the rope around their necks. A bloody club and a wicked smile. A girl broken simply for being what she was. She shook the thought away, trying to remain focused on the man before her. She cast a nervous glance at the twins she'd come to rescue. They stood motionless, almost as if they had gone through the unbinding. But there was a still a light in their eyes, something still remained of them.

"I did see. It was terrible. I won't deny that, but I've also seen the same barbarism from you. I saw the village, Nyson. I saw all those people you control. The people on the outside, they don't deserve the treatment they get, but neither do those children that trusted you, that grew up thinking you kept us safe! All this time we thought you were keeping us safe from the Darkness when we should have been kept safe from...from you!"

"Such misguided passion," Nyson cooed with an amused grin. "The Darkness was a necessary lie and one designed specifically *to* keep you safe. You think you could survive outside these walls? Do you believe any of your fellow Bonded could? We are murdered, burned, tortured for what we are. And yet here, we've stayed safe. We've been free to practice our powers, just as the Allseer meant for us to."

Kirheen shook with anger. "Then why the lies? Why unbind all these people, my friends?!"

"Sooner or later, human nature takes over. Curiosity becomes a damning thing that creates nothing but pain. All these powers we have, everything I have strived to create would be destroyed because of people like you, people who believe freedom is more important than reclaiming our place in the world. The worshippers of Zekar would have us wiped from the history books, to pretend we never existed and they'd do it under the guise of their own self-proclaimed righteousness. We could change that, Kirheen. We could infiltrate them, corrupt them from the inside and watch them fall. We could make a world that is better for our kind, a place that is safe and then we'd all be free."

There was truth to his words, Kirheen knew that. The situation beyond Sanctuary was entirely unstable. She'd seen it with her own eyes. People like her were dying because they had these powers. It was a situation that would inevitably boil over and it needed to be stopped before it got to that point. Nyson had a plan, a desire for conquest. He'd remedy the situation at the cost of countless lives, at the cost of provoking those without powers to hate and fear them more than they already did.

The man truly was insane, so bent on power and vengeance that he couldn't see the very damage he caused around him. "You already tried to create that world and look where we are. You've raised us as nothing but pawns, matching us together for power. You stripped us of our childhood; of any choice we ever had all so you could start a war. You need to be stopped!"

Nyson's face grew dark, his features a rippling pool of malice. The calm façade was cracking. "A war we could have won. If you had all stood behind me, if you'd all have stayed loyal to my cause, you would have had your precious freedom long ago. My brother corrupted this place long ago, corrupted it with a useless desire to have answers. And now you do the same. You're senseless actions have caused nothing but death and despair for your fellow Bonded. Their blood is on your hands. And now you've come back to act the hero. They'll spit on your girl, spit on you for the suffering you've created."

"None of this would have happened if it weren't for you. It's true, I pushed over your precious tower of lies and it has caused terrible things to happen to people I care about, but I came back to save them and I intend to do just that! Unlike you, I will right my wrongs. I will save them from your corruption."

"A shame there is so little left to save," he said, rising from his chair and stretching to his full height. His black robes blended with the shadows, making him look large and ominous. "Did you know, while unbinding makes a person fully under my control, it also strips them significantly of their powers. I can control only a fraction of the ability they possessed when they were whole. But if you take control of a person when there mind is whole," he said with a flourish of his hand. Fenir and Tomias raised their heads in unison. "...you get the full extent of their abilities and power. It is more taxing, certainly, but infinitely more enjoyable. They are fully aware of what they are doing, but incapable of stopping their actions. Tell me, Kirheen. What would be more painful for you?"

The twins turned towards each other, each pulling a dagger from the sash around their waist. They took exaggerated steps towards each other, looking like oversized dolls, their movements awkward and strained. They stopped within arm's reach, daggers held at their side.

"Perhaps them hurting each other?"

It took a moment for the words to sink in. It wasn't until they both raised their daggers high that she felt her blood go cold. "NO!"

They struck with their daggers at the same time, slicing each other vertically down the chest with barely a flinch. Blood followed, seeping from their wound. It made Kirheen sick and she squeezed her eyes shut, trying to block out the sight. *This is an illusion. It has to be an illusion.*

"This isn't real. Allseer tell me this isn't real." She forced herself to use her power, to strike at Nyson with all she had. She felt the power leave her, felt it driving through the air between them and then it was gone, like someone flicking a switch in her head. She'd felt it before, a mental wall that wasn't of her design. She tried to move her hand and realized with sudden terror that she couldn't move at all. Nyson had her under his control, at least partially. When she opened her mouth to speak, she found herself able to. Perhaps he wanted to be able to hear her scream. "Damn it, Nyson. Stop this. This is insane! What are you trying to prove?"

"This is power, Kirheen. This is what our kind could do, this is what we could be. We could control the world, a *new* world just for our kind."

"You can't possibly want that. You can't."

"Perhaps a further demonstration will change your mind. It would really be a shame if your act of heroics ended in their deaths, wouldn't it? Watching them cut each other to pieces must be terrible to see, but you've yet to feel true terror. Terror lies in betrayal, of having those you love turn against you."

"Nyson please, stop this!"

A flick of his hand and the twins turned towards her, daggers dripping crimson onto the floor. They marched towards her, brown eyes haunted. *Allseer, they know. They know and they can't stop.* It pained her to realize that all her training, all she'd strived for was useless to her now. She pushed against her bonds, trying desperately to flee but it was pointless. There was nothing she could do. It was as if someone had glued her legs to the floor.

Her eyes were filling with tears, her jaw clenched tightly together as she watched them approach, step by step. Walking death.

"Are you afraid, Kirheen?"

"Stop this, please," she pleaded but Nyson ignored her. She forced her way into her own mind but found that familiar space tainted; a hazy dream filled with vague shapes she couldn't comprehend. She tried to branch out her power to Tomias but like her attack on Nyson, her power fizzled out, losing life in the space between them.

"Tomias, listen to me. Look at what you're doing. You need to stop! Tomias, please!"

And he did stop. His feet slowed beneath him, his face contorting with pain as he fought against the power that held him. "I...can't..." It only halted his advance for a second before he was moving towards her, a white ghost carrying death in his hands. Fenir was only feet away from her, his fingers clenched tight around the hilt of his dagger. He raised the dagger high above his head, ready to strike.

I've been such a fool. Trying to stand against Nyson had been a hopeless task, a death wish. She'd wanted to save her friends and instead she'd gotten them trapped in a terrible nightmare. They would be forced to watch themselves cut her down, would feel her sticky blood on their skin. They'd be lost to her forever. She'd never have another moment with them. That gentle laugh from Tomias, the rare warmth in his twins eyes... All lost.

There was a swooshing noise in front of her face, a parting of the air as the dagger descended. Pain burst to life across her cheek, the cold steel biting into her flesh with intensity she hadn't expected. She felt the control over her body release and she stumbled back, raising a hand to her face. When she pulled her hand away, it was slick with blood.

Terror; pure and primal. Nyson was leaving her just enough control to fight back, to struggle against the death that was sure to come. He wanted to watch her fight for her life, wanted to see her fight against the inevitable. He meant to break her.

Tomias had fallen further behind, his hands shaking violently as he fought against his own body. His brow was covered in sweat, his eyes wild. A low growl escaped his throat, giving voice to his struggle.

Fenir launched forward, the dagger cutting through her robe and slicing across her left ribcage. It was a shallow wound. He was toying with her. Nyson meant to drag out her torture, to see her die screaming. The pain on her cheek was a burning flame, the smell of blood in the air making her nauseous.

Fenir stood over her like a wild cat, his teeth bared. Kirheen saw the dagger sweep towards her again and out of instinct she raised her right arm. The blade bit deep into her forearm at an angle, slicing through skin and muscle as if she were made of cloth. She expected more pain but her body was pumping full of adrenaline. It was a surreal feeling watching him wrench the dagger away. All she could feel was the hammering of her heart, sheer animal terror vibrating in her chest.

The blow had forced her to the ground and she scrambled back away from Fenir. She collided with the wall behind her and huddled against it, trying to make herself as small as possible. Strong fingers pushed past her shoulder, forcing her hair aside. Those same fingers found her neck and with anger she didn't know they possessed, she was lifted to her feet and pinned to the wall, a butterfly pinned to a board.

He was squeezing the air out of her and a mesh of black and white spots flickered in her vision like insects. She could see his cinnamon colored eyes swimming in her sight, saw the despair hidden there. The dagger slid forward and this time she felt the sickening slip of the blade as it drove through her right side. She thought briefly how lucky she'd be if it missed her innards when the blade was driven forward again, this time aimed at her hearts. *Forgive me*

Kirheen squeezed her eyes shut, waiting for the attack that would spell her doom. A scream from behind Fenir forced her to open them again and she saw a flash of Tomias, faced crazed as he ran forward with his dagger raised. The blade connected with flesh, driving through his brothers neck with enough force to drive his own blade off course. What should have driven straight through her heart collided with the wall behind her as she slipped from his grip and landed on the ground. Her wounds came alive as if she'd suddenly been doused in alcohol.

But there was a new wound, deeper and more painful than the rest. It tore at her heart and a cry ripped from her chest as she watched Fenir fall to the ground, his eyes wide with disbelief. His fingers fumbled at the hilt that jutted from his neck but his brother was at his side a moment later, pushing his hands away. "No, no, no, no," she heard him mumble. "Brother. Oh, Allseer. I'm so sorry. Brother, please. Don't do this."

Fenir raised a shaky hand and Tomias took it frantically. Tears streamed down his cheeks as he watched his brother fade before his eyes. "No…no…no…" A cough sent a spray of bloody saliva floating into the air and Fenir was still a moment later. Kirheen winced as Tomias let loose a scream that seemed to tear at his throat, a cry of pain that Kirheen knew she'd never know the weight of. He had just lost a part of himself, his other half, his twin. She couldn't fathom that pain. Didn't want to.

The world was growing dark at the edges of her vision as her own blood seeped out onto the floor. Every wound howled for attention, playing tug-o-war with her mind. Her head pounded, like someone hammering nails into the inside of her skull. It only grew worse as she laid flat on the floor, her chest barely rising and falling as she struggled to stay conscious. It couldn't end like this; it couldn't have been all in vain. There was flutter of movement to her right, a streak of red hair. Another cry joined the chorus of sorrow and Kirheen shut her eyes, just wanting to drown out the world that had suddenly fallen apart around her.

Chapter 39

Therin stepped into a nightmare. There was a scream as they approached the temple, something inhuman, so filled with pain and rage that he stopped walking. Trista put a hand on his back, listening intently to the sounds coming from the Temple. Therin hesitated for just an instant, hearing the wracking sobs coming from the other side of the door. He burst through a moment later, bow drawn.

He almost slid through the entrance as his boots came in contact with something dark and sticky. The smell gave it away before his sight did. There was no way to tell who or what had been injured but there were three bodies crowded around the door and all of them were covered in blood. Trista stumbled into the room behind him and her eyes grew wide. She took in the scene for barely a second before she was rushing to the side of one of the three.

"Fenir," she screamed, her hands scrabbling over the body lying before her. There was another man by his side that looked just like the man on the floor, his white hair tinged with red blood. He was sobbing, completely inconsolable, rocking back and forth next to the corpse. "Fenir! Wake up, damn you! Wake up! Allseer, please...Tomias, tell me this isn't real. Tell me...." She sobbed against Fenir, her hands grabbing the folds of his robe as she cried.

There was movement to his left and he looked over to see Kirheen, a deep gash visible in her arm. She was bleeding heavily but still alive. Lowering his bow, he stepped over to Trista and grabbed the back of her robes. He hoisted her to her feet and ignored her fury as she turned on him.

"I know your pain right now, but help those that can be helped. Grief can come later. Kirheen needs you."

Her lip quivered, tears streaking down her face in tiny rivers. She took a shuddering breath and stepped past him to help Kirheen. With that done, Therin retrieved his bow and turned to face his brother.

Nyson stood at the end of the hall, his hands calmly clasped behind his back. This was not the man that he remembered. He had grown terribly thin over the years, his features almost skeletal, his eyes a flaming ember of hatred. His lips were curved into a smile, as if he took pride in the work he'd done. It filled Therin with a rage he'd never known.

"Brother," he said through gritted teeth.

"The rebellious sibling comes crawling back to my sanctuary. You're too late."

His fingers curled tightly around his bow, his knuckles going white. "I came here to end this. This, Nyson, this is too much. I've seen what you've been up to all these years. You're a heartless fool. Whatever purpose you had, whatever hope you had for saving our kind, you lost it long ago. You're nothing but an animal now. You need to be put down."

Therin notched an arrow and raised his bow, taking a step towards his brother. Nyson regarded him with a cool stare. "You won't hurt me, brother. Even back then, with the hatred you felt towards me, you couldn't bring yourself to kill me and be done with it. Instead you fled with your tail between your legs. You even had the indecency to take my bond mate with you, a cruelty that more than just I have felt."

"And so you've done all this? You knew how she felt. She despised you, despised your desire for revenge. You've become the very thing she hated."

"It doesn't matter anymore, brother. I've become so much more than she could ever imagine. Lower the bow, I know you won't use it."

"You may have changed, brother, but so have I!" He let his fingers slip, felt the familiar thwack of the bow as it snapped the air. The arrow hit his brother in his right shoulder, forcing him back against the wall. His hand flew up to the shaft and he looked up with an expression of pure shock. A second later he retaliated with a blast of energy so powerful it manifested itself in his vision, hurtling towards him as a glowing blue ball. He almost dodged but the blast burnt his hand, ripping the bow away from him and sending it flying across the room where it landed near the others.

With no physical weapon, it was now mind against mind. He took a breath to steady himself and reinforced his walls. He felt his brother lash out, clawed fingers digging into his skull as he tried to wrench control over him. He pushed back with equal strength, their powers pushing against each other in a deadlock. He kept pushing with all his strength as he forced his feet to carry him forward. Step by step he made his way across the room until he was standing just a few feet in front of Nyson.

Another ball of energy was hurled at him but he easily side stepped it, feeling a calm wash over him. In their youth, his brother had always been the better of the two when it came to his control of his powers. He'd shown remarkable skill at a young age, able to bend others to his will by the time most people were learning how to block their minds. Despite his strength of mind, his physical strength had always been lacking.

Therin pressed hard, shoving all he had into taking a few more steps. A solid push and he broke free, lurching forward to grab his brother around the throat. He slammed him against the wall and Nyson winced as it collided with the arrow sticking from his shoulder.

"You took everything from these children. You stole from them the ability to choose."

Nyson smiled. "Are you going to kill me, brother?"

"No, Nyson. I think it's time you shared their fate."

With his free hand, he locked his fingers against the side of Nyson's face. There was a moment of panic from him as he realized what was happening but by then it was too late. Therin pushed against his mind, slicing through the delicate threads holding it together.

There was a shudder and his brother went limp. Therin released his grip, holding his brother steady while he swayed, unsteady as a newborn colt. When he raised his head, his eyes were dull, his jaw slack as he stared far off into space.

Unbinding, a power he had obtained naturally, but one he had kept hidden. Such a power wasn't meant to exist. It wasn't meant to be used. This, however, was a special case and as he turned away from his brother, he felt the ripples of the past finally still.

His rebellion had stripped them of their independence, had forced them to live a lie. Now he would show them the truth and this time, he would be setting them free.

Chapter 40

K irheen watched smoke curl from the funeral pyre, weaving through the blue wraith wood like tiny spirits seeking escape. The world seemed unnaturally still. No wind blew through the trees that night and the people standing near her seemed more like apparitions hovering on the edge of her peripheral, ghostly and silent.

There was a crackle as the wood caught fire and the dry tinder exploded into blue flame, licking upwards to claim the body that lay over it. She felt her stomach twist with guilt, felt the wounds he'd inflicted burn like the fire raging beneath him. Shame coated her skin like a film of sweat and it was hard not to think that those standing beside her weren't blaming her for the pain they were now feeling.

Tomias stood close to the fire, watching the flames with dead eyes. He hadn't spoken a word since the events in the temple. He was distant, in a world all of his own. Trapped in a prison of pain and there was no saving him from it.

Trista was nowhere to be seen. The pain was too much and grief drove her apart from them. The healer had allowed Kirheen this moment, a moment to see off a man that had been both mentor and friend. Once it was over, she'd be drugged, forced to sleep until their business in Sanctuary was over. Her wounds needed to heal, both mental and physical. Kirheen would consider herself lucky is Trista didn't poison her while she was at it.

She took a cautious step forward, her shoulder brushing Tomias. His eyes never left the flames and she felt a stab of overwhelming sadness when he refused her hand. There was nothing to be done for him. His grief was beyond comprehension. She could only stand by his side and hope that somewhere within he found comfort in her presence.

They watched the flames wash over Fenir, curling around his body as if to embrace him. He faded, claimed by the heat and smoke until he was no more. Kirheen choked back tears, biting her cheek to stop herself from crying. *Goodbye my friend.*

Even long after the flames had died and the others had fled, she stayed with Tomias. The moon was big and bright above them, her gentle light making the surrounding trees glow even brighter. She probably would have stayed there all night had Trista not come to fetch them. Grieving as she was, she was still a healer and that part of her was strong as ever.

The vial she downed was bitter but she found little heart to complain. She settled into her bed and let herself weep quietly until she couldn't fight off the effects of the medicine any longer. She was pulled into a dreamless slumber, free of the pain that had hung over her like a cloud ever since she'd learned the truth. It was the last time she'd ever sleep there. The last time she'd ever see Sanctuary.

A new life awaited her come morning and with it a new set of struggles.

There were so many broken. He forced himself to knit their minds back together one by one, driving himself to exhaustion day by day. Those that had recently undergone the unbinding returned to the world just as they had been, but those that had spent years under the control of Nyson remained much as they were. There was nothing to be done with the broken but to leave them behind.

In the end he opted for a merciful death and the others that had made the journey shared in the grim task. Each of them was given a proper burial and laid to rest, their symbols carved onto wraith wood planks so they'd never be forgotten. He only hoped Kirheen would approve.

The Bonded, broken from the control that had been exerted over them were shocked to learn the truth. Just as Kirheen had been when she'd learned the reality beyond the woods, they found their whole world suddenly turned upside down. Without purpose, the idea of freedom was overwhelming and scary but in the end, they agreed to make the journey to the outside world. They agreed to leave their powers behind and start a life anew.

They left Sanctuary as they had come, leaving the whispering woods behind once and for all. They carried the broken and battered with them and crossed the mountains that would lead them to their new lives.

Chapter 41

K irheen examined herself in the small mirror above the washbasin. A row of stitches held her cheek together, a livid red line running between them. Despite the outward look of it, it was healing nicely. The same couldn't be said for her arm and side, both of which were healing slowly. The pain came and went, washing over her in powerful waves when it did decide to strike. Leann had taken to dosing her with pain relieving tinctures to help her cope with the pain.

If the external wounds were bad, the pain she felt in her heart could have been called catastrophic. The death of Fenir was fresh in her mind and she often suffered from terrible nightmares, reliving the events in the temple as if they were real. She'd awake screaming, often waking Tomias in the process. With little place to put them, they had both been set up in the barn, beds made out of hay in two empty stalls. It wasn't the most comfortable bed she'd ever slept in, but it was a place to call home for the time being.

The space between them was palpable. Most days, Tomias would barely eat, his eyes far away and filled with a pain Kirheen wished she could fix. But there was no fixing his loss, a loss that she blamed herself for causing. He had slain his brother in order to save her and while she was grateful, she would have given anything to save him from the pain he now felt.

Each day she tried speaking to him and each day she was ignored until she finally gave up all together. Despite his silence, she laid his food out for him each day and covered him with a blanket at night. From time to time she brought him books and scrolls to keep him busy. Though a rare thing, she'd sometimes catch him reading, flipping through the pages with trembling hands.

Garild, while in considerably better health, was of no help. His anger over losing his hand had faded in part to the slender, raven haired healer that had tended to him. They had grown close in her absence. She was gentle and kind and nurturing, all the things that Kirheen was not. She didn't expect such a thing to hurt as bad as it did, but she found herself weeping for the friend she had lost, for the life with him she'd never had.

She distanced herself from her old bond mate, too consumed by her own feelings of guilt and sadness to deal with the dying embers of his anger towards her. She needed his forgiveness but it was something she was willing to wait for. It would come in time and right now she needed to be alone.

She kept herself busy, helping Leann on projects around the house to the best of her abilities. Leann claimed the movement would help her wounds heal better and though it was painful, it kept her mind busy which was more important than the pain she faced.

As she grew stronger, she became restless. She took up lessons with Therin, learning about the world that she knew so little about. She learned that the great beast she shared a barn with was called a Horse, a strange kind of pack animal that made traveling easier. She studied maps, fascinated by the alien world around her. It was so large and she struggled to wrap her head around the sheer size of it all, of the amount of people said to live within each city.

She learned of the deities, of the current Royal Family and their worship of Zekar the Nightbringer. The plight of her people was a convoluted web and the details of their struggles made her head spin. It was a struggle most of her kind tried to avoid. Having powers, Therin said, wasn't worth losing their lives.

And she learned other things; to cook and mend clothes and to tend to the horses. A gathering in the town led to a night of learning to dance and for the first time in weeks, she laughed, linked arm in arm with a boy as they twirled into the night.

And on a day just like any other, after she'd risen from her bed and brushed the hay from her hair, Tomias spoke. At first she thought she had imagined it, thinking the small croaking sound had come from Benny, the speckled horse that slept across the barn. She eyed him curiously but the horse simply stared at her, his teeth working on a clump of hay. It was only when she caught movement out of the corner of her eye that she realized it was Tomias. He had moved from his usual spot, had stood with the painful rise of a man much older than he was. He used the post of the stall to raise himself up, his face squinted painfully.

Kirheen was at his side in a flash, helping him stand. They took a few careful steps and then he sunk to his knees. She lowered him down carefully, sitting on the dusty ground with him, his arm draped around her shoulder. "Are you alright," she asked cautiously, dawdling over him as if he were a child.

He raised his dark eyes and his gaze locked on to hers. He reached out with an unsteady hand and touched the jagged red line on her cheek. "Thank you," he whispered. There were tears welling in his eyes and she looked away, feeling ashamed that the mere sight of her could cause him such pain. "Thank you," he said again. "Thank you for not leaving me. For not giving up."

She forced herself to meet his eyes and found herself lost in the beauty of them, of the strangeness of seeing life in eyes that she thought were forever dead. To see a hint of that spark took her breath away. "I wouldn't leave you, Tomias. I'll be right here."

"Can you help me back? I...don't think I'm ready for this. I thought maybe...but...I can't."

"I understand." She helped him to his feet and lowered him back onto his makeshift bed. He leaned his head back against the stall, letting his eyes drift shut. She rose quietly, intending to let him drift back to sleep.

"Kirheen," he called and she stopped, turning her head to look over her shoulder. He was staring at her intently, his cinnamon colored eyes swimming with an emotion she couldn't define. He took a shaky breath and spoke. "It was always my brother. Ever since we were young…it was always him. Every bad thing that ever happened to us, he took the brunt of. Every scrape and bruise and broken bone was his to bear. And now… he's gone, taken by my own hands."

Kirheen felt her voice crack as she spoke. "Tomias, I'm so—"

He raised a hand to stop her. "Let me finish, please. I am broken, Kirheen. I can't explain to you the pain I feel at having lost him. He was a part of me just as I was a part of him. I feel like a part of me has died. Maybe a part of me has." He looked down at his palms, examining his hands as if they were foreign things. He opened and closed them a few times, squeezing feeling back into his long fingers. When he looked back up to her, his brow was furrowed. She shuddered, knowing full well what would come next. The blame for his death, pinned on her as it should be.

"Despite this pain…despite everything that has happened, Kir, I don't regret saving you."

She felt something heavy shift in her heart, a floodgate rising and a tide of emotion finally freeing itself from some place deep within her. She swallowed the lump in her throat and turned towards him, her lip quivering. She wanted so badly to say something, to ask him to say it again so she'd know for certain it was real.

Instead he opened his arms, beckoning her to come closer. She ran forward, diving into him harder than she'd planned. He huffed, trying to reclaim the air she'd driven out of him with her elbow. Her wounds protested the movement, burning from the sudden impact. At the moment she cared little for his arms were wrapping around her, pulling her close. He settled his chin on top of her head and sighed.

After a time he leaned away from her, raising a hand to settle on her cheek. His thumb gently caressed the puckered skin of her scar and she leaned into his touch. Those same fingers traveled to her arm, running along the bandages that protected her healing wound.

"Does it hurt," he asked, his face displeased.

"It will heal in time," she said softly. *We both will.*

He nodded and pulled her against him, careful of the wound on her side. They remained that way, basking in a strange mix of hope and sadness that surrounded their world like a bubble. "What happens now," he asked. "I know you too well. You won't stay here forever."

Kirheen mused, mulling over the question. She'd thought long about her options, about what she planned to do. As much as she hated to admit it, he was right. She couldn't stay there forever. She couldn't just stay as she was, to grow old without a purpose. "I think I'll visit the city. I want to see it with my own eyes. I keep hearing so much, I want to see it all, not just hear about it."

"Hmm, a change of scenery then?" He burrowed his cheek against her forehead. "I think I may have to go with you, you know, make sure you stay out of trouble and all."

"Oh please, like I ever get into trouble." Benny neighed loudly, shaking his head. Kirheen looked over at him, her lips curling into a smile. "Yeah, a change of scenery would definitely be nice. This barn isn't doing much for our good looks, is it?"

"I'd say not," he grinned, the first genuine smile Kirheen had seen on his face in weeks. It filled her with joy. She drifted to sleep in his arms, feeling the rise and fall of his chest, the steady drumming of his heart. She dreamt of places she had yet to see, of oceans and fields of grain, of crowded streets filled with bright tents, the streets alive with sound and the smell of spices. She dreamt of spiraling towers stretching into the sky like skeletal fingers and felt hope bloom in her heart once more.

ACKNOWLEDGMENTS

Writing this novel has been by far one of the most challenging and rewarding experiences I've had in life. From the first spark of an idea to the rigorous writing/editing/designing process, I've had so much support in making this novel one that is worth sharing.

To my parents; thank you! I've received nothing but love and support from the two of you as I've gone through this process. You've both been there to pick me up and brush me off when the going got tough. Thank you for pushing me to realize my dreams. This wouldn't be a reality without you both!

To my aunt Kim; thank you for putting up with me and letting me pay rent in chapters! I promise for the next book, I won't make you wait so long. Thank you so much for all you've done to help push this project along!

To my amazing little sister; you are my star; the light in my world when I need a laugh, a hug or someone to sing obnoxiously loud in the car with. You've grown into such an amazing young lady and I can't wait to see you pursue your own dreams! I'll be there to support you along the way!

To Meghan; Words can't express how much I appreciate all the hard work you've done helping me make this book a reality. Your never ending support and dedication to this project and to our friendship is a true testament to the wonderful person you are! Thank you for everything! Ready for round 2?

To everyone else near and far; Whether it was a kind word, a helping hand or just good times, you helped shape this novel into what it is today. For that, you have my thanks!

About the Author

Author. Nerd. Lover of Bacon. Serial Hobbyist. Procrastination level: 9001.

Kaitlyn Rouhier was born and raised in Southern Oregon. She spent much of her youth working random jobs and having too many hobbies until she decided to follow her dreams and become an author.

Now she spends her days drinking tea and staring at blank word documents, all the while trying to discover the secret to being creative and motivated at the same time.
This is her first novel.

Find her on:
Facebook.com/booksbykaitlyn
Twitter.com/kaitlynrouhier
www.rouhierwrites.com

Made in the USA
Charleston, SC
21 December 2015